PENGUIN 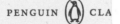 CLA

THE SAGA OF THE PEOPLE OF LAXARDAL
and
BOLLI BOLLASON'S TALE

KENEVA KUNZ was born and raised in Winnipeg, Canada. she studied Germanic languages and linguistics in Manitoba, Munich and Copenhagen, where her doctoral thesis examined translation of Icelandic medieval sagas. In addition to teaching translation for several years at the University of Iceland, she has worked as translator and editor in Reykjavík, Brussels and Stockholm since 1987.

BERGLJÓT S. KRISTJÁNSDÓTTIR is Professor of Icelandic literature at the University of Iceland.

The Saga of the People of Laxardal

and

Bolli Bollason's Tale

Translated by KENEVA KUNZ
Edited with an Introduction by
BERGLJÓT S. KRISTJÁNSDÓTTIR

PENGUIN BOOKS

PENGUIN CLASSICS

Published by the Penguin Group
Penguin Books Ltd, 80 Strand, London WC2R ORL, England
Penguin Group (USA) Inc., 375 Hudson Street, New York, New York 10014, USA
Penguin Group (Canada), 90 Eglinton Avenue East, Suite 700, Toronto, Ontario, Canada M4P 2Y3
(a division of Pearson Penguin Canada Inc.)
Penguin Ireland, 25 St Stephen's Green, Dublin 2, Ireland
(a division of Penguin Books Ltd)
Penguin Group (Australia), 250 Camberwell Road, Camberwell, Victoria 3124, Australia
(a division of Pearson Australia Group Pty Ltd)
Penguin Books India Pvt Ltd, 11 Community Centre, Panchsheel Park, New Delhi – 110 017, India
Penguin Group (NZ), 67 Apollo Drive, Rosedale, North Shore 0632, New Zealand
(a division of Pearson New Zealand Ltd)
Penguin Books (South Africa) (Pty) Ltd, 24 Sturdee Avenue, Rosebank, Johannesburg 2196, South Africa

Penguin Books Ltd, Registered Offices: 80 Strand, London WC2R ORL, England

www.penguin.com

Translations first published in *The Complete Sagas of Icelanders*, V, edited by
Viðar Hreeinsson (General Editor), Robert Cook, Terry Gunnell, Keneva Kunz
and Bernard Scudder. Leifur Eiríksson Publishing Ltd, Iceland, 1997
This edition first published by Penguin Classics 2008

021

Translation copyright © Leifur Eiríksson, 1997
Editorial matter copyright © Bergljót S. Kristjánsdóttir, 2008
All rights reserved

The moral right of the translators and editors have been asserted

Set in 10.25/12.25 pt PostScript Adobe Sabon
Typeset by Rowland Phototypesetting Ltd, Bury St Edmunds, Suffolk
Printed and bound in Great Britain by Clays Ltd, Elcograf S.p.A.

ISBN: 978-0-140-44775-0

www.greenpenguin.co.uk

Contents

Acknowledgements

Help and advice from many individuals – too numerous to mention in full – is gratefully acknowledged. Bergljót S. Kristjánsdóttir is especially grateful to Sverrir Tómasson and Aðalsteinn Eyþórsson for their constructive criticism of her Introduction; to Elísabet Snorradóttir, who translated it into English; Bernard Scudder for helping to put together the volume; and Bragi Halldórsson for his idea for the graphical representation of Gudrun's dreams and marriages.

The editor and translator jointly thank Jóhann Sigurðsson, publisher of *The Complete Sagas of Icelanders*, and likewise Marcella Edwards, Jane Robertson, Lindeth Vasey, Mariateresa Boffo and others at Penguin.

Introduction

For centuries *The Saga of the People of Laxardal* has been one of the best loved of medieval Icelandic narratives. Numerous poets have mined its content; painters have revealed their own vision of its events; plays – even a film script – have been written about its characters. The saga's enduring popularity can no doubt be explained in various ways: it deals with the archetypal themes of love, betrayal and revenge; its events are comic as well as tragic; and it paints a picture of a society in which an exceptional number of strong female characters play a decisive part in the turn of events. In fact, the role of women in the saga is such that it has even been suggested that the original story was told or composed by a woman.[1]

The timeframe of *The Saga of the People of Laxardal* spans approximately two centuries: the story begins in the latter part of the ninth century and ends in the latter part of the eleventh (see Chronology, p. 202). While its setting extends to several European countries, Norway and Ireland for example, it is chiefly centred in west Iceland, the Dales and the communities around Breidafjord (see map, p. 199). Its main characters are the descendants of Ketil Flat-nose, a powerful Norwegian landowner who refuses to submit to the overbearing Harald Fairhair, the first king to unify Norway under a single crown. Ketil therefore leaves for Scotland, accompanied by his daughter, Unn the Deep-minded. Three of his five children and a son-in-law sail to Iceland and settle there. When Unn loses her son, Thorstein, who had become ruler of half of Scotland, she sets sail again, this time for Iceland where she settles in the Dales and founds the family estate Hvamm.

The saga's main events revolve around the axis of conflict among Ketil's descendants, in particular concerning Gudrun Osvifsdottir, a descendant of Bjorn Ketilsson the Easterner. She is the saga's principal character and the focus of much of its action. At the very end, however, the story traces the fate of her beloved son Bolli Bollason, in the separate *Bolli Bollason's Tale*, which is included in this edition.

GENERAL ASPECTS OF THE
SAGAS OF ICELANDERS

The Saga of the People of Laxardal is one of the Sagas of Icelanders, the collective name given to circa forty Icelandic medieval prose narratives. A common feature of this genre is that all the sagas present Icelandic characters and events, mainly taking place in Iceland during the period 850–1050. Their authors are unknown and so is the precise time of their composition. The oldest preserved manuscript fragments date from the thirteenth century and the principal calfskin manuscripts from the fourteenth and fifteenth centuries. Among the latter is *The Modruvellir Book (Möðruvallabók)*, a collection of eleven sagas and the only manuscript to preserve *The Saga of the People of Laxardal* in its entirety. In this manuscript – and others – *Bolli Bollason's Tale* is appended to *The Saga of the People of Laxardal* as a sequel. The Tales are short prose narratives featuring Icelanders in the tenth, eleventh and twelfth centuries and events in which they were involved, both at home and abroad. This particular tale has never existed as an independent narrative and has therefore for centuries been considered an inseparable part of *The Saga of the People of Laxardal*.

Most scholars agree that the Sagas of Icelanders grew out of the rich soil of an oral story-telling tradition. Many believe that they are somewhat older than the manuscripts in which they are preserved. Numerous saga characters appear in other medieval Icelandic works such as national histories (*de origine gentis*). The inference is that some of the characters were actual men and women living roughly a millennium ago, and that some of the events they recount really happened in one way or another. Nevertheless, the sagas are indisputably works of art. As such their composition obeys narrative principles and their structure mirrors patterns derived from the Bible, hagiography, fairy tales and old epic narrative poems, to name only a few of their many sources. Additionally, they contain the inevitable re-creation and glorification introduced when people tell of the past. In other words, the past they show is the past that Icelanders – particularly during the period 1250–1450 – saw or wanted to see, perhaps compelled by a need to embellish the story of their own origin and family, to put forward Christian doctrines, to express their own interpretation of social circumstances and development, or simply to tell an exciting story.

Various attempts have been made to categorize the Sagas of Icelanders, for example by subject matter, setting or structural characteristics. Thus we have sagas of outlaws, their main subject being a man condemned to a life outside the community for years; sagas of poets, again the life story of a man, this time with a gift for poetry, and quite often significantly marked by a love triangle – two males competing for one female; sagas of (family) feud and hatred revolving around conflicts between groups of kinsmen and others, partly or wholly following a classical feud pattern; regional sagas, relating the history of a certain area; and sagas of love relating the trials and tribulations of lovers who finally are united. A number of the sagas, however, are not easily contained within a single group and *The Saga of the People of Laxardal* is one. It tells of conflict within a family, takes place to a large extent in one district, emphasizes the life of one of its many characters and is partly a tragic love story. Its place among the Sagas of Icelanders is quite distinct. It is one of very few sagas whose protagonist is not male but female, and where the strife resulting from its main love triangle is not between two men but rather between the lovers themselves: a woman and a man.[2]

SOCIETY AND STRUCTURE

Some sagas clearly reveal by their structure a specific understanding of the origin of Icelanders and the development of their society during this period. *The Saga of the People of Laxardal* is one of this type. Its opening chapters, the description of the independent-minded Ketil Flat-nose – who emigrates rather than submit to aggression and someone else's rule and begets such magnificent descendants that one of them even becomes king of Scotland – is one version of a well-known myth of origin widely found in the Sagas of Icelanders.

This myth serves many purposes, one of which is to show that the sagas' protagonists are fully equal to chieftains elsewhere in Europe. Additionally, accounts of the characters' ancestors abroad are frequently echoed in some manner in later conflicts in Iceland. *The Saga of the People of Laxardal* recounts conflicts within a clan-based society, conflicts that are to a large extent born of its inner weaknesses. At the very beginning some major thematic elements are summarized, in particular in the account of Unn the Deep-minded.

When Unn leaves Scotland she has lost a husband, a father and a son. She rescues her family, followers and flock of sheep from a life-threatening situation and marries two of her granddaughters into powerful families in the Orkneys and Faroe Islands. On arrival in Iceland her ship is wrecked. She seeks shelter with one of her brothers, but leaves there in a fit of pique when he refuses to take in her entire retinue. She stays the winter with her other brother – a forefather of Gudrun Osvifsdottir – who houses them. Later she settles in the Dales, claiming land in the manner of men instead of marking out her territory on foot with a heifer in tow, which was the traditional and accepted manner of women. Finally, she marries off her third granddaughter and bestows land upon her followers.

The account of Unn resembles structurally those of Old Testament patriarchs. At the same time it bears witness to the fact that the very foundation of *The Saga of the People of Laxardal* lies in a reversal of traditional gender roles: a woman plays the role of patriarch as if she were male and the men accept her leadership, but clashes are imminent should they neglect to show her the respect she feels is her due.

While Unn holds the reins of power, peace and lawfulness prevail. However, just like any patriarch, this matriarch declines to nominate a woman as her successor. She chooses instead a son of a king, her grandson, Olaf Feilan Thorsteinsson, but he has no intention of deferring to a female for long. When his grandmother, in old age, wants him to marry and declares that his wedding feast shall be the last banquet she gives, his reply is 'the only wife I take will be one *who will rob you of neither your property nor your authority*' (p. 9, my italics). Subsequently he marries Alfdis, whose importance may be judged from the fact that we are told nothing whatsoever about her appearance or her family; in fact her name is mentioned only once after the marriage – as the mother of Olaf's many children.

So gender roles in the community come into focus and their societal roots are laid bare. The woman (Unn) is more than capable of wielding power but the society she lives in is a patriarchal one where women (Alfdis) are expected to play the silent role of wives and mothers. After Unn's death no woman gains the same social position and power. Nor is it long before events take a turn for the worse, partly due to gender conflicts. Family strife rages and the balance of power tips: the family's leadership, handed down by Unn to Olaf Feilan – and thereby his descendants – is transferred to the offspring of his sister Thorgerd Thorsteinsdottir and her first husband, Dala-Koll. One strong female character after another now enters the stage, all cast in Unn's mould. They challenge any man who offends their honour or that of others, but they also fight each other for wealth and power, as do the men. To show us where the community is heading, three narrative strands are placed together at the beginning of the story.

1. Hoskuld Dala-Kollsson buys an Irish slave girl named Melkorka in Norway, makes her his concubine and brings her home to his farm Hoskuldsstadir where she lives under the

same roof as his wife Jorunn and gives birth to his son, Olaf. The women's fierce quarrelling leaves Hoskuld no alternative but to move Melkorka and Olaf to a neighbouring farm. Later, Melkorka marries Thorbjorn the Pock-marked, without informing Hoskuld, not only to humiliate him, but also to ensure that her son has the necessary means to travel abroad.

2. Thorkel Scarf, whose wife is closely related to Hoskuld, usurps the entire wealth and property of a neighbour named Hrapp by means of treachery and false witness. Thorkel later sells Hrapp's land to Olaf Hoskuldsson for a price far below its worth.

3. Vigdis Ingjaldsdottir, Olaf Feilan's granddaughter, gives shelter to a kinsman, Thorolf, who is on the run after killing a chieftain's brother. Her husband, Thord Goddi, accepts money for delivering Thorolf to the chieftain, but Vigdis tricks them both and Thorolf escapes. Subsequently she divorces her husband without claiming her due, one half of their wealth and property. Her relatives, the men of Hvamm, however, intend to do so, frightening Thord into seeking Hoskuld's help. He agrees and in return Thord offers to foster his son, Olaf, and make him his sole heir. By these means Hoskuld cheats his relatives from Hvamm out of wealth and property, but in so doing secures his son's social standing.

The core or the basic units of the medieval Icelandic social order were the clan, the extended family and the estate. When these were felt to be under threat or attack, with no executive authority in the country, people had only two options: prosecution or blood feud. *The Saga of the People of Laxardal* clearly shows how the blood feud, whose original purpose was to defend and protect the family, tends to backfire and cause it severe damage. The escalation of events, a common structural device in the Sagas of Icelanders, is typified by the family feuds in *The Saga of the People of Laxardal*. Three pairs of half-brothers or foster-brothers fight over wealth, social prestige and power. When the third generation arrives on the scene, however, it is a woman who pits herself against one of the 'brothers'. The

dynamics of the action are given added momentum by love –
which turns out to be inseparable from death – and the unequal
social status of the sexes. The weaknesses of the patriarchal
social order faintly outlined in the saga's beginning now
reappear in bold strokes until the climax is reached.

In the first generation the half-brothers Hrut Herjolfsson
and Hoskuld Dala-Kollsson argue because Hoskuld grabs their
mother's entire inheritance, refusing to pay Hrut his legal share.
When armed conflict seems inescapable, Jorunn, Hoskuld's
wise wife, intervenes and prevents this. Later, however, when
Hoskuld incites his son Thorleik against Hrut for settling a
former slave of his on Hoskuld's land, a conflict rises that
eventually leads to the death of Hrut's most gifted son – after
Hoskuld's own death.

The second generation sees hostility between Hoskuld's sons,
the half-brothers Thorleik and Olaf. According to medieval
feudal traditions, Thorleik, the first-born son in wedlock,
should inherit, while Olaf, the son of a concubine, should stay
in his shadow. Their father, however, bestows his favour on
Olaf, who uses his father's power, wealth and his own connection to people of power to gain for himself not only the wealth
of Thord Goddi, but also Hrappsstadir. As if that were not
enough, Hoskuld wangles Thorleik's permission to legally will
Olaf the equivalent of twelve ounces, presumably omitting to
mention his own interpretation of those as ounces of gold, as
opposed to silver. He hands over to Olaf the precious ring and
sword given him by King Hakon and therewith 'his own good
fortune and that of his kinsmen' much to Thorleik's dismay
(p. 53). Being in receipt of Hoskuld's gifts, Olaf now holds the
family's symbols of power, except the land. The gifts may also
confirm that he is the chosen head of the family – according to
medieval Christian ideas.[3] Thorleik's lack of joy is therefore
not hard to understand. Nevertheless, their enmity vanishes
when Olaf, who wants to keep the family together, offers to
foster Thorleik's son, Bolli, as a foster-father was seen as lower
in rank than a child's biological father. Bolli's fostering in
Hjardarholt does not, however, ensure peace.

In the third generation, conflict arises between the lovers

Gudrun Osvifsdottir and Kjartan, the son of Olaf, when he decides to travel abroad and refuses to take her along. Travelling with Kjartan is his foster-brother, Bolli. He returns to Iceland ahead of Kjartan, then, in order to take Gudrun for himself, implies that Kjartan might settle in Norway and marry Ingibjorg the king's sister. Bolli does marry Gudrun, not least at her father's and brothers' instigation. When Kjartan finally returns, unmarried, his relationship with Bolli becomes less than cordial. Nothing dramatic happens, however, until Kjartan marries. He then humiliates Gudrun during a banquet and she is bent on revenge. Their conflict escalates until Gudrun goads Bolli and her brothers into ambushing Kjartan. When Bolli slays Kjartan – who takes his last breath in his arms – the climax is reached.

Four years after Kjartan's slaying, Bolli is killed; twelve years later, when the fourth generation is old enough to bear arms, he is avenged. Subsequently and finally there is peace and stability among the descendants of Thorgerd Thorsteinsdottir. The family as a whole, however, is still not at peace. Thorkel Eyjolfsson and Thorstein Kuggason, descendants of Olaf Feilan, plan, by unscrupulous means, to get their hands on Hjardarholt, the former Hrappsstadir. Their attempt fails and on the way back home Thorkel is drowned in Breidafjord.

A few years later Bolli Bollason becomes the head of the family and a new dawn finally rises. Bolli is not only a descendant of Hoskuld's legitimate son, he is also descended from Gudrun Osvifsdottir and therefore also Bjorn the Easterner Ketilsson. Moreover, he is married to Thordis Snorradottir, a descendant of Olaf Feilan, and is therefore – as well as by his own merit – the heir to the wealth and power of the 'legitimate' branch in the Dales. In the marriage of Bolli and Thordis the saga's conflicting powers come together. In its last part the descendants of Ketil Flat-nose are united under one 'strong' chieftain. This seeming attempt to conciliate two assumptions is remarkable: on the one hand, that wealth and power should inevitably pass on down the male bloodline; and on the other, that people may reach a position of power through marriage and merit.

In *Bolli Bollason's Tale* no mention is made of conflict within

the family or the district. It does, however, tell of Bolli's dealings
with Northerners. He avenges a relative, a boy named after
Bolli's grandfather Olaf, but later, on his way to visit one of
the most powerful of Northern chieftains, he and his retinue are
ambushed twice. According to the tale he handles both situations
with grace. The story of the former ambush is particularly
artful: the ambushers, Northern chieftains, take flight on seeing
the number of Bolli's companions. Earlier, in *The Saga of the
People of Laxardal*, the same chieftains were compared to Olaf
Peacock: they were said to have entertained the greatest number
of guests ever at a feast in Iceland and Olaf the second greatest.
Bolli's journey can therefore be interpreted as demonstrating
that the men of the Dales have now outdone the Northerners.

The society described in *The Saga of the People of Laxardal*
is not only characterized by conflicts within families and
between the genders – it also emphasizes the meeting of
heathendom and Christianity. Dispute about the new religion
is crucial to the development of events: Kjartan's return to
Iceland is delayed by his being one of the chieftains' sons taken
hostage by King Olaf to force the Icelanders to adopt Christianity. Even more important is the way the conversion is utilized
in the saga's structure. This becomes clear in the life story of
the protagonist Gudrun Osvifsdottir.

When Gudrun enters the scene she tells her relative Gest
Oddleifsson four dreams. These he interprets as omens of her
four marriages. Subsequently her husbands appear on the scene
and quickly disappear. The course of events is, in short, a direct
confirmation of Gest's prophecies and the story of Gudrun's
life is as a frame around other stories until she is the only one
left. In old age, her son Bolli asks her which man she loved the
best and she answers (see summary, pp. xviii–xxi). Yet Gudrun's most significant love affair – with Kjartan – is nowhere
connected to these dreams. In the saga's structure it stands
alone opposite her four marriages. This contrast sharpens the
portrayal of women who are only to a limited extent able to
shape their own destiny. Simultaneously, attention is focused
on the love between Gudrun and Kjartan and made distinct –
and there Christianity plays a certain role.

Gudrun's dreams and their interpretation in the story

The first dream	Gest's interpretation
'I seemed to be standing outdoors, by a stream, wearing a tall head-dress that I felt did not suit me well at all. I wanted to change the head-dress but many people advised against it. I refused to listen to them, tore the head-dress from my head and threw it into the stream. The dream ended there.' (65)	'. . . I expect that the first man to whom you are married will not be a match to your liking. As you thought you bore a great head-dress, which you felt suited you poorly, you will care little for this man. And since you removed the head-dress and threw it into the water, this means that you will leave him. People say things have been cast to the tide when they refer to getting rid of possessions and getting nothing in return.' (66)
The second dream	*Gest's interpretation*
'In the beginning of the second dream I seemed to be standing by a lake. I seemed to have a silver ring on my arm which belonged to me and suited me especially well. I treasured it greatly and intended to keep it long and with great care. But the ring slid from my arm when I least expected it and fell into the lake and I never saw it again.' (65)	'In your second dream you thought you had a silver ring on your arm. This means you will be married to a second, fine man for whom you will care greatly and enjoy only a short time. It would not surprise me if he were drowned.' (66)

The third dream	*Gest's interpretation*
'. . . I seemed to have a gold ring on my arm; it was my own and seemed to make up for my loss. I expected to have the pleasure of owning this one longer . . . All the same it wasn't as if it suited me so very much better, not if compared with how much more costly gold is than silver. Then I fell and reached out my hand to break my fall, but the gold ring struck a stone and broke in two, and I thought I saw blood seep from the pieces. My feelings afterwards were more like grief than regret. I realized that there had been a flaw in the ring, and . . . I could see other flaws. All the same I had the impression that if I'd looked after it better the ring might still have been in one piece.' (65–6)	'In your third dream you thought you had a gold ring on your arm. This represents your third husband. He will not surpass his predecessor to the same extent that you felt that metal to be rarer and more precious. But if my guess is right, there will be a change in religion around that time and this husband of yours will have adopted the new religion, which seems to be much nobler. When the ring appeared to break in two, in part because of your own carelessness, and blood to seep from its parts, this signifies that this husband will be killed. It is then that you will see most clearly the faults of that marriage.' (66)

The fourth dream	*Gest's interpretation*
'. . . I seemed to have a gold helmet on my head, set with many gems. This treasure was mine. But it did seem to me that it was too heavy for me to bear. I could hardly manage it and held my head bowed. I didn't blame the helmet for this, however, nor did I intend to get rid of it. But it fell suddenly from my head and into the waters of Hvammsfjord, after which I woke up.' (66)	'It was in your fourth dream that you bore a gold helmet set with gems on your head, which was a heavy weight for you. This signifies that you will marry a fourth time and this husband will far surpass you. The helmet seemed to fall into the waters of Hvammsfjord, which indicates that this fourth husband will have an encounter with that same fjord on the final day of his life.' (67)

Gudrun's marriages and husbands and her comments in old age on the husbands

Thorvald Halldorsson	*Gudrun's words*
... Thorvald ... a wealthy man but hardly a hero ... asked for Gudrun Osvifsdottir's hand in marriage ... Gudrun cared little for Thorvald and was avid in demanding ... precious objects ... When Gudrun ... asked Thorvald to buy her a new treasure ... he ... slapped her in the face. (68–9) That same spring Gudrun announced she was divorcing Thorvald ... She had been married ... for two years. (69)	'Of Thorvald I make no mention.' (173)
Thord Ingunnarson	*Gudrun's words*
Thord was a fine, strapping figure of a man, highly capable, and often involved in lawsuits. (64) Thord ... proceeded to ask for Gudrun's hand in marriage. Osvif agreed readily and Gudrun raised no objection ... the marriage of Thord and Gudrun [was] a happy one. (71) Thord and all his companions were drowned ... (74)	'Thord Ingunnarson was the wisest of these men and the most skilled in law.' (173)
Bolli Thorleiksson	*Gudrun's words*
... Bolli grew into a large man. Next to Kjartan, he was the best at all skills and in other	'... none of them was more valiant and accomplished than Bolli.' (173)

accomplishments. He was strong and handsome, a top fighter, with good manners and fond of fine clothes. (57) Kjartan and Bolli were then baptized . . . (91) 'I [Bolli] want to ask for the hand of Gudrun . . .' (95) Gudrun . . . was very reluctant . . . After they were married Gudrun showed little affection for Bolli. (96–7) Bolli . . . dealt him [Kjartan] a death blow . . . '. . . I [Bolli] suspect that you [Gudrun] would be much less upset if it were me lying there slain and Kjartan who lived . . .' (116) Helgi lunged at Bolli, and the spear pierced both the shield and Bolli himself. (126)

Thorkel Eyjolfsson	*Gudrun's words*
Thorkel . . . a renowned man of prominent family . . . (129) Thorkel said . . . the match [Gudrun] was a worthy one, 'but it's her single-mindedness and fanaticism that cause me concern . . .' (131) The match . . . was . . . decided. (152) Gudrun and Thorkel grew to love one another very deeply. (154–5) His [Thorkel's] was the leading voice in the district. (155) As the party . . . sailed the length of Breidafjord . . . Thorkel . . . drowned . . . (169–70)	'Thorkel was the most powerful of men and most outstanding chieftain . . .'(173)

Certain characters in *The Saga of the People of Laxardal* are placed in the seat of honour, so to speak, because they predict the spread of Christianity or advance it in one way or another. Gest Oddleifsson foretells a change of religion when he interprets Gudrun's dreams. He also predicts his own death and that of Gudrun's father when he says: '. . . the time will come when the distance between our [Gest's and Osvif's] dwelling places will be shorter than at present. It will be easier for us to carry on a conversation then, if we are still allowed to talk' (67). This turns out to mean that he and Osvif are eventually buried in the same grave at Helgafell. Gest's prophecy is placed in the same chapter as Gudrun's dreams where he also foretells Kjartan's slaying. The conversion and the companionship of characters in another world are thus brought into focus and simultaneously arranged to coincide with the marriage of Gudrun and the slaying of Kjartan, creating dramatic tension and stimulating the reader's interest.

Last but not least it shows how meticulously events are prepared for and underpinned. Gudrun and Kjartan not only become Christianity's foremost champions, each in their own way, but it is presumed that they will be united in the next world. Kjartan's description supports this. It is partly based on the concept of Christ as a knight, the soul's lover – one source being the Anglo-Saxon *Ancrene Wisse*. In Norway, Kjartan competes with Olaf Tryggvason in a swimming contest shortly before he adopts Christianity: the act of immersion may be interpreted as taking the sign of the Cross. In Iceland he is the first to fast during Lent and finally dies a sacrificial death of sorts, throwing away his weapons rather than killing his brother. Gudrun, on the other hand, has a church built at Helgafell and later becomes 'a nun and anchoress' (173). She in fact ends her life as 'Christ's betrothed'. Her reply to Bolli's question about her former loves – 'Though I treated him worst, I loved him best' (174) – indicates that here at the story's end the motif of Tristan and Isolde appears, the lovers (Kjartan/Christ – Gudrun/the betrothed) separated in life, yet united in the hereafter. If so, Gudrun's reply also suggests the confession of a sinner repenting old sins at the end of life.

The structure of *The Saga of the People of Laxardal* is highly complex, offering its readers a variety of interpretations. The many similarities with heroic poetry have been pointed out, among them Gudrun's dreams.[4] This is no doubt correct. However, what seems to have been the guiding light in ordering events are three Christian concepts about the story of man and the world, which might be described thus.

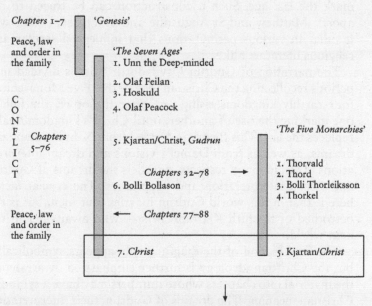

In the Saga the last period is shown
symbolically, e.g. with Kjartan's
sacrificial death and Gudrun as a nun.

'Genesis' recounts the creation of the community in the Dales. We are told the story of Gudrun Osvifsdottir's ancestors, her third husband Bolli Thorleiksson, her lover Kjartan Olafsson and the settlement of Unn the Deep-minded. These stories span six chapters just as the creation takes place over six days; and in the seventh chapter Unn rests, although her rest is somewhat different from that of the Creator.

From Unn's settlement six generations brand the course of events. After her death, the saga is a continuous account of family and gender conflict until finally Bolli Bollason becomes head of the family. With 'Genesis' marking the commencement of the structure and Kjartan described as Christ in the form of a knight, the narrative's six generations of Dalesmen can be seen to follow the old pattern of dividing the story of the world into 'Seven Ages' – where Christ's return and the Apocalypse mark the last age. Such a construction can be traced to the apostle Matthew and St Augustine and in medieval times was familiar in various permutations that influenced secular and religious literature alike.

The narration of Gudrun Osvifsdottir's life is divided into periods recollecting the Christian idea of the 'Five Monarchies': four earthly kingdoms rising one after the other, the fall of one marking the rise of another, until Christ's kingdom finally replaces the last. This theory is derived from Nebuchadnezzar's dreams, as well as from Daniel's visions and dream interpretations. This, in many respects, parallels the dreams of Gudrun and Gest's interpretation and prophecies. The crucial factor here is that in this world Gudrun marries four men, but is the betrothed of the fifth Kjartan/Christ – who awaits her in the next world.

The final section of the diagram only appears symbolically, but the Christian ideology is further emphasized by arranging the material into chapters whose numbers may have a symbolic Christian meaning. The dreams of Gudrun, their interpretation – among them the prediction of a new religion – the prediction of Gest of his own and Osvif's last place of rest as well as Kjartan's slaying are all in chapter 33 of the manuscript *The Modruvellir Book*, a holy number referring to the number of years Jesus lived. Thirty-three chapters later Gest predicts the foundation of a monastery at Helgafell (established 1184), dies and is buried there alongside Osvif. Kjartan is finally baptized in chapter 40, a number which had diverse symbolic meanings,

among them a reference to the gospels and the commandments
(the numbers 4 and 10 multiplied).

The three structural parts described above also overlap.
One of the main characteristics of the structure of *The Saga of
the People of Laxardal* is that the course of action is not a
simple consecutive series of events. Incidents are intertwined
so that time and again the story seems to deviate from its
course, but as it proceeds it becomes clear that what earlier
seemed a digression served one of its themes, possibly more
than one, simultaneously. Additionally, the medieval concept
of time was that of a spiral continuously growing upwards, the
assumption being that history repeats itself, albeit never in
precisely the same manner. Within the spiralling form it is
possible to look both forwards or backwards along a curve and
view the course of events almost horizontally (or as a continuous ring), or follow certain points from one curve to another,
vertically. This results in the past being remarkably close to the
present, in a very different way from that conceived by the
modern mind.

Various – and at times quite resourceful – methods are used
to intertwine the events in *The Saga of the People of Laxardal*.
For example, the ruffian Hrapp is introduced in chapter 10
and Thord Goddi in chapter 11: we are told of the birth of
Olaf Peacock in chapter 13 after his father has gone abroad,
but the story continues with Thord Goddi in chapters 14 and
16 and picks up Hrapp and his land again in chapters 17 and
18. Olaf is thus firmly anchored between Hrapp and Thord
Goddi as they enter the story twice in reverse order. This
method calls to mind the so-called chiasmus in rhetorics where
the same parts of a sentence are repeated in reverse, creating a
pattern like the Greek character χ. It draws attention to the
ways in which Olaf becomes wealthy and powerful and invites
readers to contemplate aspects of Christian morality – the continuous cycle of sowing and reaping. This method can be shown
graphically:

The interlacing becomes even more elaborate as Thorbjorn
Pock-marked enters the story at the same time as Thord Goddi

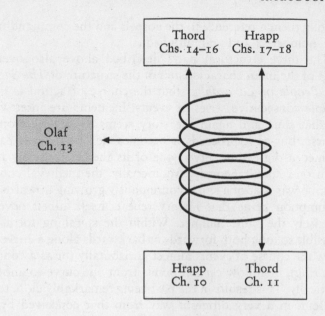

in chapter 11, returning in chapter 20 when he pays for Olaf's travel abroad and marries Melkorka. In chapter 19, on the other hand, a tale of the fight between Hrut and Hoskuld is inserted. These interwoven threads refer both backwards and forwards in the story (ill-gotten gains, travels abroad, marrying for money, a woman's revenge, conflict between brothers) in a similar manner to that in medieval architecture and romances.[5]

Medieval concepts of the progress of history along the spiral of time and the recurrence of events produce a series of parallels, contrasts and escalation of events that characterize their works. This is a powerful feature in the structure of *The Saga of the People of Laxardal*. The escalation of family and gender conflicts has already been mentioned. The parallels emerging in the conflicts of three generations of 'brothers' are obvious and the women's reactions to their husbands and loved ones travelling abroad are also marked by clear parallels and opposites. They range from silence through protesting murmurs, reaching their apex in the demands of Gudrun to accompany Kjartan, and finally end in silence.

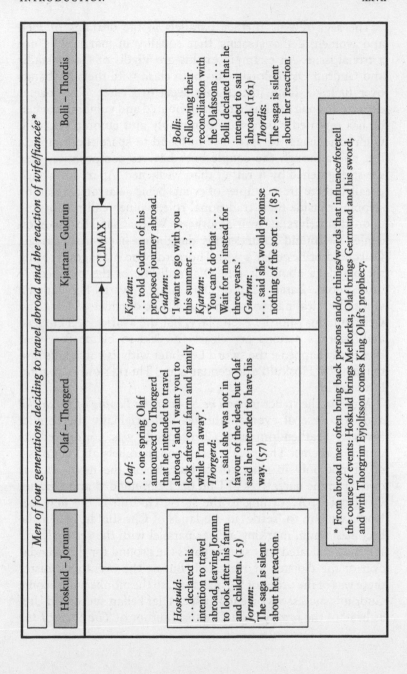

*Men of four generations deciding to travel abroad and the reaction of wife/fiancée**

Hoskuld – Jorunn	Olaf – Thorgerd	Kjartan – Gudrun	Bolli – Thordis

CLIMAX

Hoskuld:
... declared his intention to travel abroad, leaving Jorunn to look after his farm and children. (15)
Jorunn:
The saga is silent about her reaction.

Olaf:
... one spring Olaf announced to Thorgerd that he intended to travel abroad, 'and I want you to look after our farm and family while I'm away'.
Thorgerd:
... said she was not in favour of the idea, but Olaf said he was intended to have his way. (57)

Kjartan:
... told Gudrun of his proposed journey abroad.
Gudrun:
'I want to go with you this summer . . .'
Kjartan:
'You can't do that . . . Wait for me instead for three years.'
Gudrun:
... said she would promise nothing of the sort . . . (85)

Bolli:
Following their reconciliation with the Olafssons . . . Bolli declared that he intended to sail abroad. (161)
Thordis:
The saga is silent about her reaction.

* From abroad men often bring back persons and/or things/words that influence/foretell the course of events: Hoskuld brings Melkorka; Olaf brings Geirmund and his sword; and with Thorgrim Eyjolfsson comes King Olaf's prophecy.

The saga reveals further parallels in the dealings of men and women, demonstrating that equality in marriage is not a trivial issue. An example of this are Vigdis of Goddastadir and Gudrun Osvifsdottir who both clash with their husbands over fugitives from justice they wish to shelter. The former departs, leaving her husband dishonoured and vulnerable when he has repeatedly behaved abominably and ignored her will. Gudrun manages to force her husband to spare the fugitive's life, and although the couple both have to compromise, they are strengthened by it rather than weakened. Apart from such parallels there are examples of events being so arranged that by stepping outside their traditional role, women call misfortune upon themselves as well as others. When Olaf Hoskuldsson denies Geirmund Thunder his daughter's hand in marriage, Geirmund bribes Olaf's wife Thorgerd, who manages to bring the marriage about despite Olaf's dislike of the prospective bridegroom. Later Thurid Olafsdottir thwarts her father's will in her dealings with Geirmund. The conduct of Olaf and Geirmund may not be exemplary, but the avarice of Thorgerd and Thurid's actions are clearly no less to blame for what eventually happens: the sword Leg-biter with its curse falls into the hands of Hoskuld's descendants and Thurid's only daughter loses her life.

Much in the structure of *The Saga of the People of Laxardal* and its course of events indicates that originally the conflict between heathendom and Christendom was considered its principal theme. The saga's escalation, parallels and contrasts occur not only in this world, but also in the next. This is evident in the narratives of Unn the Deep-minded and Gudrun Osvifsdottir. According to the story, Gudrun is the first Icelandic woman to 'settle' in the lands of Christianity when she becomes a nun, marking a clear parallel with the settler Unn.[6] It is also indicated that she prepares the ground for the foundation of the cloister at Helgafell. But as the eventual cloister there was of the order of St Augustine, so the monks will become Gudrun's successors on earth just as Olaf Feilan succeeded Unn as head of the family. The Christian author of *The Saga of the*

People of Laxardal presumably envisaged no more glorious fate for women than to 'marry' Christ and therefore saw this destiny as the pinnacle of Gudrun Osvifsdottir's progress – and that of women as a whole. Readers not sharing that particular view of the world will doubtless interpret the story differently. For example, it could be said that Unn's and Gudrun's respective settlements show that in certain circumstances women can play the leading role in the community, while the saga as a whole reveals their proper place as 'the betrothed' – wives and mothers. While Gudrun in her old age prepares for her meeting with the 'lover', her grown-up foster-daughter Herdis Bolladottir is thought to be 'the loveliest of women' (173) and is favourably mentioned as a wife and mother, leading to a new line of descendants.

NARRATION

Narrators in the Sagas of Icelanders are more often than not observers and listeners and therefore unobtrusive. They refer to rumours rather than explaining events directly; they seldom reveal their personal thoughts, briefly describing their character and appearance when they enter the story and again when they die or crucial events take place. In most cases there is considerable congruity between the initial description of a character and later conduct. The narrator of *The Saga of the People of Laxardal* partly relies on external description, but he also looks into the mind of his characters and informs the readers what they are 'feeling'. He also describes 'practices' during the two hundred years of the story and compares the attitude of people living in those times to those at the time of writing and explains why he mentions particular matters. Last but not least, he sometimes uses a high-flown vocabulary to describe his characters that often turns out to be over-inflated as events take their course. Because of this, many have seen more than a touch of irony in the saga.

The narrative of *The Saga of the People of Laxardal* is

extremely visual and at times remarkably powerful, partly because descriptions of looks, manners and behaviour reveal the feelings of its characters. One memorable image is that of Helgi Hardbeinsson entering the farm Laugar's shieling with a weapon of such awesomeness that Bolli throws his sword down and steps towards his death holding only his shield. No less impressive is the image of Melkorka's Irish nurse, sitting, like a child, shrunken with age on the knees of Olaf Peacock.

Events are sometimes described from more than one point of view and at the same time the narration is stalled to create tension. An example of this is when Kjartan, on horseback, unexpectedly meets his slayers head-on. The viewpoint alternates between the men of Laxardal, the men of Laugar, and Thorkel, the farmer of Hafratindar, whose account may reveal what ideas the high-born of the time had about commoners and the latter's attitude to the armed clashes of chieftains. Narrative delays are exceptionally well constructed, such as when Helgi Hardbeinsson's shepherd describes in detail the appearance and clothing of Thorgils Holluson and his companions. Prophecies and dreams also magnify the tension and awaken the reader's unease. Fine examples of this are the many forebodings of Kjartan's slaying. By connecting Kjartan's death and Gudrun's life to dreams and prophecies the narrative also places them in a unique position (see Curses, p. xxxii).

Occasionally there is a direct reference to other sources, such as the mention of the saga of Thorgils Holluson (151), now lost. Sometimes events referred to are known from other sagas: of the divorce of Hrut and Unn Mardardottir we are told: 'This became the beginning of a dispute between the people of Laxardal and of Fljotshlid' (35). These are conflicts we know in detail from *Njal's Saga*. In the descriptions of individual characters there often seems to be an assumption that readers will know other stories about their relatives, for example, the dealings of Thorgerd Egilsdottir and Geirmund Thunder gain a particularly comic aspect if readers already know of her father's notorious avarice and parsimony as described in *Egil's Saga*.

The Saga of the People of Laxardal tends more to the verbose and its descriptions are frequently more detailed and precise than those of most other Icelandic sagas. Its vocabulary contains echoes of both secular literature and romance, and the story is rich in symbolism that sometimes bears witness to the different fate and experiences of males and females. Geirmund Thunder leaves Thurid and his child without securing them any means of sustenance. Thurid reacts by taking his sword, his symbol of masculinity, leaving the child in its stead. Gudrun Osvifsdottir compares her morning work to that of Bolli – weaving and killing; she also unwillingly does the laundry while Bolli fights his killers. Most of the time, however, Christianity hovers over the story, and it is quite possible to view Gudrun's womanly work in terms of Christian symbolism. It was she who planned Kjartan's killing, 'weaving his death', making her also responsible for Bolli's killing (after which she stood with 'clean' hands after all the washing – just like Pontius Pilate). Supporting this interpretation are Gudrun's words that she had woven twelve yards of woollen cloth the morning of Kjartan's slaying and the fact that its epilogue, the revenge, takes place twelve years later.

Curses, dreams, prophecies and comments that predict Kjartan Olafsson's fate

'Then I lay this curse upon it,' Geirmund said, 'that it will be the death of that man in your family who will most be missed and least deserve it.' (61)

When he [the ox Harri] had reached the age of eighteen years . . . Olaf had him slaughtered . . . The following night Olaf dreamed that a large, angry-looking woman approached him . . . The woman said: '. . . You have had my son killed and sent him to me disfigured, and for that I will make sure you see a son of yours covered with blood. I will also choose the one whom I know you will least want to part with.' (62)

Gest [Oddleifsson] answered, 'No need to mention it, but since you [Thord, Gest's son] ask, I won't conceal it from you either, as you'll live to see it happen. I wouldn't be surprised if Bolli should one day stoop over Kjartan's corpse and in slaying him bring about his own death, a vision all the more saddening because of the excellence of these young men.' (68)

Olaf [Hoskuldsson] spoke to Kjartan one day, saying, 'I don't know why your visits to the springs at Laugar to spend time with Gudrun make me uneasy. It isn't because I don't appreciate how much superior to other women Gudrun is, as she is the only woman I consider a worthy match for you. But somehow I have a feeling, although I won't make it a prediction, that our dealings with the Laugar family will not turn out well.' (83)

The king followed Kjartan with his gaze and said, 'Great is the worth of Kjartan and his kinsmen, but difficult it will be to alter that destiny which awaits them.' (98) [my italics]

CHARACTERS

The descriptions of the characters in *The Saga of the People of Laxardal* are considerably more grandiloquent than those of most other Sagas of Icelanders. The principal female characters, like Gudrun Osvifsdottir, are beautiful, exceptionally intelligent, imperious, the most desirable brides of the district, the part of the country or even the country as a whole. They do not settle for the roles other medieval Icelandic women were expected to play; they take over men's work when they consider them inadequate. The reversal of gender roles at the beginning of the saga continues throughout, and these masterful women often recall the heroines of epic poetry, such as Brynhildur Budladottir, who devises the death of the man she loves rather than see him in the arms of another woman, or Gudrun Gjukadottir who murdered her children to avenge her brothers. But the spirit of fairy tale and romance also feature, as evidenced in the figures of Melkorka, a king's daughter, and the ostentatious Gudrun Osvifsdottir. The tale of fifteen-year-old Gudrun's first prenuptial treaty is highly amusing: it seems composed for a girl who is on the one hand directly descended from the valkyrie and on the other a lady of chivalric romance; in her pride she is quite prepared to strip her husband of all his worldly goods:

> ... Gudrun should control their common finances once they were married and would acquire the right to half of the estate, whether the marriage was a brief or a lengthy one.
>
> Thorvald was also obliged to purchase whatever finery Gudrun required in order that no other woman of equal wealth should own better, although not to the point of ruining the farm. (69)

The most important male characters are well liked, wealthy and often chieftains of their districts. They are also handsome, grand or exceptionally good-looking, to the point of being the most 'handsome' men 'ever born in Iceland' (56) like Kjartan

Olafsson. They sail across the Atlantic to find fame and fortune in European courts as befits true knights. There they are said to outshine most if not all other men, are praised to the skies, receive bounteous presents and even offers of land or kingdoms. Particular attention is paid to the smallest detail of their clothing and weaponry. Olaf Peacock, Kjartan Olafsson and Bolli Bollason are presented as grand aristocrats wearing not only colourful ceremonial clothing and rare weapons but also coats of arms. These descriptions are elaborated with a clear purpose: Bolli Bollason, the last Dale chieftain described in the saga, travels further than any other in search of fortune and on his return his entire appearance – clothing as well as weaponry – shines with gold.

The merits of many characters in *The Saga of the People of Laxardal* may be unstintingly praised, but during the course of action some of them fall rather short of that promise – the men more so than the women.[7] It is hard, for instance, to understand why Kjartan is said to be 'the humblest of men' (57). His character is in fact distinctly marked by an overweening pride, obvious in his initial dealings with Olaf Tryggvason. Additionally, he seems prepared to commit one atrocious act after another – whether by the standards of heathendom or Christianity – rather than yield to another. In Norway he wants to incinerate the king; he incarcerates the men of Laugar and forces the farmer Thorarin Thorisson to break his oaths. A similar story is told of Gudrun Osvifsdottir. She is praised as a paragon of women, yet it is by her doing that two treasures are stolen from Kjartan and his wife Hrefna, and she may even have stolen one herself. The discrepancy between the characters' acts and the praise of the narrator as well as that of other characters in the saga has resulted in contradictory interpretations of the saga's characterization. Some see the men as being mocked, and shown as ignoble, while the women are described as heroines;[8] others do not see any irony in the story, the men of Laxardal simply being described as kings.[9] Yet another critic sees the discrepancy between the external magnificence of the characters and their base doings as a criticism of thirteenth-century Icelandic society: the saga is a tragic one, revealing that overweening pride leads to destruction.[10] A fourth interpretation sees a feminine awareness illuminating the characterization that is usually severely circumscribed by the masculine tradition of the sagas.[11]

The Saga of the People of Laxardal is essentially a Christian work though some of its characters are identified more closely with Christianity than others. The trinity Gest/prophet, Kjartan/Christ and Gudrun/nun, the betrothed, presumably was intended as an example for readers. The piety of Kjartan and Gudrun, his sacrificial death and her repentance, establishes a dramatic contrast to their former unChristian acts and those of others. It seems likely that readers are meant to conclude that unChristian behaviour leads to torment and death and that it is never too late to seek and follow the narrow path of virtue. Should that be the case, there are, as before, various alternative interpretations of the discrepancy between the characters' description and acts. If, however, the saga was composed or related in a convent, as has been suggested,[12] one can at least assume that the author and readers/audience viewed the inhabitants of this world and their struggle as weak – and also comic. How many of the characters particularly serve Christianity remains a matter of interpretation. Nevertheless, it is clear that after Kjartan's death Olaf Peacock tries to follow his example and prevent bloodshed; that Gudrun's son Gellir builds a church and goes on a pilgrimage, and that her granddaughter Herdis plays a part in the final destruction of heathendom.

Characters who serve Christianity*

Gest Oddleifsson: Possesses the divine gift of prophecy and foretells Christianity and cloisterlife. Also turns against sorcery.

Gudrun Osvifsdottir: The first woman in Iceland to become a nun, she studies the Psalter. She also has a church built at Helgafell and has the bones of a pagan prophetess moved from the church grounds.

Kjartan Olafsson: As a result of his initiative a group of Icelanders in Norway converts to Christianity before it is made compulsory in Iceland. He is the first Icelander to observe Lent and dies a sacrificial death.

Olaf Hoskuldsson: Gets rid of a ghost and kills sorcerers. He also tries to prevent bloodshed among relatives and friends.

Herdis Bolladottir: Dreams of a pagan prophetess who is subsequently moved from Gudrun's place of prayer at Helgafell. Like Olaf, her great-grandfather's brother, she therefore plays a part in stamping out the remains of paganism.

If the characters of *The Saga of the People of Laxardal* are viewed in the light of Christian concepts our impression of them alters. They usually lack some of the cardinal virtues or else behave in an unChristian manner. Hoskuld Dala-Kollsson is shown as lacking both temperance and righteousness. This is evident in his dealings not only outside the home but also within, where it is hard to decide which woman he treats worse, the slave girl Melkorka or Jorunn, his wife. Bolli Thorleiksson, on the other hand, violates the tenets of brotherly love when tricking Gudrun away from Kjartan. He also goes from bad to worse when, on meeting the newly arrived Kjartan, he offers him a stallion accompanied by three mares. This seems to reek of the farmyard as the mares are equal in number to the three women Kjartan is involved with (Gudrun, Ingibjorg, the king's

---

* It is matter of interpretation who belongs on this list; it could easily be longer.

sister, and Hrefna). Finally, Bolli is driven to murder his own brother.

Gudrun Osvifsdottir also breaks one commandment after another: she covets her neighbour's husband; she steals or has things stolen; and she repeatedly instigates murder. When dedicating herself to celibacy she therefore has, by Catholic standards, a multitude of sins on her conscience. But she is also given various good reasons for absolution. She is raised in a different religion and in the community of the saga women are not only given in marriage primarily to ensure the family's best interests, but blood feud is also an accepted method of guarding and preserving the family. The saga emphasizes that she is married the first time for her husband's wealth, and that her father and brothers pressure her into accepting Bolli. With every new marriage she climbs higher up the social ladder until, espousing the Christian religion, she is united with the one she loves. A key factor in Gudrun's story is that of King Olaf's attempt to force Christianity upon the Icelandic population by intimidation. That is the reason why Kjartan does not return to Iceland at the same time as Bolli. In other words, it is Christianity that initially sunders the lovers, though uniting them at the story's end.

The Catholic values of *The Saga of the People of Laxardal* are the main reason for the dulling of some of the saga's radical descriptions of women. As strange as it might seem, the acts of men often cast a shadow over the women, an example of which is the story – tragic and dramatic – of Thorgerd Egilsdottir following the death of her son, Kjartan Olafsson. Thorgerd exhorts her sons to take up arms against Bolli, her foster-son, accompanies them on horseback to the slaying like a general, and eggs them on until Bolli is dead. In the narrative, great attention is paid to revealing and explaining her feelings: 'Thorgerd . . . was filled with hatred towards Bolli, feeling she had been sorely repaid for raising him' (120). The narrator also paints an unforgettable picture of her coaxing her sons to accompany her to Bolli's farm, Saelingsdalstunga, looking towards the house and asking 'What is the name of this farm?' and 'Who is it lives here?' (122) – then sighing. Nevertheless, even though the narrative shows understanding of Thorgerd's emotions it judges her doubly guilty: on the one hand indirectly by Kjartan's sacrificial death and on the other by Olaf Peacock's attempts to prevent further armed conflict between relatives and friends.

Even when the story seems to favour women who assume the role of men after being unfairly treated, it is the men's Christian 'model behaviour' that excuses their acts. An example of this is the tale of Breeches-Aud, the saga's transvestite. When her husband Thord Ingunnarson leaves her for Gudrun Osvifsdottir, he insults her by accusing her – at Gudrun's suggestion – of dressing as a male. Aud's brothers do not react, not having 'managed to convince others to help them . . .' (71). Lack of assistance, however, does nothing to stop Aud herself going off alone to seek vengeance – unsurprisingly dressed in breeches. She strikes Thord with a short-sword as he lies in his bed, wounding him symbolically on both breasts. Osvif wants to go after her, but Thord prevents him, saying she 'was only evening the score' (73). His words not only judge both himself and Gudrun, but his placatory attitude and decision not to seek revenge contrasts starkly with the belligerent behaviour of Aud.

Various parallels and contrasts are highlighted in the saga's characterization. Hrefna, Kjartan's wife, for example, is Gudrun's counterpart. She is a woman who accepts her husband's control, only once revealing her bitterness and jealousy. She almost never attempts to influence events and finally dies of a broken heart when her husband is no longer by her side. Hrut and Hoskuld are opposites too: one tries hard to follow the law, the other breaks it with impunity.

Ghosts and sorcerers play their part in the saga's characterization too, not only because their descriptions may be memorable, but also because of the light they shed on the other characters. Hrapp's ghost is capable of murdering Thorstein Black, but is himself defeated by Olaf Peacock; Thorleik Hoskuldsson makes an alliance with notorious sorcerers in order to get the better of Hrut, but in doing so he causes the death of Hrut's own son and is subsequently forced to leave the country. Both these incidents and their consequences reveal where the saga's sympathies lie.

Certain characters in *The Saga of the People of Laxardal* also appear in other ancient Icelandic works and it is interesting to study their descriptions elsewhere. Hrut Herjolfsson is primarily a man of wisdom in *Njal's Saga*; Thorkel Scarf is treacherous in *Hen-Thorir's Saga*, but uses his tricks to help his friends; and the chieftain Snorri appears in many stories as the schemer and the power behind the throne, advancing himself and his family to the detriment of his enemies. The most notable difference, though, is that Unn the Deep-minded is a Christian in *The Book of Settlements* and there Gudrun has daughters, whereas in *The Saga of the People of Laxardal* she has only sons.

CONCLUSION

The Saga of the People of Laxardal was written in the thirteenth century, the bloodiest period in Icelandic history. Numerous intense battles were fought over wealth and power until the Icelanders became subjugated to the Norwegian crown, and subsequently the ancient order of society, the Icelandic commonwealth, vanished. The saga clearly reflects the community in which it was set. In the thirteenth century bloody conflict within families, bribery, abuse of the law, betrayal and murder plots were everyday occurrences. Many have assumed that the author must have disliked the bloodshed intensely;[13] and indeed the saga's descriptions of armed conflict are anything but admiring. The account of the killing of Bolli is characterized by brutality and Kjartan is made to fight with a sword so soft that he needs to straighten it every once in a while to be able to use it at all. Nowhere, however, does the social structure itself seem to be questioned. The marriages of Gudrun Osvifsdottir bear witness to a social hierarchy stretching from the earthly world to the Christian heaven, and when the female protagonist chooses the bridal bed of the Lord, the highest goal is reached.

Bergljót Soffía Kristjánsdóttir
Translated by Elísabet Snorradóttir

NOTES

1. Helga Kress, ' "Mj†k mun þér samstaft þykkja" Um sagnahefð
    og kvenlega reynslu í Laxdæla sögu', in *Konur skrifa til heiðurs
    Önnu Sigurðardóttur* (ed. Valborg Bentsdóttir, Guðrún Gísla-
    dóttir, Svanlaug Baldursdóttir) (Reykjavík: Sögufélag, 1980),
    pp. 97–109.

2. Ibid.

3. Helgi Skúli Kjartansson, 'Fjöldi goðorða samkvæmt Grágás',
    Félag áhugamanna um réttarsögu, in *Erindi og greinar*, 26,
    Ritstjóri Páll Sigurðsson (Reykjavík: Félag áhugamanna um
    réttarsögu, 1989).

4. Einar Ólafur Sveinsson, Introduction to *Íslenzk fornrit*, 5
    (Reykjavík: Hið íslenzka fornritafélag, 1934).

5. Eugène Vinaver, *The Rise of Romance* (Cambridge: D. S. Brewer,
    Barnes & Noble, 1984).

6. Bjarni Guðnason, 'Guðrún Ósvífursdóttir och Laxdœla saga', in
    Scripta Islandica, 50, 1999.

7. Robert Cook, 'Women and men in Laxdæla saga', in *Skáld-
    skaparmál*, 2, 1992.

8. Ibid.

9. Ármann Jakobsson, 'Konungasagan Laxdæla', in *Skírnir*, 1999.

10. Njörður P. Njarðvík, 'Laxdæla saga – en tidskritik?', in *Arkiv
    för Nordisk Filologi*, 86, 1971.

11. Helga Kress, *Máttugar meyjar. Íslensk fornbókmenntasaga*
    (Reykjavík: Háskólaútgáfan, 1993).

12. Helga Kress, ' "Mj†k mun þér samstaft þykkja" Um sagnahefð
    og kvenlega reynslu í Laxdæla sögu', in *Konur skrifa til heiðurs
    Önnu Sigurðardóttur* (ed. Valborg Bentsdóttir, Guðrún Gísla-
    dóttir, Svanlaug Baldursdóttir) (Reykjavík: Sögufélag, 1980),
    pp. 97–109.

13. Njörður P. Njarðvík, 'Um Laxdæla sögu', in *Laxdæla saga*
    (Reykjavík: Iðunn, 1984).

Further Reading

PRIMARY SOURCES IN TRANSLATION

Andersson, Theodore M., *The Problem of Icelandic Saga Origins: A Historical Survey* (New Haven: Yale University Press, 1964).

Andersson, Theodore M., *The Icelandic Family Saga: An Analytic Reading* (Cambridge: Harvard University Press, 1967).

Book of Settlements, The (*Landnámabók*), trans. Hermann Pálsson and Paul Edwards (Winnipeg: University of Manitoba Press, 1972).

Byock, Jesse L., *Feud in the Icelandic Saga* (Berkeley: University of California Press, 1982).

Byock, Jesse L., *Medieval Iceland: Society, Sagas, and Power* (Berkeley: University of California Press, 1988).

Clover, Carol J., *The Medieval Saga* (Ithaca: Cornell University Press, 1982).

Clover, Carol J., and John Lindow (eds), *Old Norse–Icelandic Literature: A Critical Guide, Islandica* xlv (Ithaca: Cornell University Press, 1985).

Complete Sagas of Icelanders, The, including 49 Tales, ed. Viðar Hreinsson, 5 vols (Reykjavík: Leifur Eiríksson Publishing, 1997).

Hallberg, Peter, *The Icelandic Saga*, trans. Paul Schach (Lincoln: University of Nebraska Press, 1962).

Hastrup, Kirsten, *Culture and History in Medieval Iceland* (Oxford: Clarendon Press, 1985).

Íslendingabók (*The Book of the Icelanders*), trans. Halldór Hermannson (Ithaca: Cornell University Press, 1930).

Jesch, Judith, *Women in the Viking Age* (Woodbridge: Boydell Press, 1992).

Jochens, Jenny, *Women in Old Norse Society* (Ithaca: Cornell University Press, 1995).

Jochens, Jenny, *Old Norse Images of Women* (Philadelphia: University of Pennsylvania Press, 1996).

Ker, W. P., *Epic and Romance: Essays on Medieval Literature*, 2nd edn (London, 1908; rpt. New York: Dover, 1957).

Kristjánsson, Jónas, *Eddas and Sagas: Iceland's Medieval Literature*, trans. Peter Foote, 3rd edn (Reykjavík: Hið íslenska bókmenntafélag, 1997).

Laws of Early Iceland: Grágás I–II, trans. Andrew Dennis, Peter Foote and Richard Perkins (Winnipeg: University of Manitoba Press, 1972).

Miller, William Ian, *Bloodtaking and Peacemaking: Feud, Law, and Society in Saga Iceland* (Chicago: University of Chicago Press, 1990).

Nordal, Sigurður, *Icelandic Culture*, trans. Vilhjálmur T. Bjarnar (Ithaca: Cornell University Press, 1990).

Ólason, Vésteinn, *Dialogues with the Viking Age: Narration and Representation in the Sagas of Icelanders*, trans. Andrew Wawn (Reykjavík: Heimskringla, 1997).

Pulsiano, Phillip, and Kirsten Wolf, et al. (eds), *Medieval Scandinavia: An Encyclopedia* (New York: Garland, 1993).

Sagas of Icelanders, The: A Selection, with a preface by Jane Smiley and introduction by Robert Kellogg (London: Allen Lane/The Penguin Press, 2000).

Sawyer, Birgit and Peter, *Medieval Scandinavia: From Conversion to Reformation, circa 800–1500* (Minneapolis: University of Minnesota Press, 1993).

Schach, Paul, *Icelandic Sagas* (Boston: Twayne, 1984).

Steblin-Kamenskij, M. I., *The Saga Mind*, trans. Kenneth H. Ober (Odense: Odense University Press, 1973).

Tucker, John (ed.), *Sagas of the Icelanders* (New York: Garland, 1989).

Turville-Petre, Gabriel, *Origins of Icelandic Literature* (Oxford: Clarendon Press, 1953).

STUDIES OF *THE SAGA OF THE PEOPLE OF LAXARDAL*

Arendt Madelung, A. M., 'The Laxdœla Saga: Its Structural Patterns', in *University of North Carolina Studies in the Germanic Languages and Literatures* 74 (1972).

Auerbach, Loren, 'Female experience and authorial intention in Laxdæla saga', in *Saga-Book of the Viking Society* 25 (part 1) (1998), pp. 30–52.

Beck, Heinrich, 'Laxdæla Saga – A Structural Approach', in *Saga-Book of the Viking Society* 19 (1977), pp. 383–402.

Bouman, A. C., 'Patterns in the Laxdœla saga', in A. C. Bouman, *Patterns in Old English and Old Icelandic Literature* (Leiden, 1962).

Conroy, Patricia '*Laxdœla Saga* and *Eiríks saga rauða*: Narrative Structure', in *Arkiv för nordisk filologi* 95 (1980), pp. 116–25.

Conroy, Patricia, and T. C. S. Langen, '*Laxdœla Saga*: Theme and Structure', in *Arkiv för nordisk filologi* 103 (1988), pp. 118–41.

Cook, Robert, 'Women and Men in Laxdæla saga', in *Skáldskaparmál* 2 (1992), pp. 34–59.

Dronke, Ursula, 'Narrative Insight in Laxdœla Saga', in *J. R. R. Tolkien, Scholar and Storyteller. Essays in Memoriam*, ed. Mary Falu and Robert T. Farell (Ithaca, 1979), pp. 120–37.

Dronke, Ursula, 'Sem jarlar forðum. The influence of *Rígspula* on two saga-episodes', in *Speculum Norroenum. Norse studies in memory of Gabriel Turville-Petre* (Odense, 1981), pp. 56–72.

Finley, Alison, 'Betrothal and women's autonomy in Laxdæla saga and the poets' sagas', in *Skáldskaparmál* 4 (1997), pp. 107–27.

Langen, T. C. S., 'Family Relationships and the Interpretation of Laxdœla saga', *Old Norse Literature II. Annual Meeting of the Society for the Advancement of Scandinavian Study* (Amherst, 1978).

Louis-Jensen, Jonna, 'A Good Day's Work: Laxdæla saga, CH. 49', *Twenty-eight papers presented to Hans Bekker-Nielsen on the occasion of his sixtieth birthday, 28 April 1993* (Odense, 1993), pp. 267–81.

McTurk, Rory, 'Guðrún Ósvífrsdóttir: An Icelandic Wife of Bath?', in *Sagnaheimur. Studies in Honour of Hermann Pálsson on his eightieth birthday, 26th May 2001*, edited by Ásdís Egilsdóttir and Rudolf Simek (Wien 2001), pp. 175–94.

Sayers, William Charles Berwick, 'An Irish descriptive topos in Laxdæla saga', *Scripta Islandica* 41 (1990), pp. 18–34.

Sørensen, Preben Meulengracht, *Saga and Society: An Introduction to Old Norse Literature*, trans. John Tucker (Odense: Odense University Press, 1993).

Sørensen, Preben Meulengracht, 'Some Traits in the Patterns of Social Balance in the Laxdœla Saga', *Alþjóðlegt fornsagnaþing*, Reykjavík 2.–8. ágúst 1973. Fyrirlestrar 2 (Reykjavík, 1973).

Taylor, Arnold R., 'Laxdæla Saga and Author Involvement in the Icelandic Sagas', *Leeds Studies in English* 7 (1974), pp. 13–21.

Young, Jean I., 'Olaf Peacock's Journey to Ireland', in *Acta Philologica Scandinavica* 8 (1933), pp. 94–6.

Note on the Translation

The text in this edition of *The Saga of the People of Laxardal* is reprinted with minor revisions from Keneva Kunz's translation as originally published in *The Complete Sagas of Icelanders* (Leifur Eiríksson Publishing, 1997) and later in *The Sagas of Icelanders* (Penguin, 2000). The saga is translated from the version printed in *Íslenzk fornrit*, vol. 5 (Reykjavík, 1934), with a few variant readings from Kristian Kålund's critical edition (*Samfund til udgivelse af gammel nordisk litteratur*, vol. 19, Copenhagen, 1896).

The translator's aim – like that of everyone engaged in *The Complete Sagas of Icelanders* project – has been above all to strike a balance between faithfulness to the original text and appeal to the modern reader. *The Complete Sagas* project as a whole also sought to reflect the homogeneity of the world of the Sagas of Icelanders, by aiming for consistency in the translation of certain essential vocabulary, for instance terms relating to legal practices, social and religious practices, farm layouts or types of ships. This translation of *The Saga of the People of Laxardal* is therefore a rendition not only of an independent literary work, but also of one strand, albeit an important one, from the tapestry of a much wider tradition.

As is common in translations from Old Icelandic, the spelling of proper nouns has been simplified, both by the elimination of non-English letters and by the reduction of inflections. Thus 'Guðrún' becomes 'Gudrun', 'Ósvifur' becomes 'Osvif' and 'Þorsteinn' becomes 'Thorstein'. The reader will soon grasp that '-dottir' means 'daughter of' and '-son' means 'son of'. Place-names have been rendered in a similar way, often with an English identifier of the landscape feature in question (e.g. 'Laxa river', in which 'Lax-' means 'salmon' and '-a' means 'river'). A translation is given in parentheses at the first occurrence of place-names when the context requires this: 'In the spring she crossed Breidafjord, arriving at a promontory where they had a morning meal and which has since been known as Dagverdarnes (Morning Meal Point)' (p. 7). For place-names outside Scandinavia, the common English equivalent is used if such exists; otherwise the Icelandic form has been transliterated. Nicknames are translated where their meanings are reasonably certain.

THE SAGA OF THE PEOPLE
OF LAXARDAL

1 | A man called Ketil Flat-nose, the son of Bjorn Buna,[1] was
a powerful hersir[2] in Norway and came from a prominent
family. He lived in Romsdal in the Romsdal district, between
South More and North More. Ketil Flat-nose was married to
Yngvild, the daughter of Ketil Ram, a man of good family.
They had five children: one of their sons was Bjorn the Easterner, another Helgi Bjolan. One of their daughters, Thorunn
Hyrna, was married to Helgi the Lean. Helgi the Lean was the
son of Eyvind the Easterner and Rafarta, the daughter of Kjar-
val, the king of the Irish. Another of Ketil's daughters, Unn the
Deep-minded, was married to Olaf the White.[3] Olaf the White
was the son of Ingjald, son of Frodi the Valiant, who was killed
by the descendants of Earl Sverting.[4] Ketil's third daughter was
called Jorunn Manvitsbrekka.[5] Jorunn was the mother of Ketil
the Lucky Fisher, who settled at the farm Kirkjubaer. His son
was Asbjorn, the father of Thorstein who was the father of
Surt, who was the father of Sighvat the Lawspeaker.

2 | During Ketil's later years King Harald Fair-hair grew so
powerful in Norway that no petty king or other man of
rank could thrive in Norway unless he had received his title
from the king. When Ketil learned that the king had intended
to offer him the same terms as others, namely to submit to his
authority without receiving any compensation for kinsmen who
had been killed by the king's forces, he called a meeting of his
kinsmen and addressed them, saying:

'All of you know of our dealings with King Harald in the

past, so there is no need to go into that here, but all the
more need to discuss the difficulties at hand. Of King Harald's
animosity towards us there is proof enough; it seems to me we
should expect little friendship from that direction. We seem to
have two choices before us: to flee the country or to be killed
off, one by one. Although I would prefer to meet my death as
my kinsmen have done, I do not wish to make a decision on
my own which will make things difficult for all of you. I know
only too well the character of my kinsmen and friends: you
would not want us to go our separate ways despite the trials
that following me would involve.'

Ketil's son Bjorn answered: 'I can tell you at once what I
want to do. I want to follow the example of other worthy men
and flee this country. I see little honour to be gained in sitting
at home waiting for King Harald's henchmen to chase us off
our lands, or even in meeting death at their hands.'

They applauded his words as being boldly spoken. Then they
decided to leave the country, since Ketil's sons were greatly in
favour of the idea and no one opposed it. Bjorn and Helgi
wanted to go to Iceland, as they claimed they had heard many
favourable reports of the country; there was enough good land
available, they said, without having to pay for it. There were
reported to be plenty of beached whales and salmon fishing,
and good fishing every season.

To this Ketil answered, 'I do not intend to spend my old age
in that fishing camp.'

Ketil said he preferred to travel to the west; there, he said,
they seemed to live a good life. He knew the country well, for
he had gone raiding through much of the area.

3 | Afterwards Ketil held an excellent feast, and it was here
  | that he gave his daughter Thorunn to Helgi the Lean in
marriage. He then prepared to leave the country and sail westward. His daughter Unn went with him, along with many of
his other kinsmen. Ketil's sons and their brother-in-law Helgi
the Lean set out for Iceland the same summer. Bjorn Ketilsson
made land in the bay of Breidafjord in the west and followed

the southern shore of the bay until he reached a fjord stretching inland. A high mountain rose up from a headland on the far side of the fjord, with an island just offshore. Bjorn said they should stop there a while. He went ashore with several others and made his way along the coast. There was only a short distance between the mountains and the sea, and he thought it looked a good place to settle. In one inlet he found his high-seat pillars had drifted ashore, and they took this to be a sign of where they should settle.

Following this Bjorn took all the land between the Stafa river and Hraunsfjord and made his home at the place which has since been called Bjarnarhofn (Bjorn's Harbour). He was called Bjorn the Easterner. Bjorn's wife was Gjaflaug, the daughter of Kjallak the Old. Their sons were Ottar and Kjallak, whose son was Thorgrim, the father of Killer-Styr and Vermund.[6] Kjallak's daughter was named Helga. She was married to Vestar of the Eyri farm, the son of Thorolf Blister-pate who settled at Eyri. Their son was Thorlak, the father of Steinthor of Eyri.[7]

Helgi Bjolan made land in the south and took all the Kjalarnes headland between Kollafjord and Hvalfjord. He lived at Esjuberg into his old age.

Helgi the Lean made land in the north of Iceland and took all of Eyjafjord between the Siglunes and Reynisnes headlands. He lived at Kristnes. The people of Eyjafjord trace their descent from Helgi and Thorunn.

4 | Ketil Flat-nose made land in Scotland, where he was well received by the men of high rank, being both renowned and of a prominent family. They offered to let him settle wherever he wished. Ketil and the rest of his kinsfolk made their homes there, with the exception of Thorstein, his grandson. He set off immediately to go plundering and raiding in many parts of Scotland, and was everywhere successful. He later made peace with the Scots and became the ruler of half of the Scottish kingdom. He married Thurid, the daughter of Eyvind and sister of Helgi the Lean. The Scots only kept the peace for a short time before breaking their pact with Thorstein. He was

killed at Caithness, according to Ari Thorgilsson the Learned.[8]

Unn was at Caithness when her son Thorstein[9] was killed. Upon learning that her son had been killed, and as her father had died as well, she felt her future prospects there were rather dim. She had a knorr built secretly in the forest. When it was finished, she made the ship ready and set out with substantial wealth. She took along all her kinsmen who were still alive, and people say it is hard to find another example of a woman managing to escape from such a hostile situation with as much wealth and so many followers. It shows what an exceptional woman Unn was.

Unn also took along with her many other people of note and from prominent families. One of the most respected was a man named Koll and called Dala-Koll. He came from a renowned family and was himself a hersir. Another man of both rank and distinction making the journey with Unn was named Hord.

Her preparations complete, Unn sailed to the Orkneys, where she stayed for a short while. There she arranged the marriage of Groa, Thorstein the Red's daughter. Groa was the mother of Grelod, who was married to Earl Thorfinn, the son of Earl Turf-Einar and grandson of Rognvald, Earl of More. Their son was Hlodver, the father of Earl Sigurd, who was the father of Earl Thorfinn, from whom all the earls of Orkney are descended. Unn then sailed to the Faroe Islands, where she also stayed a while and arranged the marriage of Olof, another of Thorstein's daughters. The most prominent family in that country, the so-called Gotuskeggi clan,[10] are descended from Olof.

5 | Unn then made ready to leave the Faroe Islands, and told her sailing companions that she intended to sail to Iceland. With her she took Olaf Feilan, Thorstein the Red's son, and his sisters who were still unmarried. She set sail and had a smooth journey, making land at Vikrarskeid on the south shore. The ship was wrecked upon landing but all those aboard survived and managed to save their property. Taking twenty men with her, Unn set off to seek her brother Helgi. He came to meet her as she approached and offered to put her up along with nine

others. She answered him angrily, saying she had hardly expected such stinginess of him, and departed. She then set off to visit her brother Bjorn in Breidafjord. When he learned of her coming, he went out to meet her with a large company, welcomed her warmly and invited her to stay with him along with all her companions, as he knew well his sister's grand style. This was much to her liking, and she thanked him for his generosity.

Unn stayed there over the winter, and was given generous treatment, as Bjorn was well off and unsparing with his wealth. In the spring she crossed Breidafjord, arriving at a promontory where they had a morning meal and which has since been known as Dagverdarnes (Morning Meal Point). The point juts out into the sea from the coast of Medalfellsstrond. Unn then sailed her ship into Hvammsfjord until she came to another promontory where she also made a brief stop. She lost a comb there and the point has since been called Kambsnes (Comb Point). Afterwards she travelled through all the valleys of Breidafjord and took as much land as she wished.

Unn sailed to the head of the fjord. Finding that her high-seat pillars had floated ashore there, she felt it was clear that this was where she should make her home. She had a farm built at the site, now called Hvamm, and lived there. The same spring that Unn was building her farm in Hvamm, Dala-Koll married Thorgerd, the daughter of Thorstein the Red. Unn held the marriage feast and gave Thorgerd all of Laxardal as a dowry. Koll set up a farm on the south bank of the Laxa river and was held in high esteem. Their son was Hoskuld.

6 | Unn subsequently gave away portions of the land she had taken to various other men. To Hord she gave all of Hordadal, as far as the Skraumuhlaupsa river. He lived at Hordabolstad and was an important man with many notable descendants. His son was Asbjorn the Wealthy, who lived at Asbjarnarstadir an Ornolfsdal. He was married to Thorbjorg, the daughter of Skeggi of Midfjord. Their daughter was Ingibjorg who was married to Illugi the Black. Their sons were

Hermund and Gunnlaug Serpent-tongue.[11] They are known as
the Gilsbakki family.

Unn spoke to her followers: 'For your services you will be
rewarded; we have now no lack of means to repay you for your
efforts and your loyalty. You are aware of the fact that I have
made a free man of Erp, the son of Earl Meldoon. It was far
from my intention that such a well-born man be called a slave.'

Unn then gave him land at Saudafell between the Tungua
and Mida rivers. His children were Orm, Asgeir, Gunnbjorn
and Halldis, who was married to Alf of Dalir. To Sokkolf she
gave the valley Sokkolfsdal, where he lived into his old age.

One of her freed slaves, Hundi, who was of Scottish descent,
was given the valley Hundadal. A fourth slave was named Vifil,
and she gave him Vifilsdal.

Thorstein the Red had a fourth daughter, Osk, the mother
of the wise Thorstein Surt (Black), who devised the 'leap week'
in summer.[12] Thorhild, a fifth daughter, was the mother of
Alf of Dalir, to whom many people trace their ancestry. Alf's
daughter was Thorgerd, the wife of Ari Masson of Reykjanes.
His father, Mar, was the son of Atli, son of Ulf the Squinter
and Bjorg Eyvindardottir, the sister of Helgi the Lean. The
people of Reykjanes are descended from them. Vigdis was the
sixth daughter of Thorstein the Red. Her descendants are
the people of Hofdi in Eyjafjord.

7 | Olaf Feilan was the youngest of Thorstein's children. He
   | was a large, strong man, handsome and highly accom-
plished. Unn was fonder of him than anyone else and let it be
known that she intended to leave all her property at Hvamm
to Olaf after her death. As Unn grew weak with advancing age,
she sent for Olaf and spoke to him:

'It has occurred to me, my grandson, that you should think
of settling down and marrying.'

Olaf agreed and said he was ready to follow her advice on
this matter.

Unn said, 'It would be best, I think, to hold your wedding
feast at the end of this summer, when it is easiest to provide

everything we need. If things turn out as I expect, our friends will attend in number, as this will be the last feast I will hold.'

Olaf answered: 'You have made me a generous offer, and the only wife I take will be one who will rob you of neither your property nor your authority.'

Olaf was married that same autumn to Alfdis and the wedding was celebrated at Hvamm. Unn went to great expense with the feast, to which she invited prominent people from distant districts. She invited her brothers Bjorn and Helgi Bjolan, both of whom attended with large followings. Koll, her granddaughter's husband, came, as did Hord of Hordadal and many other men of distinction. There were large numbers of guests, even though nowhere near as many came as Unn had invited, since those who lived in Eyjafjord had a long distance to travel.

Old age was tightening its grip on Unn. She was not up and about until noon and retired to bed early in the evening. No one was allowed to consult her from the time she went to bed in the evening until she was dressed the next day. She replied angrily if anyone asked after her health. On the day the feast began Unn slept longer than usual, but was up when the guests began to arrive and went out to give her friends and kinsmen a proper welcome. She said they had shown their affection for her by making the long journey.

'I mean Bjorn and Helgi especially, but to all of you who have come, I give my thanks.'

Unn then entered the hall, followed by a large group of people. When the hall was filled, everyone was impressed by the magnificence of the feast. Unn then spoke:

'I call upon you, my brothers Bjorn and Helgi, and my other kinsmen and friends, as witnesses. This farm, with all the furnishings you see around you, I hand over to the ownership and control of my grandson, Olaf.'

Unn then rose to her feet and said she would retire to her bedchamber. She urged them to enjoy themselves in whatever way they saw fit, and people could take pleasure in drinking. It is said that Unn was both tall and heavy-set. She walked briskly along the hall and people commented on her dignified bearing. The evening was spent feasting until everyone went to bed.

Olaf Feilan came to the sleeping chamber of his grandmother Unn the following day. As he entered the room, Unn was sitting upright among the pillows, dead. Olaf returned to the hall to announce the news. Everyone was impressed at how well Unn had kept her dignity to her dying day. The feast then continued, in commemoration of both Olaf's marriage and Unn's death. On the final day Unn was borne to the burial mound which had been prepared for her. She was placed in a ship in the mound, along with a great deal of riches, and the mound closed.

Olaf Feilan then took over the farm at Hvamm and its property with the consent of his kinsmen who had come to visit. When the feast concluded, Olaf gave generous parting gifts to his most respected guests. Olaf became an influential man and a great chieftain. He lived at Hvamm into his old age. The children of Olaf and Alfdis were Thord Bellower, who married Hrodny, the daughter of Skeggi of Midfjord. Their sons were Eyjolf the Grey, Thorarin Foal's-brow and Thorkel Kuggi. Olaf's daughter Thora was married to Thorstein Cod-biter, the son of Thorolf Moster-beard. Their sons were Bork the Stout and Thorgrim the father of Snorri the Godi. Another daughter, Helga, was married to Gunnar Hlifarson. Their daughter Jofrid was married first to Thorodd, the son of Tungu-Odd, and later to Thorstein Egilsson. Another of their daughters, Thorunn, was married to Herstein, the son of Thorkel Blund-Ketilsson. Olaf's third daughter, Thordis, was married to Thorarin Ragi's brother the Lawspeaker.

Olaf was living at Hvamm when his brother-in-law Dala-Koll became ill and died. Hoskuld, Koll's son, was still a youngster when his father died, but wise beyond his years. Hoskuld was a handsome and accomplished youth. He inherited his father's property and took over the running of the farm. His name was soon linked with the farm where Koll had lived, and it was called Hoskuldsstadir. Hoskuld was soon a well-liked farmer in the district, as he enjoyed the support of many who had been friends and relatives of his father, Dala-Koll.

His mother Thorgerd, Thorstein the Red's daughter, was still a young and good-looking woman. After the death of Koll she was unhappy in Iceland and told her son Hoskuld that she wished to take her portion of the property and go abroad. Hoskuld answered that he would deeply regret their parting, but would not oppose her in this or anything else. He proceeded to purchase for his mother a half-share in a ship which was beached at Dagverdarnes. Thorgerd arranged her passage, taking substantial wealth with her. She put out to sea and the ship had a good journey to Norway. In Norway Thorgerd had many relatives and numerous kinsmen of high birth. They welcomed her warmly and offered her whatever hospitality she cared to accept. Thorgerd accepted gladly, saying that she intended to settle in Norway.

Thorgerd did not remain a widow for long before a suitor named Herjolf asked for her hand. He had been granted the rank of landholder, and was wealthy and greatly respected. Herjolf was a large and powerful man. While not handsome, he was still an impressive-looking fellow, and the best of warriors. Under such circumstances, as a widow, Thorgerd was free to decide for herself, and on the advice of her kinsmen she decided not to refuse his offer.[13]

Thorgerd married Herjolf and went to live at his farm; they cared deeply for one another. Thorgerd soon proved herself to be a woman of firm character. Herjolf's situation was now considered better than before as he enjoyed even greater respect after having married a woman like Thorgerd.

8 | Soon after Herjolf and Thorgerd began their life together they had a son. The child was sprinkled with water and named Hrut. From his early childhood he was both big and strong for his age, and no man cut a better figure: tall, broad-shouldered and narrow at the waist, with well-formed arms and legs. Hrut was also very handsome, and in this respect took after his grandfather, Thorstein, and great-great-grandfather, Ketil. He was highly accomplished in all respects.

Herjolf fell ill and died, and was deeply mourned by everyone. Afterwards Thorgerd wanted to return to Iceland and see her son Hoskuld, whom she cared for more than anyone else. Hrut stayed behind with his kinsmen where he was in a favourable

position. Thorgerd set out on the trip to Iceland and made her
way to her son Hoskuld's farm in Laxardal. He gave his mother
a fitting welcome. Thorgerd was wealthy and spent the remainder of her life with Hoskuld. A few years later she fell ill and
died, and was buried in a mound. Hoskuld took over all her
wealth, although his brother Hrut was entitled to half.

9 | At this time Norway was ruled by King Hakon, foster-son
     of King Athelstan of England. Hoskuld was one of the
king's men and spent alternate years at court and at home on
his farm. He was a well-known person in both Norway and
Iceland.

A man named Bjorn had settled in Bjarnarfjord, which cuts
into the land north of Steingrimsfjord and is named after him.
There is a ridge between the two fjords. Bjorn was a wealthy
man and of good family. His wife was named Ljufa and they
had a daughter named Jorunn, a good-looking woman, very
proud, and no less clever. She was considered the best match in
the entire West Fjords.

Hearing of this woman and also that Bjorn was the foremost
farmer of the Strandir district, Hoskuld set out with a party of
nine men to visit him in Bjarnarfjord. Hoskuld was well received, for Bjorn had heard others speak well of him. Eventually
Hoskuld asked for his daughter's hand. Bjorn consented for his
part, and said in his opinion his daughter could not wish for a
better marriage, but referred the question to her.

When the question was put to Jorunn, she answered, 'Nothing I have heard of you, Hoskuld, would make me inclined to
refuse you, and I think any woman married to you will be well
cared for. In this, however, my father will have the deciding
say, as I will abide by his wishes.'

The long and the short of it was that Jorunn was betrothed
to Hoskuld with a large dowry. Their wedding was to be celebrated at Hoskuldsstadir. The question settled, Hoskuld rode
home to his farm, where he remained until the date set for the
wedding. Bjorn came south for the occasion, accompanied by
a sizeable following. Hoskuld had also invited a great many

guests from among both his friends and his kinsmen, and the wedding feast was a very grand one. Afterwards everyone returned home in a spirit of friendship and bearing worthy gifts.

Jorunn Bjarnardottir remained at Hoskuldsstadir and assumed her duties in running the farm along with Hoskuld. She soon showed herself to be both clever and experienced, and skilled at many things, though often somewhat headstrong. She and Hoskuld got along well together, but they seldom showed strong affection for each other.

Hoskuld soon became a great chieftain. He was both powerful and ambitious, and did not lack wealth. People felt him to be at least the equal of his father, Koll, in all respects. Not long after their marriage Hoskuld and Jorunn had a child. This son was named Thorleik and was the eldest of their children. A second son was named Bard. Their daughter Hallgerd was later called Long-legs. Another daughter was named Thurid. All their children were promising.

Thorleik was a big, strong man with striking features, who spoke little and was unruly. Judging from his character as a youngster people felt he would hardly prove to be easy to get along with. Hoskuld often said that Thorleik reminded him of his relatives in the Strandir district. Bard was exceptionally good-looking, strong and intelligent, and in character resembled more his father's side of the family. As a youngster Bard was even-tempered, and he grew up to be a popular man. Of all the children he was Hoskuld's favourite.

Hoskuld's situation was by this time extremely prosperous and he was highly respected. At this point Hoskuld married his sister Groa to Veleif the Old. Their son was Bersi the Dueller.

10 | A man named Hrapp lived north of the Laxa river, across from Hoskuldsstadir. His farm, later called Hrappsstadir, is now deserted. Hrapp was the son of Sumarlidi and was called Killer-Hrapp. He was of Scottish descent on his father's side, but his mother's family had lived in the Hebrides, where he was born. A big, strong man, he was never willing to back down,

even when facing an opponent who was considered more than his equal. He had fled from the Hebrides to Iceland and purchased the farm where he now lived because this same belligerence had led him to commit misdeeds for which he refused to make retribution. His wife was Vigdis Hallsteinsdottir and their son was named Sumarlidi.

Vigdis's brother was Thorstein Hallsteinsson, who lived at Thorsnes. Sumarlidi grew up there and was a promising youth. Thorstein had been married, but his wife had died by this time. He had two daughters, one named Gudrid and the other Osk. Gudrid was married to Thorkel Scarf who lived at Svignaskard, an important chieftain and wise man; he was the son of Red-Bjorn. Osk, Thorstein's other daughter, was married to a man named Thorarin who lived in Breidafjord. He was a robust and popular man who farmed with his father-in-law Thorstein, now an elderly man and much in need of help.

Most people cared little for Hrapp. He pushed his neighbours around and had on occasion hinted to them that they could expect trouble if they showed anyone else more respect than they did him. The farmers got together and agreed to approach Hoskuld and tell him of their difficulties.

Hoskuld told them to let him know if Hrapp did them any harm, 'for he'll deprive me of neither men nor means'.

11 | A man named Thord Goddi lived on the north side of the Laxa river on a farm which has since been called Goddastadir. He was very wealthy and had no children. He had purchased the farm where he lived. As a neighbour of Hrapp's, he was often the victim of his aggression. Hoskuld gave him protection so that he could remain on his farm. Thord's wife Vigdis was the daughter of Ingjald, who was the son of Olaf Feilan and brother of Thord Bellower. On her mother's side she was the niece of Thorolf Red-nose of Saudafell. Thorolf was a noted warrior and a man of means; his kinsmen could always look to him for support. Vigdis had been married to Thord more for his wealth than his worth.

Thord had a slave, who had immigrated to Iceland with him,

named Asgaut. He was a large and capable man, and, though
he was called a slave, there were few among those called free
men who could regard themselves as his equals. He was exceptionally loyal to his master. Thord had other slaves, but only
Asgaut is mentioned by name.

A man named Thorbjorn, who was called Pock-marked, lived
on the next farm up the valley from Thord. He was a man of
wealth, much of it in gold and silver. He was a big man, very
strong, and tight-fisted in his dealings with most people.

The buildings on Hoskuld's farm were far from his liking, as
he felt them unworthy of a man in his situation. He purchased
a ship from a man from the Shetland Islands which was beached
at Blonduos. He made the ship ready and declared his intention
to travel abroad, leaving Jorunn to look after his farm and
children. They set out to sea, had favourable winds and made
land in the south of Norway, in Hordaland, where the trading
town of Bergen was later established. He had the ship drawn
ashore there, as important kinsmen of his lived nearby, although they are not mentioned by name. King Hakon was then
in Vik. Hoskuld did not proceed on to the king, as his kinsmen
received him with open arms. Nothing of note occurred all that
winter.

12 | The coming summer was the occasion of a royal ex-
      pedition east to the Brenno Islands. Intended to keep the
peace in the region, the excursion was made every third summer, according to the law. An assembly of chieftains was called
to choose the cases on which the king was to pass judgement.
Attending the assembly was regarded as an entertainment, as
men attended from all the lands of which we have reports.

Hoskuld had his ship set afloat. He also wanted to attend the
assembly, as he had not yet paid his respects to the king that
winter. The assembly attracted a gathering of traders. People
attended in large numbers, and there was plenty of entertainment, drinking and games, and festivities of all sorts. Nothing
especially newsworthy occurred, but Hoskuld met many of his
kinsmen who lived in Denmark.

One day, when Hoskuld was on his way to the festivities with several companions, he noticed a highly decorated tent some distance away from the others. Hoskuld went over and entered the tent, where a man sat dressed in costly clothing and wearing a Russian hat.

When Hoskuld asked him his name, he replied that it was Gilli, 'but many know me better by my nickname; I am called Gilli the Russian'.

Hoskuld replied that he had often heard him mentioned and called him the richest of the merchants trading there.

Hoskuld then said, 'I suppose you can provide me with anything I might want to buy?'

Gilli asked what it was that he and his companions wished to buy.

Hoskuld said that he wanted to purchase a slave-woman, 'if you should happen to have one for sale'.

Gilli replied, 'You hope to put me on the spot by asking for something you assume I don't have. I wouldn't be too sure of that, however.'

Hoskuld then noticed an inner curtain drawn across the tent. When Gilli lifted the curtain Hoskuld saw twelve women sitting behind it. Gilli told Hoskuld to go inside and take a look, to see whether he cared to buy any of these women. Hoskuld did so. The women sat in a row across the width of the tent. When Hoskuld looked more closely he noticed one of the women sitting near the outer side of the tent. She was poorly dressed, but Hoskuld thought her to be a good-looking woman, as far as he could judge.

Hoskuld then spoke: 'Say I wanted to buy this woman, how much would she cost?'

Gilli answered: 'For her you will weigh out and pay me three marks of silver.'

'It seems to me,' said Hoskuld, 'that you value this slave-woman rather highly; that is the price of three.'

To this Gilli answered, 'Right you are, I do value her more highly than the others. Choose one of the eleven others instead, for one mark of silver; I will keep this one.'

Hoskuld said, 'Tell me first how much silver is in this purse on my belt,' and asked Gilli to bring out his scales while he sought his purse.

Gilli then said, 'I'm not out to trick you in this transaction – the woman has a major flaw and I wish you to know of it, Hoskuld, before we conclude the bargain.'

When Hoskuld asked what it was, Gilli replied: 'The woman cannot speak. I have tried in many ways to get her to speak, but never got so much as a word from her. To my mind, at least, she doesn't know how to speak.'

To this Hoskuld replied, 'Bring out your scale and we will see how much the money I have here weighs.'

This Gilli did, and weighed the silver, which proved to weigh three marks.

Hoskuld then said, 'Since that's the case, we'll call it a bargain. You take the silver, and I will take the woman. I must say you acted fairly, in not trying to trick me into a purchase.'

Hoskuld then went back to his own booth.

Hoskuld slept with the woman that same evening. The next morning, as they were dressing, Hoskuld spoke: 'There's not much sign of pride in this clothing which the wealthy Gilli has provided you with. But I suppose it's more of a burden for him to dress twelve than for me to dress one.'

Hoskuld then opened a chest from which he took fine women's clothing and gave it to her. Everyone remarked on how well fine clothing suited her.

When the leaders had concluded the business provided for by law, the assembly was dissolved. Hoskuld then approached King Hakon and offered his respectful greetings in a fitting manner.

The king looked hard at him and said, 'We would have received you well, Hoskuld, had you hailed us earlier, and so will it be even now.'

13 | This said, the king welcomed Hoskuld affectionately and suggested he come aboard his ship – 'and dwell with us as long as you wish to stay in Norway'.

Hoskuld answered, 'For your offer, many thanks, but I have

much work ahead of me this summer. My intention of acquiring building timber was the main reason for the delay in paying you my respects.'

King Hakon told Hoskuld to sail to Vik, where he spent some time as the king's man. The king gave him a supply of building timber and had it loaded aboard ship.

He then spoke to Hoskuld: 'I will not detain you here longer than you wish to stay, but it will be no easy task to find someone to take your place.'

The king then accompanied Hoskuld to his ship and spoke: 'You have proved the best of men, but I suspect that this will be the last time you sail from Norway under my rule.'

The king drew a gold ring, which weighed a full mark, from his arm and presented it to Hoskuld along with another treasure, a sword which was worth half a mark of gold. Hoskuld thanked the king for his gifts and all the honour he had shown him. He then boarded his ship and sailed out to sea.

The ship was favoured with good winds and made land on the south shore of Iceland. They sailed westward, skirting the peninsulas of Reykjanes and then Snaefellsnes, to enter the bay of Breidafjord. Hoskuld landed at the mouth of the Laxa river, had the cargo unloaded and the ship drawn up on the beach on the inland side of the river. There they constructed a boat shed for the ship, the remains of which are still visible. They built booths at the place now known as Budardal (Booth valley). Hoskuld then had the timber transported to his home, which was not difficult as it was no great distance away. Afterwards he and several other men rode home to be met with a warm reception, as might be expected. His property had also been well looked after in his absence.

Jorunn asked who the woman was accompanying him.

Hoskuld answered: 'You probably think I'm mocking you, but I do not know her name.'

Jorunn said, 'Unless the stories I've heard are lies, you must have spoken to her enough to have at least asked her name.'

Hoskuld said there was no denying that and told her the whole story. He asked her to show the woman respect and said he wanted her to live there at home with them.

Jorunn replied: 'I've no intention of wrangling with some slave-woman you have brought home from Norway who doesn't know how her betters behave, least of all since she is obviously both deaf and dumb.'

Hoskuld slept with his wife every night after returning home, and had little to do with his slave-woman. Everyone noticed the obvious air of distinction about her and realized that she was no fool. Late that winter Hoskuld's slave-woman gave birth to a boy. When Hoskuld was sought and the boy shown to him, he felt, as did others, that he had never seen a handsomer or more distinguished-looking child. Hoskuld was asked what the child should be called. He asked that the boy be named Olaf, as his uncle Olaf Feilan had died a short time earlier.

Olaf was an exceptional child and Hoskuld became extremely fond of the boy. The following summer Jorunn said that the slave-woman would either have to do her share of the farm work or leave. Hoskuld asked the woman to wait upon himself and Jorunn as well as look after her child. By the time the boy was two years old he spoke perfectly and ran about on his own like a child of four.

One morning Hoskuld had gone out on some farm business. The weather was good, and the sun still low in the sky. He heard voices and followed the sound to a place where a stream ran down the slope of the hayfield. There he saw two people whom he recognized: his son, Olaf, and the child's mother. He then realized that she was anything but dumb, as she had plenty to say to the boy. Hoskuld went over to them and asked her what her name was, saying that there was no point in pretending any longer. She agreed and they all sat down on the slope.

Then she spoke: 'If you wish to know my name, it is Melkorka.'

Hoskuld asked her for details of her family.

She answered: 'My father is Myrkjartan; he is a king in Ireland. I was taken captive there at the age of fifteen.'

Hoskuld said that she had too long concealed such noble birth.

Hoskuld then returned to the house and told Jorunn what he had learned. Jorunn said there was no way of knowing whether she spoke the truth, and that she had no use for people of dubious origin. Their discussion ended on this point. Jorunn treated the slave-woman no better than before, but Hoskuld was rather more kindly towards her from then on. Shortly afterwards, when Jorunn was getting ready for bed, Melkorka assisted her in removing her socks and shoes and laid them on the floor. Jorunn picked up the socks and struck her with them. Angered, Melkorka gave Jorunn a blow on the nose, causing it to bleed, before Hoskuld came in and separated them. After that he had Melkorka move to another farm further up the valley, which has been called Melkorkustadir ever since and is now deserted. It is on the south shore of the river. Melkorka set up household there with her son Olaf, and Hoskuld supplied her with everything she needed. As Olaf grew up it was obvious to everyone how exceptionally handsome and well mannered he was.

14 | A man named Ingjald lived on the Saudeyjar Islands in Breidafjord. He was called the Godi of Saudeyjar. He was a wealthy man who liked to throw his weight around. His brother Hall was a big and capable man. He lacked wealth, though, and few men set much store by him. The brothers seldom agreed; Ingjald felt that Hall hardly conducted himself in the manner of worthy men, while Hall felt that Ingjald failed to do what he could to improve his lot.

On the Bjarneyjar Islands in the bay of Breidafjord was a fishing camp. This is a cluster of islands rich in supplies of food. People often went there for provisions and visited in large numbers every year. Wise men said it was important to maintain harmony in fishing camps, and it was said that catches would be poorer if there was dissension, advice which was heeded by most people.

Ingjald's brother, Hall, is said to have gone to the islands one summer to fish. He rowed a boat with a man called Thorolf. He was from Breidafjord and had barely a permanent home or any property, although he was a sturdy fellow. Hall stayed there some time and behaved as if he were superior to most of the others. One evening Hall and Thorolf returned to shore and set about dividing the day's catch. Hall intended both to divide the catch into two portions and then choose his portion first, because he felt himself superior. Not mincing his words, Thorolf refused to take less than his share. After a few angry exchanges, with each of them becoming more adamant, Hall picked up a gaff lying nearby and attempted to strike Thorolf on the head with it. At this point other people intervened and separated them, restraining Hall who struggled furiously but to no avail, at least for the moment. Their catch was left undivided and when Thorolf left the island that evening, Hall took the entire catch for himself, being the more influential of the two. Hall then found someone to replace Thorolf and continued fishing as before.

Thorolf was far from satisfied with this turn of events and felt he had been shamefully treated in the exchange. He continued to work in the islands, and awaited the chance to even the score. Hall paid no heed to him, thinking that no one would dare to raise a hand against him there on his home territory. One day Hall was out fishing in his boat with two others. The fish had been biting well, and the companions were in a cheerful frame of mind as they rowed home in the evening. Thorolf learned of Hall's movements that day and waited down by the landing in the evening as Hall and his companions came in to land. Hall rowed from the bow and jumped out as the ship approached shore to draw it up on the beach. Thorolf was close by and as Hall came ashore he swung at him. The blow struck Hall on the neck, close to the shoulder, and sent his head flying. Thorolf then turned to run away but Hall's companions fell upon him. News of Hall's killing spread throughout the islands and was considered a major event, as the man came from a prominent family, although he himself had hardly been luck's favourite.

Following this Thorolf sought to get away from the islands, as he could expect no one there to offer him protection after such a deed. Nor did he have any kinsmen from whom he could expect support, while there were powerful men close at hand who were certain to wait for the chance to take his life, among them Hall's brother Ingjald the Godi of Saudeyjar.

Thorolf managed to get passage to the mainland. He kept himself hidden as much as possible and nothing is said of his movements until he arrived at Goddastadir one evening. Vigdis, Thord Goddi's wife, was distantly related to Thorolf, and this was the reason for his visit to the farm. Thorolf had already heard something of the situation there, and that Vigdis was made of sterner stuff than her husband, Thord. He approached Vigdis directly upon arriving, told her of his plight and asked for her protection.

Vigdis answered his request, saying: 'We are, of course, related, and in my opinion you have done nothing to lower my opinion of you. But it does look as if anyone who offers you protection does so at the risk of his own life and property, because such powerful men will be on your trail. My husband Thord,' she said, 'is no hero, and any help we women can offer is generally of little protection against such odds. All the same, I don't want to desert you completely, since you did come here for protection.'

Vigdis then led him to a storage shed and told him to wait there until she returned. She locked the shed, then went to Thord and said, 'A man by the name of Thorolf has come to stay with us. He is a distant relation of mine, and he needs to stay for some time, if you agree to it.'

Thord said he did not care to have anyone stay there. The fellow might rest until the following day, if he was not in any trouble, but if such was the case he must be off straight away.

Vigdis answered, 'I have already promised him lodging and do not intend to go back on my word, despite the fact that he is a man of few friends.'

She then told Thord of the killing of Hall and that it was Thorolf, who now sought shelter with them, who had slain him.

This news upset Thord greatly, and he said he knew for certain that Ingjald would make him pay a high price for the accommodation that was now offered Thorolf, 'since we have allowed the door to shut behind this man'.

Vigdis answered: 'Ingjald won't be making you pay for a single night's accommodation, for he'll be staying here all winter.'

Thord spoke: 'If you do this you put me in the utmost danger, and I am against letting such a troublemaker stay here.'

All the same, Thorolf spent the winter there.

Ingjald, who was to seek redress for his brother's killing, learned of it. He made ready an excursion into the valley late in the winter and set afloat a ferry he owned. They were a party of twelve. They sailed eastward under a strong north-westerly wind and made land at the mouth of the Laxa river. They drew the ferry ashore and headed for Goddastadir the same evening. Their arrival scarcely came as a surprise, but they were well received.

Ingjald drew Thord aside and told him of his reason for coming, that he had heard that Thorolf, his brother's killer, was there. Thord said that there was no truth to this.

Ingjald told him there was no point denying it – 'We'll make a deal, you hand the man over to me without causing me any trouble, and I have here three marks of silver which will be yours. I'll also forgive you any offence you have given me in sheltering Thorolf.'

Thord was tempted by the sight of the silver, as well as the chance to get off without paying for an offence which he had feared would cost him money.

Thord then spoke: 'I intend to keep our words a secret from the others, but you have yourself a bargain.'

They went to sleep until the night was almost at an end and daybreak only a short while off.

15 | When Ingjald and his men rose up and got dressed, Vigdis asked Thord what he and Ingjald had been talking of the previous evening.

He said they had talked of many things, and had agreed that a search of the farm would be made and their part in the matter would be considered closed if Thorolf were nowhere to be found; 'I had Asgaut, my slave, take him away.'

Vigdis said she had no use for lies, nor for having Ingjald

snooping around her household, but told him to have it his own way.

Ingjald made his search and failed to find his man. While this was going on Asgaut returned, and Vigdis asked him where he had left Thorolf.

Asgaut answered: 'I took him to our sheep sheds, as Thord told me to do.'

Vigdis spoke: 'Is there any place more directly in Ingjald's path on the way to his boat? There's little doubt that they planned this together yesterday evening. I want you to go there at once and take him away as quickly as possible. Take him to Saudafell, to Thorolf Red-nose. And if you do as I bid you, you will be rewarded. I will give you your freedom and the wealth you need to go wherever you wish.'

Asgaut agreed to this, went back to the sheep shed and found Thorolf. He told him to come quickly. Meanwhile Ingjald left Goddastadir, intending to collect his silver's worth. As they rode down from the farm they saw two men making their way towards them, Asgaut and Thorolf. It was still early in the morning and not yet fully light.

Asgaut and Thorolf were trapped, with Ingjald on the one side and the Laxa river on the other. The river was very high, with stretches of ice along both banks and a torrent of open water in the middle, making it treacherous to cross.

Thorolf spoke to Asgaut: 'It looks to me as if we have two choices. We can wait for them here on the bank and defend ourselves as long as our courage and strength last; more likely than not Ingjald and his men will put a quick end to us. Or we can take our chances with the river, a choice which is not without danger either.'

Asgaut told him to decide, and said he would not desert him 'whichever course you choose'.

Thorolf answered: 'We'll try the river.'

This they did, first ridding themselves of excess weight. They then made their way over the stretch of ice along the shore and set out to swim across the water. As they were both strong men, and fate intended them to live for some time yet, they managed to cross the river and climb up on the ice on the other side.

No sooner had they crossed the river than Ingjald and his men arrived at the bank opposite them.

Ingjald spoke to his men: 'What will we do now? Try the river or not?'

They told him to decide and said they would abide by his decision, but the river looked impassable to them.

Ingjald agreed – 'We won't attempt to cross.'

Not until Thorolf and Asgaut saw that Ingjald and his men did not attempt to cross the river did they stop to wring the water out of their clothes. They then made ready for their journey and, after walking all that day, arrived at Saudafell in the evening. They were received well, for everyone was put up at Saudafell. Asgaut went to Thorolf Red-nose the same evening and told him the whole story of their journey and that Thorolf's kinswoman, Vigdis, had sent his travelling companion to Thorolf for safe-keeping. He told him everything of Thord Goddi's dealings and produced the tokens which Vigdis had sent Thorolf.

Thorolf answered: 'These tokens are not to be mistaken, and I will certainly look after the man at her request. I think her conduct in this affair does great credit to Vigdis. It's all the more shame that a woman like her should be so poorly married. Stay here with us, Asgaut, as long as you wish.'

Asgaut said he did not intend to stay long. Thorolf then welcomed his namesake, who became one of his followers, and parted with Asgaut on good terms. Asgaut then headed homeward.

As for Ingjald, he turned back towards Goddastadir after leaving Thorolf. By that time men from the neighbouring farms, to whom Vigdis had sent word, had arrived and there were at least twenty men there. When Ingjald and his men returned to the farm, he summoned Thord and spoke to him.

'You have treated me badly, Thord,' he said, 'for I know it was you who helped this man escape.'

Thord replied that there was no truth in his accusations, and the whole scheme between Ingjald and Thord was revealed. Ingjald demanded the return of the silver which he had given Thord. Vigdis stood nearby, listening to their words, and said they had both got what they deserved.

She told Thord not to keep the money. 'For you, Thord,' she said, 'have come by it dishonourably.'

Thord replied that she obviously intended to have her way. Vigdis then went indoors and opened a chest of Thord's, where she found a heavy purse of money. She took the purse and went out, came up to Ingjald and told him to take his money. Ingjald's face brightened at the sight and he reached his hand out to take the purse. Vigdis swung the purse up into his face, striking him on the nose which bled so that drops of blood fell to the ground. While doing so she heaped abuse on him, adding that he would never again see this money, and told him to be off. Ingjald decided he had little choice but to leave as quickly as possible, and did so, hardly slowing his pace until he was at home once more. He was very displeased at the outcome of his journey.

16 | Soon Asgaut returned home. Vigdis gave him a hearty welcome and asked him whether they had been well received at Saudafell. He gave her a glowing report and told her of Thorolf's concluding words. She was highly pleased at this.

'You, Asgaut,' she said, 'have carried out your task both loyally and well. Your reward will not be long in coming. I give you your freedom, so that from this day onward you may call yourself a free man. You will take the money which Thord accepted for the head of Thorolf, my kinsman; it will be better off in your hands.'

Asgaut praised her and thanked her for this gift.

The following summer Asgaut took passage on a ship which put out to sea from Dagverdarnes. They had a brief, stormy sailing and made land in Norway. Asgaut then travelled to Denmark and settled there and was considered a capable and decent fellow; his story ends here.

After the scheme between Thord Goddi and Ingjald the Godi of Saudeyjar to bring about the death of Thorolf, Vigdis's kinsman, Vigdis showed open enmity to Thord. She announced she was divorcing him and went to stay with her kinsmen, to whom she told the story. Thord Bellower, who was their leader, was not pleased about it, but no action was taken.

Vigdis had taken nothing but her own belongings with her from Goddastadir. Her relatives at Hvamm made it known that they claimed half of the property in Thord Goddi's possession. He was very upset by this news and rode off at once to Hoskuld to tell him of his dilemma.

Hoskuld said, 'You've been stricken with fear before, even when you weren't pitted against such superior forces.'

Thord then offered Hoskuld money for his support and said he would not be petty about the payment.

Hoskuld said, 'We all know you can never stand by and look on happily while anyone else enjoys your wealth.'

Thord answered: 'You won't have to worry about that in this case, because I will gladly place you in charge of all my wealth. What's more, I'm offering to foster your son, Olaf, and make him my sole heir after my death, as I have no heirs in this country and I would rather the wealth went to him than for Vigdis's kinsmen to get their paws on it.'

Hoskuld agreed to this and they settled the agreement. Melkorka was not pleased, as she felt the fosterage was far from worthy enough. Hoskuld said she failed to see its advantages: 'Thord is an elderly man and has no children. All his wealth will go to Olaf; meanwhile, you can see the boy whenever you wish.'

After this Thord took over the raising of Olaf, who was then seven years old, and treated the boy with great affection. When news of this spread to those men who had unfinished business with Thord Goddi, they saw that it would make settling scores considerably more difficult.

Hoskuld sent Thord Bellower generous gifts and asked him not to take offence at the developments. Legally, he said, they had no right to demand payment on Vigdis's behalf, as Vigdis had not declared any grounds for her divorce which had been proven to be true and thus justified her departure.[14] 'One can hardly blame Thord for trying to seek a way to rid himself of a man who threatened to cost him dearly and whose guilt surrounded him like juniper bushes around a rowan tree.'

When Hoskuld's message was conveyed to Thord Bellower, along with substantial gifts of money, he let himself be appeased. Any property Hoskuld was in charge of was well looked after, he said. He accepted the gifts and no action was taken, although relations were somewhat cooler between them after that.

Olaf grew up with Thord Goddi and turned into a big, strong man. He was so handsome that no man could be found to equal him. At the age of only twelve he rode to the Althing, and people coming from other districts were impressed at how fine a figure he cut. Olaf dressed well and bore fine weapons, all of which set him apart from other men. Thord Goddi's situation was much better after Olaf became his foster-son. Hoskuld gave his son the nickname Peacock. The name stuck and he was known by it from then on.

17 | Hrapp was becoming increasingly difficult to deal with. By now he was so aggressive that his neighbours could hardly stand up to his attacks. Hrapp could not touch Thord after Olaf came of age. As he grew older, Hrapp's strength waned until he was confined to his bed, but his malicious nature remained the same. He summoned his wife Vigdis and spoke: 'I'm not one to catch every passing disease,' he said, 'and this illness will likely send us our separate ways. When I'm dead I want to be buried in the kitchen doorway. Have me placed in the ground upright, so I'll be able to keep a watchful eye over my home.'[15]

He died soon afterwards.

Everything was done just as he had instructed, for she dared not go against his wishes. But if it had been difficult to deal with him when he was alive, he was much worse dead, for he haunted the area relentlessly. It is said that in his haunting he killed most of his servants. To most of the people living in the vicinity he caused no end of difficulty and the farm at Hrappsstadir became deserted. Vigdis, Hrapp's wife, fled to the west of Iceland to her brother Thorstein Surt, who offered her a home and took charge of her property.

Once again, the farmers called on Hoskuld to tell him of the difficulties Hrapp was causing and ask him to find some solution. This Hoskuld promised to do and, taking several men with him, went to Hrappsstadir to disinter Hrapp and move him somewhere far away from sheep and men alike. Hrapp's haunting decreased considerably after this. Sumarlidi, Hrapp's son, inherited his property, which was both of good quality and quantity. The following spring Sumarlidi set up a farm at Hrappsstadir, but went insane after having lived there only a brief while and died shortly afterwards. Vigdis, his mother, then inherited all the property, but she refused to live on the farm at Hrappsstadir so Thorstein Surt took charge of all the property. He was an elderly man by this time, but still strong and in good health.

18 | In the meantime, Thorstein's kinsmen in the Thorsnes district, Bork the Stout and his brother Thorgrim, had become full-grown men. It was soon evident that the brothers intended to be the leading men of the district and enjoy the greatest respect. Thorstein saw this and, in order to avoid coming into conflict with them, declared his intention to move and set up house at Hrappsstadir in Laxardal. He made his preparations for the journey following the Spring Assembly and had his livestock herded along the coast.

Thorstein and eleven others boarded a ferry. Among them were his son-in-law Thorarin, his daughter Osk and Thorarin's daughter, Hild, who was then three years old. A strong south-westerly wind bore Thorstein's ship into a current known as Kolkistustraum (Coal-chest Current), the most dangerous of the Breidafjord currents. Their crossing was slow and difficult, mainly because the tide was ebbing and the wind against them. The rain came in showers, with strong winds gusting when the clouds broke and then calmer spells in between.

Thorarin was at the helm. He had the straps to control the rudder bound round his shoulders as there was little room to move about aboard ship. It was loaded with chests and cases, piled high, for they were not far from land. The boat made slow progress against the strong opposing current. They ran aground on a skerry but not hard enough to break through the hull of the ship. Thorstein told them to strike the sail quickly, take the long forks and attempt to push the ship afloat again. They tried this but without success, because the water on both sides of the ship was so deep that the forks could not reach the bottom. The only course was to await the incoming tide.

While they waited, and the tide continued to ebb around them, they saw a seal, much larger than most, swimming in the water nearby. It swam round and round the ship, its flippers unusually long, and everyone aboard was struck by its eyes, which were like those of a human. Thorstein told them to spear the seal and they tried, but to no avail.

Finally, the tide began to come in. When it had reached the point where the ship was about to float free, a great storm struck which capsized the ship. Everyone aboard was drowned except one man who managed to make his way to shore holding on to a bit of wood. His name was Gudmund and the islands where he landed have since been called Gudmundareyjar (Gudmund's Islands).

Thorstein's daughter Gudrid, who was married to Thorkel Scarf, was to inherit her father's property after his death. The news of the drowning of Thorstein Surt and the others who were with him spread quickly. Thorkel lost no time in sending for Gudmund, the survivor. When he arrived Thorkel made a secret bargain with him to have Gudmund describe according to his instructions how those aboard ship had died. Gudmund agreed to this. Thorkel then asked him, in the presence of many other people, to tell them what had happened. According to Gudmund's story, Thorstein had drowned first, followed by his son-in-law Thorarin. At this point it was Hild, Thorarin's daughter, who would have inherited everything. The next to drown, said Gudmund, was the child, which meant that the property fell to her mother Osk. Osk was the last to die, and thus the property came into the hands of Thorkel Scarf, as Osk's sister, Gudrid, who inherited her sister's property, was his wife.

Thorkel and his followers spread this story, but Gudmund had earlier given a slightly different version of the events. Thorarin's kinsmen found the new version rather suspicious and said they were not convinced. They demanded that Thorkel split the property with them. Thorkel maintained that it was all his by right and offered to undergo an ordeal[16] to prove it, according to the custom of the time.

The usual ordeal took the form of walking under an arch of raised turf. A long piece of sod was cut from a grassy field but the ends left uncut. It was raised up into an arch under which the person carrying out the ordeal had to pass. Thorkel Scarf knew there was reason to doubt the truth of the later version of the drownings which he and Gudmund had reported. Heathen men were no less conscious of their responsibility when they underwent ordeals than are Christian men who perform them nowadays. A person managing to pass under the arch of turf without its collapsing was absolved of guilt.

Thorkel arranged for two men to pretend to start a dispute, for some reason or other, near the place where the trial was to be held. They were to knock against the arch with enough force that the onlookers could plainly see that they had caused it to collapse. The trial began, and at the moment when Thorkel passed under the arch these accomplices charged at each other with their weapons in the air, collided near the arch of turf and naturally caused it to collapse. Other men ran up to separate the combatants, which was an easy enough matter as they were hardly fighting in earnest. Thorkel Scarf then appealed to the onlookers for their verdict. All of his followers were quick to say that the ordeal would have been successful if these others had not spoilt things. Thorkel then took possession of all the property, but the farm at Hrappsstadir remained deserted.

19 | The story now turns to Hoskuld. His situation was such that he enjoyed great respect and was an important chieftain. He was in charge of considerable wealth that belonged to his brother, Hrut Herjolfsson. More than one man pointed out that it would make a sizeable dent in Hoskuld's property if he had to pay out all of his mother's portion of the inheritance.

Hrut had become one of the followers of King Harald Gunnhildarson.[17] He was held in high esteem by the king, mainly because he had proved his fighting prowess in dangerous situations. He was such a favourite with Gunnhild, the queen mother, that she maintained that none of the king's followers was his equal, either in word or deed. People might make comparisons of men,[18] and praise men's excellence, but it was obvious to everyone that Queen Gunnhild considered it nothing but lack of judgement, if not envy, if anyone was compared to Hrut.

As Hrut knew that in Iceland there awaited him both well-born kinsmen and a share in great wealth, he wanted very much to go and seek both out. In parting the king presented him with a ship and said Hrut had proved a stalwart fellow.

Gunnhild accompanied Hrut to his ship and said, 'It's no secret that I regard you as an exceptional man; you are as capable as the best of our men, and far exceed them in intelligence.'

She then gave him a gold arm ring in farewell, hid her face in her shawl and walked stiffly and rapidly towards town, while Hrut boarded his ship and sailed out to sea.

He had a good journey and made land in Breidafjord. He sailed to the islands [at the mouth of Hvammsfjord], then into Breidasund, and landed at Kambsnes, where he laid a gangway from ship to shore. News of a ship's arrival, and the fact that Hrut Herjolfsson was at the helm, spread quickly. Hoskuld was little pleased by the news and did not go to meet and welcome him. Hrut had the ship drawn ashore and secured. He built a farmstead at Kambsnes, then approached Hoskuld to demand his mother's share of the inheritance. Hoskuld said he was not obliged to pay him anything, as his mother had not left Iceland empty-handed when she returned to Norway and married Herjolf. Hrut was far from happy at his reply, but rode off. All of Hrut's kinsmen, apart from Hoskuld, gave him a proper welcome.

Hrut lived at Kambsnes for three years and sought continually to press Hoskuld for his property at assemblies or other legal gatherings, where he put his case well. Most men said that Hrut was in the right, but Hoskuld maintained that Thorgerd had not obtained his consent to marry Herjolf, and that he was legally his mother's guardian. On this note they parted.

The following autumn Hoskuld accepted an invitation to
visit Thord Goddi. Hrut learned of it and rode to Hoskuldsstadir with eleven followers. He took twenty head of cattle,
leaving behind an equal number, and sent a messenger to
Hoskuld to tell him where the missing cattle could be found.
Hoskuld's farmhands lost no time in arming themselves and
others nearby were summoned, until fifteen men had gathered.
They rode after Hrut, each with as much speed as he could
muster.

Hrut and his men did not notice the pursuers until they were
only a short distance from the farm at Kambsnes. When they
did, they dismounted, tethered their horses and went over to a
gravelly stretch of land where Hrut said they would face their
pursuers. He said that although he had made slow progress in
regaining his property from Hoskuld he would not let it be said
that he had fled from his lackeys. Hrut's companions said they
would be facing superior numbers. Hrut replied that this was
nothing to worry about and said that the more they were, the
worse they would fare.

The men of Laxardal jumped down from their horses and
prepared to do battle. Hrut told his men to forget the difference
in numbers, and led the way against the pursuers. He had a
helmet on his head, his sword raised in one hand and a shield
in his other. No man fought better. Hrut was so aroused that
few of his men could keep up with him. Both sides fought
determinedly for a while, but after Hrut had killed two men in
a single charge, the men of Laxardal realized that they were no
match for him. They then surrendered, and Hrut said their lives
should be spared. All of Hoskuld's farmhands who were still
alive had been wounded by this time and four of them had been
killed. Hrut returned home with substantial wounds but his
companions were hardly hurt at all, as he had borne the brunt
of the fighting. The site has been called Orrustudal (Battle
valley) ever since. Hrut then had all the cattle butchered.

As for Hoskuld, upon hearing of the theft he collected his
men together quickly and rode home. They arrived at nearly
the same time as the farmhands returned – with a sorry tale to
tell. Hoskuld was furious and swore that he did not intend to

be robbed by Hrut of livestock and men again. He spent the day gathering supporters. His wife Jorunn approached him and asked what he planned to do.

'I haven't decided on any plan yet, but I hope to give people more to talk about than the death of my farmhands.'

Jorunn answered, 'Your intention is vile if it includes killing a man of your brother's stature. Many people feel that Hrut is only taking what is his by right, and that he should have taken the livestock sooner. His actions show that he does not intend to be written off as a bastard with no claim to property which is rightly his. Nor would he have set out on this errand, and placed himself in open conflict with you, if he did not have reason to expect that powerful men would back him up. I've been told that Hrut has secretly exchanged messages with Thord Bellower, which I find very ominous. Thord Goddi will be more than interested in supporting such a case where so much is at stake. You know only too well, Hoskuld, that since the split between Thord and Vigdis there's been no love lost between you and Thord Bellower and his kinsmen, though you managed to lessen their hostility towards you temporarily with gifts. And I think, Hoskuld,' said Jorunn, 'that they take offence at the way you and your son Olaf have been denying them their share.

'I think you'd better do right by your brother Hrut, for a hungry wolf is bound to wage a hard battle. Hrut will, I'm sure, be more than ready to accept an offer of settlement, as I'm told he is no fool. He must see that it would do honour to both of you.'

Listening to Jorunn's counsel, Hoskuld calmed down and saw the truth of her arguments. Mutual friends were then able to intervene and convey to Hrut Hoskuld's offer of settlement. Hrut responded positively, saying he was certainly willing to reach an agreement with Hoskuld; he had long since been ready to reach an agreement as brothers should, so long as Hoskuld granted him his rights. Hrut also said Hoskuld was entitled to compensation for the damage he had done him. The matters were discussed and an agreement reached between the two brothers, Hoskuld and Hrut. From that time onward the two got along as kinsmen should.

Hrut settled down to farm and became a powerful figure. He was not one to intervene often in other men's affairs, but when he did get involved he was determined to have his way. Hrut moved his farm site a short distance to the south to where the farm Hrutsstadir is located and lived there into his old age. He erected a temple in the hayfield nearby, the remains of which can still be seen. The site is called Trollaskeid (Trolls' path), and is now on the public road.

Hrut married and his wife was Unn, the daughter of Mord Gigja. She later divorced him and this became the beginning of a dispute between the people of Laxardal and of Fljotshlid.[19] Hrut's second wife was Thorbjorg Armodsdottir. He was married to a third woman, whose name is not recorded. With his two later wives Hrut had sixteen sons and ten daughters. It is said that one summer Hrut attended the Althing accompanied by fourteen of his sons. Mention is made of the fact because it was considered an indication of his wealth and power. All of his sons were accomplished men.

20 | By now Hoskuld was an elderly man and his sons full-grown. Thorleik built a farm at Kambsnes and Hoskuld turned over to him his share of the property. He then married Gjaflaug, the daughter of Arnbjorn, the son of Sleitu-Bjorn, and his wife Thorlaug Thordardottir from Hofdi. Gjaflaug was both a good-looking and a haughty woman, and was thought a fine match. Thorleik was anything but a peaceable man and was a great warrior. There was no love lost between Thorleik and his kinsman Hrut. Bard, Hoskuld's other son, lived at home with his father and the running of the farm was as much in his hands as Hoskuld's. There is little mention made of Hoskuld's daughters here, although they are known to have descendants. Olaf Hoskuldsson was also a young adult by this time and the most handsome man people had ever seen. He always dressed well and carried fine weapons. Melkorka, Olaf's mother, lived at Melkorkustadir, as was previously mentioned. Hoskuld became more and more reluctant to look after Melkorka's affairs, saying he felt it was just as much Olaf's responsibility

as his, and Olaf said he would offer her whatever help and advice he could.

Melkorka, however, felt humiliated by Hoskuld and made up her mind to repay him in kind. Thorbjorn Pock-marked had looked after most of the farming for Melkorka. Only a short time after she settled on the farm he had asked for her hand in marriage, but Melkorka had refused even to consider the offer. At this time there was a ship beached at Bordeyri in Hrutafjord. The skipper was a man called Orn, a follower of King Harald Gunnhildarson.

The next time Melkorka saw Olaf, she brought up the subject of his journeying abroad to seek out his high-born kinsmen, 'as everything I have told you is true, Myrkjartan is my father and he is king of the Irish. You could take the ship at Bordeyri.'

Olaf said, 'I have mentioned it to my father, and he was not in favour of the idea. And as far as my foster-father goes, his property consists mainly of land and livestock, and he has little in the form of Icelandic export goods.'

Melkorka answered: 'I've had my fill of people calling you the son of a slave-woman. If it's concern about trade goods that is preventing you from making the journey, then I would rather help you out by marrying Thorbjorn, if it means you'll make the journey. I'm sure he'll contribute whatever goods you feel you need for the journey if he gets me as his wife into the bargain.

'There is another advantage to this as well – it will give Hoskuld a double sting when he learns that you have left the country and I am married.'

Olaf said it was up to his mother to decide. Soon afterwards he spoke to Thorbjorn and asked him to provide him with a large quantity of export goods on loan.

Thorbjorn replied: 'Only on one condition, that I reach a marriage agreement with Melkorka. Then you can consider my property to be just as much yours as anything else you have at your disposal.'

Olaf told Thorbjorn he had himself a bargain. They discussed the details of the transaction, and agreed that it should remain a secret.

Hoskuld asked Olaf if he would accompany him to the Althing but Olaf replied that he was too occupied on the farm. He said he had to see about having a pasture walled off for his lambs down by the river Laxa. Hoskuld was pleased at Olaf's reply, and his apparent interest in the farm. No sooner had Hoskuld departed for the Althing than wedding feasting got under way at Lambastadir. Olaf set the conditions of the wedding agreement himself. He chose thirty hundreds of goods off the top, before the property was divided [between Thorbjorn and Melkorka], for which he was to make no payment. Bard Hoskuldsson attended the wedding and knew of their plans.

When the ceremonies were over, Olaf rode to the ship, met with Orn, the skipper, and arranged his passage. Before he left, his mother Melkorka handed Olaf a heavy gold arm ring, saying: 'This treasure my father gave me when I cut my first tooth, and he'll surely recognize it when he sees it again.'

She also gave him a knife and belt which he was to hand over to her nurse – 'who will not fail to know what these tokens mean'.

'I've now done all I can to help you,' Melkorka continued. 'I've also taught you to speak Irish, so that you'll be able to speak to people anywhere you make land in Ireland.'

They then parted. A favourable wind rose as Olaf reached the ship and they put out to sea at once.

21 | Hoskuld returned from the Althing to be told the news. He was far from pleased, but as his own family were involved, he soon calmed down and took no action. Olaf and his shipmates had a good passage and made land in Norway.

Orn urged Olaf to go to pay his respects to King Harald, saying that men who had less to recommend them than Olaf had been handsomely received by the king. Olaf said he would take his advice. Olaf and Orn then proceeded to where the king sat and were well received; the king welcomed Olaf warmly as soon as he learned who his kinsmen were, and lost no time in offering him a place among his followers. Upon hearing he was Hrut's nephew, Gunnhild also took a great liking to him. Some people even said that she would have enjoyed Olaf's company regardless of who his kinsmen were. As the winter progressed, Olaf grew moody and Orn asked what was troubling him.

Olaf answered: 'I have to make the journey to the Western Isles. It's very important to me that you arrange it so that we make the voyage this summer.'

Orn told Olaf to forget the idea, saying he knew of no ship journeying westward.

As they were talking, Gunnhild came up and spoke: 'Now I hear something I have never heard before: the two of you disagreeing on anything.'

Olaf welcomed Gunnhild warmly but did not change the subject of their discussion. Orn left, and Olaf and Gunnhild continued the conversation. Olaf told her of his intentions and how important the journey was for him. He said he knew for certain that King Myrkjartan was his grandfather.

To this Gunnhild replied: 'I will support your journey so that you can go as well equipped as you wish.'

Olaf thanked her for the offer. Gunnhild then ordered a ship to be made ready and manned, asking Olaf how many men he wished to have accompany him on his journey. Olaf asked for sixty men, and stressed the importance of choosing men who were more like warriors than merchants. She promised to see to this. Of Olaf's companions only Orn is named.

The company was well turned out. King Harald and Gunnhild accompanied Olaf to his ship and said they hoped their own good fortune would follow him, along with their goodwill. King Harald added that this would not be difficult, as he had seen no young man more promising among the Icelanders of the time. King Harald then asked how old Olaf was.

Olaf replied: 'I am now eighteen years old.'

The king spoke: 'You will make the finest of men, as capable as you are and still barely more than a child. Come to us directly upon your return.'

Then the king and Gunnhild said farewell.

Olaf boarded his ship and they sailed out to sea. They had poor winds during the summer, the breezes light and blowing from the wrong direction, and spells of thick fog. They drifted long distances at sea. Most of the men on board soon lost their sense of direction. Eventually the fog lifted and a wind came up. The sail was hoisted and a discussion began on which direction to take to head to Ireland. There was no agreement among the men on the question: Orn was of one opinion, but most of the men were opposed and declared that Orn was wrong and that the majority should determine their course.

The question was put to Olaf, who said, 'Let the man of best judgement determine our course; the counsel of fools is the more misguided the more of them there are.'

The question was considered decided by Olaf's words, and from then on Orn decided on their course. They sailed night and day for several days, with little wind, until one night the men on watch leapt up and woke the others. They said they had seen land very close to the bow of the ship, and the sail was still up and only a light breeze blowing. The others jumped up at once and Orn told them to steer out to sea at once if they could.

'There's no point in us doing that,' Olaf said. 'I can see from the way the waves break there are skerries on all sides; reef the sail as quickly as you can. We'll discuss what course to take when it grows light and we can see what land this is.'

They cast the anchor, which struck bottom at once.

During the night there was considerable discussion as to where they might be, and when the day dawned they saw that it was Ireland.

Orn then spoke: 'I'm afraid we won't be well received. We're far from any port or merchant town where foreigners are assured of trading in peace, and now the tide has gone out and left us stranded here like a minnow. It's my guess that, according to Irish law, they'll lay claim to all the property we have on board; they call it a stranded ship when less than this has ebbed from the stern of the ship.'

Olaf said they would come to no harm. 'But I did see a group of men up on shore today, and the arrival of our ship is obviously news to the Irish. I checked the coastline carefully while the tide was out. There is a river flowing into the sea

beside this point and water in the estuary even when the tide
ebbs. If our ship is not damaged, I think we should put out our
boat and draw the ship over there.'

The beach was clay where the ship lay at anchor, so that not
a single plank was damaged. They moved the ship as Olaf
suggested and dropped anchor there.

Later that day a large crowd of people came down to the
beach. Two of them approached in a boat to ask who was in
command of the ship. Olaf replied to them in Irish, as they had
spoken in that tongue. When the Irish learned that they were
Norse, they referred to their laws on ship strandings and said
that if the ship's company handed over all the property on
board they would be unharmed until the king had pronounced
his judgement in their case. Olaf said that this was indeed the
law if there was no interpreter among the traders.

'I warn you, we are men of peace but we don't intend to give
up without a fight.'

Giving a war cry, the Irish charged into the sea, intending to
wade out to the ship and draw it ashore with them aboard. The
water was so shallow that it only came up to their armpits and
just above the belts of the tallest of them. The pool where the
ship was anchored was so deep, however, that they could not
touch bottom. Olaf told his men to get their weapons out and
form a line along the sides of the ship. They stood so close
together that their shields formed an unbroken row, with a
spear point extending from the lower end of each shield. Olaf
took up position in the bow. He wore a coat of mail and on his
head a helmet with golden plates. At his waist was a sword, its
hilt inlaid with gold, and in his hand he held a spear with a
hooked blade, also highly decorated. Before him he held a red
shield, with the design of a lion in gold.

The sight of their readiness for battle struck fear into the
hearts of the Irish, and they realized that the ship was not the
easy prey they had imagined. They turned back and gathered in
a group. Many were greatly upset, thinking this was obviously a
vessel of war and likely to be followed by a number of others.
They sent word to the king, who was visiting nearby. He came
at once to the spot where the ship lay at anchor, accompanied

by a group of followers. The distance between ship and shore was so narrow that it was possible to call from one to the other. The Irish had made several attacks, shooting arrows and casting spears, without any of Olaf's men coming to harm. Olaf stood in the bow attired as previously described, and people were greatly impressed by the imposing-looking leader of the ship.

Olaf's companions fell silent when they saw a group of horsemen approach, well armed and valiant-looking, as it now appeared they would have to face far superior forces.

When Olaf heard the words of concern expressed by his companions, however, he told them to pull themselves together – 'as our situation has taken a turn for the better. The Irish are now welcoming their king, Myrkjartan.'

The procession on shore then came near enough to exchange words with the men on board ship. The king asked who the skipper of the ship was. Olaf gave his name and asked in return who this valiant knight was with whom he spoke.

'My name is Myrkjartan,' he answered.

When Olaf asked, 'Are you then the king of the Irish?', he replied that he was.

Then the king asked for general news and Olaf provided suitable answers to all his questions, following which the king asked where they had sailed from and who they were. He enquired more carefully into Olaf's kin than before, as he realized that this man was both proud and careful to say no more than he was asked.

Olaf said, 'For your information we set sail from Norway, and the men on board are followers of King Harald Gunnhildarson. As to my own kin, my lord, my father who lives in Iceland is named Hoskuld, and is a man of a prominent family. As far as my mother's kinsmen are concerned, I expect you know more about them than I do; her name is Melkorka and I have been told truly that she is your own daughter, King. This was my reason for making such a lengthy journey, and it is of great importance to me to hear what reply you make to my words.'

Upon hearing this the king fell silent and went to speak to his followers. Learned men asked the king what truth there was in the words the man spoke. The king answered: 'This Olaf is obviously a man of high birth, whether or not he is our kinsman, and no one speaks better Irish.'

The king then got to his feet and spoke: 'My reply to your words is to grant protection to all of your companions on board. As to your kinship with us, we will have to discuss the question more fully before I can give you an answer.'

Gangways were then put out to the ship and Olaf went ashore, followed by his men. The Irish were impressed by their rugged appearance.

Olaf greeted the king courteously, removed his helmet and knelt before him, and the king welcomed him warmly. They began a discussion; Olaf repeated his story, speaking at length and with effect.

In conclusion he referred to the gold ring on his arm, which Melkorka had handed over to him at their parting in Iceland, 'saying that you, my lord, had given it to her when she cut her first tooth'.

The king took the ring in his hand and upon examining it, his face grew very red.

He then spoke: 'These tokens are irrefutable, and are even more convincing because you resemble your mother so much that you could be recognized by that alone. Such being the case, I do not hesitate to acknowledge you as my kinsman, Olaf, and may all who hear my words bear witness. I therefore invite you, and all your men, to my court. What honour you receive there will depend upon the man you prove yourself to be when I put you to the test.'

The king obtained horses for them and appointed men to stand guard over their ship and cargo. The king then rode to Dublin and the news that the king was accompanied by his grandson, the son of his daughter who had been taken prisoner at the age of fifteen years, caused great stir. No one was more affected by the news than Melkorka's nurse. Despite being bedridden with old age and illness, she rose and went, without the aid of her stick, to meet Olaf.

The king then told Olaf: 'The woman approaching was Melkorka's nurse and she will ask you for news of her.'

Olaf received her with open arms, set her upon his lap and

told her that her former charge was living in comfort in Iceland. Then Olaf handed her the belt and knife, which the old woman recognized at once, and tears of joy came to her eyes.

She said her happiness was doubled by seeing this outstanding young son of Melkorka's – 'just like you'd expect from one of his kin'.

The old woman enjoyed good health for the rest of that winter.

The king seldom remained long in one place, as there was generally fighting somewhere in the British Isles. He spent the winter warding off both Vikings and other raiders. Olaf and his men fought with the king on his ship, and those they were pitted against found them hard to handle. The king soon came to seek the advice of Olaf and his men in all decisions, for he discovered him to be a clever and daring commander. As the winter drew to a close, the king called an assembly, which great numbers of people attended. The king addressed the assembly, beginning his speech with the following words: 'As you know, this past autumn a man came to us who proved to be the son of my daughter, and of good family on his father's side as well. Olaf has since shown himself to be highly accomplished and a man of such determination that we have no one in our kingdom to equal him. I wish Olaf to inherit the crown after my day, as he is better suited to rule than are my sons.'

Olaf thanked him for his offer with many well-chosen words and fair praise, but said he would not take the chance of having to deal with the reaction of Myrkjartan's sons after his death. He would rather, he said, enjoy a brief spell of honour than a long rule of shame. He said he intended to return to Norway as soon as the weather made it safe for ships to make the journey between the countries, and it would bring little joy to his mother should he fail to return. The king said it was up to Olaf to decide, and the assembly was then dissolved.

When Olaf was ready to sail, the king accompanied him to the ship and gave him a spear with gold inlay, a decorated sword and much other wealth. Olaf asked to take Melkorka's nurse with him, but the king said there was no need to do so, and so she remained. Olaf and his men boarded their ship and he and the king parted as great friends. Then Olaf and his men put to sea and had favourable winds until they made land in Norway, where news of Olaf's voyage spread widely. They beached their ship and Olaf obtained horses for himself and his companions to make the journey to King Harald.

22 | When Olaf Hoskuldsson came to him, King Harald received him well, but Gunnhild better still. They invited him to stay with them, and pressed him to accept. Olaf agreed and both he and Orn became king's men. The king and Gunnhild showed Olaf more honour than any other foreigner had ever been shown. Olaf gave them a number of rare and precious objects which he had brought with him from Ireland. At Christmas the king gave Olaf a complete suit of clothes made from scarlet.[20]

Olaf remained with the king over the winter, but as spring passed he spoke privately to the king and asked his leave to journey to Iceland that summer.

'Many prominent kinsmen await me there,' he said.

'If I could decide,' the king answered, 'I would rather you settled here with me on whatever terms you choose.'

Olaf thanked the king for the honour he showed him but said he would prefer to go to Iceland, if the king did not oppose it.

Then the king answered, 'I'll not detain you against your wishes, Olaf. You will journey to Iceland this summer, as I can see your heart is set on doing so, but don't bother about making the preparations, for I will have that taken care of.'

On this note their conversation concluded.

King Harald had a ship set afloat that spring, a knorr, of good size and seaworthy. He had it loaded with timber and all necessary provisions and, when the ship was ready, he sent for Olaf and said, 'This ship is yours, Olaf. I won't have you sail from Norway this summer as another man's passenger.'

Olaf thanked the king profusely for his generosity. After completing his preparations to leave, he sailed his ship out to sea, taking leave of King Harald on the best of terms. Olaf was favoured by good winds that summer. His ship sailed south into Hrutafjord and landed at Bordeyri. News of the ship's arrival, and of its skipper, spread quickly. Hoskuld was very glad to learn of his son's return and set out at once northwards towards Hrutafjord, accompanied by several men. After a warm reunion, Hoskuld invited Olaf to come home and stay with them, and Olaf accepted. He had his ship beached and his property sent south, then rode with eleven men to Hoskuldsstadir. Hoskuld gave his son a warm welcome, and his half-brothers also received him well, especially Bard.

Olaf became renowned as a result of his journey and the news that he was the grandson of Myrkjartan, king of the Irish. The story spread throughout Iceland, together with reports of the honour the powerful men whom he had visited had shown him. Olaf had also brought great wealth home.

He spent the winter at his father's farm. Melkorka soon came to meet her son and Olaf welcomed her warmly. She had much to ask him about Ireland, beginning with news of her father and other kinsmen. Olaf answered all her questions. She soon enquired whether her nurse was still alive, and Olaf replied, that yes, she was still living. Then Melkorka asked why he had not done her the favour of bringing the woman to Iceland.

To this Olaf replied: 'They did not want me, Mother, to bring your nurse with me to Iceland.'

'As you say,' Melkorka said, but it was evident that she was very disappointed.

Melkorka and Thorbjorn had a son called Lambi. He was a big, strong man, much like his father both in appearance and disposition.

The next spring following Olaf's return to Iceland, father and son discussed plans for his future.

'I suggest, Olaf,' said Hoskuld, 'seeking a wife for you and having you take over the farm at Goddastadir from your foster-father. It's still a good piece of property; you would take over the farm under my direction.'

Olaf replied: 'I haven't thought about it very much yet, nor do I know where I should find a woman it would do me honour to marry. As you can imagine, I won't be satisfied with anything but the best of matches. But I'm sure you wouldn't have brought

the matter up, had you not already decided where it should
come down.'

Hoskuld said, 'You're right about that. A man named Egil,
the son of Skallagrim,[21] lives at Borg in Borgarfjord. Egil has a
daughter named Thorgerd whom I intend to seek as a wife for
you, as there's no better match in all of Borgarfjord, or far
beyond, for that matter. What's more it will strengthen your
position to make an alliance with the Myrar family.'

Olaf replied: 'I'll take your advice in the matter, as it seems
a good enough proposal – if it's accepted. But I warn you,
Father, that if we bring up the question only to be turned down,
I'll be very annoyed.'

Hoskuld said, 'I'll take the risk of raising the question.'

Olaf said he would take his advice.

The time of the Althing approached and Hoskuld prepared to
make the journey with a large number of followers, including his
son Olaf. They set up their booth at the Althing. A great number
of people were there, among them Egil Skallagrimsson. Everyone
who saw Olaf remarked on how handsome and imposing a
figure he was. He was well dressed and carried fine weapons.

23 | One day, it is said, Olaf and Hoskuld paid a visit to Egil's
     | booth. Egil received them warmly, for he and Hoskuld
knew each other well. Hoskuld brought up the question of a
match between Olaf and Egil's daughter Thorgerd, who was
also attending the Althing. Egil responded positively to the idea,
saying he had heard nothing but favourable reports of both
father and son.

'I know, Hoskuld,' Egil said, 'that you're highly respected
and a man of prominent family, while Olaf has become renowned for his journey abroad. It hardly comes as a surprise
that such men, lacking neither good looks nor a good family,
should set their sights high. But the question will have to be
taken up with Thorgerd, because there's no man who could
make Thorgerd his wife should she be set against it.'

Hoskuld said, 'I would like you, Egil, to discuss it with your
daughter.'

Egil agreed and later spoke to Thorgerd privately.

'There's a man called Olaf, the son of Hoskuld,' Egil said, 'one of the most renowned in the country. His father has asked for your hand in marriage on his son's behalf. I have referred the question to you, and wait to hear what you say, but it seems to me that such a request deserves a good answer, as it's a good match.'

Thorgerd answered: 'I have heard you say, Father, that of all your children I was your favourite. It seems to me that can hardly be true if you intend to marry me to some slave-girl's son, however handsome and renowned he may be.'

Egil said, 'Your nose for news doesn't seem to have served you as well as usual in this instance; haven't you heard that he is the grandson of the Irish king, Myrkjartan? He's of even better family on his mother's side than his father's, which by itself would be more than good enough for us.'

Thorgerd was unconvinced, and the conversation ended in disagreement.

The following day Egil went to Hoskuld's booth where he was well received. The two men spoke privately and Hoskuld asked for news of the marriage proposal. Egil said the prospects looked glum and related what had happened.

Hoskuld agreed that it did look difficult – 'but I still think you are doing the right thing'.

After Egil had left, Olaf, who had been elsewhere while they talked, asked for news of the marriage proposal. Hoskuld replied that Thorgerd seemed reluctant.

Olaf spoke: 'It's turned out just as I feared, Father, and as I told you I am hardly pleased at being disgraced by a refusal. It was your idea to start this business; now I intend to carry it through to the proper end. It's true enough as they say, when one wolf hunts for another he may eat the prey. I'm going to pay Egil a visit.'

Hoskuld said it was up to him to decide.

Olaf was wearing the suit of scarlet which King Harald had given him, a gold-plated helmet on his head and the sword given to him by King Myrkjartan. Father and son set out for Egil's booth, with Hoskuld in the lead and Olaf following. Egil

welcomed them warmly and Hoskuld sat down beside him, but
Olaf remained standing and looked about the tent. He noticed
a woman, seated on a cross-bench, who was both good-looking
and well attired, and decided this must be Egil's daughter,
Thorgerd.

Olaf approached the cross-bench and took a seat beside her.
Thorgerd greeted him and asked who he was.

Olaf told her his own name and his father's, and added, 'You
must think it bold of a slave-girl's son to dare to sit down beside
you and strike up a conversation with you.'

Thorgerd replied, 'You must think you've done more dangerous things in your life than talk to women.'

The two of them then spent most of the day in conversation
but no one else heard what they spoke about. Before they were
finished, however, Hoskuld and Egil were called over, and
discussion of the proposal of marriage began anew. Thorgerd
agreed to abide by her father's decision and, as his consent was
given readily, the two were betrothed then and there. The bride
was to be brought to the wedding as an indication of respect
for the people of Laxardal. It was agreed the wedding should
be at Hoskuldsstadir when seven weeks of summer were
remaining.

The families then parted, and Olaf and Hoskuld rode home
to Hoskuldsstadir where the summer passed without event.
Preparations commenced for the wedding, with nothing spared,
for this was a wealthy family. The guests arrived at the
appointed time. People from Borgarfjord came in great number,
led by Egil and his son Thorstein, the bride and the leaders of
the entire district. Hoskuld's own guests also attended in great
number. The festival was outstanding and the visitors given
handsome gifts at parting. Olaf gave the sword, Myrkjartan's
Gift, to Egil, who made no attempt to conceal his great pleasure
at the gift. Everything proceeded without incident and afterwards people all returned to their homes.

24 | Olaf and Thorgerd stayed at Hoskuldsstadir and cared greatly for each other. Everyone soon realized what a woman of strong character Thorgerd was: though she was not one to waste words, once she set her mind on something there was no swaying her – things had to go the way she wanted. Olaf and Thorgerd spent the winter months either at Hoskuldsstadir or with Olaf's foster-father, Thord Goddi. In the spring Olaf took over the farm at Goddastadir, and that summer Thord was taken ill and died. Olaf had him buried in a mound at the spot called Drafnarnes on the banks of the Laxa river. A stone wall near the site was called Haugsgard (Mound wall).

Olaf soon had no lack of supporters and became an important chieftain. Hoskuld in no way resented this, and even urged that Olaf be consulted in all affairs of importance. Olaf's farm was soon the most impressive in Laxardal. Among the members of his household were two brothers, both of whom were named An – one An the White, the other An the Black. A third servant was known as Beinir the Strong. They were good carpenters and capable men. Thorgerd and Olaf had a daughter named Thurid.

The lands which Hrapp had owned were deserted, as was previously written. Olaf thought this a likely piece of land, as it bordered on his own, and suggested to his father that they pay a visit to Thorkel Scarf to purchase the land at Hrappsstadir and other property connected to it. Their offer was readily accepted and the purchase concluded, as Thorkel felt that a bird in the hand was better than two in the bush. According to the terms of the bargain, Olaf was to pay three marks of silver for the lands, which was far below their worth. They included large stretches of prime pasture and plenty of other benefits, including salmon fishing and seal hunting, and large forests as well.

A short distance upriver from Hoskuldsstadir, on the north side of the Laxa, a grove had been cleared in the forest. Olaf's sheep could, more often than not, be found gathered in this clearing in both fair weather and foul. One autumn Olaf had a

house built in this same clearing, using wood from the forest as
well as driftwood. The large and imposing house stood empty
the first winter. The following summer Olaf moved his household there, after having rounded up his stock beforehand. This
was no small herd, as no one in the Breidafjord district owned
more livestock.

Olaf sent a request that his father stand outside where he
could watch them go by on their way to the new farm and wish
them good fortune, and Hoskuld agreed. Olaf then organized
the procession: the men at the front drove the sheep which
were most difficult to handle. Next came the milking ewes and
cattle from the home pastures, followed by steers, calves and
heifers, with the packhorses bringing up the rear. The members
of the household were placed at close intervals to keep the
livestock from straying off course. Those at the front had
reached the new farm when Olaf himself rode out of the yard
at Goddastadir, and the line stretched unbroken between them.

Hoskuld and his household stood outside the farm.

He spoke words of congratulation, wishing his son Olaf fair
tidings and good fortune in his new residence, 'and unless I
guess wrongly things will turn out that way, and his name be
long remembered'.

His wife Jorunn responded, saying 'with his wealth the slave-
woman's son should be able to make a name for himself'.

The farmhands had just finished taking the packs off the
horses when Olaf rode into the yard.

He addressed his household: 'You must be curious to know
what the farm is to be called, and I know there has been a lot
of speculation about it all winter. It will be called Hjardarholt
(Herd wood).'

Everyone thought it a very good idea to take a name linked
to the events which had occurred on the site. Olaf set about
building up his farm at Hjardarholt, and the farm was soon an
impressive one, lacking nothing. Olaf's own repute grew for a
number of reasons: he himself was very popular, especially since
he managed to resolve the disputes in which his advice was
sought in such a manner that everyone was satisfied. His father
did much to increase his honour, and his marriage alliance with

the Myrar family was also to his credit. Olaf was thought to be the most outstanding of Hoskuld's sons.

During the first winter in Hjardarholt Olaf had a large number of resident servants and other farmhands. The farm chores were divided among the servants: some looked after the non-milking stock, others the milking cows. The cowshed was located in the forest some distance away from the farmhouse.

One evening the farmhand in charge of the non-milking cattle came to Olaf and asked him to assign the task to someone else and 'give me other duties'.

Olaf answered, 'I want you to look after your own duties.'

The man replied he would rather leave the farm.

'Then you must think something is seriously wrong,' Olaf said. 'I'll accompany you tonight when you tie the animals in their stalls, and if you've any cause for complaint, I won't blame you. Otherwise you'll pay for causing trouble.'

Olaf then took the spear known as the King's Gift in his hand and went out, the servant following him. Quite a lot of snow had fallen.

They reached the cowshed, which stood open, and Olaf told the servant to go inside, saying, 'I'll herd the animals inside for you and you tie them in their places.'

The servant went towards the door of the cowshed but suddenly came running back into Olaf's arms.

When Olaf asked what had frightened him so, the servant answered, 'Hrapp is standing there in the doorway, reaching out for me, and I've had my fill of wrestling with him.'

Olaf approached the door and prodded with his spear in Hrapp's direction. Hrapp gripped the spear just above the blade in both his hands and gave it a wrench, breaking the shaft. Olaf made a run at him, but Hrapp let himself sink back down to where he had come from, putting an end to their struggle. Olaf stood there with the spear shaft in his hand, for Hrapp had taken the blade.

Olaf and the servant tied the cattle in their places and returned to the farm where Olaf said the servant would not be punished for complaining. The following morning Olaf went out to where Hrapp had been buried and had him dug up.

Hrapp's body was perfectly preserved and Olaf found his spear blade there. He then had a large bonfire prepared, and had Hrapp's body burned and his ashes taken out to sea. No one else was harmed by Hrapp's haunting after that.

25 | The story now turns to Hoskuld's sons. Before he settled on his farm, Thorleik Hoskuldsson had been a successful merchant. He consorted with many men of noble birth abroad, and was considered a man of some note. He had also gone on Viking expeditions and earned himself a good reputation as a bold fighter. Bard Hoskuldsson had also been a merchant, and was both liked and respected everywhere he went, for he treated others fairly and was easy-going about everything. Bard married a woman of Breidafjord named Astrid, who was of good family. Bard had a son named Thorarin and a daughter, Gudny, who was married to Hall, the son of Killer-Styr. They had a great number of descendants.

Hrut Herjolfsson gave his slave, Hrolf, his freedom, along with some livestock and a home-site on the border of his land and Hoskuld's. It lay so near the borderline, in fact, that Hrut and his men miscalculated and placed the freed slave on property that was actually Hoskuld's. He prospered and soon had a great deal of wealth.

Hoskuld was not pleased at Hrut settling his freed slave practically in his backyard and demanded that the man pay him for the land upon which he dwelt, 'as it is my property'.

Hrolf went and told this to Hrut, who said he should pay no attention to Hoskuld and refuse to pay him. 'I'm not at all sure,' he said, 'which of us actually owned that land.'

The freed slave returned home and continued his farming as before. Shortly afterwards, Thorleik Hoskuldsson, acting on his father's bidding, went to Hrolf's farm with several men and killed him. Thorleik claimed for himself and his father all the wealth which the freed slave had acquired while dwelling there.

Hrut and his sons heard of this and were very angry. Many of his sons were now grown up and the family was an intimidating lot. Hrut tried prosecution to achieve compensation, but when men learned in law investigated the case, they gave Hrut scant hope of success. The main point was that Hrut had placed the freed slave on land belonging to Hoskuld without his permission and there his wealth had increased. Thorleik had killed a trespasser on land belonging to him and his father. Hrut was not happy with his lot, but so it was.

Afterwards Thorleik built a farm on the border of the lands owned by his father and Hrut, which was called Kambsnes, where he lived for some time, as has been mentioned. A son was born to Thorleik and his wife, sprinkled with water and given the name Bolli. He soon showed himself to be a promising child.

26 | Hoskuld Dala-Kollsson fell ill in his old age and sent for
   | his sons and other kinsmen.

When they arrived Hoskuld spoke to the brothers, Bard and Thorleik: 'An affliction has settled over me, although I've seldom been ill, and I expect this illness will put an end to me. Both of you know how things stand: as my legitimate sons you inherit all my property. I have a third son, who is illegitimate, and I ask you brothers to allow Olaf to be recognized so that each of you will inherit a third of my property.'

Bard was the first to answer and said that he would do as his father wished, 'as I expect Olaf to treat us fairly, the more so as he is much wealthier'.

Thorleik then said, 'I won't have Olaf acknowledged as heir. He has plenty of wealth already. You, Father, have given him many things and for some time now discriminated greatly between us brothers. I won't voluntarily give up my birthright.'

Hoskuld spoke: 'You can't wish to deprive me of my legal right to give my son twelve ounces[22] for his inheritance, if only in recognition of Olaf's high birth on his mother's side.'

Thorleik consented to this. Hoskuld then took his gifts from King Hakon, a gold arm ring which weighed a mark and sword which was worth half a mark of gold, and gave them to his son Olaf, wishing him all his own good fortune and that of his kinsmen. Hoskuld added that despite his words he was not unaware that this fortune had already found its way to Olaf.

Olaf said he would take a chance on Thorleik's reaction
and accepted the gifts. Thorleik was very angry, and felt that
Hoskuld had tricked him.

Olaf answered: 'I don't intend to return the objects, Thorleik,
as you consented to the gift in the presence of witnesses. I'll
take my chances on keeping them.'

Bard said he would abide by his father's wishes. Hoskuld
died soon afterwards and was greatly mourned, especially by
his sons and all his kinsmen, in-laws and friends. His sons had
a suitable mound built for his burial, but buried little wealth
with him. Afterwards, the brothers discussed among themselves
the holding of a memorial feast, a custom which had become
fashionable at that time.

Olaf said, 'To my mind we won't be able to hold this feast
right away, if we intend to make it grand enough to do us
credit. It's late autumn already and not easy to collect the
provisions we need. Many people, who have a long way to
travel, will think making the journey in the autumn too difficult,
and we can be sure that a lot of the people we want most to
attend wouldn't come in fact. I suggest we announce the feast
at the Althing next summer instead. I'll pay a third of the cost.'

The brothers agreed to this and Olaf returned home. Thorleik
and Bard divided the inheritance between them. Bard took over
their father's farm, as he had more supporters and was the more
popular, while Thorleik received a larger share of the goods
and livestock. Relations between Olaf and Bard were warm,
but rather cool between Olaf and Thorleik. The winter passed
and summer came and soon it was time for the Althing. When
the Hoskuldssons got ready to attend the Althing it was evident
that Olaf would take the lead. Upon arriving they set up their
booth in fine style.

27 | It is said that one day, as men were gathering at the Law
     | Rock, Olaf got to his feet and called for attention.

He began by recalling his father's death: 'As many of his
kinsmen and friends are here today, my brothers and I would
like to invite all of you godis to a feast in honour of our father,

Hoskuld, as most of you leading men were connected to him by marriage. I can also promise you that no man of influence will leave empty-handed. In addition, we invite farmers and any others who care to come, whether beggars or their betters, to attend this fortnight's feast at Hoskuldsstadir when ten weeks of summer remain.'

When Olaf had finished speaking, there was general approval of his speech and generosity. He returned to the booth and told his brothers of his plans, but they were not at all enthusiastic and felt he had gone too far. After the assembly the brothers returned home. The summer passed and they began preparations for the feast. Olaf contributed his third and more, and the feast was very sumptuous. Great quantities of supplies were needed, as large numbers of guests were expected. Most of the prominent people who had promised to come attended the feast at the appointed time. There were so many people that most reports put the figure at over a thousand guests. It was the second-largest feast ever held in Iceland, the largest being the memorial feast held by the Hjaltasons[23] in memory of their father, which was attended by over fourteen hundred people.

The feast was grand in every respect and a great credit to the brothers, especially Olaf. For the parting presents, which were given to all the important men, he contributed a share equal to that of both his brothers.

When most of the guests had left, Olaf turned to his brother Thorleik and said, 'Brother, as you well know, we have shown each other little affection in the past. I wish we could do better in the future. I know you resented my accepting the gifts from our father on his deathbed and if you still feel yourself hard done by, I would like to make it up to you by fostering your son, as he who raises the child of another is always considered as the lesser of the two.'

Thorleik was pleased by the offer, and agreed that it did him great honour. Olaf then took over the upbringing of Thorleik's son Bolli, who was three years of age at the time. They parted on the best of terms, with Bolli returning home to Hjardarholt with Olaf. Thorgerd welcomed him warmly and Bolli grew up with them. They loved him no less than their own children.

28 | Olaf and Thorgerd had a son. He was sprinkled with
     water and given the name Kjartan, after his grandfather
Myrkjartan, and was almost the same age as Bolli. They had
other children as well: their sons were Steinthor, Halldor and
Helgi, and the youngest was Hoskuld. Two of their daughters
were Bergthora and Thorbjorg. All their children grew up into
promising youngsters.

In Saurbaer, on the farm called Tunga, there lived a man
called Bersi the Dueller. He came to Olaf and offered to foster
his son Halldor. Olaf accepted the offer and Bersi took Halldor,
who was a year old at the time, home with him. That same
summer Bersi grew ill, and was bedridden for most of the
summer. It is said that one day the household at Tunga were
out haying and only the two of them, Halldor and Bersi, at
home. Halldor lay in a cradle, which fell on one side and the
youngster rolled out. Bersi couldn't get up to help him, and
spoke the following verse:

1.   Both of us lie,
      flat on our backs,
      Halldor and I
      helpless and frail.
      Old age does this to me,
      but youth to you,
      you've hope of better,
      but I, none at all.[24]

People soon returned home and picked Halldor up off the
floor, and Bersi got better again. Halldor grew up at Tunga and
was a large and robust man.

Kjartan Olafsson grew up with his parents at Hjardarholt.
No fairer or more handsome man has ever been born in Iceland.
He had a broad face and regular features, the most beautiful
eyes and a fair complexion. His hair was thick and as shiny as
silk, and fell in waves. He was a big, strong man, much like his
grandfather, Egil, or Thorolf. No man cut a better figure than
Kjartan, and people were always struck by his appearance when

they saw him. He was a better fighter than most, skilled with his hands, and a top swimmer. He was superior to other men in all skills, and yet he was the humblest of men, and so popular that every child loved him. He also had a generous and cheerful disposition. Of all his children, Kjartan was Olaf's favourite.

His foster-brother, Bolli, grew into a large man. Next to Kjartan, he was the best at all skills and in other accomplishments. He was strong and handsome, a top fighter, with good manners and fond of fine clothes. The foster-brothers cared deeply for one another. Olaf stayed at home on his farm for many years after that.

29 | It is said that one spring Olaf announced to Thorgerd that he intended to travel abroad, 'and I want you to look after our farm and family while I'm away'.

Thorgerd said she was not in favour of the idea, but Olaf said he intended to have his way. He bought a ship which was beached at Vadil and sailed abroad that summer. He made land in the Hordaland district. A short distance from shore lived a man known as Geirmund Thunder, a powerful and wealthy man and a great Viking. He was a troublemaker, who had settled down and become a follower of Earl Hakon the Powerful.

Geirmund went down to the ship and, on hearing his name, recognized Olaf from the stories he had heard of him. He invited Olaf to come and stay with him and bring as many men as he wished. Olaf accepted his offer and went to stay with him, taking five others with him. The rest of the crew were placed on various farms in Hordaland. Geirmund treated Olaf well. He had a large farmhouse and a large household; in the winter there was plenty of entertainment.

As spring approached, Olaf told Geirmund that the purpose of his voyage was to get building timber and that it was of great importance to him to get a prime selection of timber.

Geirmund replied: 'Earl Hakon owns the best forest around. I'm sure that if you seek his help, it'll be within your reach. Men who have less to recommend them than you, Olaf, have been handsomely received by the earl when they paid him a visit.'

In the spring Olaf prepared for his journey to Earl Hakon. He was warmly received by the earl, who invited him to stay with him as long as he wished.

Olaf told the earl the reasons for his voyage. 'I would like to request permission to cut lumber in your forest, my lord.'

The earl replied: 'It's an honour for me to fill your ship with wood from the forest, as it is not every day we receive guests like you from Iceland.'

In parting the earl gave Olaf an axe inlaid with gold, a prize weapon, and they parted the best of friends. Geirmund had secretly put others in charge of his lands and planned on going to Iceland that summer aboard Olaf's ship. He had kept this a secret from everybody, and before Olaf realized what was happening Geirmund had had all his wealth, which was no small sum, loaded aboard the ship.

Olaf said, 'You'd not be travelling aboard my ship if I'd known of your plans earlier, as I suspect it would be better if some people in Iceland never laid eyes upon you. But since you're here, with all your property, I can hardly run you off my ship like some stray dog.'

Geirmund said, 'I'm not about to turn back, despite your harsh words, and I'm not asking you for free passage.'

Both he and Olaf boarded the ship and sailed out to sea. They had favourable winds and made land in Breidafjord, setting the gangways ashore at the mouth of the Laxa river. Olaf had the timber unloaded and the ship drawn up into the boatshed which his father had had built. He invited Geirmund to stay at his farm.

That summer Olaf had a fire-hall built at Hjardarholt which was larger and grander than men had ever seen before. On the wood of the gables, and the rafters, ornamental tales were carved. It was so well crafted that it was thought more ornamental without the tapestries than with them.

Geirmund was a sullen man and made little effort to get along with most people. He usually wore a red woollen tunic with a grey fur cloak about his shoulders, and had a hat of bearskin on his head and a sword in his hand. His sword was a fine weapon, with a hilt of walrus ivory. It had no silver overlay, but the blade was sharp and without a spot of rust. He called the sword Leg-biter and never let it out of his sight.

Geirmund had only stayed with Olaf a short time when he began to fancy his daughter Thurid. He put a proposal of marriage to Olaf, who turned him down. Geirmund then approached Thorgerd and offered her money if she would support his suit. She accepted the money, which was no petty sum, and soon raised the subject with Olaf.

She said that in her opinion, their daughter could not wish for a better match – 'He's a great warrior, rich and generous with his money.'

To this Olaf replied, 'Have it your own way then, as you do in most things, but I would rather marry Thurid to someone else.'

Thorgerd went off highly satisfied with her efforts and told Geirmund of the results. He thanked her for interceding on his behalf and for her determination. When he approached Olaf a second time he received his consent. Geirmund was then engaged to Thurid, and their wedding was held later that winter at Hjardarholt. A great number of people attended the feast as the fire-hall was finished by that time. Among the guests was a poet, Ulf Uggason, who had composed a poem about Olaf Hoskuldsson and the tales carved on the wood of the fire-hall which he recited at the feast. It is called 'House Drapa'[25] and is a fine piece of verse. Olaf rewarded him well for the poem, and gave all the important people who attended the feast fine gifts, gaining considerable respect as a result.

30 | There was little affection in the relations between Geirmund and Thurid, and the coolness was also mutual. Geirmund stayed at Olaf's farm for three years before declaring he wished to go abroad and leave behind Thurid and their daughter Groa, who was a year old, without any means of support. This pleased neither mother nor daughter and both of them complained to Olaf.

Olaf said, 'Why, Thorgerd, is your easterner not quite as

generous now as he was that autumn when he asked you for your daughter's hand?'

They could not provoke Olaf into taking action, as he sought to resolve differences wherever possible and avoided trouble. He said that in any case the child should remain there until she was of an age to travel. In parting, Olaf made Geirmund a present of the merchant ship, completely outfitted. Geirmund thanked him well and said it was a most generous gift. He made ready and sailed from the mouth of the Laxa river on a light north-easterly breeze, but the wind died as they reached the islands. The ship lay at anchor off Oxney for a fortnight, without gaining a favourable wind for its departure.

During that time Olaf had to leave to oversee the collecting of driftwood on beaches he owned. After his departure Thurid summoned several servants and told them to accompany her. They were a party of ten, counting her infant daughter, whom she also took along. She had them launch a ferry which Olaf owned, and sail or row out to the mouth of Hvammsfjord. When they reached the islands, she told them to set out the boat which was on board the ferry. Thurid got into the boat along with two others, telling those who remained behind to look after the ferry until she returned. Taking the child in her arms, Thurid instructed the men to row across the current so that they could reach the ship. From the storage chest in the bow of the boat Thurid took an auger which she handed to one of her companions. She told him to make his way to the ship's boat and bore holes in it, so that it would be unusable if it were needed in a hurry. She then had them row her and the child ashore. By this time it was dawn. She walked up the gangway and on board the ship. Everyone aboard was asleep. Thurid made her way to Geirmund's leather sleeping sack where his sword Leg-biter hung. She placed the child in the sack, took the sword and made her way off the ship and back to her companions.

The child soon began to cry and woke Geirmund. He sat up and, recognizing his daughter, suspected who was behind all this. Jumping to his feet, he reached for his sword, only to find it gone, as might be expected. Running up on deck he saw

Thurid and her companions rowing their boat away. Geirmund called out to his men to jump into the ship's boat and row after them. They did so, but hadn't gone far when they noticed the sea water flooding in and turned back to the ship.

Geirmund then called to Thurid to come back and return his sword Leg-biter – 'and take your daughter with you and whatever wealth you want'.

Thurid said, 'Do you mind the loss of your sword so much?'

Geirmund replied, 'I'd have to lose a great deal of money before I minded it as much as the loss of that sword.'

She said, 'Then you will never have it, as you have treated me dishonourably in more ways than one. This will be the last you'll see of me.'

Geirmund then spoke: 'That sword will bring you no luck.'

She replied that she would take that chance.

'Then I lay this curse upon it,' Geirmund said, 'that it will be the death of that man in your family who will most be missed and least deserve it.'

Thurid then returned to Hjardarholt. Olaf had returned and was not at all pleased at her escapade, but no action was taken. Thurid gave the sword Leg-biter to her kinsman Bolli, as she was no less fond of him than of her own brothers, and Bolli wore the sword for many years afterwards.

A favourable wind arose, and Geirmund and his men sailed out to sea, making land in Norway that autumn. One night they ran aground on rocks near Stad, and Geirmund and all aboard were drowned, bringing Geirmund's story to an end.

31 | As written earlier, Olaf Hoskuldsson lived on his farm and enjoyed the respect of others.

A man named Gudmund Solmundarson lived at Asbjarnarnes in Vididal in north Iceland. Gudmund was a wealthy man. He asked for Thurid's hand in marriage and she was betrothed to him with a large dowry. Thurid was a shrewd, determined woman, quick to anger and demanding. They had four sons, named Hall, Bardi, Stein and Steingrim, and two daughters, Gudrun and Olof.

Olaf's daughter, Thorbjorg, was a good-looking, heavy-set woman. She was called Thorbjorg the Stout and was married to Asgeir Knattarson, a man of good family, in Vatnsfjord in the West Fjords. Their son Kjartan was the father of Thorvald, who was the father of Thord, who was the father of Snorri, who was the father of Thorvald. The people of Vatnsfjord trace their descent to them. Thorbjorg was married a second time, to Vermund Thorgrimsson. Their daughter Thorfinna was married to Thorstein Kuggason.

A third daughter, Bergthora, was married to Thorhall, a godi in Djupifjord in the West Fjords, who was the son of Oddi Yrarson. Their son was Kjartan, the father of Smid-Sturla, who fostered Thord Gilsson, the father of Sturla.[26]

Olaf Peacock had many prime animals among his livestock. One of them was an ox, called Harri, which was dapple grey in colour and larger than other steers, with four horns. Two of them were large and well formed, but a third grew straight out and the fourth curved from his forehead down below his eyes. He used it as an icebreaker. He pawed the snow away to get at the grass like the horses.

During one long, hard winter, which killed off great numbers of livestock, Harri went from the farm at Hjardarholt to a place now called Harrastadir in the valley of Breidafjord. He ranged there all winter with sixteen steers and managed to find enough grass for all of them. In the spring he returned to the pastureland now known as Harrabol (Harri's Lair) at Hjardarholt. When he had reached the age of eighteen years the icebreaker fell from his forehead. Olaf had him slaughtered that autumn. The following night Olaf dreamed that a large, angry-looking woman approached him.

She spoke to him: 'Are you asleep?'

He replied that he was awake.

The woman said, 'You are asleep but you might just as well be awake. You have had my son killed and sent him to me disfigured, and for that I will make sure you see a son of yours covered with blood. I will also choose the one whom I know you will least want to part with.'

She then disappeared.

Olaf woke up with the image of the woman still before him. The dream made a strong impression on him and he told it to friends, but no one could interpret it for him to his satisfaction. He was most inclined to believe those who said that his dream was only a false indication of things to come.

32 | A man named Osvif was the son of Helgi, the son of Ottar, the son of Bjorn the Easterner, the son of Ketil Flat-nose, the son of Bjorn Buna. His mother was Nidbjorg, the daughter of Kadlin, the daughter of Hrolf the Walker, the son of Ox-Thorir, who was a hersir of good family in Vik [in Norway]. He was called Ox-Thorir because he owned three islands with eighty oxen on each of them. He gained much renown by giving one of the islands, together with its oxen, to King Hakon.

Osvif was a very wise man. He lived at Laugar in Saelingsdal. The farm is located to the south of the Saelingsdalsa river, across from the Tunga farm. His wife was Thordis, the daughter of Thjodolf the Short. They had five sons, Ospak, Helgi, Vandrad, Torrad and Thorolf, all of them bold fighters.

They had a daughter named Gudrun. She was the most beautiful woman ever to have grown up in Iceland, and no less clever than she was good-looking. She took great care with her appearance, so much so that the adornments of other women were considered to be mere child's play in comparison. She was the shrewdest of women, highly articulate, and generous as well.

One member of Osvif's household, a woman named Thorhalla, called the Chatterbox, was distantly related to him. She had two sons named Odd and Stein, hardy men who shouldered their load and more on the farm. They were as talkative as their mother but unpopular, although they could always rely on the support of Osvif's sons.

The farmer at Tunga was Thorarin, the son of Thorir Saeling, and a successful farmer himself. Thorarin was a big man and strong. He had plenty of land but not enough livestock. Osvif had plenty of livestock and not enough land, and wanted to purchase land from Thorarin. They agreed that Osvif should purchase from Thorarin all the land on both sides of the valley extending from the Gnupuskord pass as far up as Stakkagil. This is good, fertile grassland and Osvif used it for a shieling. He had a fair number of servants and enjoyed great respect in the district.

West at Saurbaer, two brothers named Thorkel Pup and Knut lived with their brother-in-law on a farm called Hol. Their brother-in-law, Thord, was identified with his mother Ingunn and called Ingunnarson. His father was Glum Geirason. Thord was a fine, strapping figure of a man, highly capable, and often involved in lawsuits. Thord was married to the brothers' sister Aud, a woman who was neither good-looking nor exceptional in other ways, and Thord had little affection for her. He had married primarily for wealth, which Aud had brought him in quantity. The farm had prospered ever since Thord had joined up with the others.

33 | A man called Gest Oddleifsson[27] lived at Hagi on the Bardastrond coast of the West Fjords. He was an important chieftain and especially wise man, who could foretell many events of the future. Most of the foremost men of the country were on good terms with him and many sought his advice. He attended the Althing every summer and generally spent the night at Hol on his way.

On one occasion when Gest was on his way to the Althing and had stayed overnight at Hol, as usual, he was up and preparing to continue his journey early the next day, as he still had a long way before him. He intended to ride as far as the farm at Thykkvaskog that evening to his brother-in-law Armod, who was married to his sister Thorunn. They had two sons, Ornolf and Halldor.

He rode from Saurbaer and came to the hot springs Saelingsdalslaug, where he stopped awhile. Gudrun came down to the springs to greet her kinsman. Gest was pleased to see her and they struck up a conversation; their discussion was both shrewd and lengthy.

Later in the day, however, Gudrun said, 'I'd like to invite you, kinsman, to ride up to the farm, along with all your followers, and spend the night with us. It's my father's suggestion as well, but he's done me the honour of making me his messenger, and he also wanted to invite you to stop with us every time you journey through.'

Gest thanked her well, saying the offer was a generous one indeed, but said he would continue according to his original plan.

Gudrun said, 'I've had many dreams this winter, and four of them especially have caused me much concern. No one has yet been able to interpret them to my satisfaction, although I don't insist that they be favourably interpreted.'

Gest then replied, 'Tell me your dreams. I might be able to make something of them.'

Gudrun said, 'I seemed to be standing outdoors, by a stream, wearing a tall head-dress that I felt did not suit me well at all. I wanted to change the head-dress but many people advised against it. I refused to listen to them, tore the head-dress from my head and threw it into the stream. The dream ended there.'

She continued: 'In the beginning of the second dream I seemed to be standing by a lake. I seemed to have a silver ring on my arm which belonged to me and suited me especially well. I treasured it greatly and intended to keep it long and with great care. But the ring slid from my arm when I least expected it and fell into the lake and I never saw it again. I was filled with a sense of loss much greater than I should have felt at losing a mere object. After that I awoke.'

To this Gest replied only: 'No less remarkable is this dream.'

Gudrun continued on: 'In the third dream I seemed to have a gold ring on my arm; it was my own and seemed to make up for my loss. I expected to have the pleasure of owning this one longer than the previous one. All the same it wasn't as if it suited me so very much better, not if compared with how much more costly gold is than silver. Then I fell and reached out my hand to break my fall, but the gold ring struck a stone and broke in two, and I thought I saw blood seep from the pieces. My feelings afterwards were more like grief than regret. I realized that there had been a flaw in the ring, and upon examining the pieces I could see other flaws. All the same I had the impression that if I'd looked after it better the ring might still have been in one piece. The dream ended here.'

Gest answered: 'The source of your dreams is far from drying up.'

Once more Gudrun spoke: 'In my fourth dream I seemed to have a gold helmet on my head, set with many gems. This treasure was mine. But it did seem to me that it was too heavy for me to bear. I could hardly manage it and held my head bowed. I didn't blame the helmet for this, however, nor did I intend to get rid of it. But it fell suddenly from my head and into the waters of Hvammsfjord, after which I woke up. Now I have told you all the dreams.'

Gest replied: 'I can clearly see what the dreams mean, but you may find the fare lacking in variety, as I would interpret them all in a very similar way. You will have four husbands; I expect that the first man to whom you are married will not be a match to your liking. As you thought you bore a great head-dress, which you felt suited you poorly, you will care little for this man. And since you removed the head-dress and threw it into the water, this means that you will leave him. People say things have been cast to the tide when they refer to getting rid of possessions and getting nothing in return.'

Gest continued: 'In your second dream you thought you had a silver ring on your arm. This means you will be married to a second, fine man for whom you will care greatly and enjoy only a short time. It would not surprise me if he were drowned. There is no need to dwell any longer on this dream. In your third dream you thought you had a gold ring on your arm. This represents your third husband. He will not surpass his predecessor to the same extent that you felt that metal to be rarer and more precious. But if my guess is right, there will be a change in religion around that time and this husband of yours will have adopted the new religion, which seems to be much nobler. When the ring appeared to break in two, in part because of your own carelessness, and blood to seep from its parts, this signifies that this husband will be killed. It is then that you will see most clearly the faults of that marriage.'

Once more Gest spoke: 'It was in your fourth dream that you bore a gold helmet set with gems on your head, which was a heavy weight for you. This signifies that you will marry a fourth time and this husband will far surpass you. The helmet seemed to fall into the waters of Hvammsfjord, which indicates that this fourth husband will have an encounter with that same fjord on the final day of his life. I can make no more of this dream.'

Gudrun had grown blood-red while listening to her dreams being interpreted, but kept silent until Gest had finished.

Then she spoke: 'You would have made a prettier prediction if I had given you the material for it, and I thank you for interpreting the dreams for me. I will have plenty to think about if all of this comes to pass as you say.'

Gudrun then repeated her invitation to Gest to visit them for the day, saying he and Osvif would have many interesting things to discuss.

He answered, 'I will ride onwards as I have planned, but give my greetings to your father and tell him that the time will come when the distance between our dwelling places will be shorter than at present. It will be easier for us to carry on a conversation then, if we are still allowed to talk.'

Gudrun then returned home, while Gest rode off. He met a servant of Olaf's near a hayfield wall, who invited him to Hjardarholt on his master's bidding. Gest said he wished to see Olaf but would be staying the night at Thykkvaskog. The servant returned home at once and gave Olaf the message. Olaf had horses brought and rode to meet Gest along with several other men. They met near the Lja river. Olaf welcomed Gest and invited him and all his men to stay with them. Gest thanked him for the offer and said he would accompany him home and have a look at the farmhouse, but would stay the night with Armod. Gest made only a short visit, but was shown around much of the farm, which he admired, saying Olaf had obviously spared no expense.

Olaf followed him a short distance along his onward journey, down to the Laxa river. The two foster-brothers had been swimming in the river that day, a sport in which the Olafssons took the lead. Many other young men from nearby farms had joined them in swimming. As the group approached, Kjartan and Bolli came running back from their swim and were almost fully dressed when Gest and Olaf came riding up. Gest looked at the two young men a moment and then told Olaf which was Bolli and which Kjartan. After that he pointed his spear at and identified each of the other Olafssons who were there. But although there were many other handsome young men who had come out of the water and sat on the riverbank near Kjartan and Bolli, Gest said that he could not see any resemblance to Olaf in any of them.

Olaf then said, 'The stories of your cleverness are hardly exaggerated if you can identify men whom you have never seen before. I want to ask you which of these young men will be the most outstanding.'

Gest replied, 'It will be much as your own affections predict, as Kjartan will be thought the most outstanding of them, as long as he lives.'

With that Gest prodded his horse and rode off.

A short while later his son Thord drew alongside him and asked, 'Why, Father, are there tears in your eyes?'

Gest answered, 'No need to mention it, but since you ask, I won't conceal it from you either, as you'll live to see it happen. I wouldn't be surprised if Bolli should one day stoop over Kjartan's corpse and in slaying him bring about his own death, a vision all the more saddening because of the excellence of these young men.'

They rode on to the Althing which passed without event.

34 | A man named Thorvald, the son of Halldor the Godi of Garpsdal, lived at Garpsdal in Gilsfjord. He was a wealthy man but hardly a hero. He asked for Gudrun Osvifsdottir's hand in marriage at the Althing when she was fifteen years of age. His suit was not rejected but Osvif felt the difference in their means would be evident in the marriage conditions. Thorvald spoke indulgently, though, and maintained he was seeking a wife and not a fortune. Gudrun was eventually be-

trothed to Thorvald according to conditions which Osvif himself decided upon. He declared that Gudrun should control
their common finances once they were married and would
acquire the right to half of the estate, whether the marriage was
a brief or a lengthy one.

Thorvald was also obliged to purchase whatever finery
Gudrun required in order that no other woman of equal wealth
should own better, although not to the point of ruining the farm.
Having agreed to this, the men rode home from the Althing.
Gudrun was not asked for her opinion and, although she was
rather against the idea, nothing was done. The wedding was to
be held at Garpsdal at hay-time. Gudrun cared little for Thorvald and was avid in demanding purchases of precious objects.
There were no treasures in all the West Fjords so costly that
Gudrun felt she did not deserve them, and she vented her anger
on Thorvald if he failed to buy them, however dear they were.

Thord Ingunnarson made a point of befriending Thorvald
and Gudrun and spent a great deal of time at their farm, until
soon rumours of the growing affection between Thord and
Gudrun spread. When Gudrun subsequently asked Thorvald
to buy her a new treasure, he retorted that there was no limit
to her demands and slapped her in the face.

To this Gudrun replied: 'Fine rosy colour in her cheeks is just
what every woman needs, if she is to look her best, and you
have certainly given me this to teach me not to displease you.'

When Thord came to the farm that same evening, Gudrun
told him of her humiliation and asked how she should repay
Thorvald.

At this Thord smiled and replied, 'I know just the thing.
Make him a shirt with the neck so low-cut that it will give you
grounds for divorcing him.'[28]

Gudrun did not oppose the idea and their conversation
ended.

That same spring Gudrun announced she was divorcing
Thorvald and went home to Laugar. When their estate was
divided Gudrun received half of all the property, which was
larger than before. She had been married to Thorvald for two
years. The same spring Ingunn sold her farm in Kroksfjord,

which has since then been called Ingunnarstadir, and moved west to Skalmarnes. She had been married to Glum Geirason, as was previously mentioned.

At this time Hallstein the Godi lived at Hallsteinsnes on the western shore of Thorskafjord. Although he was a powerful man he was not especially popular.

35 | A man named Kotkel had only recently immigrated to Iceland, along with his wife, Grima, and their sons Hallbjorn Slickstone-eye and Stigandi. They were from the Hebrides,[29] all of them skilled in witchcraft and accomplished magicians. Hallstein had received them on their arrival and settled them at Urdir in Skalmarfjord, where their presence was anything but welcome.

That summer Gest attended the Althing, travelling by boat to Saurbaer as he was accustomed to do. He stayed the night at Hol where he borrowed horses for the journey as usual. Thord Ingunnarson accompanied him in this instance and came to Laugar in Saelingsdal. Gudrun Osvifsdottir was going to the Althing and Thord accompanied her.

One day, as they were riding across the Blaskogar heath in fine weather, Gudrun asked Thord 'whether the rumour is true, that your wife Aud is often dressed in breeches, with a codpiece and long leggings?'

He replied that he had not noticed.

'You can't pay her much attention, in that case,' said Gudrun, 'if you haven't noticed such a thing, or what other reason is there then for her being called Breeches-Aud?'

Thord said, 'She can't have been called that for long.'

Gudrun replied, 'What is more important is how long the name will follow her.'

They arrived at the Althing soon after that, where the proceedings were without event. Thord spent most of his time at Gest's booth talking to Gudrun. One day he asked her what consequences it could have for a woman if she wore trousers like the men.

Gudrun answered: 'If women go about dressed as men, they

invite the same treatment as do men who wear shirts cut so low that the nipples of their breasts can be seen – both are grounds for divorce.'

Thord then asked, 'Would you advise me to announce my divorce from Aud here at the Althing or at home before the local assembly? I'll have to collect a number of supporters because those whom I will offend by so doing will be determined on revenge.'

After only a moment, Gudrun replied, 'Tarry-long brings little home.'

Thord then jumped to his feet and made his way to the Law Rock. He named witnesses and announced he was divorcing Aud on the grounds that she had taken to wearing breeches with a codpiece like a masculine woman.[30] Aud's brothers were not at all pleased but nothing was done. Thord rode home from the Althing with the Osvifssons.

When Aud learned the news she said,

2. Kind of him to leave me so
    and let me be the last to know.

Thord rode west to Saurbaer with a party of eleven men to claim his share of the property, which was accomplished without difficulty since Thord was prepared to be generous about his wife's share. He drove a large herd of livestock back to Laugar and proceeded to ask for Gudrun's hand in marriage. Osvif agreed readily and Gudrun raised no objection, so they decided to hold the wedding feast at Laugar when ten weeks of summer remained. The feast was impressive and the marriage of Thord and Gudrun a happy one. Thorkel and Knut would have made an attempt to start a case against Thord but hadn't managed to convince others to help them do so.

The following summer Aud and other people from Hol were staying in the shieling with the milking ewes in Hvammsdal. The people of Laugar took their ewes to a shieling in Lambadal, which runs west up the mountain from the main valley of Saelingsdal. Aud asked the farmhand who looked after the ewes how often he expected to meet his counterpart from Laugar.

The boy replied that this would probably happen frequently as there was only a single ridge separating the two valleys.

Aud then said, 'See if you can't run into the shepherd from Laugar today, then, and find out for me who is staying in their shieling and who is at home. Make sure you always speak of Thord in the friendliest of terms.'

The boy promised to do as she asked. When he returned that evening Aud asked what he had discovered.

The shepherd replied: 'I learned such news as will be pleasing to your ears, that there is a great distance separating the beds of Thord and Gudrun these days, since she is in the shieling while he is working feverishly at building a hall; only he and Osvif are at home.'

'You've done a fine job of spying,' Aud said. 'Have two horses saddled for me when the others go to bed.'

The shepherd did as she asked and shortly before sundown Aud mounted her horse, dressed in breeches, to be sure. The boy followed her on the second horse, but could hardly keep up with her flying pace. She rode southward over the Saelingsdal heath, not stopping until she reached the wall of the hayfield at Laugar. There she dismounted and told the shepherd to look after the horses while she proceeded to the house. She went up to the door, which was unlocked, into the fire-hall and found the bed closet where Thord lay sleeping. The door was closed but not latched. She entered the bed closet, where Thord slept on his back facing upwards. She woke Thord, but he only turned over on his side when he saw some man had come in. She drew her short-sword and struck him a great wound on his right arm which cut across both breasts. She struck with such force that the sword lodged in the wood of the bed. Aud then returned to her horse, sprang into the saddle and rode home. Roused by the attack, Thord tried to get to his feet, but was weakened by the wound and loss of blood. Osvif woke up at the disturbance and asked what was happening, and Thord replied that he had been wounded. While he dressed Thord's wound, Osvif asked if he knew who had attacked him. Thord replied that he suspected it was Aud, and Osvif offered to ride after her, as she would have brought few followers and deserved punishment. Thord told him not to think of doing so, as what Aud had done was only evening the score.

It was sunrise when Aud returned home, and her brothers asked where she had gone. Aud told them she had gone to Laugar and the news of her visit there. They were pleased but said Thord deserved worse. Thord was a long time recuperating from the wounds; the ones on his chest healed well but he never regained much use of his right arm.

The winter passed without event, but in the spring Thord's mother Ingunn came from her farm at Skalmarnes to visit him. Thord welcomed his mother warmly. She said she had come to him for help and protection, as Kotkel and his wife and sons were making her life miserable, stealing her livestock and practising sorcery under the protection of Hallstein the Godi. Thord responded at once and said he would not allow these thieves to get away with this even if Hallstein opposed him. He got ready to travel west immediately with Ingunn and nine others to accompany him. He took a ferry from Tjaldanes and they continued west to Skalmarnes.

Thord had all the property there which belonged to his mother loaded on the ferry and ordered men to herd the livestock overland. There were twelve of them aboard the boat, including Ingunn and one other woman. Thord rode to Kotkel's farm with nine men. Kotkel's two sons were not at home. Before witnesses, Thord charged Kotkel and his wife and sons with theft and sorcery, an offence punishable by full outlawry. They would have to answer the charges at the Althing. This accomplished he went back to the boat. Hallbjorn and Stigandi returned home just after Thord and the others had set sail, and were only a short distance from shore. Kotkel told his sons what had happened. The two brothers were furious and claimed none of their enemies had ever dared treat them like this. Kotkel then prepared a high platform for witchcraft which they all mounted. Then they chanted powerful incantations, which were sorcery. A great blizzard came up.

Thord Ingunnarson and his companions at sea felt how the force of the weather was directed at them and the ship was driven west beyond the headland at Skalmarnes. Thord struggled valiantly on board the ship. People on shore saw him throw everything overboard that could weigh the ship down except the travellers themselves. They expected that the ship would be able to make land after that, as they had passed the worst of the skerries, but all of a sudden a breaker rose where no one could ever recall having seen a skerry and rammed the ship so that it capsized at once. Thord and all his companions were drowned and the ship smashed into small pieces, the keel washing ashore on an island which has since been called Kjalarey (Keel Island). Thord's shield drifted ashore on an island called Skjaldarey (Shield Island). His body and the bodies of his companions drifted ashore directly afterwards and are buried in a mound at Haugsnes (Mound Point).

36 | The news of these events spread and was condemned; men capable of such sorcery as Kotkel and his family had performed were considered truly evil. Gudrun, who was pregnant and had only a short time left before she gave birth, was stricken with grief at Thord's death. She soon gave birth to a boy, who was sprinkled with water and named Thord.

At this time Snorri the Godi lived at Helgafell. He was Osvif's kinsman and friend and a source of great support to both him and Gudrun. When he visited them Gudrun told him of her dilemma and he promised to help her in the way he thought best. To give Gudrun some consolation he offered to foster her son, which she accepted; she agreed to follow his advice. The boy Thord was later given the nickname 'the Cat' and was the father of the poet Stuf.[31]

Gest Oddleifsson then approached Hallstein and offered him a choice: Hallstein would either have to get rid of these sorcerers or else Gest would kill them, 'even though it's already too late'.

Hallstein was not long in choosing and told the family they would have to find another dwelling place at least as far away as the other side of the highlands of the Dalir heath, though they did not deserve to escape with their lives. Kotkel and his family then left, taking no possessions except a stud of four horses with them. The stallion was black, large and powerful and had proven its fighting prowess.[32] Nothing is mentioned of their journey until they arrived at the farm of Thorleik Hoskuldsson at Kambsnes. He expressed an interest in purchasing the horses, which he could see were prime animals.

Kotkel answered, 'I'll give you the chance to own them: you provide me with a place to live near you and the horses are yours.'

Thorleik replied, 'I'll end up paying a high price for the horses if I do that – aren't you a wanted man in this district?'

Kotkel answered, 'The men of Laugar have told you that.'

Thorleik admitted this to be true.

Kotkel then spoke: 'The truth of our doings against Gudrun and her brothers is somewhat different from what you've been told. Accusations have been heaped on us of deeds we had no part in – accept the stallions in return for protecting us. If all the stories we hear of you are true, we won't be helpless prey for the dwellers of this district if we have your backing.'

Thorleik decided to accept the offer, as he was drawn both by the fine horses and Kotkel's cleverly convincing speech. He found the family a place to live at Leidolfsstadir in Laxardal, and supplied them with livestock, taking the horses into his charge in return.

When the men of Laugar learned of this, Osvif's sons wanted to attack Kotkel and his family at once.

Their father, however, said, 'We should take the advice of Snorri the Godi and leave this to others. It won't be long before their neighbours will have new complaints against them, and it will be Thorleik who'll suffer for it, which is so much the better. He'll soon have enemies where he once had supporters. But I won't try and dissuade you from doing whatever you like with Kotkel and his clan if three years pass without anyone driving them out of the district or putting an end to them once and for all.'

Gudrun and her brothers agreed to this.

Although Kotkel and his family were seldom seen working, they purchased neither hay nor food during the winter. They were anything but popular with the people of the district, but no one dared to raise a hand against them because of Thorleik.

37 | One summer when Thorleik was attending the Althing, a
     | large man entered his booth and greeted him. Thorleik
returned the greeting and asked the man his name or origin. He
said his name was Eldgrim and he lived in the Borgarfjord
district on the farm called Eldgrimsstadir, located in the valley
now called Grimsdal which runs westward up the mountain
between the farms of Muli and Grisartunga.

Thorleik said, 'I've heard of you, and if the stories are true
you're a man to be reckoned with.'

Eldgrim responded: 'My purpose in coming here is to purchase those fine horses which Kotkel made you a present of last
summer.'

Thorleik answered, 'The horses are not for sale.'

Eldgrim said, 'I'm offering you an equal number of horses in
exchange, plus a sizeable additional payment. Some people
would say you'd be getting double the normal price.'

Thorleik answered, 'I'm not much of a horse-dealer, and
you're not going to get those horses even if you offer me triple
the price.'

Eldgrim said, 'People who told me you were arrogant and
headstrong were obviously not lying. If I had my way you'd
end up losing the horses and getting considerably less than I've
been offering you.'

Thorleik grew very red in the face at his words, and replied,
'You'll need more than threats, Eldgrim, if you intend to take
the horses from me by force.'

Eldgrim responded, 'You may think it unlikely that I should
end up getting the better of you, but I'll go and take a look at
the horses this summer, and we'll see which one of us ends up
owning them after that.'

Thorleik answered, 'You can make good your threat any
time, so long as you don't intend to outnumber me when you
make your attack.'

The conversation ended on that note. People who overheard
them said the two would end up with no more than they
deserved. The Althing came to a close and everyone returned
home without incident.

Early one morning a farmhand at Hrutsstadir returned from his morning chores and Hrut Herjolfsson asked him whether he had any news to tell.

The man replied that he had seen nothing except someone riding across the far side of the tidal flats towards where Thorleik's horses were grazing, 'then he dismounted and caught the horses'.

Hrut asked where the horses had been and the farmhand replied, 'They kept to their usual grazing area; they were in your meadow below the hayfield wall.'

Hrut answered, 'It's true that my kinsman Thorleik is not one to be choosy about his pasture, and I don't think those horses will have been herded off with his consent.'

With that Hrut sprang to his feet, dressed only in a shirt and linen breeches, pulled on a grey fur garment and took up a gold-inlaid halberd which King Harald had given him. He walked briskly out and saw a man driving several horses below the hayfield wall. He approached them and recognized the man as Eldgrim. When Hrut greeted him Eldgrim responded somewhat reluctantly, and Hrut then asked where he was taking the horses.

Eldgrim answered, 'I won't try to conceal from you, although I know you and Thorleik are close kin, that I intend to see to it that he won't get his hands on these horses again. I am only carrying out what I told him at the Althing that I intended to do, and I've not sought the horses by means of superior forces either.'

Hrut replied, 'There's hardly much prestige in driving the horses off while Thorleik is in bed asleep. If you really intend to keep your word, as the two of you agreed, you should face him before you ride off with his horses.'

Eldgrim said, 'Tell Thorleik if you wish; as you can see, I left home prepared to meet him,' and brandished the barbed spear which he held in his hand.

He was also wearing a helmet and coat of mail, with a sword at his waist and a shield at his side.

'I'm not about to make the journey to Kambsnes on my slow legs, but I don't intend to stand by while Thorleik is robbed, if

I can do anything about it, even if he's no favourite relation of mine,' said Hrut.

'You don't mean you intend to take the horses from me?' asked Eldgrim.

'I'll offer you other horses instead, if you let these loose again, although they're no match for them,' said Hrut.

'Good of you to make the offer, Hrut,' Eldgrim replied, 'but now that I've got my hands on these horses of Thorleik's, neither bribes nor threats will make me let go of them again.'

Hrut then answered, 'Then I'm afraid your choice will turn out badly for both of us.'

Eldgrim was about to leave and prodded his horse, but when Hrut saw this he raised his halberd and struck Eldgrim between his shoulder blades. The mail-coat split asunder at the blow and the halberd cut right through the body. Eldgrim fell from his horse dead, as might be expected. Hrut buried the corpse at the spot called Eldgrimsholt (Eldgrim's rise), south of Kambsnes.

Afterwards Hrut rode to Kambsnes to tell Thorleik the news. Thorleik responded with anger and felt that he had been put to shame, while Hrut thought he had done him a real service. Thorleik said his actions were not only badly meant, they would also have serious consequences. Hrut said he could do as he chose, and the two parted on the worst of terms.

Hrut was over eighty when he killed Eldgrim, and gained a great deal of respect as a result of the deed. The fact that Hrut rose in esteem did not improve Thorleik's feelings towards him. Thorleik was convinced that he himself would have had the best of Eldgrim, since Hrut had made short work of him.

Thorleik then approached his tenants, Kotkel and Grima, to ask them to take some action to discredit Hrut. They agreed readily and promised to get right to work. Thorleik returned home and shortly afterwards Kotkel, Grima and their sons set out at night for Hrut's farm, where they began to practise strong magic rites. As the magic proceeded, the inhabitants of the farmhouse were puzzled by the sounds. The chants were sweet to the ear.

Only Hrut realized what the sounds meant and told his

household that no one was to leave the house to see what was going on, 'but everyone is to remain awake, if he possibly can, and if we manage to do so no harm will come to us'.

Eventually, however, they all fell asleep. Hrut managed to keep awake the longest, but finally even he fell asleep. Hrut's son Kari was twelve years old at the time and the most promising of his children. He was a great favourite with his father. Kari slept lightly and uneasily, as the incantations were directed at him. Eventually he sprang to his feet and looked outside. He went outside into the magic and was struck dead immediately. The next morning Hrut awoke, along with the rest of his household, to find his son was missing. His dead body was found a short distance from the entrance to the house. It was a great blow to Hrut and he had a burial mound made for Kari.

He then paid a visit to Olaf Hoskuldsson to tell him what had happened. Olaf was furious at the news and said it showed great foolishness to have allowed such evildoers as Kotkel and his clan to settle so close by. He also said that Thorleik had repaid Hrut badly for his actions, and that things had doubtless turned out worse than Thorleik intended.

Olaf said that Kotkel and his sons should be put to death at once – 'even though it's already too late'.

Olaf and Hrut set out with fifteen others, but when Kotkel and his family saw riders approaching they fled towards the mountains. Hallbjorn Slickstone-eye was the first to be caught, and a sack was pulled over his head. Several men were left behind to guard him while the others went after Kotkel, Grima and Stigandi. Kotkel and Grima were taken on the ridge between Haukadal and Laxardal. They were stoned to death and their bodies placed in a shallow grave heaped with stones,[33] the remains of which are still visible. It is called 'Sorcerers' Cairn'. Stigandi managed to make it through the pass and into Haukadal, where they lost sight of him. Hrut and his sons rowed out to sea with Hallbjorn. They removed the sack and tied a stone about his neck.

As they did so, Hallbjorn looked landwards with anything but a gentle gaze, saying, 'It was no lucky day for us, when my family approached Thorleik here on Kambsnes. I lay this curse that Thorleik will know little enjoyment here for the rest of his days, and that anyone who takes his place will know but ill fortune.' Events are thought to have proved how effective was his curse. They then drowned him and rowed back to shore.

Shortly afterwards Hrut went to Olaf and told him that he did not feel he had settled his affairs with Thorleik, and asked Olaf to lend him men to accompany him in a foray to Kambsnes.

Olaf replied, 'It's not right that you kinsmen should come to blows, even though Thorleik's actions have turned out very badly. I would rather try to negotiate a settlement between you. You have more than once had to wait to receive your due.'

Hrut answered, 'There's no question of that now; things will never be settled between us, and I don't want both of us to live here in Laxardal in the future.'

Olaf answered, 'It won't do you any good to attack Thorleik against my wishes; if you do you may find you've bitten off more than you can chew.'

Hrut then realized there was little he could do in this situation, and returned home very dissatisfied with the results. The following years passed without event.

38 | To return to Stigandi, he became an outlaw and difficult to deal with. A man named Thord lived in Hundadal, a rich man but hardly exceptional. One summer the number of sheep rounded up in Hundadal was lower than normal. People noticed that a slave-woman who looked after the sheep in Hundadal had acquired many new possessions, and had often disappeared for hours at a time without anyone knowing of her whereabouts. Thord had her threatened to try to find out the truth.

When suitably frightened, the woman revealed that a man came to her, 'a large man, and handsome, he seemed to me'.

Thord then asked when she thought this man would return and she said she expected him to come soon.

Thord then approached Olaf and told him that it was very likely Stigandi was not far away and asked him to gather some men together and go after him. Olaf was quick to respond and went up to Hundadal, where the slave-woman was brought before him. Olaf asked where Stigandi's camp was, but she said she did not know. He then offered to buy her her freedom if she would deliver Stigandi into their hands, and she accepted his offer.

That day she watched over her sheep as usual and Stigandi came to her. She welcomed him warmly and offered to search his hair for lice. He lay down with his head in her lap and soon fell asleep. She then crawled out from under him and went to Olaf and his men to tell them how matters stood. They went to where Stigandi lay and were determined not to let him see anything he could put a curse on, as his brother had done, so they drew a sack over his head. Stigandi awoke and offered no resistance for there were many of them against him alone. There was a tear in the sack through which Stigandi could see the slope opposite. It was a fertile bit of land, green with grass, but suddenly it was as if a tornado struck it. The land was transformed and never again did grass grow there. It is now called 'The Fire-Site'. Following this they stoned Stigandi to death and placed him in a shallow grave there. Olaf kept his promise to the slave-woman and gave her her freedom, and she returned to Hjardarholt with them.

Hallbjorn Slickstone-eye's body washed up on the beach a short while after he was drowned. He was placed in a shallow grave at the spot called Knarrarnes, and haunted the area frequently.

A man called Thorkel the Bald lived at Thykkvaskog on a farm he had inherited from his father. He was a courageous man and extremely strong. One evening a cow was missing at Thykkvaskog and Thorkel and one of his farmhands went to look for her. It was after nightfall and there was a moon in the sky. Thorkel said they should split up and divide the area between them. When Thorkel was alone he thought he saw a cow on a rise before him. As he approached it turned out to be Slickstone-eye rather than a cow and they fought with one another. Hallbjorn had to give way and, just when Thorkel least expected it, he slipped out of his hands and let himself sink down into the ground. Thorkel returned home afterwards. His servant had already come home with the cow. After this Hallbjorn did no more harm.

By this time both Thorbjorn the Pock-marked and Melkorka were dead. They were buried in a mound in Laxardal and their son Lambi lived on their farm. He was a bold fighter and well off. He enjoyed more respect than his father had because of his mother's family, and the relations between him and Olaf were warm.

The winter following the killing of Kotkel and his family passed and the next spring the brothers Olaf and Thorleik met. Olaf asked whether Thorleik intended to continue farming at Kambsnes, and Thorleik replied that this was his intention.

Olaf said, 'I would like to ask you instead, kinsman, to change your plans and sail abroad. You will enjoy the respect of everyone wherever you go. But I'm afraid our kinsman Hrut cares little for your company, and I would rather not take the chance of having the two of you at such close quarters much longer. Hrut is a powerful man, and his sons are bold warriors and hotheads. For the sake of our family ties, I would rather avoid a clash between you two kinsmen.'

Thorleik replied, 'I'm not afraid of not being able to stand up to Hrut and his sons, and won't leave the country because of that. But if it makes a great difference to you, kinsman, and has put you into a difficult position, then I will do so at your request, and because I was more contented when I was abroad. Nor do I fear that you will treat my son Bolli any less well though I am not nearby, and he is dearer to me than anyone else.'

Olaf answered, 'You're doing the right thing in agreeing to my request in this matter. And, as far as Bolli is concerned, I intend to continue as before, and treat him no less well than I do my own sons.'

Following this the brothers parted with great affection. Thorleik sold his property and used the proceeds to prepare for his journey abroad. He purchased a ship which was beached at Dagverdarnes, and when it was ready to sail went aboard accompanied by his wife and others of his family. They had a good passage and made land in Norway that autumn. From

there he travelled south to Denmark, as he did not feel satisfied
in Norway; his friends and relatives had died or been driven
out of the country. From Denmark he travelled to Gotland.
According to most people, Thorleik was not one to grow old
gracefully, but was nevertheless respected as long as he lived.
The story of Thorleik ends here.

39 | Word spread of the dispute between Hrut and Thorleik,
      and most people in the dales of Breidafjord felt that Kotkel
and his sons had dealt Hrut a heavy blow. Osvif reminded
Gudrun and her brothers of his earlier words, and his advice
that they avoid jeopardizing their own lives by taking on such
fiends as Kotkel and his family.

Gudrun said, 'No one can be ill-advised, Father, who has the
advantage of your advice.'

Olaf now enjoyed great respect on his farm. All of his sons
lived at Hjardarholt, as did their kinsman and foster-brother,
Bolli. Kjartan was the leader of Olaf's sons, and he and Bolli
were very close. Kjartan never went anywhere without Bolli at
his side.

Kjartan often went to the hot springs at Saelingsdal, and it
usually happened that Gudrun was there as well. Kjartan
enjoyed Gudrun's company, as she was both clever and good
with words. Everyone said that, of all the young people of the
time, Kjartan and Gudrun were best suited for one another.
Olaf and Osvif were also good friends, and exchanged visits
regularly, which did little to decrease the growing affection
between the youngsters.

Olaf spoke to Kjartan one day, saying, 'I don't know why
your visits to the springs at Laugar to spend time with Gudrun
make me uneasy. It isn't because I don't appreciate how much
superior to other women Gudrun is, as she is the only woman I
consider a worthy match for you. But somehow I have a feeling,
although I won't make it a prediction,[34] that our dealings with
the Laugar family will not turn out well.'

Kjartan replied that he would do his utmost not to go against
his father's wishes, but said he expected things would turn out

better than Olaf anticipated. He continued his visits as before, with Bolli usually accompanying him. The year passed.

40 | A man named Asgeir, who was called Scatter-brain, lived on the farmstead Asgeirsa in Vididal. His father, Audun Shaft, was the first of his family to make the journey to Iceland and had taken land and settled in Vididal. Another of Audun's sons was Thorgrim Grey-head who was the father of Asmund, the father of Grettir the Strong.[35]

Asgeir had five children: one of his sons was Audun, the father of Asgeir, the father of Audun, the father of Egil who was married to Ulfheid, the daughter of Eyjolf the Lame. Their son was Eyjolf, who was killed at the Althing. Another of Asgeir's sons was Thorvald, whose daughter Dalla was married to Bishop Isleif and was the mother of Bishop Gizur. A third son was named Kalf. Asgeir's sons were all promising. At this time Kalf was sailing on trading voyages and had earned a good name for himself. Thurid, one of Asgeir's daughters, was married to Thorkel, the son of Thord Bellower, and their son was named Thorstein. His other daughter was named Hrefna. She was the finest-looking woman in the northern districts of Iceland and very well liked. Asgeir was a powerful figure.

Kjartan Olafsson set out on a journey to Borgarfjord, of which nothing is reported until he arrived at Borg. Thorstein Egilsson, his mother's brother, was farming at Borg at the time. Bolli accompanied Kjartan, as the affection between the two foster-brothers was such that both of them felt something was missing in the other's absence. Thorstein welcomed Kjartan warmly and said he hoped he would make his visit a long one, and Kjartan stayed at Borg for some time.

That summer a ship that was owned by Kalf Asgeirsson was beached at the mouth of the Gufua river. He had spent the winter with Thorstein Egilsson.

Kjartan confided to Thorstein that his main purpose in coming south to Borg had been to purchase a half-share in the ship from Kalf, 'as I want to journey abroad', and he asked Thorstein for his opinion of Kalf.

Thorstein replied that he considered Kalf to be a decent fellow, 'but it's a shame you long to go abroad and learn of foreign ways. Your journey will likely prove to be of importance in more ways than one. For your kinsmen a great deal depends upon how the journey turns out.'

Kjartan said that it would turn out well. He then purchased a half-share in the ship from Kalf and they reached an agreement to share the profits equally. They would set sail when Kjartan returned after the tenth week of summer. On departing from Borg, Kjartan was given fine gifts and he and Bolli rode home. When Olaf learned of the plans he felt that Kjartan had made a hasty decision, but said he would not fail to offer his support.

A short while later Kjartan rode to Laugar and told Gudrun of his proposed journey abroad.

Gudrun said, 'You were in a hurry to make this decision, Kjartan', and other words which made it clear to Kjartan that Gudrun was not at all pleased about it.

Kjartan said, 'Don't get angry about this and I'll make it up to you by doing anything you ask that would please you.'

Gudrun said, 'Make sure you mean that, because I'll hold you to it.'

Kjartan told her to go ahead and name whatever she wished, and Gudrun said, 'I want to go with you this summer, and by taking me you can make up for deciding this so hastily, for it's not Iceland that I love.'

'You can't do that,' Kjartan answered. 'Your brothers are inexperienced and your father is an old man. If you go abroad there'd be no one to look after things. Wait for me instead for three years.'

Gudrun said she would promise nothing of the sort, and they parted in disagreement. Kjartan returned home.

Olaf attended the Althing that summer, and Kjartan accompanied his father from Hjardarholt as far as the Nordurardal valley, where they parted ways. Kjartan rode to his ship, accompanied by his kinsman Bolli. There were ten Icelanders who went with Kjartan on his journey because they were so attached to him. With this group of followers Kjartan approached the ship, where Kalf Asgeirsson gave them a warm welcome. Kjartan and Bolli took with them goods of great value. They set about making their preparations, and as soon as a favourable wind arose they set sail from Borgarfjord out to the open sea.

They had a good crossing and made land in Norway north of Nidaros, at Agdenes, where they sought news of recent events from the people they met. They were told that there had been a change of rulers in the country, of the fall of Earl Hakon and the rise of King Olaf Tryggvason, who had managed to bring all of Norway under his rule. King Olaf decreed that the Norwegians should adopt a new religion, and far from all of his subjects were prepared to agree to this.

Kjartan and his men docked their ship at Nidaros. There were a great number of prominent Icelanders in Norway at this time, and the three ships already docked there were all owned by Icelanders. Brand the Generous,[36] the son of Vermund Thorgrimsson, owned one of them, Hallfred the Troublesome Poet[37] a second, and the third was owned by two brothers, Bjarni and Thorhall, who were the sons of Skeggi of Breida in Fljotshlid. All of them had intended to sail to Iceland that summer, but the king had forbidden all of the ships to put to sea because the owners refused to adopt the new religion[38] which he had decreed. All the Icelanders welcomed Kjartan, especially Brand, as he and Kjartan were old acquaintances.

The Icelanders held counsel and agreed among themselves to refuse to adopt the new religion which the king had decreed. All of the men mentioned were party to the decision. Kjartan and his men then docked, unloaded their ship and saw to their goods. King Olaf, who was in town, learned of the arrival of the ship and that among those on board were a number of highly capable men.

One fine day that autumn, Kjartan and his men saw many people leaving the town to go swimming in the river Nid. Kjartan suggested to his men that they also go on a swimming outing, which they did. One of the swimmers was by far the best, and Kjartan asked Bolli if he wouldn't care to match himself against the local swimmer.

Bolli answered: 'I doubt that I'm good enough.'

'I don't know what's become of your sporting spirit,' Kjartan replied. 'I'll challenge him then.'

Bolli answered, 'Go ahead and do as you please.'

Kjartan then dived out into the river and swam over to the man who was such a strong swimmer, pushed him underwater and held him down for some time, before letting him come up again. The other had not been above water long before he grasped Kjartan and forced him underwater and held him under so long that Kjartan felt enough was enough. They both emerged once more, but neither spoke to the other. On the third try both of them went underwater and were under much longer. Kjartan was far from certain what the outcome would be and realized that he had never before been in such a tight situation. Finally, both of them came up and swam ashore.

The local man then asked, 'Who is this man?'

Kjartan told him his name and the local man replied, 'You're a fair swimmer; are you as good at other skills?'

Kjartan answered, after a pause, 'It was said, in Iceland, that I was – not that it makes any difference now.'

The man spoke: 'It does make a difference who your opponent is; why haven't you asked me any questions?'

Kjartan replied, 'I don't care who you are.'

The man said, 'You're not only highly capable, but highly confident of yourself as well; but I intend to tell you my name, all the same, and who it is you have been swimming against. You have before you King Olaf Tryggvason.'

Kjartan made no answer but turned to leave without putting on his outer cloak. He was wearing an inner shirt of scarlet. By this time the king was practically fully dressed. He called out to Kjartan, asking him not to hurry off, and Kjartan turned back reluctantly. The king then removed a fine cloak from his own shoulders and gave it to Kjartan, saying it wouldn't do for him to return to his men without a cloak. Kjartan thanked the king for the gift, went back to his followers and showed them the cloak. They were not at all pleased, as they felt Kjartan had put himself in the king's debt, but nothing more occurred.

The weather was especially harsh that autumn, with long spells of heavy frost and cold.

The heathen men said it was hardly surprising that the weather should be bad – 'It's because of the new king and his new religion, that the gods have grown angry.'[39]

All of the Icelanders spent the winter in the town, and Kjartan was the leader among them. When the weather improved a great number of people began arriving in town in answer to the summons of King Olaf. Some people in Nidaros had converted to Christianity, but the great majority were still opposed.

One day the king called a meeting at Oyr where he made a long and very eloquent speech to urge men to convert. The men of the Nidaros district had collected a small army and maintained they were prepared to do battle with the king rather than convert. The king told them to keep in mind that he had dealt with greater opponents than a bunch of local farmers from Nidaros. This was enough to strike fear into the hearts of the farmers and they all surrendered to him. A great number of people were baptized before the assembly was dissolved.

That same evening the king sent men to the quarters of the Icelanders to listen in on their conversations. Inside there was a great deal of noise.

Kjartan could be heard speaking to Bolli, 'How eager are you to adopt this religion that the king has decreed, kinsman?'

'I'm not eager at all,' Bolli answered, 'as this religion seems very weak to me.'

Kjartan asked, 'Didn't you think the king was threatening anyone who wasn't prepared to submit to his will?'

Bolli answered, 'I think the king left no doubt about his intentions to use force against them if need be.'

'No one is going to force me to do anything against my will,' said Kjartan, 'as long as I can stand on my own two feet and wield a weapon. Only a coward waits to be taken like a lamb from the fold or a fox from a trap. The other course looks better to me; if a man's got to die anyway, he might as well make a name for himself before it comes to that.'

Bolli asked, 'What is it you want to do?'

'I won't keep it from you,' Kjartan said. 'Burn down his quarters with the king inside.'

'I wouldn't call that a cowardly plan,' Bolli said, 'but something tells me little good will come of it. This king is not only favoured by destiny and fortune, he is also securely guarded both day and night.'

Kjartan replied that even courageous men lost their nerve now and again, to which Bolli answered that he wasn't so sure who should be taunted about lack of courage. Many of their followers then told them to stop this pointless arguing. After listening to this, the king's spies left to report the entire exchange to the king.

The next morning the king called a meeting and summoned all the Icelanders. When they had assembled, he stood up and thanked all those men who were his loyal friends and had converted to Christianity for answering his summons to the meeting. He ordered the Icelanders to come before him and asked whether they wished to be baptized. Not really, they replied.

He said they were choosing a course for themselves that would turn out badly for them – 'and which of you was it who expressed the wish to set fire to my quarters?'

At this Kjartan replied, 'You no doubt expect that the speaker of these words will not dare to admit to them, but he stands here before you.'

'I know you,' the king replied, 'and your daring, but you are not destined to stand over my dead body. You are guilty of enough in ignoring the advice of those who would teach you a better faith, without threatening to burn alive the king who attempts it. Since, however, I am not certain that you meant what you said, and you have honestly admitted to it, I will not have you put to death for the offence. Perhaps when you do convert you will keep your faith better than others – to the same extent you expressed more opposition to it than they did. I realize as well, that it will mean entire ship's crews will turn up for baptism the day that you decide of your own free will to convert. I think it very likely that your friends and kinsmen will pay heed to what you say when you return to Iceland, and if my guess is right, Kjartan, you will leave Norway under a better faith than you had when you arrived. Leave this meeting then in peace and proceed in safety, whatever course you choose; no

one will force you to adopt Christianity for the time being, for
God has said that he wishes no man to be forced to turn to him.'

There was general approval at the king's speech, especially
among the Christians. The heathens, however, left it to Kjartan
to answer as he saw fit.

Kjartan then spoke: 'We thank the king for promising us a
fair peace. You tempt us most to adopt your faith by forgiving
us our offences with gentle words, when our fate is completely
in your hands. I do not intend to adopt the Christian faith here
in Norway unless my regard for Thor remains just as low the
next year after I return to Iceland.'

The king then said with a smile, 'From the way Kjartan
behaves it is apparent that he puts more trust in his own strength
and his weapons than in Thor and Odin.'

The meeting was then adjourned. Many men close to the
king urged him to force Kjartan and his men to convert, and
felt it unwise to have so many heathen men at such close
quarters.

To this the king responded angrily, saying that to his mind
many of the Christians did not conduct themselves as well as
Kjartan or his men, 'and such men are worth waiting for'.

That winter the king had many useful works carried out. He
had a church built and the town enlarged considerably. This
church was completed by Christmas, and Kjartan suggested to
his men that they go near enough to observe the services held
by Christian men. Many of his men supported the idea, which
they felt would prove amusing. The group included Kjartan
and Bolli, along with Hallfred and many other Icelanders.

The king was urging listeners to convert. He spoke both
eloquently and at length, and his speech met with general
approval among the Christians.

When Kjartan and his men had returned to their quarters,
they began discussing what they thought of the king during
this festival which Christian men regarded as the second most
important to their religion – 'since the king did say, in our
hearing, that it was on this night that the prince was born in
whom we are to believe, if we do the king's bidding'.

Kjartan said, 'The king gave me the impression from the first time I saw him that he was an exceptional man, and that impression has been confirmed every time that I have seen him in public since. But I have never been so impressed by him as I was today. It seems to me that our welfare depends upon our believing this God whom the king supports to be the one true God. I doubt that the king is now any more eager to have me convert than I am to be baptized. The only thing that keeps me from going to see him right away is how late in the day it is, as the king will be dining. We will need a whole day if all of our company are to be baptized.'

Bolli expressed his full agreement and said Kjartan should decide for them.

The king learned of the discussion between Kjartan and his men before his dinner was over, for he had an informer in each of the heathen men's quarters.

He was extremely pleased at the news and said, 'Kjartan has proved the truth of the saying, "Festivals are a time of fortune."'

Early that next morning, as the king was on his way to church, Kjartan approached him on the street with a large following. He greeted the king warmly and said he had a request to make of him.

The king replied just as warmly, and said he knew of his request, and 'I will grant it with pleasure.'

Kjartan said they should not waste time but fetch the holy water, and warned they would need plenty of it.

The king answered with a smile, 'Yes, Kjartan, and we wouldn't say you charged too high a price though it cost us more than that water.'

Kjartan and Bolli were then baptized along with all their crew and many others. It took place on the second day of Christmas, before morning service. Afterwards the king invited Kjartan, along with his kinsman Bolli, to his Christmas feast. According to most of the reports, Kjartan swore his allegiance to King Olaf the same day as he removed his white baptismal clothing, as did Bolli. Hallfred was not baptized that day,[40] because he demanded that the king himself should bear witness to his baptism, which the king did two days later.

Kjartan and Bolli remained among the king's followers for the remainder of the winter. Both because of his family and his prowess, Kjartan was the king's favourite, and it is said that he was so popular that none of the king's men was jealous of him. It was also generally agreed that never had a man come from Iceland who could compare with Kjartan. Bolli was also a very capable man and was highly thought of by worthy men. The winter passed and as spring came everyone made ready for his journey, whatever direction that might take.

41 | Kalf Asgeirsson approached Kjartan to ask him what his plans were for the summer.

'I had been thinking,' Kjartan answered, 'that we might sail to England, where there are good trade markets for Christians. But I want to discuss it with the king before I make a firm decision, because he did not seem much in favour of my journey when we spoke of it this spring.'

Kalf then left and Kjartan went to speak to the king, greeting him warmly. The king responded just as warmly and asked what he and his comrade had been speaking of. Kjartan told him of their plans and said that he had come to bid the king give him leave to make the journey.

The king replied, 'I will give you a choice, Kjartan: you can travel to Iceland this summer to convert the people there to Christianity, either by persuading them or by force. If you feel this journey to be too difficult, then I will not let you go elsewhere. I consider your talents should be put to better use by serving noble men than in making your fortune as a merchant.'

Kjartan chose to stay with the king rather than go on a missionary voyage to Iceland.

He said he did not wish to set himself up against his kinsmen. 'And I can well imagine that my father, and the other chieftains who are my close kin, will be less unwilling to do your bidding while I am here in your hands and enjoying your hospitality.'

The king said, 'You are making a wise and honourable choice.'

The king gave Kjartan a complete suit of newly made clothes

of scarlet. They suited him very well, as people said that he and King Olaf were men of the same size when measured.

King Olaf sent his own royal cleric, a man named Thangbrand, to Iceland. His ship sailed into Alftafjord, where he spent the winter at Thvotta with Hall of Sida. He preached the Christian faith with both fair words and dire punishments. Thangbrand killed two men who most opposed his teachings.

Hall converted that spring and was baptized the Saturday before Easter along with all of his household. Gizur the White was also baptized, along with Hjalti Skeggjason and many other chieftains, but the great majority were opposed, and relations between the Christians and heathens soon grew dangerously tense. A number of chieftains made plans to kill Thangbrand and others who supported him. The hostilities eventually drove Thangbrand to Norway, where he made a report on his journey to King Olaf and added that the Icelanders would not adopt Christianity.

The king grew very angry at his words and said that many an Icelander would feel the consequences if they failed to come to their senses. At the Althing that same summer Hjalti Skeggjason was sentenced to outlawry for blasphemy.[41] The case was prosecuted by Runolf Ulfsson, one of the country's leading men, who lived at Dal under the Eyjafjoll mountains. That summer Gizur sailed abroad, accompanied by Hjalti, made land in Norway and travelled directly to King Olaf and his followers. The king received them well, and praised their actions and invited them to become his men, which they accepted.

Sverting, the son of Runolf of Dal, had been in Norway that winter and had intended to sail for Iceland in the summer. His ship was loaded and moored at the dock awaiting favourable winds. The king forbade him to sail and said that no ship would sail for Iceland that summer. Sverting then went to the king and pleaded his case, asked for his leave to sail and said that it meant a great deal for him not to have to unload the cargo again.

The king answered him angrily, 'Fitting enough that the son of that sacrificing heathen stays where he least wants to be,' and Sverting remained.

The winter passed without event.

The following summer the king sent Gizur and Hjalti to Iceland as missionaries once more, but he kept four men behind as his hostages: Kjartan Olafsson, Halldor, the son of Gudmund the Powerful, Kolbein, the son of Thord Frey's Godi, and Sverting, the son of Runolf of Dal.

Bolli arranged passage for himself with Gizur and Hjalti and went to his kinsman Kjartan. 'I've made preparations to leave now. I'd wait for you over the winter, if there was much chance you'd be freer to travel then than now, but I'm fairly sure that the king is determined to keep you here. I also take for granted that you remember little that might entertain you in Iceland when you're conversing with the king's sister Ingibjorg.'[42]

Ingibjorg was staying with the king at the time and was considered to be among the most beautiful women in Norway.

Kjartan replied, 'Don't go saying things like that, but do give my regards to our kinsmen and friends.'

42 | After that Kjartan and Bolli parted. Gizur and Hjalti sailed from Norway and had a good voyage. They made land at the time of the assembly in the Westman Islands and went from there to the mainland, where they called a meeting and spoke to their kinsmen. Later they went to the Althing and urged men to convert to the new religion, both eloquently and at length, after which all the people of Iceland converted to Christianity.[43]

Bolli rode home to Hjardarholt with his uncle Olaf who had welcomed him heartily. After he had been home for some time he rode to Laugar for a visit, and was given a good welcome. Gudrun asked in detail about his journey, and of Kjartan.

Bolli answered all her questions readily, and said there was little to report of his own travels, 'but as far as Kjartan is concerned, there's splendid news of his situation. He is King Olaf's man and none of the king's followers is in higher favour. But it wouldn't surprise me if we saw little of him here at home during the coming years.'

Gudrun asked if there was any reason for this other than the friendship between him and the king. Bolli told her of the stories about the friendship between Kjartan and Ingibjorg, the king's sister, and said in his opinion the king would rather marry Kjartan to Ingibjorg than let him leave, if he had his way.

Gudrun said that this was good news, 'as only the best of wives is a fair match for Kjartan', and ended the conversation.

She walked away blushing. Other people suspected that she hardly thought the news as good as she said.

Bolli stayed at home at Hjardarholt that summer and had earned himself a great deal of respect as a result of his journey. All of his kinsmen and acquaintances valued his strength and courage highly. Bolli had also made a large profit from his voyage. He often went to Laugar to visit Gudrun. Bolli once asked Gudrun what her answer would be if he asked her to marry him.

Gudrun replied quickly, 'There's no point in even discussing that, Bolli; I'll marry no man as long as I know Kjartan is still alive.'

Bolli answered, 'It's my guess that you'll have to sit here alone for a few years yet, if you wait for Kjartan. He could have asked me to give you a message, if he thought it important enough.'

They exchanged a few more words, then parted in disagreement, and Bolli returned home.

43 | Some time afterwards Bolli was speaking to his uncle Olaf and said, 'Uncle, I've been thinking, now that I feel myself a full-grown man, that I should settle down and get married. I want to ask for your advice and assistance to accomplish this, as I know that most men here listen to what you have to say.'

Olaf answered, 'I'd think most women would consider you more than a fitting match. But you wouldn't have brought the question up if you hadn't already decided where it should come down.'

Bolli said, 'I won't have to go looking for a wife in distant districts as long as there are such fine women nearby. I want to ask for the hand of Gudrun Osvifsdottir; she is the most renowned of women.'

Olaf answered, 'That's a matter I want no part in. You know, Bolli, just as well as I do that the affection between Kjartan and Gudrun was spoken of everywhere. But if you consider this very important, then if you and Osvif reach an agreement I won't oppose it. Have you raised the question with Gudrun?'

Bolli said he had brought the question up on one occasion and she had been rather reluctant – 'but I expect that it will be first and foremost Osvif who will decide the question'.

Olaf said he would have to do as he wished.

Not long after this Bolli rode from Hjardarholt to Laugar, accompanied by eleven followers, among them Olaf's sons, Halldor and Steinthor. Osvif and his sons welcomed them. Bolli asked to speak to Osvif privately and brought up the question of marriage, asking for the hand of his daughter Gudrun.

Osvif replied, 'As you know, Bolli, Gudrun is a widow and as such she can answer for herself, but I will give it my support.'

Osvif then approached Gudrun and said that Bolli Thorleiksson had arrived, 'and has asked for your hand in marriage. You are to answer him. I can say without hesitation that if I were to decide, Bolli would not be turned down.'

Gudrun answered, 'You've been quick to decide this. Bolli brought the question up once with me and I tried to discourage him, and I still feel the same way.'

Osvif then said, 'If you refuse a man like Bolli many people will say that your answer shows more recklessness than foresight. But as long as I'm still alive, I intend to direct my children's actions in matters where I can see more clearly than they.'

Since Osvif opposed her so, Gudrun did not, for her part, refuse, although she was very reluctant in all respects. Osvif's sons were also very eager for her to make the match and felt it was an honour for them to have Bolli as their brother-in-law. The upshot of it was that they were betrothed and the date of the wedding set for the Winter Nights.

Bolli then rode home to Hjardarholt and told his foster-father Olaf of the arrangement. Olaf was not enthusiastic at the news. Bolli was at home until the time came for him to leave for the wedding. He invited his foster-father Olaf and, although Olaf was reluctant to attend, he agreed to it for Bolli's sake. The feast at Laugar was impressive and Bolli remained there after the wedding for the remainder of the winter. After they were married Gudrun showed little affection for Bolli.

When summer came and ships began to sail between the two countries, the news that Iceland was completely Christianized travelled to Norway. The news pleased King Olaf exceedingly and he gave his permission for all the men who had been his hostages to sail to Iceland or anywhere else they pleased.

Kjartan replied to the king, for he had been the spokesman for all the men who had been held hostages, 'We give you our thanks, and will be heading for Iceland this summer.'

The king answered, 'I don't intend to go back on my word, Kjartan, but I meant it more for the others than for you. In my view you have dwelt here more in amity than detention. I would rather you did not wish to go to Iceland, despite the fact that you have prominent kinsmen there, because I can offer you opportunities in Norway far beyond anything that awaits you in Iceland.'

To this Kjartan replied, 'May our Lord reward you for the honour you have shown me from the time I entered your service. But I expect you will grant me permission to leave no less than the others whom you have held here for some time.'

The king replied that so it would be, but said it would be difficult to find a man the equal of Kjartan outside of the ranks of the noblemen.

Kalf Asgeirsson had spent the winter in Norway after returning from England with their ship and trading goods. When Kjartan had received the king's leave to sail to Iceland he and Kalf began to make the ship ready. When it was ready to sail, Kjartan paid a visit to the king's sister Ingibjorg. She received him warmly and made room for him to sit beside her and they conferred together. Kjartan told Ingibjorg that he had made his ship ready for the journey to Iceland.

To this she answered, 'I suspect, Kjartan, that you have done so more on your own initiative than because others urged you to leave Norway and return to Iceland.'

After that they had little to say to one another. Ingibjorg then reached for a nearby casket, from which she took a white head-dress, embroidered with golden threads, which she gave to Kjartan and said she hoped Gudrun Osvifsdottir would enjoy winding this about her head.

'You are to give it to her as a wedding present, as I want Icelandic women to know that the woman you have consorted with here in Norway is hardly the descendant of slaves.'

There was a covering of fine fabric around the head-dress. The gift was a great treasure.

'I won't come to see you off,' said Ingibjorg, 'but farewell and godspeed.' Kjartan then stood up and embraced Ingibjorg, and people say the truth is that both of them regretted having to part.

Kjartan then left to go to the king and tell him he was ready to leave. King Olaf and a large following accompanied Kjartan to his ship where it lay at anchor, with only a single gangway remaining between it and the shore.

The king then spoke: 'This sword, Kjartan, I wish to give you as a parting gift. May you carry it with you always, and I predict that no weapon will wound you while you bear it.'

The sword was very precious and highly decorated. Kjartan thanked the king graciously for all the honour and respect he had shown him while he had been in Norway.

The king said, 'Make sure, Kjartan, to keep your faith well.'

After saying this they parted as the warmest of friends, and Kjartan boarded his ship.

The king followed Kjartan with his gaze and said, 'Great is the worth of Kjartan and his kinsmen, but difficult it will be to alter that destiny which awaits them.'

44 | Kjartan and Kalf set sail and had favourable winds and a speedy passage. They cast anchor at the mouth of the river Hvita in Borgarfjord. The news of Kjartan's arrival was quick to spread, and his father Olaf and other kinsmen were very glad to learn of it. Olaf rode south to Borgarfjord from the Dalir district at once and the meeting of father and son was a joyous one. Olaf invited Kjartan to come home with him and

bring as many men as he wished. Kjartan gladly accepted and said that was the only place in Iceland he wanted to stay. Olaf and his men then returned home to Hjardarholt, while Kjartan stayed with the ship during the summer. He learned of Gudrun's marriage and showed no sign of response, although many people had been dreading his reaction.

Kjartan's brother-in-law Gudmund Solmundarson and his sister Thurid came to see them at the ship, and Kjartan welcomed them well. Asgeir Scatter-brain came to welcome home his son Kalf, accompanied by his daughter Hrefna, a lovely woman. Kjartan offered his sister Thurid the pick of the wares. Kalf said the same to Hrefna, opened up a large chest and told them to look over the contents.

That same day the winds grew strong and both Kjartan and Kalf had to hurry out to moor the ship better; when they returned to the booths, Kalf entered ahead of him. Thurid and Hrefna had gone through most of the contents of the chest. Hrefna snatched up the head-dress and began to unwind it, and both of them admiringly said what a beautiful object it was. Hrefna said she would like to try it on, and after Thurid advised her to go ahead, she did so.

Kalf noticed them and said she should not have done that, and told her to take it off at once: 'That's the only thing that's not both of ours to give.'

As he was saying this Kjartan entered. He had heard what they said and said at once that there was no harm done. Hrefna sat there still wearing the head-dress.

Kjartan looked her over closely and said, 'To my mind the head-dress suits you very well, Hrefna. I expect the best thing for me would be to own both the head-dress and the comely head it rests upon.'

Hrefna replied, 'People would expect you to take your time choosing a wife, and get the wife you choose.'

Kjartan said it mattered little what woman he married, but implied that he would not remain a suitor for long. Hrefna then removed the head-dress and handed it to Kjartan who put it away.

Gudmund and Thurid invited Kjartan to pay them a visit

where they lived in north Iceland during the coming winter, and he promised to do so. Kalf Asgeirsson decided to head north with his father, so he and Kjartan each took their share of their common fund and parted the best of friends. Kjartan left the booths to ride to Dalir with eleven others, and everyone was pleased to see him when they arrived home at Hjardarholt. Kjartan had his property brought north from the ship in the autumn. They all spent the winter in Hjardarholt. Olaf and Osvif continued their usual custom of taking turns inviting each other to feasts in the autumn. This autumn Olaf and his family were to visit Laugar.

Gudrun now told Bolli that she felt not everything he had told her about Kjartan's return was true, but Bolli maintained he had told her what he knew as the truth. Although Gudrun hardly spoke of the matter, it was obvious that she was anything but happy, and most people assumed that she regretted having lost Kjartan, though she tried to conceal it.

Eventually the date of the feast at Laugar came. Olaf made ready for the journey and asked Kjartan to come along, but he said he intended to stay at home and look after the farm.

Olaf asked him to avoid hard feelings where kinsmen were concerned. 'Remember, Kjartan, that no one was as close to you as your foster-brother, Bolli. I want you to come and I'm sure you two will sort out your differences once you sit down together.'

Kjartan did as his father wished, and took out the suit of scarlet that King Olaf had given him in parting and other finery. He put on his sword, King's Gift, and on his head had a helmet with gold plating, and a shield with a red front and a gold cross marked on it. He also held a spear, the socket of which was inlaid with gold. All of his followers wore brightly coloured clothes. They made a party of more than twenty in all, who rode from Hjardarholt to Laugar, where a large number of people had already gathered.

45 | Bolli and the Osvifssons went to meet Olaf and his party
and welcomed them warmly. Bolli went up to Kjartan
and welcomed him with a kiss, and Kjartan responded in like
fashion. They then accompanied the party indoors. Bolli was
in high spirits and Olaf was very pleased, although Kjartan
seemed less enthused, and the feast was a success.

Bolli had a stud of horses regarded as the finest of animals.
The stallion was large and handsome and had never been
known to give way in a fight. It was white with red ears and
forelock. Bolli said he wished to give the horse, along with three
mares which were the same colour, to Kjartan, but Kjartan said
he was no man for horses and refused to accept them.

Olaf asked him to accept the horses, saying 'They're a fine
gift', but Kjartan absolutely refused.

They parted without warmth, and the people of Hjardarholt
returned home. The winter proceeded without event. Kjartan
was more withdrawn than usual; the others had scant pleasure
conversing with him, and Olaf was concerned about the change
in him.

After Christmas Kjartan made preparations to journey to the
north of Iceland with eleven followers. They travelled as far as
Vididal, to the farm at Asbjarnarnes, where Kjartan was given
a warm welcome. The farm buildings there were very imposing.
Hall, the son of Gudmund the Powerful, was then in his teens,
and much resembled the men of Laxardal. It was said that
a stauncher man was not to be found in all of the northern
quarter. Hall gave Kjartan a very warm welcome, and organized
games at Asbjarnarnes to which people from many parts of the
surrounding region were invited. People came from Midfjord
in the west, Vatnsnes and Vatnsdal and all the way from
Langadal. A great number of people gathered, and everyone
commented on how outstanding a man Kjartan was. Players
were to be divided into teams under Hall's direction.

He invited Kjartan to take part. 'We hope you'll be gracious
enough to join us, kinsman.'

Kjartan replied, 'I haven't had much practice at games recently, as in the service of King Olaf we had other things to

keep us occupied, but I don't want to refuse your request in this instance.'

Kjartan then got ready to take part, and the men placed against him on the opposing team were those who were considered the strongest players. The game lasted all day, and no man could match Kjartan in strength or agility. In the evening, when the game was over, Hall Gudmundarson stood up and spoke: 'It is the wish of myself and my father that all of those people who have travelled a long distance should stay the night so that we may continue our entertainment tomorrow.'

His offer was well received and considered a handsome one indeed. Among the guests was Kalf Asgeirsson, and he and Kjartan enjoyed each other's company especially. Also there was his sister Hrefna, dressed in the finest of clothes. There were over a hundred people who stayed the night. The following day teams were formed again. This time Kjartan sat and watched the game.

His sister Thurid approached him and said, 'I've been told, brother, that you have been rather quiet this winter, and that people say it's because you regret the loss of Gudrun. They also say you and Bolli have little to do with each other, although the two of you were always inseparable friends. Do the right and fitting thing and try to put any malice behind you. Don't begrudge your foster-brother a good match. I think it would be best if you got married, as you yourself suggested last summer, even if Hrefna is not quite your equal, because in this country you won't find a woman who is. Her father, Asgeir, is a worthy man and of very good family, and has enough wealth to make the match an appealing prospect; his other daughter is already married to a powerful man. You yourself have told me what a capable man Kalf Asgeirsson is, and their situation is generally a fine one. I want you to have a talk with Hrefna. I'm sure you'll find her as clever as she is lovely.'

Kjartan concurred, saying that what she said made good sense, and it was arranged for him to meet Hrefna. They conferred together all that day. In the evening Thurid asked Kjartan what he thought of his conversation with Hrefna. He was very pleased and said that, as far as he could tell, she was the finest of women in all respects. The following morning messengers were sent to invite Asgeir to Asbjarnarnes, and discussions of a marriage settlement began, with Kjartan asking for the hand of Asgeir's daughter Hrefna in marriage. Asgeir responded positively to the proposal as he was no fool and realized what an honour the match was.

Kalf supported the proposal energetically, saying, 'I'll spare nothing to help bring it about.'

Hrefna, for her part, did not refuse but said her father should decide. Eventually an agreement was reached and witnessed. Kjartan would not hear of holding the wedding anywhere else but in Hjardarholt, and, as Asgeir and Kalf raised no objection, it was decided that the feast should take place there in the sixth week of summer. Kjartan then rode home bearing worthy parting gifts.

Olaf brightened at the news, for Kjartan was now in much better spirits than when he had left home. Kjartan fasted on dry foods alone during Lent, the first man known to have done so in Iceland. People found it so incredible that Kjartan could live for such a long time on such food, that they came from far and wide to witness it. In this, as in other ways, Kjartan's conduct surpassed that of other men. When Easter had passed, Kjartan and Olaf organized the wedding feast. Asgeir and Kalf rode down from the north at the appointed time, accompanied by Gudmund and Hall, and all together they made a party of sixty. Many other guests awaited them. The feast was a grand one and lasted a week.

Kjartan gave Hrefna the head-dress as a wedding present, and the gift was renowned throughout the country, as no Icelander was so cultured that he had seen, or so wealthy that he had possessed, such a treasure. According to reliable reports, there were eight ounces of gold woven into the head-dress.

Kjartan was in such high spirits at the wedding feast that he entertained everyone with his conversation and stories of his travels abroad. People were very impressed by how much he had to tell, after serving under that most worthy of rulers, King Olaf Tryggvason. When the feast came to an end Kjartan chose suitable gifts for Gudmund and Hall and the other men of distinction. Both Kjartan and Olaf gained much respect from the feast, and Kjartan and Hrefna's marriage was one of great affection.

46 | Despite the ill-feelings between the younger members of
     | their families, Olaf and Osvif remained good friends. Olaf held a feast two weeks before the beginning of winter and Osvif had organized a similar feast for the Winter Nights. Each of them invited the other to attend with as large a following as he felt did him the greatest honour.

It was Osvif's turn first to visit Olaf and he arrived at the appointed time in Hjardarholt. Among his company were Gudrun and Bolli and Osvif's sons. The following morning, as they walked towards the outer end of the hall, one of the women was discussing the women's seating plan. The discussion took place at just the moment when Gudrun had reached a point opposite the bed where Kjartan usually slept. Kjartan was dressing at that moment, and drew on a tunic of red scarlet.

To the woman who had mentioned the women's seating plan he called out – as no one was quicker to respond than he – 'As long as I'm alive, Hrefna will have the seat of honour and be treated in every way with the greatest respect.'

Previously it had always been Gudrun who had enjoyed the privilege of sitting in the seat of honour at Hjardarholt as elsewhere. Gudrun heard his words, looked at Kjartan and changed colour but said nothing.

The following day Gudrun asked Hrefna to put on the head-dress so everyone would be able to see one of the greatest treasures ever brought to Iceland.

Kjartan was not far off and, hearing Gudrun's words, was quicker to respond than Hrefna: 'She won't be wearing the head-dress at this feast, as it's more important to me that Hrefna should possess this treasure than to provide our guests at this time with a moment's diversion.'

Olaf's feast that autumn was to last a week. The following day Gudrun spoke to Hrefna privately and asked to see the head-dress, and Hrefna agreed. Later that day the two went to the outbuilding used for the storage of fine possessions. Hrefna opened a chest and took up a case made of costly woven material, out of which she took the head-dress and showed it to Gudrun. Gudrun unwound the head-dress and looked at it awhile, without either praising or criticizing it, until Hrefna took it and put it away. They then returned to their places in the hall for the evening's entertainment.

When the day came for the guests to depart, Kjartan was busy helping people who had come a long way to exchange their horses for fresh ones and assisting others in whatever way they needed. He was not carrying his sword, King's Gift, while he was doing this, despite the fact that he seldom let it out of his reach. When he finally returned to the place where he had left it, it was gone. Kjartan went directly to his father to tell him of its disappearance.

Olaf said, 'We must keep this as quiet as possible. I'll send men with each group which leaves to spy on their actions.'

This he did, sending An the White with Osvif's company to note whether anyone left the group or tarried on the way. They rode past Ljarskogar and the farm called Skogar and stopped at another farmstead called Skogar, where they dismounted. Thorolf Osvifsson and several other men left the farmhouse and disappeared into some bushes while the group stopped at Skogar.

An accompanied them when they continued their journey, riding as far as the Laxa river, where it runs out of Saelingsdal. There he said he would turn back, and Thorolf said it would not have done much harm if An had not come with them at all. The preceding night a light snow had fallen, so that it was possible to follow men's tracks. An rode back to Skogar, where he traced Thorolf's footsteps to a bog or marsh. Feeling around under the surface, he managed to grasp the hilt of a sword. He wanted to have other people witness what he did and rode to Saelingsdalstunga, to have the farmer Thorarin accompany him to recover the sword.

An presented the sword to Kjartan, who wrapped it in cloth and placed it in a chest. The spot where Thorolf and his companions had hidden King's Gift has been called Sverdskelda

(Sword bog) ever since. The sheath was never recovered. Nothing was done about the theft but Kjartan valued the sword much less highly than before.

He was upset and did not want to let things go unanswered, but Olaf said, 'Don't let it disturb you. It's a poor trick they've played, but you've come to no real harm. Let's not give others something to laugh at by starting an argument with friends and kinsmen over a thing like this.'

Kjartan let himself be persuaded by Olaf's words and took no action.

Soon afterwards Olaf was preparing to make the journey to Laugar for the feast at the Winter Nights and asked Kjartan to come as well. Kjartan was reluctant to go but eventually agreed at his father's urging.

Hrefna was to go as well, and had planned to leave her head-dress behind, but her mother-in-law, Thorgerd, asked, 'When do you plan on using this treasure if it is to lie at home in a chest whenever you attend a feast?'

Hrefna answered, 'Many people say that I could well choose a place to visit where fewer people envy me than at Laugar.'

To this Thorgerd answered, 'I don't pay much heed to people who spread such gossip in the neighbourhood.'

As Thorgerd was so determined, Hrefna agreed to take the head-dress, and Kjartan did not oppose it when he saw it was what his mother wanted.

They set out soon afterwards and reached Laugar in the evening where they were given a hearty welcome. Thorgerd and Hrefna turned over their clothing to be put away but the following morning, when the women dressed and Hrefna looked for the head-dress where she had placed it, it had disappeared and was nowhere to be found although a search was made. Gudrun said it was most likely that she had either left the head-dress at home or failed to pack it carefully enough and lost it on the journey. Hrefna then told Kjartan that the head-dress had disappeared. He responded by saying that this time it would not be easy to keep an eye on their movements, told her to do nothing more for the moment and then told his father what had happened.

Olaf answered, 'As before, I want to ask you to take no action; try to ignore what has happened, and let me see what I can do privately. I will do everything I can to prevent a split between you and Bolli. Least said, soonest mended,' he added.

Kjartan replied, 'Of course you only want to do well by everyone here, but I'm not sure whether I'm prepared to let the people of Laugar ride roughshod over me.'

The day they were to leave Kjartan addressed his hosts and said, 'I warn you, Bolli, as my kinsman, to treat us more honourably in the future than you have up to now. This time I won't keep silent, because everyone already knows about the things which have disappeared here, and we suspect will have found their way into your possession. This autumn, when we hosted the feast at Hjardarholt, my sword was taken; I managed to recover it, but without the sheath. Once more, property which could be described as valuable has disappeared. I want them both returned.'

Bolli answered, 'Neither of these things you accuse us of, Kjartan, are we guilty of, and least of all would I have expected you to accuse us of stealing.'

Kjartan said, 'In that case I imagine you might have offered those people here who were involved better advice, had you wanted to. You are going out of your way to insult us, and we've tried to ignore your enmity towards us for long enough. From now on, I warn you, I will suffer it no longer.'

Then Gudrun responded, saying, 'You're stirring up embers that would be better left to die out. And even if it were true someone here was involved in the disappearance of the head-dress, in my opinion they've done nothing but take what rightfully belonged to them. Believe what you like as to the whereabouts of the head-dress. I won't shed any tears if the result is that Hrefna will have little ornament from the head-dress from now on.'

After this exchange they parted rather stiffly, and the people of Hjardarholt rode homeward. The paying of visits ceased, but nothing else of event happened. Nothing more was ever heard of the head-dress, although people said Thorolf had burned it on his sister Gudrun's orders. Early in the winter Asgeir Scatter-brain died, and his sons took over his farm and wealth.

47 | After Christmas that winter Kjartan collected a group of sixty men, without saying anything to his father of his plans. Olaf, for his part, showed little curiosity. Taking tents and provisions with him, Kjartan and his men set out for Laugar, where he told his men to dismount. He ordered some of them to watch the horses and others to set up the tents.

At this time it was fashionable to have outdoor privies some distance from the farmhouse, and such was the case at Laugar. Kjartan stationed men at each of the doors and prevented everyone from going outside so that they had to relieve themselves indoors for three whole days. Afterwards Kjartan rode home to Hjardarholt and all of his followers returned to their homes. Olaf expressed his displeasure at the journey, but Thorgerd said there was no need for any reproach, and the people of Laugar deserved the dishonour they had received, if not worse.

Hrefna then asked, 'Did you speak to any of the people at Laugar, Kjartan?'

He answered, 'Not really,' but added that he had exchanged a few words with Bolli.

Hrefna said, with a smile, 'I was told for a fact that you and Gudrun had a talk, and I also learned how she was dressed, that she had put on the head-dress and that it became her extremely well.'

At this Kjartan's colour rose, as Hrefna's bantering tone had obviously angered him.

'I was not aware of what you refer to, Hrefna,' Kjartan said, 'but Gudrun would not need the head-dress to look more becoming than any other woman.'

Hrefna said no more on the subject.

The men of Laugar were very upset and felt that Kjartan had done them a greater offence by these actions than if he had killed one or two of their men. Osvif's sons were the most infuriated, while Bolli tried to make little of it. Gudrun said little, but the few words she did let fall showed that it was not necessarily of less concern to her than to others. After this there was open enmity between the people of Laugar and those of Hjardarholt. Late in the winter Hrefna gave birth to a son who was named Asgeir.

Thorarin, the farmer at Tunga, declared that he wanted to sell his farm. He was in need of money, but he was also concerned at the growing hostilities in the district and was fond of both families. Bolli felt he needed a farm of his own, as the men of Laugar owned a great deal of livestock but little land. Acting on Osvif's advice, Bolli and Gudrun rode over to Tunga. They thought it highly fortunate to get this piece of land close by, and Osvif had told them not to let a small difference in price cause them to miss the opportunity.

They discussed the purchase with Thorarin and reached an agreement on the price and how payment was to be made, and the bargain with Gudrun and Bolli was concluded. There were no witnesses, however, because there were not enough people present to make it legal. Afterwards Gudrun and Bolli rode home.

When Kjartan Olafsson learned of this he rode off immediately with a party of eleven others and reached Tunga early in the morning. Thorarin welcomed him warmly and invited him to stay, and Kjartan replied that he would stop awhile but would return home that evening.

Thorarin asked what his business was and Kjartan answered, 'I came here to discuss with you the agreement you made with Bolli, because I'm opposed to your selling your land to Gudrun and Bolli.'

Thorarin said he could hardly do otherwise – 'the price Bolli offered me for the land was high and is to be paid in a short time'.

Kjartan said, 'You won't suffer financially by not selling the land to Bolli, for I'll buy it for the same price. Nor will it do you much good to refuse to do as I wish, for people will soon realize that I intend to determine the course of events in this district, and show more respect for the views of other people than those of the men of Laugar.'

Thorarin answered, 'The master's word is law in that case, but if I had my way the agreement I made with Bolli would stand unchanged.'

Kjartan replied, 'I wouldn't call it an agreement if it wasn't witnessed. Now either you agree to hand this land over to me on the same terms that you've already agreed to with the others, or keep the land for yourself.'

Thorarin chose to sell him the property, and the agreement was witnessed at once. After purchasing the land, Kjartan rode home.

The news was not long in spreading through all the valleys surrounding Breidafjord.

At Laugar they learned of it the same evening, and Gudrun said to Bolli, 'It looks to me, Bolli, as if Kjartan has given you a choice even less attractive than the one he gave Thorarin: either to turn over the district to him and gain little respect from it, or to show yourself less spineless when your paths cross in the future than you have up to now.'

Bolli made no answer, but walked away at once. Things remained quiet for the remainder of Lent.

On the third day of Easter Kjartan left Hjardarholt accompanied by An the Black. They arrived at Tunga the same day, where Kjartan wanted to have Thorarin make the journey to Saurbaer with him to agree to the debts he was to take over [as payment for his land], for Kjartan had considerable sums owed to him there. As Thorarin had gone to a nearby farm, Kjartan remained at Tunga awhile and waited for him to return. That day Thorhalla Chatterbox was at Tunga and asked Kjartan where he was headed.

He told her he was on the way to Saurbaer and she asked, 'What route will you follow?'

'Through Saelingsdal on the way there, but coming back I'll go through Svinadal,' Kjartan replied.

She asked how long he would stay, and Kjartan answered, 'I expect to return on Thursday.'

'Could you do me a service on the way?' Thorhalla then asked. 'A kinsman of mine, who lives to the west of Hvitadal in the Saurbaer district, has promised me half a mark of homespun cloth. Could I ask you to fetch it for me and bring it back with you?'

Kjartan promised he would do so.

Thorarin returned home then and joined them for the journey. They rode west over the Saelingsdal heath and reached the Hol farm in the evening. Kjartan was given a hearty welcome by the brothers and sister there, who were good friends of his. Thorhalla Chatterbox returned to Laugar that evening, and Osvif's sons asked for news of those she had met that day. She said she had met Kjartan Olafsson and they asked where he was going.

She told them what she knew, adding, 'and I've never seen him look so dashing. It's no wonder men like that feel themselves a cut above.' Thorhalla continued, saying, 'It was also clear that there were few things Kjartan would rather talk about than his purchase of Thorarin's farm.'

Gudrun answered, 'Kjartan can well afford to act as boldly as he likes, as experience has shown that no matter what offence he chooses to commit, no one dares to take him to task for it.'

Both Bolli and the Osvifssons heard their words. Ospak and his brothers gave little answer apart from a few scornful words about Kjartan as usual, but Bolli acted as if he had not heard, as was his custom. As a rule, if anyone criticized Kjartan, he kept silent or argued in his defence.

48 | Kjartan spent the Wednesday following Easter at Hol, where there was plenty of entertainment and feasting. The following night An tossed and turned in his sleep, until others woke him.

They asked what he had been dreaming, and he replied, 'A horrible-looking woman approached me and tugged me sharply out of bed. She had a cleaver in one hand and a wooden meat tray in the other. Placing the cleaver on my chest, she slit me open right down the front, took out all my entrails and put in twigs instead. Then she went off.'

Kjartan and the others laughed at his story and said they would call him An Twig-belly from then on. They even grabbed him and said, teasingly, they wanted to see if they could feel the twigs in his stomach.

Aud said, however, that it was nothing to joke about, and suggested 'that Kjartan should either stay here a bit longer or, if he's determined to ride off straight away, take a few more men with him than he came with'.

Kjartan replied, 'You may value the words of An Twig-belly highly, since he sits here all day entertaining you with his stories, and think that his every dream is prophetic. But I intend to continue on my way as planned, dream or not.'

Kjartan got ready to leave early Thursday, along with Aud's brothers Thorkel Pup and Knut, at her insistence. Kjartan and his followers made a party of twelve altogether. As he had promised, he stopped in Hvitadal to pick up the homespun cloth for Thorhalla Chatterbox before heading southwards through Svinadal.

Meanwhile, at Laugar, Gudrun had risen early before the sun had come up and went to where her brothers slept. She roused Ospak, who was quick to awake, and then her other brothers. When Ospak recognized his sister he asked why she was up and about so early.

Gudrun said she wanted to know what their plans for the day were, and Ospak said he intended to remain at home, 'as there's not much farm work at the moment'.

Gudrun replied, 'With your temperament, you'd have made some farmer a good group of daughters, fit to do no one any good or any harm. After all the abuse and shame Kjartan has heaped upon you, you don't let it disturb your sleep while he goes riding by under your very noses, with only one other man to accompany him. Such men have no better memory than a pig. There's not much chance you'll ever dare to make a move against Kjartan at home if you won't even stand up to him now, when he only has one or two others to back him up. The lot of you just sit here at home, making much of yourselves, and one could only wish there were fewer of you.'

Ospak said she was anything but spare of words, but it was hard to protest against the truth of what she said. He sprang to his feet at once and got dressed and the other brothers followed him. They made preparations to ambush Kjartan. Gudrun asked Bolli to go with them, but he replied that it was not right for him to attack his kinsman and reminded her of how lovingly Olaf had raised him.

Gudrun replied, 'What you say is true enough, but you're not fortunate enough to be in a position where you can please everyone, and if you refuse to go along it will be the end of our life together.'

At Gudrun's urging, Bolli's resentment of Kjartan and his offences grew, and he quickly gathered up his weapons. They were nine in number: Osvif's five sons, Ospak, Helgi, Vandrad, Torrad and Thorolf, Bolli was the sixth, the seventh was Gudlaug, Osvif's nephew and a promising young man. Odd and Stein, the sons of Thorhalla Chatterbox, completed the party. They rode to Svinadal and stopped by the ravine called Hafragil, where they tethered their horses and sat down to wait. Bolli was silent all day and lay up near the top of the ravine.

When Kjartan and his party had passed Mjosund and entered the part of the valley where it widens out, he told Thorkel and his men they should turn back. Thorkel said he would follow them all the way to the mouth of the valley. When they had passed the shielings called Nordursel, Kjartan told the brothers they should not ride any further: 'I won't have that thief, Thorolf, laughing at me for not daring to go my way with only a few men.'

Thorkel replied, 'We'll do as you tell us and go no further, but we'll regret it if we aren't there to help you today if you need it.'

Kjartan then said, 'I'm sure my kinsman Bolli won't be out to kill me, and if the Osvifssons are planning on ambushing me the outcome is anything but a foregone conclusion, even if I'm a bit outnumbered.'

The brothers then headed back.

49 | Kjartan continued south through the valley along with An the Black and Thorarin. At that time a man called Thorkel lived on the Hafratindar farm in Svinadal which is now

deserted. He had gone to see to his horses that day, taking his shepherd along with him. They could see both the men of Laugar lying in wait and Kjartan as he rode down the valley with his two companions. The boy suggested they change their course and ride towards Kjartan, saying it would be very fortunate if they could prevent such a disaster as was now looming on the horizon.

Thorkel said to him, 'Do shut up! Do you think, you fool, that you could save the life of one doomed to die? To tell you the truth, I won't be sorry to see them do whatever damage they please to one another. We're better off finding a spot where we're in no danger ourselves, but have the best view of their meeting so we can enjoy the sport. Everyone says that Kjartan is the best fighter there is; well, I expect he'll need all the fighting prowess he can muster, as we can see they are considerably outnumbered.'

They did as Thorkel wished.

Kjartan and his party were now approaching the ravine Hafragil. By this time the Osvifssons had begun to suspect that Bolli had taken up a position where anyone approaching from the north could see him. They conferred together and felt that Bolli might be going to betray them, so they went up to him on the slope and, pretending it was all in jest, began to wrestle with him, took hold of his feet and drew him further down the slope.

Kjartan and his followers, however, were riding at a good speed and approached quickly. They caught sight of the ambushers when they reached the ravine and recognized them. Kjartan jumped down from his horse immediately and turned towards the Osvifssons. There was a very large rock where Kjartan said they should stand to meet the attack. Before they met, Kjartan threw his spear and struck Thorolf's shield above the handle, forcing it back against him. The point of the spear went through the shield and into Thorolf's arm above the elbow where it severed the large muscle. Thorolf dropped his shield and his arm was of no use to him that day.

Next Kjartan drew his sword – but he was not bearing the one called King's Gift. The two sons of Thorhalla Chatterbox grappled with Thorarin, as this was the role which had been assigned to them. Their struggle was a hard one, for Thorarin was very strong, but the brothers were sturdy men as well. It was difficult to say who would come out on top.

The Osvifssons and Gudlaug attacked Kjartan. There were six of them[44] against Kjartan and An. An defended himself valiantly and tried his best to protect Kjartan. Bolli stood back and watched, holding his sword Leg-biter. Kjartan struck powerful blows, which proved to be more than his sword could bear, and more often than once he had to straighten it by standing on it. The Osvifssons and An had all been wounded, but Kjartan was still untouched. Kjartan fought so fiercely that the Osvifssons had to fall back under the force of his onslaught and instead turned on An. After having fought for some time with his entrails exposed, An finally fell.

At the same moment Kjartan severed Gudlaug's leg above the knee, a wound which proved fatal. Four of the Osvifssons then charged at Kjartan, but he defended himself so valiantly that he did not give way under their attack at all.

Then Kjartan called out, 'Why did you leave home, kinsman Bolli, if you intended only to stand and watch? You're going to have to decide whose side you're on and then see what Leg-biter can do.'

Bolli acted as if he had not heard.

When Ospak saw that they would not be able to overcome Kjartan, he began to urge Bolli in every way he knew to join in, saying that Bolli could not wish it to be said of him afterwards that he had promised to help them in the attack and then failed to do so. 'Kjartan has proved hard enough to handle, even when we'd done much less than this to offend him, and if he should manage to escape now, a harsh punishment will await you, Bolli, no less than us.'

At this Bolli drew the sword Leg-biter and turned towards Kjartan.

Kjartan then said to him, 'An evil deed this is, that you're about to do, kinsman, so much is certain. But I'd rather receive my death at your hands than cause yours.'

With that Kjartan threw down his weapons and refused

to defend himself further. He was only very slightly injured, although exhausted from fighting. Bolli made no response to Kjartan's words, but dealt him a death blow, then took up his body and held him in his arms when he died. Bolli regretted the deed immediately and declared himself the slayer.

Bolli told the Osvifssons to return home but himself remained there with Thorarin by the bodies. When they arrived at Laugar they told the news to Gudrun, who was very pleased. Thorolf's wounded arm was bandaged but took a long time healing and was always a handicap to him.

After Kjartan's body was taken to the farm at Tunga, Bolli rode back to Laugar. Gudrun went out to meet him, and asked how late in the day it was.

Bolli replied that it was almost mid-afternoon, and Gudrun said, 'A poor match they make, our morning's work – I have spun twelve ells of yarn while you have slain Kjartan.'

Bolli replied, 'I'll not soon forget this misfortune, even without you to remind me of it.'

Gudrun then said, 'I wouldn't consider it misfortune. I think you were held in much greater esteem the winter Kjartan was still in Norway than now, after he returned to Iceland and has walked all over you. And last but most important, to my mind, is the thought that Hrefna won't go to bed with a smile on her face this evening.'

At this Bolli was furious and replied, 'I wonder whether she'll pale at the news any more than you, and I suspect that you would be much less upset if it were me lying there slain and Kjartan who lived to tell the tale.'

Gudrun then realized how angry Bolli was and said, 'Don't say things like that. I'm very grateful for what you have done. Now I know that you won't go against my will.'

The Osvifssons then went into hiding in an underground shelter which had been secretly prepared for them, and Thorhalla Chatterbox's sons were sent to Helgafell to tell the news to Snorri the Godi. They were also to ask him to send them assistance quickly for support against Olaf and others seeking recourse for Kjartan's slaying.

A surprising event occurred at Saelingsdalstunga the night

after the battle. An, whom everyone had thought to be dead, suddenly sat upright.

The people keeping watch over the bodies were very frightened and thought this a wondrous event, but An spoke to them, saying, 'Fear not, I tell you, in God's name. I was alive and in my right mind up until the moment when I lost consciousness. Then I dreamed this same woman came to me as before, and now she removed the twigs from my stomach and replaced my entrails, after which I became whole again.'

The wounds he had received were then bandaged and healed well, but he was ever afterwards known as An Twig-belly.

For Olaf Hoskuldsson the news of Kjartan's killing was a heavy blow, although he took it with dignity.

His sons wanted to attack and kill Bolli immediately, but Olaf replied, 'That's the last thing I want. It's no compensation for my son though Bolli be slain, and though I loved Kjartan more dearly than any other person, I can't agree to Bolli being harmed. I can give you something worthwhile to do; you should go after those two sons of Thorhalla's who were sent to Helgafell to gather forces against us. Anything you do to punish them will please me.'

The Olafssons lost no time in setting out. First, taking a ferry that belonged to Olaf, they rowed towards the mouth of Hvammsfjord. They were a party of seven, and made speedy progress. The light wind that blew was in their favour and they used their oars as well as the sail until they came to Skorey Island. They stopped there for a while to ask about the movements of people of the district. A short time later they saw a boat being rowed down from the north of the fjord and recognized the men aboard as Thorhalla's sons. Halldor and his men set out to attack them at once and met with little resistance. After boarding the ship, the Olafssons seized Stein and his brother, killed them and threw their bodies overboard. They then returned home and their journey was thought to have been very effectively carried out.

50 | Olaf went out to meet Kjartan's body as it was borne home. He sent messengers south to Borg to tell Thorstein Egilsson the news and ask him for support in prosecuting the slayers. In case powerful men were to throw their weight behind the Osvifssons, he said, he wanted to make sure he would still be able to determine the course of events. He sent similar messages north to his son-in-law Gudmund in Vididal and to the Asgeirssons, and told them that he had declared all of the men guilty of the slaying who had taken part in the assault, with the exception of Ospak Osvifsson. Ospak had previously been outlawed for seducing a woman named Aldis,[45] the daughter of Ljot the Dueller of Ingjaldssand. Their son Ulf later became a steward among King Harald Sigurdarson's followers. His wife was Jorunn Thorbergsdottir, and their son Jon was the father of Erlend the Torpid, who was the father of Archbishop Eystein.

Olaf had declared his intent to prosecute the case at the Thorsnes Assembly. He had Kjartan's body brought home and a tent raised over it, as no church had been built in Dalir district at this time. When Olaf learned that Thorstein had responded to his message at once and collected a large number of men, as had the men of Vididal, he sent word asking his neighbours throughout the Dalir for their support.

Many men gathered in answer to his call and Olaf sent them all to Laugar, saying, 'I want you to show Bolli no less support, should he need it, than you would offer me, because if my guess is right the men from the other districts, who will soon be upon us, will feel they need to wreak their vengeance on him.'

Soon after things had been arranged in this manner, Thorstein and his company arrived, followed by the men of Vididal, all in a state of fury. Hall Gudmundarson and Kalf Asgeirsson were the most adamant in demanding that they attack Bolli and search out the Osvifssons until they were found, saying they could hardly have left the district. But when Olaf spoke determinedly against it, a message of conciliation was sent. Bolli agreed readily, and said Olaf should decide the terms for him. Osvif saw no possibility of protesting, as no support had come from Snorri. At a conciliation meeting held at Ljarskogar the judgement was awarded entirely to Olaf. He was to name whatever compensation he chose for Kjartan's slaying, either fines or outlawry. The conciliation meeting was then dissolved. Bolli did not attend, on Olaf's advice. The sentences were to be pronounced at the Thorsnes Assembly. Both the Myrar people and those from Vididal then rode back to Hjardarholt. Thorstein Kuggason offered to foster Kjartan's son Asgeir, as consolation for Hrefna, who returned north with her brothers. She was wracked with grief, but maintained a dignified and courteous manner, conversing cheerfully with everyone. Hrefna did not marry again after Kjartan's death. After returning north she lived only a short while, and it was generally said that she had been shattered by her grief.

51 | Kjartan's body had remained a week at Hjardarholt. As Thorstein Egilsson had had a church built at Borg, he took the body home with him, and Kjartan was buried at Borg in the graveyard of the newly consecrated church, still in its white drapings.

The time soon came for the Thorsnes Assembly. The case against the Osvifssons was presented and all of them sentenced to outlawry. Atonement was made so that they might be transported from the country, but they were not allowed to return as long as any of the Olafssons or Asgeir Kjartansson were alive. No compensation was to be paid for Osvif's nephew Gudlaug having taken part in the ambush or the attack upon Kjartan, nor was Thorolf to receive any redress for the bloody wounds inflicted on him. Olaf refused to have Bolli outlawed and pronounced a fine as his compensation. His sons, especially Halldor and Steinthor, protested angrily at this, and said they would find it difficult to dwell in the same district as Bolli in the future. Olaf said that as long as he were alive no difficulties would arise.

A ship beached at Bjarnarhofn belonged to a man called Audun Halter-dog. He was attending the assembly and spoke out, saying, 'It could turn out that these men will be treated as much as outlaws in Norway if Kjartan's friends there are still alive.'

Osvif then replied, 'You, Halter-pup, will not prove much of a prophet, as my sons will gain the respect of worthy men, while you'll be wrestling with the trolls before this summer is out, Halter-dog.'

Audun Halter-dog sailed abroad that summer and his ship was wrecked near the Faroe Islands. Everyone aboard was drowned and people said that Osvif's prophecy had certainly been proven true.

The Osvifssons journeyed abroad that summer and none of them ever returned to Iceland. With the case thus concluded, it was Olaf who gained in stature as a result of having ensured that those who deserved the most severe punishment, the Osvifssons, paid the price, while sparing Bolli because of his close family ties. Olaf thanked his supporters warmly for their assistance. At Olaf's suggestion Bolli purchased the farm at Tunga. Olaf is said to have lived another three years after Kjartan's slaying. After his death, his sons divided up the property, with Halldor taking over the farm at Hjardarholt. Thorgerd, their mother, lived with Halldor and was filled with hatred towards Bolli, feeling she had been sorely repaid for raising him.

52 | The following spring Gudrun and Bolli set up house at Saelingsdalstunga, which soon became an impressive farm. A son born to them was named Thorleik. Even as a young lad he was very handsome and precocious.

Halldor Olafsson lived at Hjardarholt, as was mentioned earlier, and acted as leader for his brothers in most matters. The spring Kjartan was slain Thorgerd Egilsdottir sent a young lad related to her to work as a servant for Thorkel of Hafratindar. The boy looked after the sheep during the summer. Like others, he was very grieved at the loss of Kjartan, but he could never mention his name in the presence of Thorkel, who generally spoke scornfully of Kjartan, saying he was cowardly and lacked daring. He often imitated Kjartan's reaction at being dealt his wound. The boy was greatly upset by this and went to

Hjardarholt to report it to Halldor and Thorgerd and ask them
to take him in.

Thorgerd told him he should remain in the position until
the winter came, but the boy said he could not hold out any
longer, 'and you wouldn't ask me to if you knew how much it
tortures me'.

At that Thorgerd sympathized with him and said that, for
her part, she could offer him a place.

Halldor said, 'Don't pay any attention to the boy; he's of no
consequence.'

To this Thorgerd replied, 'The boy may be of little consequence, but Thorkel's behaviour has been nothing but des-
picable. He knew of the men of Laugar waiting there to ambush
Kjartan and wouldn't warn him, but instead enjoyed himself
watching their encounter and now adds insult to injury. There's
little chance of you brothers ever doing much to get revenge
against a more powerful opponent if you can't even deal with
a miserable swine of the likes of Thorkel.'

Halldor had little to say in reply but told his mother to do as
she liked regarding the boy's position.

A few days later Halldor left Hjardarholt accompanied by
several men and went to Hafratindar where he attacked Thorkel
in his farmhouse. When Thorkel was brought outside to be
killed, his behaviour was anything but courageous. Halldor
prevented the men from taking anything and returned home
afterwards. Thorgerd expressed her pleasure at his actions,
feeling that this action was better than none at all.

The summer passed without event, despite the strained
relations between Bolli and the Olafssons. The brothers showed
Bolli nothing but hatred, while he attempted to avoid coming
into conflict with the Olafssons and their relatives in every way
he could without sacrificing his own honour, for he had no lack
of ambition himself. Bolli kept a large number of servants and
lived in style, for he did not lack wealth.

Steinthor Olafsson farmed at Donustadir in Laxardal. His
wife was Thurid Asgeirsdottir, who had earlier been married to
Thorkel Kuggi. Their son Steinthor was called Groslappi
(Groa's Layabout).

53 | Late in the winter following the death of Olaf Hos-
kuldsson, Thorgerd Egilsdottir sent word to her son
Steinthor, asking him to pay her a visit. When he answered her
summons, his mother told him she wished to travel to Saurbaer
to visit her friend Aud. She told Halldor to accompany them as
well. They made a party of five, with Halldor escorting his
mother. They rode along until they were passing the farm at
Saelingsdalstunga.

Thorgerd turned her horse towards the farm and asked,
'What is the name of this farm?'

Halldor replied, 'You're hardly asking for an answer you
don't already know, Mother; the farm is called Tunga.'

'Who is it lives here?' she asked.

He answered, 'You also know that only too well, Mother.'

She answered with a snort. 'What I do know,' she said, 'is
that here lives Bolli, your brother's slayer, and not a shred of
resemblance do you bear to your great ancestors since you
won't avenge a brother the likes of Kjartan. Never would your
grandfather Egil have acted like this, and it grieves me to have
such spineless sons. You would have made your father better
daughters, to be married off, than sons. It shows the truth of
the saying, Halldor, that "every kin has its coward". I see only
too well now that fathering such sons was Olaf's great failing.
I address my words to you, Halldor,' she said, 'because you've
taken the lead among your brothers. We will turn back now;
I made the journey mainly to remind you of what you seem to
have forgotten.'

Halldor then answered, 'You're the last person we could
blame, Mother, if it did slip from our minds.'

Halldor had little else to say, although his hatred for Bolli
swelled.

The winter passed and the summer came. When the time of
the Althing approached, Halldor declared he and his brothers
would attend. They rode together in a large company and set
up their booth at Olaf's site. The Althing was uneventful.
Also attending were the northerners from Vididal, the sons of
Gudmund Solmundarson. Bardi Gudmundarson was eighteen

at the time and a big, strapping man. The Olafssons invited him to come back to Hjardarholt and urged him to accept. His brother Hall was not in the country at the time, and Bardi was more than willing to accept their invitation, as the kinsmen were good friends. After the Althing Bardi rode westward with the Olafssons to Hjardarholt, where he stayed for the remainder of the summer.

54 | Halldor soon confided to Bardi that the brothers were planning an attack on Bolli, adding that he could no longer stand merely to listen to his mother's taunts – 'I won't try to hide the fact, kinsman Bardi, that it was not least because we hoped for your help and support that we invited you to come home with us.'

Bardi replied, 'It will bring you no credit if you renege on a settlement made with your own kinsman. Besides that, Bolli will be no easy mark; he always has a large number of men about him, and is himself the best of fighters. Nor does he lack clever advice, both from Gudrun and Osvif. All in all it looks like anything but an easy task to me.'

Halldor said, 'We scarcely need anyone to make things more difficult for us. I wouldn't have brought the matter up if we weren't already determined to seek our revenge on Bolli. And I don't expect you, kinsman, to back out of making this trip with us.'

Bardi replied, 'I know you'd think it unsuitable for me to refuse, and if I can't manage to convince you otherwise, I won't let you down.'

'You make me a good answer,' Halldor said, 'just as I'd expect of you.'

When Bardi said that they would have to plan the attack wisely, Halldor said he had learned that Bolli had sent most of his servants off, some north to a ship in Hrutafjord and others down to Strond[46] – 'I'm also told that Bolli himself is at the shieling up in Saelingsdal with only some servants who are making hay there. It looks to me as if there'll be no better time to confront him.'

Halldor and Bardi agreed on this.

A man named Thorstein the Black lived in Hundadal in the Dalir district of Breidafjord. He was both wealthy and wise and had long been a friend of Olaf's. Thorstein's sister Solveig was married to a man called Helgi, the son of Hardbein. Helgi was a big, strong man who had sailed on many merchant voyages. He had only recently settled in Iceland and was staying on his brother-in-law Thorstein's farm. Halldor sent word to Thorstein and Helgi, and when they arrived in Hjardarholt he told them of his plans and preparations and asked them to come along.

Thorstein was not in favour of the plan. 'It's a terrible loss if you kinsmen continue killing one another off. There are now few men the equal of Bolli in your family.'

Thorstein's words were to no avail. Halldor sent word to Lambi, his father's half-brother, and told him of his plans when he arrived. Lambi supported the project enthusiastically. Thorgerd, mistress of the house, was another who never flagged in encouraging them to make the journey. Kjartan would never be properly revenged to her mind, she said, until Bolli paid with his life.

Soon afterwards they made ready for the journey. The four Olafssons, Halldor, Steinthor, Helgi and Hoskuld, were accompanied by Bardi, Gudmund's son, Lambi was the sixth, Thorstein the seventh, Helgi his brother-in-law the eighth, and An Twig-belly made up the ninth. Thorgerd also got ready to accompany them.

When they protested, saying this was no errand for a woman, she replied that she intended to go along, saying, 'No one knows better than I do that it is likely my sons will require some urging yet.' They replied that she would have to decide for herself.

55 | The nine of them then set out from Hjardarholt, with Thorgerd making it a party of ten. Following the shore, they reached Ljarskogar early in the night, but did not slow their pace until they arrived in Saelingsdal shortly after dawn. In those days the valley was thickly wooded. As Halldor had

been told, Bolli was in the shieling. The buildings stood down
by the river, on the spot now known as Bollatoftir (Bolli's
ruins). There is a large hill which extends back from the shieling
up to the ravine Stakkagil. Between this hill and the mountain
slopes there is a large meadow, called Barm, where Bolli's
farmhands were haying.

Halldor and his followers approached Oxnagrof, across the
plain Ranarvellir and above Hamarengi, which was opposite
the shieling. They knew that there were many people staying
at the shieling, so they dismounted and planned to wait there
until they had left to pursue their day's tasks.

Bolli's shepherd had gone out to see to the flocks up on the
mountain early that morning. He caught sight of the men in
the wood and their tethered horses, and suspected that anyone
who moved so secretively could hardly be on a peaceful errand.
He headed straight back to the shieling to tell Bolli of the men's
arrival. Halldor, who was a man of keen sight, saw him running
down the hillside towards the shieling.

He told his companions that this would be Bolli's shepherd,
'who will have seen our movements. We'll have to cut him off
so he won't be able to give them a warning at the shieling.'

They did as he suggested. An Twig-belly was the first to catch
up with the boy. He lifted him up into the air and then threw
him forcefully to the ground, breaking his spine when he fell.
They then rode up to the two buildings of the dairy, a sleeping
cabin and a storehouse. Bolli had been up early that morning
to give instructions for the day's work, then had gone back to
bed after the farmhands had set off. The two of them, Gudrun
and Bolli, were alone in the sleeping cabin. They awoke at the
noise of the men dismounting and heard them discussing who
should be the first to enter the building and attack Bolli. Bolli
recognized the voices of Halldor and several of his companions
and told Gudrun to leave the cabin. The encounter at hand, he
said, could only prove to be poor entertainment for her.

Gudrun replied that she felt she could look upon whatever
happened, and said she would not prove any hindrance to Bolli
though she remained near him. Bolli said he intended to have
his way this time, and Gudrun left the building. She walked

down the slope to a small stream and began to wash some linen. When Bolli was alone in the cabin he collected his weapons, placed his helmet on his head and picked up his shield and sword Leg-biter. He had no coat of mail.

Halldor and the others discussed how to go about the attack, as no one was eager to be the first to enter the cabin.

An Twig-belly then spoke: 'Others in this company may be closer kin to Kjartan, but in none of your minds do the events of Kjartan's death stand out as clearly. I remember thinking, as I was carried home to Tunga and assumed to be dead, and Kjartan was slain, how gladly I would strike back at Bolli if I got the chance. So I'll be the first one to enter.'

To this Thorstein the Black answered, 'Those are courageous words, but discretion is the better part of valour. Bolli is not simply going to stand still when attacked. Despite the fact that he has few men to back him up, you can expect him to put up a good defence. Bolli is not only strong and an excellent fighter, he also has a sword that never fails him.'

An Twig-belly then entered the cabin in a quick rush, holding his shield over his head with the narrow end foremost. Bolli struck him a blow with Leg-biter, cutting off the tail of the shield and splitting An right down to his shoulders and killing him immediately. Lambi followed on An's heels, with his sword drawn and a shield before him. At that moment Bolli jerked Leg-biter loose from An's wound, and as he did so his shield slipped to one side. Lambi used the moment to strike him in the thigh, giving him a bad wound. Bolli responded with a blow at Lambi's shoulder. The sword cut down his side and put him out of action. He never regained the full use of his arm. At this same instant Helgi Hardbeinsson entered, bearing a spear whose blade was a full ell in length, with iron wound around the shaft. When Bolli saw this, he threw down his sword, took his shield in both hands and went towards the doorway to meet Helgi. Helgi lunged at Bolli, and the spear pierced both the shield and Bolli himself. Bolli leaned against the wall of the cabin. Halldor and his brothers then came rushing in, followed by Thorgerd. Bolli spoke: 'Now's the time, brothers, to come a bit closer than you have done,' and added that he expected that his defence would soon be over. It was Thorgerd who answered, and urged them not to hesitate to finish Bolli off and to put some space between trunk and head.

Bolli was still leaning against the wall of the cabin, holding his cloak tightly to contain his entrails. Steinthor Olafsson rushed at him and struck him a blow on the neck just above the shoulders with a great axe, severing his head cleanly.

Thorgerd said, 'May your hands always serve you so well,' and said Gudrun would be busy awhile combing Bolli's bloody locks.

They then left the cabin.

Gudrun then walked away from the stream and came up towards Halldor and his party, and asked for news of their encounter with Bolli. They told her what had happened. Gudrun was wearing a long tunic, a close-fitting woven bodice and a mantle on her head. She had bound a shawl about her that was decorated in black stitching with fringes at the ends. Helgi Hardbeinsson walked over to Gudrun and used the end of her shawl to dry the blood off the spear with which he had pierced Bolli. Gudrun looked at him and merely smiled.

Halldor said to him, 'That was a vile thing to do, and merciless of you.'

Helgi told him to spare his sympathy, 'as something tells me that my own death lies under the end of that shawl'.

Gudrun followed them a short way and talked to them as they untied their horses and rode off, then turned back.

56 | Halldor's companions remarked that Gudrun had seemed to care but little that Bolli had been slain, since she followed them on their way and even spoke to them as if they had done nothing at all to offend her.

Halldor answered them, saying, 'I suspect that it was not because Bolli's killing meant little to her that she saw us off, but rather that she was intent on finding out exactly who had taken part in the attack. It's no exaggeration when people say that Gudrun is a woman of exceptionally strong character. Besides, it's only natural that she should greatly regret losing

Bolli, because there's no denying that a man of Bolli's stature is a severe loss, despite the fact that we kinsmen were not destined to get along together.'

After this they rode back to Hjardarholt.

The news of these events soon spread and created plenty of comment. Bolli was mourned widely. Gudrun sent men to Snorri the Godi immediately, because she and Osvif felt they could place all their trust in Snorri. Snorri lost no time in answering Gudrun's summons and arrived at Tunga with a party of sixty men.

Gudrun was very glad to see him, but when he offered to seek a reconciliation she was anything but eager to accept payment for Bolli's killing on behalf of her son Thorleik. 'The best help you could offer me, Snorri,' Gudrun said, 'would be to exchange residences with me, so that I won't have the Hjardarholt clan in the next field to me.'

At this time Snorri was involved in extensive disputes with his own neighbours, the people of Eyrar.

He replied that he would make the change for Gudrun's sake, 'but you'll have to remain at Tunga for a year yet'.

Snorri then prepared to leave and Gudrun gave him worthy gifts at parting. He returned home and the year followed without event. Gudrun gave birth to a child the winter after Bolli's death, a boy, who was named Bolli. Even as a young child he was large and handsome and Gudrun loved him deeply. The winter passed and spring arrived, and the time came for the exchange of lands which had been agreed upon between Gudrun and Snorri. Snorri settled down at Tunga and lived there for the remainder of his life, while Gudrun and Osvif moved to Helgafell, where they built up a substantial farm. Gudrun's sons, Thorleik and Bolli, grew up there. Thorleik was four years of age when his father Bolli was slain.

57 | There was a man named Thorgils who was identified with his mother and known as Halla's son (Holluson), because she had outlived his father. His father Snorri was the son of Alf from Dalir, while his mother Halla was the daughter of Gest

Oddleifsson. Thorgils's farm Tunga was in Hordadal. He was a large, handsome man, very haughty, and not at all fair in his dealings. There was no love lost between him and Snorri the Godi, who considered Thorgils to be an interfering fellow who liked to make his presence felt.

Thorgils often travelled to the district to the west on one pretext or another. He was a frequent visitor at Helgafell and offered Gudrun his assistance. She answered him politely enough but refrained from giving any definite answer. Thorgils offered to have her son, Thorleik, come and stay with him, and the boy was at Tunga for quite some time, where he learned law from Thorgils, who was clever at the law.

Thorkel Eyjolfsson, a renowned man of prominent family and a great friend of Snorri the Godi, was sailing at this time on merchant voyages. When in Iceland he generally stayed with his kinsman, Thorstein Kuggason. Once, when Thorkel's ship was beached at Vadil on the coast of Bardastrond, the son of Eid of As was slain by the sons of Helga of Kropp. The killer himself was named Grim and his brother Njal. Njal was drowned soon afterwards in the Hvita river, while Grim was sentenced to full outlawry for the killing and fled to the mountains after being outlawed. He was a big, strong man. Eid was an old man when this occurred and no action was taken against the outlaw and many people criticized Thorkel Eyjolfsson for not acting in the case.

The following spring,[47] when Thorkel had made ready to sail, he went south to Breidafjord, where he got himself a horse and rode alone all the way to his kinsman Eid at As without slowing his pace. Eid welcomed him with great pleasure. Thorkel told him that the reason for his coming was to seek out the outlaw Grim, and asked Eid if he had any idea where his lair might be.

'I'm not sure I like this idea,' Eid answered. 'It seems to me you're taking quite a chance on the outcome in confronting a fiend like Grim. If you must go, at least take some other men with you, so you will control the course of events.'

'There's little prestige to be gained from it,' said Thorkel, 'if a whole group attacks a single man, but I would like you to

lend me your sword Skofnung.[48] With it, I'm sure I'll manage
to deal with a single man, no matter how capable a fighter
he is.'

'Please yourself, then,' Eid said, 'but I wouldn't be surprised
if you ended up regretting your stubbornness sooner or later.
And since you feel you are doing this for my sake, I won't refuse
your request, as I think Skofnung will be in good hands with
you. But the sword can only be used under certain conditions:
the sun must not be allowed to shine on its hilt, nor may it be
drawn in the presence of women. Any wound it inflicts will not
heal unless rubbed with the healing stone which accompanies
it.' Thorkel promised to follow these instructions carefully and
took the sword, asking Eid to show him where Grim had his
lair. Eid said it was most likely that he hid east of As, on the
Tvidaegra heath by the Fiskivotn lakes. Thorkel then rode
northwards up into the highlands following the trail Eid had
pointed out to him. After travelling a long distance he saw a
hut by a large lake and headed towards it.

58 | As Thorkel approached the hut he caught sight of a man
     | wearing a fur cloak who sat fishing near the mouth of a
stream emptying into the lake. Thorkel dismounted and tethered his horse by the wall of the hut, then headed towards the
lake where the man sat fishing.

Grim saw the shadow of a man on the water and sprang to
his feet. By that time Thorkel was right beside him and struck
a blow at him. The blow landed on his arm just above his wrist,
but the wound was not deep. Grim took hold of Thorkel and
as they wrestled with one another the difference in strength
soon became apparent, with Thorkel falling to the ground and
Grim on top of him.

Grim then asked who he was, but Thorkel replied that it was
none of his concern.

Grim said, 'Things have turned out differently than you
expected, and now it's your life which seems to be in my hands.'

Thorkel replied that he wouldn't ask to be spared. 'Things
have turned out unluckily for me.'

Grim replied that he had caused enough misfortune already, even if this deed were to go undone. 'Fate has other things in store for you than to die at this meeting of ours, so I'll spare your life. You can reward me in whatever way you wish.'

They both then got to their feet and walked back to the hut. Thorkel saw that Grim was weakened by the loss of blood and took Skofnung's healing stone, rubbed it on the wound and bound the stone against it. All the pain and swelling disappeared from the wound immediately. Both of them spent the night there, and the next morning Thorkel prepared to leave and asked Grim if he wished to come along. When Grim accepted, Thorkel rode westward, without returning first to Eid. They did not stop until they reached Saelingsdalstunga, where Snorri the Godi gave him a warm welcome.

Thorkel told him that his journey had turned out badly, but Snorri said things had gone well, 'and to my mind Grim has a lucky look about him. I want you to treat him generously. And if you take my advice, my friend, you'll put an end to your voyaging, settle down and get married and become the leader that a man of such good family should.'

Thorkel replied, 'Your counsels have served me well often enough', and asked whether Snorri had given thought to what woman he should propose to.

Snorri answered, 'You should propose to the woman who is the finest possible match and that is Gudrun Osvifsdottir.'

Thorkel said there was no denying the match was a worthy one, 'but it's her single-mindedness and fanaticism that cause me concern; she will presumably be intent on seeking revenge for Bolli, her husband. Thorgils Holluson seems to be involved in this with her and I'm not sure that he would like this. Not that I don't find the prospect of Gudrun appealing.'

Snorri replied, 'I'll see to it that you won't be in any danger from Thorgils, and I expect we'll see developments in the matter of Bolli's revenge before the end of the coming winter.'

Thorkel answered, 'You may be speaking more than just empty words when you say that, but I can't see that there's any more likelihood of Bolli's being avenged now than before, unless some of the leading men are ready to lend a hand in it.'

Snorri said, 'I think you should sail abroad once more this summer, and we'll see what happens.'

Thorkel agreed to this and on this note they parted company.

Thorkel travelled west across Breidafjord to his ship. He took Grim along with him on his voyage abroad. They had good winds that summer and made land in the south of Norway.

Thorkel then spoke to Grim: 'You know well enough the events and circumstances of our acquaintance, so that there is no need for me to speak of it. But I would like it to end with less hostility than we once showed each other. You have proved a staunch fellow, and I would like to part with you as if I had never borne any ill will towards you. Money enough will you have to enable you to join a company of courageous men. But you should avoid dwelling in the north of this country, as many of Eid's kinsmen sail on merchant voyages and they will bear you ill will.'

Grim thanked him for his words and said he had been offered more than he could ask for. Thorkel gave Grim plenty of trading goods at parting, and many men called his act a very generous one. After this Grim went east to the Vik region where he settled and was considered a valiant man. This is the last that is said of Grim.

Thorkel spent the winter in Norway and was regarded as a man of importance. He was both very wealthy and boldly ambitious. This scene will now be left for a while, and the thread taken up again once more in Iceland, with news of the events taking place while Thorkel was abroad.

59 | At hay-time Gudrun Osvifsdottir left home and rode to the Dalir district and to Thykkvaskog. At the time Thorleik either stayed at the farm at Thykkvaskog with the Armodssons, Halldor and Ornolf, or at Tunga with Thorgils. That same night Gudrun sent word to Snorri the Godi that she wished to meet him straight away the following day. Snorri responded at once and taking a companion with him rode off directly until he came to the Haukadalsa river. There is a cliff on the north bank of the river known as Hofdi, on the land

belonging to the Laekjarskog farm. Gudrun had said they should meet there. They arrived at much the same time. Only one person followed Gudrun as well, Bolli Bollason. He was twelve years old at the time, but had the strength and wit of a full-grown man, and many a man would never be more mature though fully grown. He also bore Leg-biter.

Snorri and Gudrun spoke to each other privately, while Bolli and Snorri's companion sat at the top of the cliff to keep watch for people travelling in the district. When Snorri and Gudrun had exchanged the usual news, Snorri asked what Gudrun's purpose was – what had happened recently to bring about this sudden summons?

Gudrun replied, 'Nothing could be fresher in my mind than the event which I intend to refer to although it occurred twelve years ago. It is Bolli's revenge I intend to discuss, and it cannot come as a surprise to you, as I have reminded you of it now and again. And I remind you as well that you promised me your assistance, if I waited patiently. By now I have lost all hope of you giving your attention to our case, and I have waited as long as my patience admits. I want to ask your advice in deciding where to take revenge.'

Snorri asked what she had in mind, and Gudrun answered, 'That not all the Olafssons will remain unscathed.'

Snorri said he would forbid any action against those men who were of highest standing in the district, 'as their close kinsmen will take no small revenge and it is important to put an end to this feud'.

Gudrun said, 'Then Lambi should be attacked and killed, and that will get rid of the most malicious of them.'

Snorri answered, 'Lambi is certainly guilty enough to be killed, but I don't feel it would avenge Bolli to have Lambi killed, nor will you get the difference in compensation that Bolli's death deserves if those killings are equalled out.'

Gudrun spoke: 'It may well be that we won't be able to take an equal toll of the men of Laxardal, but someone is going to pay the price, whatever dale he dwells in. Let's turn then to Thorstein the Black; no one has played a less honourable part in this affair than he.'

Snorri spoke: 'You have no more complaint against Thorstein than any of the others who went along on the attack but inflicted no wound on Bolli. But you pass over completely men who to my mind are more worthy of taking revenge upon, and actually dealt Bolli his death-blow, such as Helgi Hardbeinsson.'

Gudrun said, 'That is true enough, but I am not content to let off all the others against whom I've nurtured such hostility.'

Snorri answered, 'I see a good plan. Lambi and Thorstein will assist your sons in the attack, as a fair way of settling their debt to you. If they refuse, I won't attempt to protect them or deter you from punishing them in any way you wish.'

Gudrun asked, 'How do we go about getting these men you have named to take part?'

Snorri replied, 'Those who head the attack will have to look after that.'

Gudrun said, 'I should like you to suggest who is to lead and direct the attack.'

Snorri smiled at this and said, 'You have already picked the man for the job.'

Gudrun replied, 'By that you mean Thorgils?'

Snorri said that indeed he did. Gudrun replied, 'I have spoken of this to Thorgils, but the subject is as good as closed. He set the one condition that I could not consider: he would not refuse to avenge Bolli, if I would agree to marry him. Of that there is no hope at all, and so I will not ask him to make the journey.'

Snorri spoke: 'I will tell you a way to go about it, because I would not mind Thorgils making this journey. He will, naturally, be promised a match, but with the catch that you should otherwise marry no other man in the country. That promise you can keep, as Thorkel Eyjolfsson is not in this country at the moment, and it is he whom I intend you to marry.'

Gudrun replied, 'Surely he will see the catch.'

Snorri replied, 'He surely will not. Thorgils is a man more given to acting than thinking. Make the agreement with him in the presence of only a few witnesses; have Halldor, his foster-brother, present but not Ornolf, who is cleverer, and I'll take the blame if it doesn't work.'

Snorri and Gudrun then brought their conversation to an end and said their farewells to one another. Snorri rode home and Gudrun to Thykkvaskog. The following morning Gudrun left Thykkvaskog in the company of her sons, and as they travelled westward along the Skogarstrond shore they noticed men following them. As these men were riding hard, they soon caught up and proved to be Thorgils Holluson and followers. They greeted each other warmly and rode on together to Helgafell that day.

60 | Several nights after returning home, Gudrun asked her sons to come and speak to her in her leek garden. When they arrived they saw spread out garments of linen, a shirt and breeches much stained with blood.

Gudrun then spoke: 'These very clothes which you see here reproach you for not avenging your father. I have few words to add, for it is hardly likely that you would let the urging of words direct you if unmoved by such displays and reminders.'

Both brothers were greatly shaken by Gudrun's words, but answered that they had been too young to seek revenge and had lacked someone to lead them. They had neither been able to plan their own actions nor those of others, 'though we well remember what we have lost'.

Gudrun said she suspected that they gave more thought to horse-fights or games. After this the brothers left, but they could not sleep that night. Thorgils noticed this and asked what was troubling them. They told him everything of the conversation with their mother, adding that they could no longer bear their grief and her reproaches.

'We wish to seek revenge,' said Bolli. 'We brothers are mature enough now that people will begin to count it against us if we fail to take action.'

The following day Gudrun and Thorgils were talking privately together.

Gudrun began by saying, 'It looks to me, Thorgils, as if my sons have had their fill of inaction, and will be looking to avenge their father. Things have had to wait until now mostly because I felt Thorleik and Bolli were too young to go about slaying men. There was certainly more than enough cause to have retaliated earlier.'

Thorgils answered, 'You have no reason to discuss this matter with me, since you have absolutely refused to marry me; I'm still of the same mind, however, as before when we discussed this. I don't think it too tall an order to knock off one or both of the men who played a major part in Bolli's killing if I can get you to marry me.'

Gudrun spoke: 'It seems that Thorleik feels no one is better suited as the leader for any difficult undertaking. But I will not conceal from you that the lads intend to attack the berserk Helgi Hardbeinsson, who lives on his farm up in Skorradal, and is completely off his guard.'

Thorgils spoke: 'It makes no difference to me whether his name is Helgi or anything else. I don't feel it beyond me to take on Helgi or any other man. I've said my last word on it; you promise before witnesses to marry me if I manage to help your sons get their revenge.'

Gudrun replied that she would keep any promise she gave, though it were made before but a few witnesses, and said they should agree on this bargain. She asked that Thorgils's foster-brother Halldor be summoned and then her sons.

Thorgils asked that Ornolf be present as well, but Gudrun said there was no need for that – 'I am more suspicious of Ornolf's loyalty towards you than I expect you are.'

Thorgils said she should have her way.

The brothers then approached Gudrun and Thorgils, who were talking to Halldor as they came.

Gudrun explained the situation to them, that 'Thorgils has promised to offer his leadership on a journey to attack Helgi Hardbeinsson, along with my sons, to avenge Bolli. Thorgils made it a condition for the journey that I agree to marry him. Now I declare in your presence as witnesses, that I promise Thorgils to marry no other man in this country than him; nor do I intend to marry abroad.'

Thorgils was satisfied that the promise was binding enough and saw nothing questionable about it. They then brought the conversation to an end. It was now settled that Thorgils would lead the attack. He made preparations to set out from Helgafell, accompanied by Gudrun's sons. They rode eastward to the Dalir district, stopping first at Thorgils's Tunga farm.

61 | The next Lord's Day the local Autumn Meeting was held, which Thorgils attended with his party. Snorri the Godi did not attend the assembly, but a large crowd was there.

During the day Thorgils managed to speak to Thorstein the Black, saying, 'Since, as you know, you went along with the Olafssons when Bolli was slain, you owe his sons some unpaid compensation. And although it's a long time since the events took place, I don't imagine they have forgotten those men who took part. In the opinion of the two brothers, it would hardly be to their honour to seek revenge on the Olafssons, for the sake of kinship. So they now intend to attack Helgi Hardbeinsson, as it was he who dealt Bolli his death blow. We want to ask you, Thorstein, to accompany them on their journey, and in so doing buy your own settlement.'

Thorstein answered, 'It does me little honour to plot an attack on my brother-in-law Helgi; I would much rather give money to buy peace, and I'll make it enough to serve as an honourable settlement.'

Thorgils answered, 'I scarcely expect the brothers are doing this for the sake of money. Make no mistake, Thorstein, you have two choices before you: either you make the journey or face harsh punishment when it's dealt out. I also want you to accept this offer, despite your obligations to Helgi. Each man must look out for himself in a tight situation.'

Thorstein said, 'Will you be making such an offer to others, with whom Bolli's sons have a score to settle?'

Thorgils answered: 'It's the same choice Lambi will have to make.'

Thorstein said he thought it better if he were not the only one involved.

After that Thorgils sent word to Lambi to meet him, and invited Thorstein to be present at their conversation.

He said, 'I intend to speak to you, Lambi, about the same matter which I have already raised with Thorstein. What honour are you ready to do Bolli's sons for the grievance they have against you? I have been told truthfully enough that you wounded Bolli, and, in addition, you share a major portion of the guilt for having strongly urged that he be killed. You were admittedly among those with the most cause for offence, next to the Olafssons.'

Lambi asked what would be demanded of him. Thorgils answered that he would be offered the same choice as Thorstein, to accompany the brothers on an attack or face punishment.

Lambi replied, 'This is a poor and ignoble way of buying one's peace. I'm not willing to make this journey.'

Thorstein then said, 'It's not so simple a question, Lambi, that you should refuse so quickly. Important and powerful men are involved, who feel they have received less than their due for a long time. I am told that Bolli's sons are promising young men, bursting with pride and eagerness, and with cause enough to seek revenge. We can only expect to have to make them some redress after such a deed. People will place most of the censure on me, in any case, because of my connections to Helgi. And like most others I am ready to do almost anything to save my own skin. Each pressing problem that arises demands its own solution.'

Lambi spoke: 'It's clear which way you're leaning, Thorstein. I suppose it's just as well to let you decide, if you're so determined about it; we're old partners in troublemaking. But I want to make it a condition, if I agree to this, that my kinsmen, the Olafssons, will be left alone and in peace, if revenge against Helgi is successful.'

Thorgils agreed to this on behalf of the brothers.

Thus it was decided that Thorstein and Lambi would accompany Thorgils in the attack. They agreed to meet early in the day at Tunga in Hordadal three days later. After this they parted and Thorgils returned to his farm at Tunga that evening. The appointed time for the men intending to make the journey to meet Thorgils came. Before sunrise on the third morning Thorstein and Lambi arrived at Tunga. Thorgils gave them a warm welcome.

62 | Thorgils now made ready to set out and the party of ten rode off up Hordadal, with Thorgils Holluson leading the group. Others making the journey included Bolli's sons, Thorleik and Bolli. The fourth man was their half-brother Thord the Cat, Thorstein the Black was the fifth, Lambi the sixth, Halldor and Ornolf the seventh and eighth, Svein and Hunbogi, both sons of Alf from Dalir, were the ninth and tenth. All of them looked like fighters to be reckoned with. They set out on their way, up the Sopandaskard pass and over Langavatnsdal, then cut straight across the Borgarfjord district. They crossed the river Nordura at Eyjarvad ford, and the Hvita river at the Bakkavad ford, just above Baer. They rode through Reykjadal and over the ridge to Skorradal where they followed the woods to the vicinity of the farm at Vatnshorn. There they dismounted; it was late in the evening.

The farmhouse at Vatnshorn stands a short distance from the water's edge on the south side of the river.

Thorgils told his companions they would spend the night there. 'I intend to go up to the farm and look around, and try to learn whether Helgi is at home. I am told that he usually keeps few servants, but is always very much on his guard and sleeps in a sturdily built bed closet.'

His companions said Thorgils should decide their course.

Thorgils then had a change of clothes, removing his black cloak and pulling on a hooded cowl of grey homespun. He went up to the farm and when he had almost reached the hayfield wall he saw a man approaching.

When they met, Thorgils asked, 'You may think my question an ignorant one, comrade, but what district is this I'm in, and what is the name of that farm or the farmer who lives there?'

The man replied, 'You must be very foolish and ignorant indeed, if you haven't heard of Helgi Hardbeinsson, such a great warrior and important man as he is.'

Thorgils then asked what sort of welcome Helgi gave strangers who knocked at his door, especially those in much need of assistance.

The man replied, 'I can in truth give you a good answer there, as Helgi is the most generous of men, both in taking men in as in other dealings.'

'Would he be at home now?' asked Thorgils. 'I was hoping to ask him to take me in.'

The other man asked what his problem was and Thorgils replied, 'I was made an outlaw this summer at the Althing. I wanted to seek the protection of someone who had enough power to offer it. In return I can offer him my service and support. Now, take me to the farm to meet Helgi.'

'I can easily enough,' he said, 'take you home, and you'll be allowed to stay the night. But you won't meet Helgi, because he's not at home.'

Thorgils then asked where he was.

The man answered, 'Helgi is at his shieling, in the place called Sarp.'

Thorgils asked where that was, and who were there with him. He replied that Helgi's son, Hardbein, was there and two other men Helgi had taken in who were also outlaws.

Thorgils asked him to show him the straightest route to the shieling, 'as I want to meet Helgi right away, wherever he can be found, and put my request to him'.

The servant then showed him the way and they parted after that.

Thorgils returned to the wood to his companions and told them what he had learned of Helgi's circumstances. 'We'll stay here overnight and wait until morning to make our way to the shieling.'

They did as he proposed. In the morning Thorgils and his men rode on up through the wood until they were only a short way from the shieling. Thorgils then told them to dismount and eat their breakfast, which they did, stopping there awhile.

63 | Now to news of the shieling, where Helgi and those men previously mentioned were staying. In the morning Helgi spoke to his shepherd, telling him to look around in the woods near the shieling and see if there were any men about or any-

thing else worthy of reporting. 'My dreams last night were troubled.'

The boy did as Helgi said. He disappeared awhile and when he returned Helgi asked him what he had seen.

He answered: 'I have seen something which I think is news-worthy enough.'

Helgi asked what this was. He said he had seen no small number of men, 'and they look like men from another district to me'.

Helgi said, 'Where were they when you saw them, and what were they doing? Did you notice their appearance, or how they were dressed?'

He answered, 'I was not so stricken with fear that I didn't observe things like that, because I knew you would ask about them.'

He added that they were only a short distance away from the shieling and were eating breakfast. Helgi asked whether they sat in a circle or in a row. The boy replied that they sat in a circle on their saddles.

Helgi said, 'Tell me what they looked like. I want to see if I can guess from their descriptions what men these are.'

The boy said, 'One of the men sat on a saddle of coloured leather and wore a black cloak. He was a large man of manly build, balding at the temples and with very prominent teeth.'

Helgi said, 'I recognize that man clearly from your words; you have seen Thorgils Holluson from Hordadal. What can that fighter want with us?'

The boy spoke: 'Next to him sat a man in a gilded saddle; he was wearing a tunic of red scarlet and a gold ring on his hand. About his head was fastened a band of gold-embroidered cloth. This man had fair hair, falling in waves down to his shoulders. He was also fair-complexioned, with a bent nose, somewhat turned up at the end, handsome eyes, blue and piercing and restless, a wide forehead and full cheeks. His hair hung down in the front and was clipped at the eyebrows, and he was well built at the shoulders and broad across the chest. His hands were well formed, his arms strong, and his entire bearing refined. I must say in conclusion that no other man have I seen so valiant-looking in all respects. He was also a youthful man, with hardly a hair on his face yet. He seemed to me as if he were burdened with sorrow.'

Helgi then answered, 'You've observed this man carefully and he appears to be a man of great worth. I doubt that I have ever seen him, but I imagine it will be Bolli Bollason, because I am told he is a very promising young man.'

The boy then said, 'Another man sat on an enamelled saddle, wearing a yellow-green tunic and a large ring on his hand. He was a most handsome youngster, with brown hair which suited him well and everything about him was very refined.'

Helgi answered, 'I think I know who this man you have described is. This will be Thorleik Bollason. You're a clever lad, with a keen eye.'

The boy said, 'Next to him sat a young man in a black tunic and black breeches girded at the waist. He had a straight face and pleasing features, with light hair, slender and refined.'

Helgi answered, 'I recognize this man and have likely seen him before; he will have been fairly young in age. This is Thord Thordarson, Snorri the Godi's foster-son. A well-mannered group they have here, these men of the West. Any more?'

The boy then said, 'Next was a man in a Scottish saddle, with a greying beard and bushy brows. His hair was black and curly, and he was not very good-looking, although he had the look of a fighter all right. Over his shoulders he wore a grey gathered cape.'

Helgi said, 'I can see clearly who this man is. This is Lambi Thorbjarnarson from Laxardal. I don't know what he is doing accompanying the two brothers.'

The boy said, 'Next was a man sitting on a stand-up saddle with a black outer garment and a silver ring on his hand. A farmer by the look of him, he was no longer young, with dark brown and very curly hair and a scar on his face.'

'Your tale is taking a turn for the worse,' said Helgi. 'This man you have seen must be my brother-in-law Thorstein the Black, and I find it very surprising that he should have come along on such a journey. I wouldn't pay him a visit like this. But were there any more of them?'

The boy answered, 'Next there were two men of similar appearance and about middle age. They were both of them powerful men, with red hair and freckled faces, but handsome all the same.'

Helgi said, 'I know well who these men are. These are the Armodssons, Halldor and Ornolf, Thorgils's foster-brothers. You have given a thorough report – are these all of the men you saw?'

The boy answered, 'There's little more left to tell. The next man looked away from the group. He wore a plated coat of mail and a steel helmet with a brim as wide as the width of your hand. He held a gleaming axe over his shoulder, the blade of which was an ell in length. This man was dark, with black eyes and the appearance of a Viking.'

Helgi answered: 'This man I recognize clearly from your report. It was Hunbogi the Strong you saw, the son of Alf from Dalir. I can't quite see their intentions but they have certainly a choice selection of men for their journey.'

The boy spoke: 'Yet another man sat next to this strong-looking one; he had dark brown hair, a round and ruddy face and heavy brows, just over medium height.'

Helgi spoke: 'You need not say more; it will have been Svein, the son of Alf from Dalir and brother of Hunbogi. We had better be prepared for these men, as it's my guess that they will intend to pay me a visit before they leave the district; some of them making the journey would have thought it more fitting had our paths crossed earlier. Those women who are here in the shieling must throw on some men's clothes, take the horses close to the shieling and ride as fast as they can to the main house. Those men waiting nearby may not be able to tell whether it is men or women who go riding off. We need only gain a little time to seek more help, and then we'll see whose position is the better.'

All four women rode off together.

Thorgils suspected that their presence may have been reported and told his men to mount their horses and ride up to the shieling at once, which they did. But before they could mount, a man rode up to them in plain view. He was short in stature and brisk in his movements. His eyes darted about in a strange manner, and his horse was a strong one. This man greeted Thorgils like an old acquaintance. Thorgils asked him his name and who his kinsmen were, and where he had come from.

The man said his name was Hrapp and his mother's family hailed from Breidafjord, 'where I have been raised. I am named for Killer-Hrapp, and the name fits, for I am no man of peace, although I am small in size. My father's people are from the south of Iceland, and I have spent the last few winters there. It's a lucky chance I happened upon you here, Thorgils, as I was going to seek you out, even if I'd had to go to more trouble to do so. I'm in some difficulty; I've quarrelled with my master, as his treatment of me left much to be desired. As my name indicates, I'm not one to put up with such insults, so I tried to kill him, although with little or no success, I think. I didn't wait to find out, as I felt I was better off astride this horse I took from the farmer.' Hrapp spoke at length, but asked few questions. He soon became aware of their intention to attack Helgi, however, which he supported eagerly, saying no one should look for him in the back ranks of the attackers.

64 | After mounting their horses, Thorgils and his men set out at good speed and soon left the wood behind. They saw four riders leave the shieling, urging their horses on quickly.

Some of Thorgils's companions said they should give chase at once, but Thorleik Bollason replied, 'Let's go up to the shieling first and see what men are there. I think these riders are hardly Helgi and his companions – they look to me only to be women.'

More of the men opposed him than agreed, but Thorgils said that they should follow Thorleik's advice, for he knew him to be the most keen-sighted of men. They then approached the shieling.

Hrapp charged onward ahead of them, brandishing a puny spear he held in his hand, lunging forward with it and saying it was high time to show what they could do. Before Helgi and his men knew what was happening, Thorgils and his party attacked the shieling. Helgi and his men shut the door and took up their weapons. Hrapp ran up to the shieling straight away and asked whether Reynard was at home.

Helgi answered, 'You will find the fox here inside fierce enough, since he dares to bite so near his lair.'

As he said this, Helgi thrust his spear from the shieling window right through Hrapp, who fell to earth dead.

Thorgils told his men to approach with caution and protect themselves from injury. 'We should have more than enough strength to take the shieling and Helgi there inside it, as I think there are few men with him.'

The shieling was built with a single roof beam, which reached from one gable to the other and protruded at the ends, with a thatch of turf only a year old which had not yet fully taken root. Thorgils told several men to take each end of the roof beam and put enough pressure on it to break it or loosen the rafters from it. Others were to watch the doors, in case they should attempt to come out. Helgi and his companions in the shieling were five in number, including his son Hardbein, who was twelve years old, his shepherd and two other men, named Thorgils and Eyjolf, who were outlaws and had sought his protection that summer. Thorstein the Black stood at the door of the shieling along with Svein, the son of Alf from Dalir, while their companions set to work in two groups tearing the roof off the shieling. Hunbogi the Strong took hold of one end of the roof beam along with the Armodssons; Thorgils and Lambi and Gudrun's sons took the other. When they lifted the beam upwards sharply it split apart in the middle. At that moment Hardbein thrust his halberd out through a gap where the door had been broken. The point struck Thorstein's steel helmet and pierced his forehead, causing a bad wound. At this Thorstein said, as was true enough, that there must be men inside.

Helgi then charged out through the door so forcefully that those men standing next to it fell back. Thorgils was standing close by and struck at him with his sword, landing a blow on his shoulder that left a large wound.

Helgi turned towards him with a wood-axe in his hand, saying, 'This old fellow still dares to face others.'

He threw the axe at Thorgils, striking him on the foot and

giving him a severe wound. When Bolli saw this he charged at Helgi with Leg-biter in his hand and thrust it through Helgi, dealing him his death wound. At once Helgi's companions and Hardbein rushed out of the shieling. Thorleik Bollason turned to face Eyjolf, who was a strong man. Thorleik struck him a blow with his sword on the thigh just above the knee which cut off his leg, and he fell to the ground dead. Hunbogi the Strong charged at Thorgils and swung his axe at him, striking him on the spine and splitting him in two in the middle. Thord the Cat was standing nearby when Hardbein ran out of the shieling and wanted to charge at him.

When he saw this, Bolli ran up and told him not to harm Hardbein, saying, 'No base deeds are to be done here; Hardbein is to be spared.'

Helgi had another son called Skorri. He was being brought up on the farm called England in southern Reykjadal.

65 | After these events Thorgils and his men rode over the ridge into Reykjadal to declare responsibility for the killings. They then took the same route back as they had come, not slowing their pace until they had come to Hordadal. There they related what had happened on their journey. The foray became renowned and the slaying of a fighter the likes of Helgi was thought a deed of great note. Thorgils thanked the men warmly for making the journey, as did both of Bolli's sons. The men who had accompanied Thorgils then went their separate ways. Lambi rode northward to Laxardal, stopping on his way at Hjardarholt, where he told his kinsmen the details of the events which had taken place in Skorradal. They were greatly upset by his part in it and criticized him angrily. His actions, they maintained, showed him to be more the descendant of Thorbjorn the Pock-marked than Myrkjartan, king of the Irish. Lambi grew very angry at their words and said their scolding him showed their own lack of manners, 'as I have managed to have all of you spared from certain death'. They exchanged few more words, with both sides even more displeased than before, and Lambi rode home to his farm.

Thorgils Holluson then rode to Helgafell, accompanied by Gudrun's sons and his foster-brothers, Halldor and Ornolf. When they arrived late in the evening everyone had gone to his bed. Gudrun got up at once and told the servants to get up and wait upon them. She went into the main room to greet Thorgils and all his party and hear their news. Thorgils responded to Gudrun's greeting after removing his cloak and weapons and sat leaning against the posts of the wall. He was dressed in a reddish brown tunic with a wide belt of silver. Gudrun sat down on the bench beside him and Thorgils spoke this verse:

3. Home to Helgi we rode,
   gorged ravens on blood;
   reddened shining shields' oak,   *shields' oak*: weapons
   when we went with Thorleik.
   There we felled three
   skilful helmet-trees   *helmet-trees*: warriors, men
   of rare renown.
   Bolli's vengeance is done.

Gudrun asked more closely about the events occurring on their journey. Thorgils answered whatever she asked. Gudrun said their journey had turned out splendidly and thanked them all. After that they were waited upon and when they had had their fill they were shown to their beds, where they slept until the night was past.

The following day Thorgils spoke to Gudrun alone, saying, 'The situation is, as you know, Gudrun, that I have carried out this foray as you asked me to. I feel I have done my part completely and I hope it has been worth my while. You will remember what you have promised me in return, and I feel that I am now entitled to collect my bargain.'

Gudrun then spoke: 'Hardly has the time which has passed since we spoke of this been so long as to make me forget it. I have no intention of doing otherwise than fulfilling the bargain we agreed upon completely. Do you remember what it was that we agreed upon?'

Thorgils said she must remember that.

Gudrun answered, 'I think I promised you I would marry no other man in the country except you; do you have any objection to make to that?'

Thorgils said she remembered correctly.

'It is well that we both are agreed on this. I will not conceal from you any longer that I do not intend you to be so fortunate as to have me for your wife. I keep every word of my promise to you though I marry Thorkel Eyjolfsson, for he is at present not in this country.'

Thorgils then spoke, becoming very flushed as he did so. 'Clearly do I see where the current came from that sent this wave; they have generally been cold, the counsels that Snorri the Godi has sent my way.'

Thorgils broke off the conversation, sprang to his feet in fury, went to his companions and told them he wished to leave at once. Thorleik was displeased at the way Thorgils had been offended, but Bolli supported his mother's wishes. Gudrun offered to give Thorgils handsome gifts to soften his anger, but Thorleik said that this would be to no avail.

'Thorgils is too proud a man to bow down for a few trinkets.'

Gudrun said he would then have to return home and console himself. On this note Thorgils made his departure from Helgafell along with his foster-brothers. He returned home to Tunga highly displeased with his lot.

66 | Osvif was taken ill and died that winter. His passing was thought a great loss, for he had been among the wisest of men. Osvif was buried at Helgafell, where Gudrun had had a church built.

Gest Oddleifsson became ill that same winter and as his condition worsened he summoned his son Thord the Short and spoke to him, saying, 'If my suspicions are correct, this illness will make an end of our life together. I wish to have my body taken to Helgafell, as it will be the most prominent seat in the district. I have also often seen brightness there.'[49]

Gest died soon afterwards.

The winter had been a cold one, and there was a thick layer

of ice along the shore and far out into the bay of Breidafjord, preventing ships from setting out from the Bardastrond shore. On the second night Gest's body had lain at Hagi, a storm blew up with winds so strong that the ice was driven from the shore. The following day the weather was mild and calm. Thord laid Gest's body in a boat and that day they headed south across the bay of Breidafjord, reaching Helgafell in the evening. Thord was well received and stayed the night there. Gest's body was buried the following morning in the same grave as Osvif. The prediction made by Gest now came true, as the distance between the two was now much shorter than when one lived at Bardastrond and the other in Saelingsdal. Thord the Short returned home after concluding his errand. The following night a wild storm raged, driving all the ice back to the shore. It remained thus for most of the winter, preventing all journeys by boat. That the chance to transport Gest's body had arisen was thought to be a great omen, as all travelling was impossible both before and afterwards.

67 | A man named Thorarin lived in Langadal. He held a godord, but was a man of no influence. His son Audgisl was a man quick to act. Thorgils Holluson had dispossessed them of their godord and they considered this a grievous insult. Audgisl approached Snorri, told him of the ill-treatment which they had suffered and asked for his support.

Snorri replied positively, but made light of it all saying, 'So Halla's layabout is getting ambitious and pushing people around, is he? When is Thorgils going to run into someone who won't let him have his way in everything? It's true enough that he's a tough, strong fellow but other men of the sort have been done away with before now.'

When Audgisl departed, Snorri made him a present of an inlaid axe.[50]

That spring Thorgils Holluson and Thorstein the Black journeyed south to Borgarfjord and offered Helgi's sons and kinsmen compensation for his slaying. A settlement was reached in the matter which gave them honourable recompense. Thorstein

paid two-thirds of the compensation for the killing, and
Thorgils was to pay one-third, with payment to be made at the
Althing. Thorgils rode to the Althing that summer, and as he
and his party reached the lava field at Thingvellir they saw a
woman coming towards them of very great size. Thorgils rode
towards her, but she turned aside, speaking this verse:

4.   Let them take pains,
     these men of note,
     to protect themselves
     from Snorri's plots;
     none will escape,
     so wily is Snorri.

She then proceeded on her way.

Thorgils said, 'Seldom did you, when the future looked bright
for me, leave the site of the Althing as I arrived.'

Thorgils then rode on to the Althing and to the site of his
booth, and the first days of the session passed without incident
until a portent occurred one day during the Althing. Clothing
had been hung out to dry. A black, hooded cloak belonging to
Thorgils had been spread out on the wall of the booth. People
heard the cloak speak this verse:

5.   Wet on the wall it hangs
     yet knows of wiles, this hood;
     it will not dry again,
     I do not hide that it knows of two.

This was thought a great wonder. The following day Thorgils
crossed over to the west side of the river where he was to
pay his compensation to Helgi's sons. Accompanied by his
foster-brother Halldor and several other men, he sat down on
the rock above the booth sites. Helgi's sons came to meet
them. Thorgils had begun counting out the silver when Audgisl
Thorarinsson passed by, and, just as Thorgils said ten, Audgisl
swung at him; everyone thought they could hear his head say
eleven as it flew off his body.

Audgisl ran off immediately to the booth of the men of Vatnsfjord, but Halldor ran after him and dealt him his death blow in the entrance way. News of these events, and that Thorgils Holluson had been slain, soon came to Snorri the Godi's booth.

Snorri said, 'You can't have understood; Thorgils will have done the slaying.'

The man replied, 'Still, it was his head that flew off his body.'

'Then perhaps the news is true,' said Snorri.

A settlement was reached regarding the slaying, as is related in the saga of Thorgils Holluson.[51]

68 | The same summer that Thorgils Holluson was slain a ship owned by Thorkel Eyjolfsson arrived in Bjarnarhofn. By that time he was a man of such wealth that he owned two knorrs making voyages to Iceland. The other sailed into Hrutafjord and landed at Bordeyri. Both of them were laden with timber. When Snorri learned of Thorkel's arrival he rode to his ship at once. Thorkel welcomed him warmly. He also had a good supply of drink aboard his ship and it was served up generously. They had much to talk of. Snorri asked for news from Norway and Thorkel spoke both at length and in detail.

In return, Snorri told him of the events which had occurred while he had been abroad. 'Now seems to me a suitable time,' Snorri said, 'to do as I advised you before you sailed abroad: make an end to your sailing, settle down and take yourself the wife that we spoke of then.'

Thorkel answered, 'I understand what you're about, and I'm of the same mind now as I was when we spoke then. Far be it from me to pass up the chance of such a worthy match if it can be arranged.'

Snorri spoke: 'I am more than ready and willing to support this proposal on your behalf. Both of the difficult obstacles which you felt prevented your marrying Gudrun have now been removed. Bolli has been avenged and Thorgils done away with.'

Thorkel spoke: 'Your counsels run deep, Snorri, and I'll certainly follow this course.'

Snorri stayed on board the ship for several nights, after which they took a ten-oared boat floating alongside the merchant vessel, made their preparations and set out for Helgafell, a party of twenty-five in number.

Gudrun received Snorri especially warmly and they were waited on amply.

When they had spent the night there, Snorri asked to speak privately with Gudrun and said, 'The situation is this. I made this journey on behalf of my friend Thorkel Eyjolfsson. He has come here, as you can see, and for the purpose of asking for your hand in marriage. Thorkel is a worthy man; you know all about his family and his deeds, and he has no lack of wealth. To my mind he's the man most likely to have the makings of a leader in him here, if he has a mind to become one. Thorkel is held in high esteem out here in Iceland, but in much higher repute when he is in Norway among noblemen.'

Gudrun then answered, 'My sons, Thorleik and Bolli, will have the deciding say in this matter, but you are the third man to whom I look most for counsel, Snorri, when I feel the outcome to be important, as for many years now you have proved a good adviser to me.'

Snorri said he thought it very clear that Thorkel should not be rejected. He then had Gudrun's sons summoned and raised the question with them, explaining how much a match with Thorkel would strengthen their position, both because of his money and guidance, putting his case very convincingly.

Bolli answered, 'My mother will know what is best and I agree to her wishes, but we certainly feel the fact that you support this proposal, Snorri, lends it considerable weight, for you have done much to our great benefit.'

Gudrun then spoke: 'We should make every effort to follow Snorri's guidance in this matter, because your counsel has been good counsel to us.'

Snorri's every word was an encouragement, and the match between Thorkel and Gudrun was thus decided.

Snorri offered to hold the wedding feast, which suited Thorkel well – 'I have no lack of supplies to provide whatever you please.'

Gudrun then spoke: 'It is my wish that this feast be held here at Helgafell. I am not concerned about the cost involved, and I will ask neither Thorkel nor anyone else to take a hand in it.'

'You have shown more than once, Gudrun,' Snorri said, 'that you are the most determined of women.'

It was decided that the wedding should be held at Helgafell, when seven weeks remained of summer. Both Snorri and Thorkel then departed, Snorri to return home and Thorkel to his ship. He divided his time that summer between his ship and visiting Snorri at Tunga.

The time of the feast approached. Gudrun had made extensive preparations and laid in great stores of provisions. Snorri the Godi accompanied Thorkel to the wedding feast and their party numbered almost sixty people. It was a select group, as almost all of them wore fine, coloured clothing. Gudrun had invited well over a hundred guests herself. The brothers Bolli and Thorleik went out to receive Snorri and his party, accompanied by their mother's guests. Snorri and his followers were given a good welcome; they were relieved of their horses and their outer garments and led into the main room. Thorkel and Snorri were given the positions of highest honour on one upper bench, while Gudrun's guests occupied the opposite one.

69 | That autumn Gunnar, who was called Thidrandabani[52] (Slayer of Thidrandi), had been sent to Gudrun for shelter and protection; she had accepted him into her household and concealed his true name. Gunnar had been outlawed for slaying Thidrandi Geitisson of Krossavik, as is related in the saga of the People of Njardvik. He took great pains to conceal himself, as there were many powerful men who sought recourse in the case. The first evening of the feast, when people went to wash, a large man stood by the water, broad-shouldered and deep-chested, wearing a hat on his head. When Thorkel asked who he was, he answered with the first thing that came into his head.

Thorkel answered, 'You won't be telling the truth. You are more like the descriptions of Gunnar Thidrandabani, and if

you are as much of a warrior as people say, you can't wish to
conceal your name.'

Gunnar answered, 'Since you press the point so forcefully, I
suppose I need not conceal it from you. You have spotted your
man fairly enough – what do you have in mind for me?'

Thorkel said he intended to make that known soon enough,
and ordered his men to seize him.

Gudrun sat in the centre of the cross-bench with the other
women, all with linen veils on their heads. When she realized
what was happening she stood up from the bridal bench and
urged her followers to assist Gunnar. She also told them to
spare no one who brought on violence. Gudrun had a much
larger following and things appeared to be headed in a direction
other than that intended.

Snorri interceded between them and told them to calm the
storm – 'You, Thorkel, should obviously not pursue this matter
so forcefully. You must see just how determined a woman
Gudrun is, as she dares to overrule us both.'

Thorkel protested, saying that he had promised his namesake, Thorkel Geitisson, 'who is a great friend of mine', to kill
Gunnar if he made his way to the west of Iceland.

Snorri said, 'You're under a greater obligation to do my
bidding, and it's absolutely necessary for your own sake – you'll
never get another woman the likes of Gudrun for your wife,
though you search far and wide.'

At Snorri's urging, and since he could see for himself that
Snorri spoke the truth, Thorkel calmed down, while Gunnar
was escorted away that evening. The feast proceeded well, and
was highly impressive. At its conclusion people prepared to
depart. Thorkel had rich gifts to give Snorri at parting, and for
all the other worthy guests. Snorri invited Bolli Bollason to
come and stay with him whenever and for as long as he wished.
Bolli accepted his offer and rode back to Tunga with him.

Thorkel settled in at Helgafell and took over the running of
the farm. It soon became obvious that he was no less adept at
this than at merchant voyages. He had the hall torn down that
autumn, and the rafters were raised over a new one, large and
impressive, by the next winter. Gudrun and Thorkel grew to

love one another very deeply. The winter passed and the following spring Gudrun asked him what he wished to do about
Gunnar.

Thorkel said she should decide that. 'You have taken such
strong measures that you won't be satisfied unless he is given
decent treatment at parting.'

Gudrun said that he had drawn the right conclusion on that
point. 'I want you,' she said, 'to give him your ship and with it
anything that he cannot do without.'

Thorkel answered with a smile, 'You're not one to think on
a small scale, Gudrun. A petty husband would never suit you;
nor would he be a match for a spirit like yours. It will be as
you wish.'

When the arrangements were made, Gunnar accepted the gift
with great thanks: 'Never will my reach extend far enough to
repay you all the honour that the two of you have shown me.'

Gunnar then sailed abroad, making land in Norway whence
he proceeded to his own estate. He was very wealthy, and a
truly worthy and trusty man.

70 | Thorkel Eyjolfsson became a prominent chieftain, and did
   | much to make himself popular and respected. His was the
leading voice in the district and he often took part in lawsuits.
No mention is made of his legal disputes here, however. Next
to Snorri, Thorkel was the most powerful man in Breidafjord,
until his own death. Thorkel looked after his farm well; he
rebuilt all the buildings at Helgafell, making them large and
sturdy. He also marked out the foundations for a church and
declared his intention to go abroad to obtain the timber for it.
Thorkel and Gudrun had a son called Gellir. From a young age
he was extremely promising. Bolli Bollason divided his time
between Tunga and Helgafell, and Snorri treated him exceedingly well. His brother Thorleik lived at Helgafell. The two
brothers were large and capable men, with Bolli the more
outstanding of the two. Thorkel treated his stepchildren well.

Of all her children, it was Bolli whom Gudrun loved the
most. He was now sixteen years of age and Thorleik twenty.

Thorleik then spoke to his stepfather Thorkel and his mother of his wish to travel abroad. 'I am bored by sitting at home like the women do. I want to ask you to provide me with the means to journey abroad.'

Thorkel answered, 'To my mind, I've seldom opposed the wishes of you brothers since our family bonds were tied. And I can understand only too well your longing to go abroad and learn foreign ways, since I expect you will be considered a stalwart fellow among capable men everywhere.'

Thorleik said he did not wish to take a great amount of wealth, 'because it's far from certain that I would be able to handle it properly; I'm young and inexperienced in many ways.'

Thorkel told him to take what he wished.

Thorkel then purchased a share in a ship, which had been beached at Dagverdarnes, for Thorleik. He accompanied Thorleik to his ship and made sure he was well equipped in every respect. Thorleik sailed abroad that summer and his ship made land in Norway. At that time King Olaf the Saint ruled in Norway. Thorleik made his way directly to King Olaf. The king received him well and recognized his lineage. He invited him to join him and Thorleik accepted. He spent the winter with the king and became his follower. The king thought highly of him. Thorleik was considered the most courageous of men and spent a number of years with the king.

The story now returns to Bolli Bollason. In the spring when he turned eighteen he told Thorkel, his stepfather, and his mother that he wished to be given his share of his father's inheritance. Gudrun asked what he was planning that made him ask them to make over the money.

Bolli answered, 'I want to have a request of marriage made on my behalf, and I want you, Thorkel,' he said, 'as my stepfather to do the asking, so that it will be successful.'

Thorkel asked what woman he intended to seek and Bolli answered, 'The woman is named Thordis, and she is the daughter of Snorri the Godi. She is the woman I have my mind set on marrying, and I won't be marrying in the near future if I don't make this match. It means a great deal to me that this should succeed.'

THE SAGA OF THE PEOPLE OF LAXARDAL

Thorkel answered, 'You're entitled to my support in this, stepson, if you think it will make a difference. I expect Snorri will be more than willing to give his consent, as he will see well enough that in your case he'll be making a fine match.'

Gudrun spoke: 'I can say at once, Thorkel, that I wish nothing to be spared in order that Bolli obtain the wife he wishes. Both because he is dearest to me and because he has always been the one among my children most loyal in doing as I wished.'

Thorkel said he intended to see to it that Bolli received proper treatment at parting, 'and he deserves it for more than one reason, especially since I expect he will prove the best of men'.

Shortly after that Thorkel and Bolli, together with a large number of followers, set out on a journey to Tunga. Snorri welcomed them well and warmly, and showed them the greatest hospitality. Thordis Snorradottir lived at home with her father. She was both fine-looking and a woman to be taken seriously. When they had been at Tunga several nights, Thorkel brought up the question of a family alliance with Snorri on Bolli's behalf by proposing his marriage to Snorri's daughter, Thordis.

Snorri answered, 'You have made a worthwhile proposal, as I would have expected of you. I want to answer it well, because I think Bolli is the most promising of men, and any woman married to him is well married, to my mind. But it will depend mainly on how Thordis feels about it, because she will only be betrothed to a man of her liking.'

When the question was put to Thordis she replied that she would abide by her father's guidance. She would rather, she said, marry Bolli, a local man, than a stranger from far away. When Snorri realized that she was not opposed to a marriage with Bolli, he then agreed to the proposal and the two were betrothed. Snorri was to hold the wedding feast, which was to be at midsummer. This done, Bolli and Thorkel rode home to Helgafell where Bolli remained until the date of the wedding arrived.

Bolli and Thorkel then made their preparations for the journey, along with the others who were to attend. It was both a large and imposing group who rode to Tunga where they were given a fine welcome. There was a great number of guests and the wedding feast was highly impressive. After the conclusion of the feasting, as people were preparing to depart, Snorri gave both Thorkel and Gudrun worthy gifts, and did the same for his other friends and kinsmen. Everyone who had attended the feast then returned home. Bolli stayed at Tunga, and he and Thordis soon came to love one another dearly. Snorri was also determined to do well by Bolli and treated him in all respects better than he treated his own children. Bolli responded well to his kindness and spent the next year in comfort at Tunga.

The following summer an ocean-going vessel sailed into the Hvita river. Thorleik Bollason owned a half-share in the ship and Norwegians the other half. When Bolli learned of the arrival of his brother, he rode immediately south to Borgarfjord to the ship. The brothers were very glad to see each other, and Bolli spent several nights there. They then rode west to Helgafell. Both Thorkel and Gudrun gave them the warmest of welcomes, and invited Thorleik to spend the winter with them, which he accepted. Thorleik stayed at Helgafell awhile, then returned south to the Hvita river to have his ship beached and the goods transported westward. Thorleik had got on well in the world, earning both wealth and respect, as he had become the follower of that most noble of men, King Olaf. He spent that winter at Helgafell and Bolli at Tunga.

71 | That winter the brothers met regularly, spending their time talking privately to one another and showing little interest in games or other entertainment. Once, when Thorleik visited Tunga, the two brothers spent days talking. Snorri felt that they were certain to be planning some major venture, and eventually he approached them while they were talking. They greeted him well and immediately broke off their conversation.

He responded well to their greetings and said, 'What are you planning that makes you forget about eating and sleeping meanwhile?'

Bolli answered, 'You would hardly call it planning, for there is little point in what we are discussing.'

Snorri realized that they wished to conceal from him what-

ever it was that occupied their thoughts, but suspected that
what they spoke most about would cause major problems if it
materialized.

Snorri spoke to them, saying, 'I suspect all the same that you
wouldn't spend so much time speaking of nonsense or jesting,
and I can understand that well enough. But I ask you now to
tell me about it without concealing anything from me; the three
of us will be no less capable of making plans, as I will not
oppose anything that will be to your greater honour.'

Thorleik was pleased by Snorri's response. He said briefly
that the brothers had been planning to attack the Olafssons,
and mete them out a harsh punishment. He said they felt that
in their present position they lacked nothing to enable them
to even scores with the Olafssons, since Thorleik had become
the follower of King Olaf and Bolli the son-in-law of a godi of
Snorri's stature.

Snorri answered, 'Bolli's killing has been avenged fully
enough with the vengeance on Helgi Hardbeinsson. More
than enough hostility has already resulted without pursuing the
question further.'

Bolli then said, 'How does it happen, Snorri, that you aren't
as ready to offer your support as you professed to be just a
short while ago? Thorleik wouldn't have told you of the plan
if he had asked me about telling you first. And regarding your
contention that Bolli was avenged with the killing of Helgi,
everyone knows that compensation was paid for Helgi's killing,
whereas my father remains unredressed.'

When Snorri saw that he would not be able to change their
minds, he offered to seek a settlement with the Olafssons to
avoid any killing and the brothers agreed to this.

Snorri then rode with several men to Hjardarholt where
Halldor received him well and asked him to stay the night with
them.

Snorri said he would be returning that same evening, 'but
I have something I must discuss with you'.

The two of them then conferred and Snorri explained the
purpose of his visit, saying he had learned that Bolli and Thorleik were no longer content to have received no compensation

from the Olafssons for their father, 'but I wanted to seek a settlement and see if it weren't possible to bring the ill fortunes of your family kinsmen to an end'.

Halldor did not reject the possibility, and answered, 'I know well enough that Thorgils Holluson and the brothers intended to attack me or my brothers before you turned their vengeance aside, with the result that they decided to kill Helgi Hardbeinsson. You have for your part acted well in that instance, whatever your earlier involvement in the dealings between us kinsmen.'

Snorri spoke: 'To my mind it's very important to achieve my purpose in coming here, and to accomplish what I have in mind, to reconcile you and these kinsmen of yours properly, because I know the natures of these men you are dealing with; they will abide well and fully by any settlement which they conclude.'

Halldor answered, 'I will agree, if it is the wish of my brothers as well, to pay such compensation for the slaying of Bolli as is awarded by the men selected as arbitrators. But this must exclude all outlawry, together with my godord and farm property. This also applies to the farms where my brothers dwell; I wish them to be excluded from any award of compensation.'

Snorri said, 'This is an honourable and generous offer. The brothers will accept it if they pay any heed to my advice.'

Snorri then returned home and told the brothers the outcome of his journey, adding that he would offer them no further support if they failed to agree to this.

Bolli said that he should decide for them, 'and I want you to arbitrate on our behalf'.

Snorri then sent word to Halldor that a settlement had been arranged and asked him to choose someone to serve as his counterpart in deciding the terms. Halldor chose Steinthor Thorlaksson from Eyri to act on his behalf. The settlement was to be decided at Drangar on the Skogarstrond shore when four weeks of the summer had passed. Thorleik Bollason returned to Helgafell and the winter passed without event. When the time set for the meeting approached, Snorri accompanied the Bollasons to the site; they made a party of fifteen, the same number as Steinthor and his party. Snorri and Steinthor discussed the matter and reached agreement. They then decided on the compensation, but it is not reported here how high was the figure they set, only that it was paid as stipulated and the men honoured the settlement. Payment took place at the Thorsnes Assembly. Halldor gave Bolli a handsome sword and Steinthor Olafsson gave Thorleik a shield, both of which were fine weapons. Following this the assembly was dissolved, and both parties were felt to have risen in esteem as a result.

72 | Following their reconciliation with the Olafssons, and after a year had passed since Thorleik returned from abroad, Bolli declared that he intended to sail abroad.

Snorri tried to discourage him, saying, 'It seems to me you are risking a lot on the outcome. If you feel you want more responsibility than you now have, then I will provide you with a farm of your own and obtain a godord for you, and help you rise in importance in every way. I expect it will be easy enough, as most people are well inclined towards you.'

Bolli answered, 'For a long time now I have wanted to make a journey south; a man is considered ignorant if he has explored no more than the shores of Iceland.'

When Snorri saw that Bolli had his mind so set on this that there was no point trying to dissuade him, he offered Bolli as much wealth as he wished for the journey.

Bolli agreed to take a great deal of wealth, 'as I want charity from no man, either here or abroad'.

Bolli then rode south to Borgarfjord to the Hvita river, where he purchased a half-share in Thorleik's ship from the men who owned it. The two brothers then owned the ship together. Bolli then rode home again.

Bolli and Thordis had a daughter named Herdis, whom Gudrun offered to foster. She was one year old when she went to Helgafell. Thordis also stayed there much of the time and Gudrun treated her very well.

73 | The two brothers then proceeded to their ship. Bolli took a great deal of wealth aboard with him. They made the ship ready and after everything was prepared they set sail out to sea. It was some time before they got favourable winds, and their passage was a lengthy one. They made land in Norway in the autumn and made land in the north at Nidaros. King Olaf was in the east of the country, in Vik, with his followers, where he had collected provisions for the winter. When the brothers learned that the king would not be coming north to Nidaros that autumn, Thorleik said he wanted to head to the east of the country to seek out the king.

Bolli answered, 'I'm not excited at the prospect of tramping around from one town to another in the autumn; it seems like nothing but bondage and servitude. I want to spend the winter here in town. I'm told the king will be coming north in the spring, and if he doesn't I won't deter you from taking us to meet him then.'

They did as Bolli wished, unloading their ship and settling down in the town for the winter. It was soon apparent that Bolli was a man of ambition, who intended to be a leader among men. This he managed to do, not the least through his generosity. He was soon held in high esteem in Norway. That winter in Nidaros Bolli kept a company of men, and was recognized at once whenever he went drinking, as his men were better armed and dressed than other townspeople. He alone paid for the drinks of all his company when they went drinking. This was typical of his generosity and grand style. The brothers spent the winter in the town.

King Olaf spent that winter in Sarpsborg in the east of his kingdom, and according to news of him, the king was not expected to head northwards. Early in the spring the brothers made ready their ship and sailed eastward following the coast. Their journey went well and when they arrived in Sarpsborg they proceeded directly to meet King Olaf. He gave his follower Thorleik and his companions a good welcome, and then asked him who this impressive-looking man was who accompanied him.

Thorleik replied, 'This is my brother, who is named Bolli.'

'He certainly looks to be a most outstanding man,' said the king.

The king then offered to have both of the brothers to stay with him, and they accepted gratefully, remaining with him that spring. The king treated Thorleik as well as before, but held Bolli in much higher regard, as the king felt him to be among the most exceptional of men.

As the spring advanced the brothers discussed their travelling plans, and Thorleik asked Bolli whether he wished to sail for Iceland that summer, 'or do you wish to remain in Norway longer?'

Bolli answered: 'I intend to do neither, and to tell you the truth, when I left Iceland I had intended that people would not hear of me settling down next door. I want you, brother, to take over our ship.'

Thorleik was saddened at the prospect of their parting, 'but you will have your way in this as everything else, Bolli'.

When they told these same plans to the king, he answered, 'Do you not wish to dwell here with us any longer, Bolli? I would prefer you to stay here with me for a while, and I will offer you the same title that I have conferred upon your brother Thorleik.'

To this Bolli answered: 'More than willing enough am I, my lord, to enter your service, but I intend first to travel to the destination which I originally set out for and where I have long wished to go. Should I manage to return I will gladly accept this offer of yours.'

'You will decide your course yourself, Bolli, as you Icelanders usually intend to have your own way in most things. But I have to say that I regard you, Bolli, as the most remarkable man to have come from Iceland during my day.'

Once Bolli had received the king's leave, he made ready for his journey and boarded a cog heading south to Denmark. He took a great deal of wealth with him and was accompanied by several of his companions. He and King Olaf parted the best of friends, and the king gave Bolli worthy farewell gifts. Thorleik remained behind with King Olaf, while Bolli proceeded south to Denmark. He spent the winter there and was shown great honour by powerful men. He conducted himself there in a style no less luxurious than he had in Norway. After a year in Denmark, Bolli began his journey through foreign countries, not stopping until he reached Constantinople. After a short time there he entered the company of the Varangian guard, and we know no reports of northerners having entered the service of the Byzantine emperor before Bolli Bollason. He spent many years in Constantinople, where he was regarded as the most valiant of fighters in any perilous situation, where he was among the foremost of them. The Varangians thought highly of Bolli during his stay in Constantinople.

74 | The story now returns to Thorkel Eyjolfsson, who had become a leader of prominence in Iceland. Gellir, son of Thorkel and Gudrun, grew up at home and was from an early age a very manly and well-liked lad.

It is said that Thorkel once told Gudrun of a dream he had: 'I dreamt,' he said, 'that I had such a long beard that it spread over all of Breidafjord.'

Thorkel asked her to interpret the dream.

Gudrun asked, 'What do you think the dream means?'

'It seems to me obvious that it means my domain will extend over the whole of Breidafjord.'

'That may well be the case,' said Gudrun, 'but I am inclined to expect that it means that you will be dipping your beard into Breidafjord.'

That same summer Thorkel had his ship launched and made preparations to sail to Norway. His son Gellir was twelve years old at the time and sailed abroad with his father. Thorkel declared that he intended to obtain timber for his church and put out to sea as soon as everything was ready. He had light winds and the passage was anything but brief. They made land in the north of Norway. King Olaf was in Nidaros at the time, and Thorkel made his way directly to the king, taking his son Gellir along with him. They were well received and Thorkel was held in such high regard by the king during the winter that it was widely said that the gifts the king gave him were worth no less than five score marks of refined silver. At Christmas the king gave Gellir a wonderfully crafted cloak that was truly a treasure. That same winter King Olaf had a church built of wood in the town. It was large and very impressive, and care taken with its every aspect. The following spring the timber which the king had given Thorkel was loaded aboard ship. The timber was both of fine quality and in great quantity, for Thorkel spared no pains with its selection.

One morning when the king had risen early and was accompanied by only a few men, he saw a man up on the church which was then under construction. He was very surprised at this, for the morning had not yet advanced to the time when his carpenters were accustomed to rise. The king recognized the man: it was Thorkel Eyjolfsson, who was measuring all the largest beams, the cross-ties, joists and supports.

The king went over to him immediately and said, 'What are you up to, Thorkel? Do you plan to cut timber for your church in Iceland on this model?'

Thorkel answered, 'Right you are, my lord.'

Then King Olaf spoke: 'Chop two ells off the length of each beam and your church will still be the greatest in Iceland.'

Thorkel answered, 'Keep your timber then, if you fear you have given of it too generously, or regret making the offer, but I'll not chop so much as an ell's length off it. I lack neither the energy nor the means to obtain my timber elsewhere.'

The king then said, in a pacifying tone, 'You are a man of great worth, and of no small ambition. Of course it's absurd for a farmer's son to compete with us. But it is not true that I begrudge you the timber. If you should manage to build a church with it, it will never be so large as to contain your own conceit. But unless I am mistaken, people will have little use of this timber, and even less so will you be able to build any structure with it.'

With that their conversation came to an end. The king walked away and it was clear that he disliked Thorkel's disregard for his advice. The king let the matter drop, however, and he and Thorkel parted as the best of friends. Thorkel boarded his ship and sailed out to sea. They had favourable winds and a brief passage.

Thorkel's ship made land in Hrutafjord, and he rode promptly to Helgafell. Everyone was very glad to see him and he gained a great deal of honour from his journey. He had his ship beached and secured for the winter and the timber set in secure storage, as he would be too busy that autumn to have it transported westward. Thorkel spent that winter at home on his farm. He held a Christmas feast at Helgafell attended by a great number of people. Everything he did that winter was done extravagantly, with no opposition from Gudrun, who said that wealth was well spent if people gained esteem as the result, and anything Gudrun needed in order to have things in grand style was made available. That winter Thorkel gave as gifts to his friends many valuable objects he had brought with him from abroad.

75 | After Christmas Thorkel prepared to set out for the journey north to Hrutafjord to transport his timber home. He rode first up into the Dalir district, then to his kinsman Thorstein at Ljarskogar to borrow both men and horses. He then went north to Hrutafjord where he stayed a while and planned his journey. He collected horses from the farms along the fjord, as he hoped to make only a single trip if this were possible. This was not accomplished quickly, and Thorkel was kept busy past the beginning of Lent before he could set out. He had the wood drawn southward by more than twenty horses to Ljaeyri, where he intended to load it aboard a ship for the rest of the journey to Helgafell. Thorstein owned a large ferry which Thorkel intended to use for his homeward journey.

Thorkel stayed at Ljarskogar during Lent, as he and his kinsman Thorstein were close friends.

Thorstein suggested to Thorkel that he make a journey with him to Hjardarholt – 'I want to ask Halldor to sell me land, as he has little livestock left after paying the Bollasons compensation for their father, and it's his land that I want to obtain the most.'

Thorkel said he would oblige him, and they set out with a party that numbered over twenty men.

When they arrived at Hjardarholt, Halldor received them well and kept up a lively conversation. Only a few members of the household were at home, as Halldor had sent many of them north to Steingrimsfjord, where a whale had been stranded, and he was entitled to a share. Beinir the Strong was at home, the only one still alive of those who had served Olaf, Halldor's father.

When he saw Thorstein and his men approaching, Halldor said to Beinir, 'I know well enough what brings those kinsmen here. They are going to ask me to sell them my land, and if they do so they will ask to speak to me privately. I expect they will sit down, one of them on each side of me, and if they show me any hostility, you will attack Thorstein the moment I turn on Thorkel. You have shown my family many years of loyalty. I have also sent men to seek help from neighbouring farms. I hope they will arrive at much the same moment as we make an end of the conversation.'

Later that day Thorstein suggested to Halldor that they speak privately, 'as we have something to discuss with you, Halldor'.

Halldor said that was fine with him and Thorstein told his companions that they need not follow them. Beinir went along with them, nevertheless, as he thought things were turning out much as Halldor had predicted. They walked a long way out into the hayfield. Halldor wore a cloak fastened with a long clasp, as was common at that time. He sat down in the field, with a kinsman on either side of him, sitting practically on his cloak. Beinir stood behind them with a large axe in his hand.

Thorstein then said, 'My purpose in coming here was to purchase your land from you. I bring this up now while my kinsman Thorkel is here. I thought it should suit both of us, because I'm told you have insufficient livestock and good land is going to waste. I offer you in return a suitable farm, as well as whatever sum we both agree upon to make up the difference.'

Halldor did not reject the idea, and they began discussing possible details of the bargain. Once Halldor had shown some interest, Thorkel became very involved in the discussion and wanted to get them to agree on a bargain. Halldor then began to retreat, at which they pressed their suit more forcefully, and eventually the more they pressed the more he withdrew.

Thorkel then said, 'Don't you realize where this is heading, Thorstein? He's just been leading us on all day. We've been sitting here letting him mock and delude us. If you intend to have anything come of this attempt at purchasing land, we're going to have to spare no pains.'

Thorstein said that he wanted to know clearly how things stood, and told Halldor to make it clear whether or not he was willing to sell him the land.

Halldor answered, 'I think I can state plainly the fact that you will be returning home empty-handed this evening.'

Thorstein then said, 'And I think I need not wait to tell you what I have planned, and that is to offer you two possibilities to choose from, as I think we'll have our way by force of numbers. The first choice is to agree to this purchase of your own accord, and enjoy our friendship in return; the second and clearly poorer choice is to be forced to shake my hand and thus agree to the sale of the Hjardarholt land.'

No sooner had Thorstein spoken this than Halldor sprang to his feet, so abruptly that the clasp was torn from his cloak, and said, 'Something else will happen before I utter words that I have no wish to speak.'

'And what might that be?' Thorstein asked.

'A wood-axe, wielded by the worst of men, will be wedged in your skull, and put an end to your high-handedness and bullying.'

Thorkel answered, 'This is an evil prophecy, and we hardly expect it to be fulfilled. I'd say that you've done enough now, Halldor, to deserve to hand over your land without any payment for it.'

To this Halldor replied, 'And you'll have the bladderwrack of Breidafjord in your arms before I'll be forced to sell my land.'

After that Halldor returned home to the farm, just as the men for whom he had sent came rushing up.

Thorstein was enraged and wanted to attack Halldor at once, but Thorkel asked him not to, saying, 'It would be a serious offence at this time, but when Lent is over I won't try to prevent any settling of differences.'

Halldor replied that he would be ready for them anytime.

After this they rode off and talked a great deal about the events of their journey. Thorstein said it was true enough that this excursion had turned out very badly, 'and why did you, Thorkel, hesitate to attack Halldor and do him some damage?'

Thorkel answered, 'Did you not see Beinir standing over you with his axe aloft? It would have been a fatal move; he would have brought his axe down on your head the moment I appeared likely to make a move.'

They then rode home to Ljarskogar. Lent passed and Easter week approached.

76 | Early on the morning of Maundy Thursday Thorkel made preparations to leave.

Thorstein tried hard to dissuade him, saying, 'It looks as if unfavourable weather is brewing.'

Thorkel said the weather would serve him fine, 'and don't attempt to advise me against it, kinsman, for I intend to be home before Easter'.

Thorkel had the ferry set afloat and loaded. Thorstein immediately unloaded again all that Thorkel and his companions loaded on board – until Thorkel spoke: 'Now stop delaying our journey, kinsman; you won't have your way this time.'

Thorstein answered, 'The one of us who decides, then, will be the worse for it; this will be a journey of great event.'

Thorkel wished him farewell until they met again, and Thorstein returned home very sadly. He went into the main room and asked for something to rest his head upon, and the servant woman saw the tears streaming from his eyes on to the cushion.

A short while later the roar of a great wind could be heard in the room, and Thorstein spoke: 'There you can hear the roaring of my kinsman Thorkel's killer.'

The story now returns to Thorkel and his journey. As the

party of ten sailed the length of Breidafjord that day, the wind began to rise and turned into a great storm before it subsided again. They pressed on determinedly, as they were the hardiest of men. Thorkel had his sword Skofnung with him, in a chest. They sailed onwards until they reached Bjarnarey – with people watching their crossing from both shores – but when they had reached the island, a gust of wind filled the sail and capsized the boat. Thorkel was drowned there along with all the men who were with him. The timber was washed ashore on islands all around: the corner posts on an island which has been called Stafey (Pillar Island) ever since. Skofnung had lodged in the inner timbers of the ferry itself and washed ashore on Skofnungsey (Skofnung's Island).

In the evening of the same day that Thorkel and his men were drowned Gudrun went to the church at Helgafell after the household had gone to bed. As she passed through the gate of the churchyard, she saw a ghost standing before her.

It bent down towards her and spoke: 'News of great moment, Gudrun,' it said, and Gudrun answered, 'Then keep silent about it, you wretch.'[53]

Gudrun went towards the church as she had intended, and when she had reached the church she thought she saw that Thorkel and his companions had arrived home and stood outside the church. She saw the seawater dripping from their clothing. Gudrun did not speak to them but entered the church and stayed there as long as she cared to. She then returned to the main room, thinking that Thorkel and his companions would have gone there. When she reached the house there was no one there. Gudrun was then very shaken by all these occurrences.

On Good Friday Gudrun sent men to check on Thorkel's journey, some in along Skogarstrond and others out to the islands. By that time the timber had drifted ashore on many islands and on both sides of the bay. On the Saturday before Easter Sunday the news reached them, and was thought momentous, as Thorkel was a great chieftain. Thorkel had completed the eighth year of his fifth decade when he died, and it was four years before the fall of King Olaf the Saint. Gudrun was greatly stricken by Thorkel's death, but bore her grief with dignity.

Only a little of the timber for the church was recovered. Gellir was fourteen years old at the time. He took over the running of the farm, together with his mother, along with Thorkel's duties as godi. It was soon clear that he had the makings of a leader of men.

Gudrun became very religious. She was the first Icelandic woman to learn the Psalter, and spent long periods in the church praying at night. Herdis Bolladottir usually went with her to her nightly prayers, and Gudrun loved Herdis dearly. It is said that one night young Herdis dreamed that a woman approached her. She wore a woven cape and a folded head-dress, and her expression was far from kindly.

She said to Herdis, 'Tell your grandmother that I care little for her company; she tosses and turns on top of me each night and pours over me tears so hot that I burn all over. I am telling you this because I prefer your company, although you have a strange air about you. All the same I could get along with you, if the distress caused me by Gudrun were not so great.'

Herdis then awoke and told Gudrun her dream. Gudrun thought it was a revelation and the following morning she had the floorboards in the church removed at the spot where she was accustomed to kneel in prayer and the ground below dug up. There they found bones, which were blackened and horrible, along with a chest pendant and a large magician's staff. People then decided that a prophetess must have been buried there. The bones were moved to a remote place little frequented by men.

77 | Four winters after the drowning of Thorkel Eyjolfsson, a ship owned by Bolli Bollason sailed into Eyjafjord. Most of the crew were Norwegians. Bolli had brought with him a great deal of wealth from abroad and many treasures given him by princes. He had become such a fine dresser by the time he returned from his journey abroad that he wore only clothes of scarlet or silk brocade and all his weapons were decorated with gold. He became known as Bolli the Elegant. He declared to his crew that he intended to go westward to visit his own district

and left the ship and its cargo in their hands. He took eleven men with him, and all of them were dressed in clothes of scarlet and mounted on gilded saddles. They were all comely men, but Bolli was in a class by himself. He wore a suit of silk brocade given to him by the emperor of Byzantium, with a cloak of red scarlet outermost. About his waist he had girded the sword Leg-biter, now inlaid with gold at the top and shank, and gold bands wound about its hilt. On his head he wore a gilded helmet and he held a red shield at his side with the figure of a knight drawn on it in gold. He had a lance in his hand, as is common in foreign parts. Wherever the group stopped for the night, the women could do nothing but gaze at Bolli and the finery which he and his companions bore.

In such style did Bolli ride westward, until he and his companions reached Helgafell, where Gudrun was delighted to receive her son. Bolli did not stay there long before riding to Saelingsdalstunga to his father-in-law, Snorri, and his wife Thordis. Their reunion was a joyous one. Snorri invited Bolli to stay there with as many of his companions as he wished and Bolli accepted. He and the men who had ridden south with him stayed with Snorri that winter. Bolli became renowned for this journey abroad. Snorri made no less effort to treat Bolli with great affection now than when he had stayed with him in former times.

78 | After Bolli had been a year in Iceland, Snorri the Godi was taken ill. His illness advanced only slowly and Snorri lay abed for a lengthy time. When his illness had worsened he summoned his kinsmen and dependants.

He then addressed Bolli, 'It is my wish that you take over my farm and godord after me, as I wish to show you no less honour and affection than my own sons. The son of mine whom I expect to be foremost among them, Halldor, is not in this country now.'

Snorri then died, aged threescore years and seven, one year after the fall of King Olaf the Saint, according to the priest Ari the Learned.[54] Snorri was buried at Tunga and Bolli and Thordis took over the farm at Tunga,[55] as Snorri had requested. Snorri's sons were not displeased, and Bolli became a highly capable and popular man.

Herdis Bolladottir grew up at Helgafell and was the loveliest of women. Orm, the son of Hermund Illugason, asked for and received her hand in marriage. Their son Kodran married Gudrun Sigmundardottir, and Kodran's son Hermund married Ulfheid, the daughter of Runolf, the son of Bishop Ketil. Their sons were Ketil, who became the abbot at Helgafell, Hrein, Kodran and Styrmir. Thorvor, the daughter of Herdis and Orm, was married to Skeggi Brandsson and their descendants are the people of Skogar.

Bolli and Thordis had a son named Ospak, whose daughter Gudrun was married to Thorarin Brandsson. Their son Brand endowed the church at Husafell. His son Sighvat became a priest and lived there for a long time.

Gellir Thorkelsson married Valgerd, the daughter of Thorgils Arason of Reykjanes. Gellir journeyed abroad and served with King Magnus the Good, receiving from him twelve ounces of gold and a great deal of additional wealth. Gellir's sons were named Thorgils and Thorkel, and Ari the Learned was the son of Thorgils. Ari's son was named Thorgils and his son was Ari the Strong.

Gudrun was now well advanced in years and burdened with her grief, as was related earlier. She was the first woman in Iceland to become a nun and anchoress. It was also widely said that Gudrun was the most noble among women of her rank in this country.

It is said that once when Bolli was visiting Helgafell, he sat with his mother, because Gudrun was always pleased when he came to see her, talking of many things for a long time.

Then Bolli spoke: 'Will you tell me something, Mother, that I'm curious to know? Which man did you love the most?'

Gudrun answered: 'Thorkel was the most powerful of men and most outstanding chieftain, but none of them was more valiant and accomplished than Bolli. Thord Ingunnarson was the wisest of these men and the most skilled in law. Of Thorvald I make no mention.'

Bolli then spoke: 'I understand clearly enough what you say of the qualities of each of your husbands, but you have yet to answer whom you loved the most. You've no need to conceal it any longer.'

Gudrun answered, 'You press me hard on this point, my son,' she said. 'If I wished to say this to anyone, you would be the one I would choose.'

Bolli asked her to do so.

Gudrun then spoke: 'Though I treated him worst, I loved him best.'

'That I believe,' said Bolli, 'you say in all sincerity', and thanked her for satisfying his curiosity.

Gudrun lived to a great age and is said to have lost her sight. She died at Helgafell and is buried there.

Gellir Thorkelsson lived at Helgafell into his old age and many remarkable stories are told of him.[56] He figures in many sagas, although he is mentioned but little here. He had a very fine church built at Helgafell, as is stated explicitly by Arnor the Earl's Poet[57] in the memorial poem he composed about Gellir. When Gellir had reached an advanced age he made preparations for a journey abroad. He went first to Norway, but stayed there only briefly before leaving to travel south to Rome on a pilgrimage to St Peter the Apostle.[58] His journey was a lengthy one; he returned northwards as far as Denmark where he was taken ill and, after a lengthy illness, received the last rites. He then died and is buried in Roskilde. Gellir had taken Skofnung abroad with him, and the sword was never recovered after that. It had been taken from the burial mound of Hrolf Kraki. When news of Gellir's death reached Iceland, his son Thorkel took over his father's estate at Helgafell. Thorgils, another of Gellir's sons, had drowned in Breidafjord at an early age, along with all those who were with him aboard ship. Thorkel Gellisson was a practical and worthy man and was said to be among the most knowledgeable of men.

Here ends the saga.

Translated by KENEVA KUNZ

BOLLI BOLLASON'S TALE

1 | At the same time as Bolli Bollason lived at Tunga,¹ as was
  | spoken of earlier, a man called Arnor Crone's-nose,² the
son of Bjarni Thordarson of Hofdi, lived on the farm Miklabaer
in Skagafjord.

Another man, named Thord, lived with his wife Gudrun at
Marbaeli. They were fine, upstanding farmers with wealth in
plenty. Their son Olaf was still a boy at the time and a most
promising young man. Gudrun, Thord's wife, was a near relative of Bolli Bollason, as her mother was his aunt. Gudrun's
son Olaf was named after Olaf Peacock of Hjardarholt.

At Hof in Hjaltadal lived Thord and Thorvald Hjaltason,
two prominent leaders.

A man called Thorolf Stuck-up lived at Thufur. He had an un-
friendly nature and was often uncontrollable when angry. He
owned a very aggressive grey bull. Thord of Marbaeli had sailed
on merchant voyages with Arnor. Thorolf Stuck-up was married
to a kinswoman of Arnor's and was one of the thingmen of the
Hjaltasons. He was on hostile terms with his neighbours and
was used to making trouble, of which the people of Marbaeli
bore the brunt. After he was driven home from the summer
pastures, Thorolf's bull caused a great deal of trouble. He
wounded farm animals and could not be chased off with stones.
He also damaged stacks of hay and did much other mischief.

Thord of Marbaeli went to Thorolf and asked him to see to
it that the bull did not wander around loose. 'We don't want to
have to put up with his rampages.'

Thorolf said he did not intend to stand guard over his livestock, and Thord returned home with this reply.

Not long afterwards Thord noticed that the bull was tearing apart stacks of peat. He ran over to the spot with a spear in his hand, and when the bull caught sight of him it began moving towards him with such heavy steps that it sank into the ground almost over its hooves. Thord lunged at it with his spear and the bull fell to the earth dead. Thord then went to Thorolf to tell him the bull was dead.

'The deed does you little honour,' Thorolf replied, 'and I should like to treat you to something just as unpleasant.'

Thorolf was furious and his every word bore menace.

Soon Thord had to leave his farm. His son Olaf, then seven or eight years of age, went off some distance from the farmhouse to build himself a play house, as children often do. There Thorolf came upon him and pierced him with his spear. He then returned home and told his wife of it.

She replied, 'This is a vile and unmanly deed and you'll reap an ill reward.'

Since his wife responded so negatively, Thorolf rode off and did not slow his pace until he came to Arnor at Miklabaer.

They exchanged news and Thorolf told him of the slaying of Olaf, saying, 'I look to you for support because of our family connections.'

'You'll go looking blindly for that in this case,' Arnor said, 'as I do not value my connections with you more highly than my own honour. No protection can you expect from me.'

Thorolf then went to Hof in Hjaltadal, where he sought out the Hjaltasons.

He told them of his situation and that 'I look to the two of you for support.'

Thord answered, 'This is a base deed, and I will give you no protection in this matter.'

Thorvald had nothing to say, and Thorolf got nothing from them in this instance. He rode off and further up into Hjaltadal to Reykir where he bathed in the hot spring. That evening he rode down the valley again and as he neared the fence around the farmhouse at Hof he spoke to himself, as if to someone standing there, who greeted him and asked who he was.

'My name is Thorolf,' he said.

'Where are you headed and what is your problem?' asked the unseen man.

Thorolf told him of all that had happened – 'I asked the Hjaltasons for protection,' he said, 'as I'm in need of help.'

The man who was supposed to be there with him answered, 'They have now left the place where they held the wake attended by so many people[3] that there were twelve hundred at table; such leaders have surely fallen in stature if they won't now offer a single man protection.'

Thorvald was standing outside and heard the conversation.

He came over and took hold of the reins of Thorolf's horse and told him to dismount, 'though it is hardly likely to bring much honour to help a man as feckless as you'.

2 | The story now turns to Thord who returned home to learn of the slaying of his son, for whom he grieved deeply.

His wife Gudrun said, 'You had better declare Thorolf responsible for slaying the lad,[4] and I will ride south to Tunga to my kinsman Bolli to see what help he is willing to offer us to gain redress.'

This they did. Gudrun was given a good welcome when she arrived at Tunga. She told Bolli of the slaying of her son Olaf and asked him to take over the prosecution of the case.

He answered, 'It doesn't look to me as if it will be easy to obtain honourable redress from those Northerners. What's more, I have also learned that this man is now keeping himself where it will not be easy to search him out.'

Bolli did, however, eventually agree to take on the case, and Gudrun returned north. When she arrived home she told her husband Thord how things stood and for some time nothing more happened.

After Christmas a meeting was to be held in Skagafjord at the Thvera farm, to which Thorvald had summoned Starri of Guddalir,[5] a friend of the Hjaltason brothers. Thorvald and his followers set out for the meeting, and as they passed Urdskriduholar a man came running down the slope towards them. It proved to be Thorolf, who joined Thorvald and his men.

When they had only a short distance remaining to Thvera, Thorvald spoke to Thorolf: 'Take three marks of silver with you and wait here above the Thvera farmhouse. It will be a sign to you, when I turn the inside of my shield towards you, that it is safe for you to approach. The shield is white on the inside.'[6]

When Thorvald arrived at the meeting he met Starri and they conferred together.

Thorvald spoke: 'The situation is this: I want you to accept Thorolf Stuck-up for safekeeping and support. In return you will have three marks of silver and my friendship.'

'The man you speak of,' answered Starri, 'is neither popular in my eyes nor likely to bring much luck. But for the sake of our friendship I will take him in.'

'You act well, in that case,' said Thorvald.

He then turned his shield so that the inside faced away from him. When Thorolf saw this he came forward, and Starri took him under his protection. Starri had an underground shelter at Guddalir because he often sheltered outlaws. He himself had also been charged with offences left unsettled.

3 | Bolli Bollason prepared to prosecute the slaying of Olaf.
    | He made preparations for the journey and set out north to Skagafjord, accompanied by thirty men. He was warmly received when he arrived at Miklabaer.

He explained the reason for his journey, saying, 'I intend to bring the case against Thorolf before the Hegranes Assembly, and I would like you to assist me.'

Arnor answered, 'I don't think, Bolli, that you're headed for fair sailing, if you intend to prosecute a case here in the north against men as unjust as the ones involved here. They will defend the case by any means, whether just or not. But your case is certainly a pressing one, so we'll do what we can as well to see it successfully concluded.'

Arnor collected a large number of men and accompanied Bolli to the assembly. The brothers also attended the assembly with a large number of followers. They had learned of Bolli's journey and intended to defend the case. When people had assembled, Bolli presented the charges against Thorolf. When it was the turn of the defence, Thorvald and Starri came forward with their followings, intending to block Bolli's prosecution by force of arms and numbers.

Upon seeing this, Arnor led his followers between them, saying, 'It is clear that so many good men should not be involved in the dispute as now appears likely, so that people fail to obtain justice in their cases. It is misguided to support Thorolf in this case, and you, Thorvald, will have scant backing if it comes to a show of force.'

Thorvald and Starri now saw that the case would be concluded, since they lacked the numbers to match Arnor and his men, so they withdrew. Bolli had Thorolf outlawed there at the Hegranes Assembly for the slaying of his kinsman Olaf and then returned home. He and Arnor parted the warmest of friends. Bolli remained on his farm awhile.

4 | A man named Thorgrim owned a ship which had been drawn ashore in Hrutafjord. Starri and Thorvald went to pay him a call.

Starri spoke to the captain: 'I have a man here whom I want you to transport abroad. You will have three marks of silver and my friendship as well.'

Thorgrim said, 'It looks to me as though it will prove a problem to do so, but since you urge me to, I will take him on. He doesn't look to me like a man to bring much luck, though.' Thorolf then joined the merchants while Starri returned home.

To turn now to Bolli, who had been considering what to do about Thorolf, he felt he would hardly have followed the case to a proper end if Thorolf were to escape. He then learned that passage had been obtained for Thorolf aboard a ship. At that he made preparations to set out, placed his helmet on his head and his shield at his side. He held a spear in one hand and buckled on the sword Leg-biter. He rode north to Hrutafjord and arrived just as the merchants were completing preparations for their voyage. Soon a wind came up. As Bolli rode up to the entrance of the camp, Thorolf came out carrying his bedroll.

Bolli drew Leg-biter and struck a blow right through him. Thorolf fell backwards into the camp and Bolli jumped on to the back of his horse. The merchants ran out and towards him.

Bolli spoke to them: 'You would be best advised to leave things as they are, since it will prove too great a task for you to bring me down, and I'm likely to trim off one or two of you before I'm done in.'

Thorgrim answered, 'I expect that's true.'

They took no action, and Bolli returned home. He earned himself a great deal of honour by this, as men thought it quite an accomplishment to have the man outlawed in another district and then venture alone into the hands of his enemies and kill him there.

5 | That summer at the Althing Bolli met Gudmund the Powerful,[7] and the two conversed together at length.

Gudmund said, 'I want to say, Bolli, that it's men like you that I want to count among my friends. I invite you to come north for a fortnight's feast, and will be disappointed if you fail to accept.'

Bolli answered that he would certainly accept this honour from a man such as him and promised to make the journey. There were others who made him offers of friendship as well. Arnor Crone's-nose invited him to a feast at Miklabaer. A man named Thorstein who lived at Hals, the son of Hellu-Narfi,[8] invited Bolli to stay with them on his way south again, as did Thord of Marbaeli. When the Althing ended Bolli rode home.

That summer a ship made land at Dagverdarnes and was drawn ashore there. Bolli lodged twelve of the merchant crew at Tunga over the winter and provided for them generously. They all remained there until Christmas had passed. Bolli then intended to make his promised visits to the north, had horses shod and made preparations for the journey. They were a party of eighteen, with all of the merchant sailors bearing arms. Bolli was wearing a black cape with his splendid spear, King's Gift, in his hand. They rode northward until they reached Marbaeli, where Thord gave them a good welcome. They spent three nights there in festive hospitality. Then they rode to Miklabaer, where Arnor received them warmly. The festivities there were superb.

Arnor then spoke: 'You have done well, Bolli, in paying me this visit. In doing so, I feel you have declared your great comradeship for me. And no better gifts will remain here with me than the ones you accept at parting. My friendship is also yours for the asking. But I suspect not everyone in this district feels well inclined towards you. Some of them, especially the Hjaltasons, feel they have been robbed of their honour. I intend to follow you north as far as the Heljardal heath when you leave here.'

Bolli answered, 'I wish to thank you, Arnor my host, for all the honour you have shown me, and it will certainly improve our company if you ride along with us. We plan on proceeding peacefully through this district, but if anyone should make any attempt to attack us, we may well repay them in kind for their trouble.'

Arnor then got ready to accompany them, and they set out on their way.

6 | To return to Thorvald, he spoke to his brother Thord: 'You likely know that Bolli is now here in the district making visits. There are eighteen of them altogether in his party at Arnor's, and they will be heading north over Heljardal heath.'

'I know that,' Thord replied.

Thorvald said, 'The idea of Bolli passing by under our noses, without our making any attempt to confront him, irks me. I don't know of anyone who has done more to diminish my honour than he has.'

Thord said, 'You're a great one for getting more involved in things than I care to. This is one road to be left untravelled, if I am the one to decide. I think it's far from certain that Bolli won't know how to answer any attack you make.'

'You won't talk me out of it,' Thorvald replied, 'but you must decide your own course.'

Thord said, 'You won't see me sitting at home, brother, if

you set out. And I'll give you the credit for any honour we reap from the journey, or any other consequences.'

Thorvald began collecting men for the journey and formed a party of eighteen. They set out towards the route of Bolli and his party where they intended to wait in ambush.

Arnor and Bolli rode their way with their companions.

When they were only a short distance from the Hjaltasons, Bolli said to Arnor, 'Isn't it best if you turn back now? You have given us a more than fitting escort, and the Hjaltasons won't try any treachery with me.'

Arnor said, 'I won't turn back, because something tells me Thorvald is intending to seek you out. What is it I see moving there? Aren't those shields shining? That will be the Hjaltasons, and we will see to it that they will get no honour from this journey as it can be taken as a plot against your life.'

Thorvald and his brother and their men now saw that Bolli and his party were anything but fewer than they themselves were and realized that any show of aggression on their behalf would put them in a bad position. Their best course appeared to be to turn back, since they were not able to carry out their intentions.

Thord then spoke, 'Things have now turned out as I feared, that this journey would make a mockery of us and we'd have done better to sit at home. We have shown our hostility to men and accomplished nothing.'

Bolli and his companions continued on their way. Arnor accompanied them up on to the heath and did not leave them until the route began to slope downwards to the north. He then returned home, while they continued down through Svarfa-dardal until they reached the farm called Skeid. There lived a man named Helgi, who was ill-tempered and not of good family, though wealthy enough. His wife Sigrid, who was a kins-woman of Thorstein Hellu-Narfason, was the more outstanding of the two.

Bolli and his party noticed a store of hay nearby. They dis-mounted and began to take hay to give their horses,[9] taking rather little, and Bolli restrained them even more.

'I don't know,' he said, 'what sort of nature this farmer has.'

They took handfuls of hay and let the horses eat them.

One of the farm workers came out of the house, and then returned indoors and said, 'There are men at your haystack, master, trying the hay.'

Sigrid, the farmer's wife, said, 'The only ones who would do that are men on whom one shouldn't spare the hay.'

Helgi sprang to his feet and said furiously he would never let her allow others to steal his hay. He ran out immediately as if he were crazed and came up to where the men had paused in their journey. Bolli got to his feet when he saw the man approach, supporting himself with his spear, King's Gift.

When Helgi reached him, he spoke: 'Who are these thieves that harass me so, stealing what is mine and tearing apart my haystack for their mounts?'

Bolli told him his name.

Helgi replied, 'That's an unsuitable name and you must be an unjust man.'

'That may well be true,' said Bolli, 'but you will have your justice.'

Bolli then drove the horses away from the hay, and told his men they would stay no longer.

Helgi said, 'I declare that what you have taken has been stolen from me and you have committed an offence liable to outlawry.'

'You will want us, farmer,' said Bolli, 'to make you compensation so that you will not prosecute us. I will pay you double the price of your hay.'

'That's nowhere near enough,' he answered. 'My demands will become more rather than less when our ways part.'

'Are there any objects of ours, farmer, that you would accept as compensation?' Bolli said.

'I think there might be a possibility,' Helgi answered, 'that I would have that gold-inlaid spear which you hold in your hand.'

'I'm not sure,' Bolli said, 'whether I care to give it up. I had other plans for it. And you can hardly ask me to hand over my weapon to you. Take instead as much money as you feel does you honour.'

'There's no chance of that,' Helgi said, 'and it's best that you be made to answer properly for what you have done.'

Helgi then pronounced his summons and charged Bolli with theft and made it liable to outlawry. Bolli stood there listening with a slight smile.

When Helgi had finished his accusation, he asked, 'When did you leave home?'

Bolli told him and the farmer then said, 'In that case I consider you to have lived on others for more than a fortnight.'

Helgi then pronounced another summons, charging Bolli with vagrancy.[10]

When he had finished, Bolli said, 'You're making much of this, Helgi, and I'd better make a move against you.'

Bolli then pronounced a summons, charging Helgi with slander, and another summons accusing him of trying to get hold of his property by treachery. His companions said they should kill this rogue, but Bolli said they should not. Bolli made the offences liable to outlawry.

After concluding the summons he said, 'You will take this knife and belt from me to Helgi's wife, as I'm told she spoke up for us.'

Bolli and his men then rode off, leaving Helgi behind. They came to Thorstein's farm at Hals where they were given a fine welcome and a goodly feast awaited them.

7 | Helgi, on the other hand, returned to the farmhouse at Skeid and told his wife of the dealings between him and Bolli.

'I have no idea,' he said, 'what I should do to deal with a man like Bolli, as I'm no man of law. And I don't have many who will support me in the case.'

Sigrid his wife said, 'It's a proper fool you've made of yourself. You have been dealing with the noblest of men and you made a spectacle of yourself. You'll end up as you deserve, losing all your wealth and your life as well.'

Helgi listened to her words, which he found rather hard to take, but he suspected they would prove true, as he was a

cowardly wretch, despite his bad temper and foolishness. He
saw no way out of the impasse he had talked himself into and
became more than a little cowed by it all.

Sigrid had a horse sought and rode to seek out her kinsman
Thorstein Narfason. Bolli and his men had arrived by then. She
asked to speak to Thorstein privately and told him how the
situation stood.

'This has turned out very badly,' Thorstein replied.

She told him as well how handsome Bolli's offers had been,
and how stupidly Helgi had acted. She asked Thorstein to use
all his influence to see to it that things were straightened out.
Afterwards she returned home, and Thorstein went to speak to
Bolli.

'What's this I hear, my friend?' he said. 'Has Helgi of Skeid
been provoking you unjustly? I want to ask you to drop the
charges and dismiss the incident, at my request, as the words
of simpletons are not worthy of notice.'

Bolli answered, 'It's true enough that this is nothing of worth.
Nor do I intend to let it upset me.'

'Then I want to ask you,' said Thorstein, 'to drop the charges
against him for my sake, and accept my friendship in return.'

'There's no threat of disaster right away,' Bolli said. 'I intend
to take things calmly and we'll wait until spring.'

Thorstein spoke: 'Then I will show you how important it is
to me to have my way in this. I will give you the best horse here
in the district, and his herd, twelve altogether.'

Bolli answered, 'It's a fine offer, but you don't have to go to
such lengths. I wasn't upset by it, nor will it be upsetting when
the judgement comes.'

'The truth is,' said Thorstein, 'I want to offer you self-
judgement in the case.'

Bolli answered, 'I expect the truth to be that there is no use
making the offer, because I do not wish to accept a settlement
in the case.'

'Then you're choosing the course that will prove bad for all
of us,' said Thorstein. 'Although Helgi is hardly a worthy man,
I am related to him by marriage. I won't deliver him into your
hands to be killed since you refuse to pay heed to my words.

And as far as the charges that Helgi brought against you, I can hardly see that they will do you honour by being presented at the assembly.'

Thorstein and Bolli then parted rather coldly. Bolli rode off with his companions, and there is no mention of him receiving parting gifts.

8 | Bolli and his companions arrived at the farm of Gudmund the Powerful at Modruvellir. He came out to meet them and welcomed them warmly and was in the best of spirits. They remained there a fortnight and enjoyed festive hospitality.

Gudmund then said to Bolli, 'Is there any truth to the rumour that you and Thorstein have had a disagreement?'

Bolli said there was little truth in it and changed the subject.

Gudmund said, 'What route do you intend to take homeward?'

'The same one,' answered Bolli.

Gudmund said, 'I would advise you against it, as I'm told that you and Thorstein parted rather stiffly. Stay here with me instead and ride south in the spring, and let things run their course then.'

Bolli said he did not intend to alter his travel plans because of their threats.

'While that fool Helgi was carrying on so stupidly, speaking one slanderous charge after another, and hoping to take my spear King's Gift off me for a mere tuft of hay, I thought to myself that I would see to it that he got what he deserved for those words. I have other plans for my spear and intend to give it to you, along with the gold arm ring that the emperor gave me. I feel that the treasures are better off in your hands than in Helgi's clutches.'

Gudmund thanked him for the gifts, and said, 'The gifts you receive in return are much less worthy than they should be.'

Gudmund gave Bolli a shield decorated with gold, a gold arm ring and a cape made of the costliest material and embroidered with gold threads wherever this could add to its beauty. All of the gifts were very fine.

Gudmund then said, 'I think you're doing the wrong thing, Bolli, choosing to ride through Svarfadardal.'

Bolli replied that no harm would come of it. They then rode off, with Bolli and Gudmund parting the best of friends, and he and his party rode north along Galmarstrond.

That evening they came to the farm known as Krossar, where a man named Ottar lived. He was standing outside, a bald man wearing an outer jacket of skin. Ottar greeted them well and invited them to stay the night, and they accepted. They were waited upon well and the farmer was in the best of spirits. They spent the night there.

When Bolli and his party were ready to leave the next morning, Ottar said, 'You have done me an honour, Bolli, in visiting my farm. I would also like to do you a small favour, give you a gold arm ring, and would be grateful if you accept it. Here is also a ring to accompany it.'

Bolli accepted the gifts and thanked the farmer. Then Ottar mounted his horse and rode ahead to show them the way, as there had been a light fall of snow during the night. They continued on their way up to Svarfadardal.

They had not ridden far when Ottar turned back to them and said to Bolli, 'I want to show you how much I desire your friendship. Here is another arm ring of gold which I wish to give you. I would like to be of help to you in any way I can, as you are going to need it.'

Bolli said the farmer was treating him far too generously, 'but I will accept the ring all the same'.

'You're doing the right thing,' said the farmer.

9 | To return to Thorstein of Hals. When he expected Bolli to be returning southward again, he collected a party of men and intended to lie in ambush for Bolli, wishing to alter the situation between him and Helgi. Thorstein and his men, who made up a party of thirty, rode out to the river Svarfadardalsa where they took up position.

A man named Ljot lived at Vellir in Svarfadardal.[11] He was a prominent chieftain, a popular man and much involved in lawsuits. For everyday pursuits he wore a dark brown tunic and carried a light pole axe, while if he were preparing for a fight he had a black tunic and a broad-bladed axe, with which he appeared more than a little intimidating.

Bolli and his men rode westward in Svarfadardal. Ottar followed them past the Hals farm and out to the river. There Thorstein and his men were waiting for them, and when Ottar saw the ambush he responded abruptly, turned his horse and rode off to one side at top speed. Bolli and his party rode on boldly, and when Thorstein and his men saw this they sprang forward. They were on opposite sides of the river. The ice had broken up along its banks, but there was still a frozen patch down the middle. Thorstein and his men ran out on to the ice.

Helgi of Skeid was also there and urged the men on energetically, saying it was time to see whether Bolli's ambition and eagerness would be enough to carry the day, or whether there were any men of the north there who would dare to take him on.

'There's no reason to hesitate in killing all of them. It will also,' said Helgi, 'deter others from attacking us.'

Bolli heard Helgi's words and saw where he had advanced out on the ice. He threw his spear at Helgi and it struck him in the middle of his body, driving him backwards into the river. The spear struck the bank on the opposite side where it stuck fast, with Helgi hanging from it down into the water. A hard battle then began. Bolli pressed forward so boldly that men nearby were forced to give way. Thorstein then came forward against Bolli, and when they came together Bolli struck Thorstein a blow on the shoulder, giving him a severe wound. Thorstein received another wound on the leg. The struggle was a fierce one. Bolli himself had been wounded but not severely.

The story now turns to Ottar.

He rode up to Vellir, to Ljot, and when they met Ottar spoke: 'No cause to sit about, Ljot,' he said, 'what's at stake is to prove yourself a man of honour.'

'What would that involve, Ottar?'

'I expect them to be fighting here down at the river, Thorstein of Hals and Bolli, and it would be a most fortunate thing to put a stop to their hostilities.'

Ljot said, 'You've proved your worth more often than once.'

He reacted quickly and he and several others hurried back with Ottar. When they reached the river, Bolli and the others were fighting furiously. Three of Thorstein's men had been killed. Ljot and his men quickly ran between the fighters and held them back from attacking each other.

Then Ljot spoke: 'You are to separate at once,' he said; 'more than enough harm has been done. I intend to decide the terms of a settlement between you in this case, and if either of you refuses, he will be attacked.'

Ljot's decisive action caused them to cease their fighting, and both sides agreed that he should decide the terms of settlement in the dispute between them. They then went their separate ways, Thorstein returned home and Ljot invited Bolli and his men home to his farm, which they accepted. Bolli and his men rode up to Ljot's farm Vellir.

The site where they had fought is known as Hestanes. Ottar did not take his leave of Bolli and his party until they had reached Ljot's farm. Bolli gave him generous gifts at their parting and thanked him warmly for his assistance. He also promised Ottar his friendship. Ottar returned home to his farm at Krossar.

10 | After the fight at Hestanes, Bolli and all his men had returned home with Ljot to Vellir, where Ljot bandaged their wounds. They healed quickly because they were well looked after. When they had recovered from their wounds, Ljot called together a large assembly. He and Bolli rode to the assembly, as did Thorstein of Hals, along with his companions.

When the assembly had convened, Ljot spoke: 'No longer will I postpone the announcement of the settlement I have arrived at in the dispute between Thorstein of Hals and Bolli. To begin with, Helgi is deemed to have fallen without right to compensation because of his slanderous remarks and behaviour towards Bolli. The wounds received by Thorstein and Bolli will balance each other out. But for those three of Thorstein's men who were slain Bolli will pay compensation. And for his attempt on Bolli's, life, Thorstein will pay him the value of fifteen hundred three-ell lengths of homespun. When this is concluded they will be fully reconciled.'

After this the assembly was dissolved. Bolli told Ljot that he intended to head homeward and thanked him well for all his assistance. They exchanged fine gifts and parted as good friends. Bolli took custody of the livestock and property at Skeid on Sigrid's behalf, as she wished to accompany him westward. They rode on together until they came to Miklabaer and met Arnor. He welcomed them warmly. They stayed there awhile and Bolli told Arnor everything of his dealings with the men of Svarfadardal.

Arnor said, 'You have been very lucky in this journey, and in your dealings with a man like Thorstein. It can be truly said that few if any chieftains from other districts will have gained more honour here in the north, especially considering how many men bore grudges against you beforehand.'

Bolli then left Miklabaer and headed southward with his companions. He and Arnor pledged each other friendship anew at parting. When Bolli returned home to Tunga, his wife Thordis was relieved to see him. She had already heard some news of their skirmishes with the Northerners and thought they were at great risk as to the outcome. Bolli now lived quietly on his farm and enjoyed great respect.

This journey of Bolli's became the subject of new stories in all districts. Everyone felt that hardly any journey had been made to equal it. He gained in respect from this and many other things. Bolli found a worthy match for Sigrid and treated her generously.

We have heard no more of the story than this.

Translated by KENEVA KUNZ

Notes

THE SAGA OF THE PEOPLE OF LAXARDAL

1. *Bjorn Buna*: Bjorn and his descendants are frequently referred to in the sagas and tales. *The Book of Settlements* says: 'Almost all the prominent Icelanders are descended from Bjorn Buna' (p. 22).
2. *hersir*: A local leader in western and northern Norway; his rank was hereditary. Originally the hersirs were probably those who took command when the men of the district were called to arms.
3. *Olaf the White*: A warrior king of late ninth-century Dublin.
4. *Frodi the Valiant ... the descendants of Earl Sverting*: Also known from the *Gesta Danorum* by the Danish historian Saxo Grammaticus (*c.* 1150–1220).
5. *Jorunn Manvitsbrekka*: The byname 'Manvitsbrekka' is thought to suggest wisdom.
6. *Killer-Styr and Vermund*: Thorgrim's sons are known from several sagas, e.g. *The Saga of the People of Eyri*.
7. *Steinthor of Eyri*: One of the principal characters in *The Saga of the People of Eyri*; he also appears in other sagas.
8. *according to Ari Thorgilsson the Learned*: It is not clear which work is referred to here. *The Book of Settlements* tells of Thorstein's death, but how much in that account derives from Ari the Learned is not known.
9. *her son Thorstein*: He was also known by the byname 'the Red'.
10. *Gotuskeggi clan*: Described in *The Saga of the People of the Faroe Islands*.
11. *Gunnlaug Serpent-tongue*: Poet, hero of *The Saga of Gunnlaug Serpent-tongue*.
12. *the 'leap week' in summer*: The addition of an extra week to the summer season was an attempt to readjust the calendar to fit the solar seasons. As the settlers of Iceland had only fifty-two weeks to a year, or 364 days, their calendar was a day and a quarter short of the proper length. As the calendar and solar seasons

became more and more out of joint, the idea of adding an extra week every six years in compensation was adopted.

13. *Under such circumstances, as a widow ... his offer*: According to the legal code *Grágás* ('Grey Goose') from 1284, a widow could not accept a proposal of marriage without her legal guardian's prior consent. An exception could be made if it was deemed proven that her guardians had twice before deprived her of a marriage settlement comparable to the third. According to the Norwegian Laws of Gulathing and the Icelandic law codes *Járnsíða* ('Iron-side') and *Jónsbók*, a widow was allowed to decide this for herself, but should seek the approval of her male kinsmen.

14. *as Vigdis had not declared any grounds for her divorce*: The legal code 'Grey Goose' stipulates a husband's sexual negligence as grounds for divorce. Should he fail to sleep with his wife for six seasons in a row, she and her male kinsmen could claim back her property and transfer of legal rights.

15. *so I'll be able to keep a watchful eye over my home*: Similar arrangements for a burial place are made in *Hen-Thorir's Saga*, *The Saga of the People of Svarfadardal* and *The Saga of the People of Vatnsdal*. The practice derives from the belief that the spirits of the dead dwell near the place where their bodies are buried.

16. *ordeal*: In trials where evidence was lacking, a suspect sometimes had to undergo a test of some description to establish his guilt or innocence. The most common method was for people to carry a red-hot piece of iron: those who did not burn themselves were pure, i.e. innocent; see, for example, *The Saga of Grettir the Strong*.

17. *Harald Gunnhildarson*: A king of Norway, probably 961–74. In the sagas he is variously associated with his mother Gunnhild, as here, or named Eiriksson after his father, Eirik Blood-axe. He also had the byname 'Grey-cloak'.

18. *comparisons of men*: A game in which men exaggerated their virtues, accomplishments and physical prowess until the other player conceded defeat. Discord was generally the result.

19. *a dispute between the people of Laxardal and of Fljotshlid*: Related in the first part of *Njal's Saga*.

20. *a complete suit of clothes made from scarlet*: Brightly dyed woollen material. The original *skarlat* is somewhat deceptive as the cloth could be red, but also dark brown, blue, grey or even white.

21. *A man named Egil, the son of Skallagrim*: Warrior and poet Egil Skallagrimsson, the hero of *Egil's Saga*.

22. *deprive me of my legal right to give my son twelve ounces*: According to 'Grey Goose', 'a man has the right to give his illegitimate child twelve ounce-units' and no more, unless the legitimate heirs agree. This presumably refers to twelve ounces of silver, the legal tender, and not of gold. Hoskuld thus tricks his legitimate sons into leaving Olaf not only more money than the law allows, but also in effect his emblems of power, apart from the land itself.

23. *the Hjaltasons*: Hjalti's sons Thord and Thorvald, from Hof in Hjaltadal, also appear in *Bolli Bollason's Tale*.

24. *Both of us lie ... none at all*: A variant of this occasional verse appears in *Kormak's Saga*, describing the same event.

25. *'House Drapa'*: A fragment of this poem is preserved in Snorri Sturluson's *Prose Edda*. It includes a description of Thor's battle with the Midgard Serpent, the cremation of Balder and the fight over the Brising necklace. Of the author, Ulf Uggason, little is known. He is mentioned in *The Book of Settlements* and a single verse in *Njal's Saga* is attributed to him.

26. *Sturla*: Sturla of Hvamm, the progenitor of the Sturlungs, the most powerful family in thirteenth-century Iceland.

27. *Gest Oddleifsson*: Appears in many tales and sagas, e.g. *The Saga of Havard of Isafjord* and *The Saga of Ref the Sly*.

28. *a shirt with the neck so low-cut that it will give you grounds for divorcing him*: In medieval times men's shirts were high-necked, but women's usually low-necked. We can assume from Thord's words that, by dressing as a woman, a man would give lawful grounds for divorce. Icelandic laws preserved from these times make no mention of this, but 'Grey Goose' states that the penalty for cross-dressing should be three years' exile for both men and women.

29. *from the Hebrides*: In the sagas, Hebrideans tend to be sorcerers and evil-doers.

30. *a masculine woman*: Possibly an insinuation of homosexuality.

31. *the poet Stuf*: The hero of two tales, *Stuf's Tale* and *The Longer Tale of Stuf*.

32. *fighting prowess*: In the ancient game of the horse-fight, which was commonly practised in Iceland and Norway, according to clear procedural rules, two horses were goaded to fight against each other until one was killed or ran away. Horse-fights often had violent consequences; see *Njal's Saga*.

33. *a shallow grave heaped with stones*: In heathen times, corpses were usually placed in turfed mounds. However, stones and rocks

were thrown on the bodies of evil-doers and sorcerers, and little care was lavished on their final resting places.

34. *I won't make it a prediction*: Olaf's turn of phrase indicates his fears that a prediction would be more likely than a foreboding to become reality.

35. *Grettir the Strong*: The most renowned outlaw in the saga tradition. He is the hero of *The Saga of Grettir the Strong* and his exploits are also referred to in a number of other sagas.

36. *Brand the Generous*: Also known from his own *Tale of Brand the Generous*.

37. *Hallfred the Troublesome Poet*: A follower of King Olaf and hero of *The Saga of Hallfred the Troublesome Poet*.

38. *the king had forbidden all of the ships to put to sea . . . adopt the new religion*: In other sources, e.g. *The Saga of Olaf Tryggvason* (an Icelandic translation of a lost Latin work) by Odd Snorrason and *The Saga of Christianity*, these events are recounted in much the same way. This, however, is the only place where the sons of Skeggi are mentioned.

39. *hardly surprising that the weather should be bad . . . the gods have grown angry*: In ancient times, kings were often considered responsible for the weather. They were extolled if the season was favourable, but if it was not, they were sometimes even executed, e.g. as in *The Saga of the Ynglings* in *Heimskringla*.

40. *Hallfred was not baptized that day*: *The Saga of Hallfred the Troublesome Poet* tells of his baptism and its prelude.

41. *Hjalti Skeggjason was sentenced to outlawry for blasphemy*: These events are described in other works, e.g. *Njal's Saga* and *The Book of Icelanders*.

42. *the king's sister Ingibjorg*: Mentioned in *The Saga of St Olaf* in *Heimskringla*, where she is said to be the wife of Earl Rognvald Ulfsson of western Gotland and a staunch supporter of the king.

43. *all the people of Iceland converted to Christianity*: The primary source for most accounts of the conversion is *The Book of Icelanders*.

44. *There were six of them*: A puzzling statement, as by now Thorolf seems to be too wounded to take part in the battle and Osvif's sons should therefore number four, or at most five if their kinsman Gudlaug is included. The likeliest explanation is that this is simply a scribal error, because shortly afterwards, when Gudlaug is badly wounded, four sons of Osvif attack Kjartan.

45. *Aldis*: In *The Book of Settlements* it is Asdis, the sister of Ljot

of Ingjaldssand, who is said to have been abducted by Ospak Osvifsson, whom Ljot subsequently summoned.

46. *Strond*: The name means 'coast' and probably refers to Fellsstrond, but possibly to Skardsstrond.

47. *The following spring*: The ensuing account of Thorkel Eyjolfsson and his dealings with Grim is very similar to that found in one version of *The Saga of Thord Menace*. Their dealings are also mentioned in *The Saga of Grettir the Strong*.

48. *your sword Skofnung*: According to *The Saga of Hrolf Kraki*, the sword Skofnung originally belonged to Hrolf, but in *The Book of Settlements* Skeggi from Midfjord is said to have stolen it from his burial mound. The sword's attributes are described in further detail in *Kormak's Saga*. It is common in the sagas for magical properties to be associated with certain weapons.

49. *I have also often seen brightness there*: Gest's vision alludes to the establishment of a cloister at Helgafell in 1184.

50. *Snorri made him a present of an inlaid axe*: This is not the only instance when Snorri is said to have given weapons to men bent on revenge. In *The Saga of the People of Eyri*, shortly after it is implied that he sent a spy to Arnkel the Godi, he gives Thorleif Kimbi an axe. Generally, characters who appear in more than one saga maintain consistent personalities, although Hrut's portrayal in *The Saga of the People of Laxardal* and *Njal's Saga* is a notable exception. Wherever Snorri the Godi appears, he is described as intelligent and wise, but also devious.

51. *as is related in the saga of Thorgils Holluson*: This saga is lost.

52. *Gunnar, who was called Thidrandabani*: Features in *The Tale of Gunnar, the Slayer of Thidrandi*.

53. *Then keep silent about it, you wretch*: A reference to the belief that a ghost's words must be replied to immediately. The idea was common in folktales and popular belief, even in later centuries.

54. *according to the priest Ari the Learned*: This seems to be a reference to *The Life of Snorri the Godi*, which some scholars have conjectured was written by Ari Thorgilsson the Learned.

55. *Bolli and Thordis took over the farm at Tunga*: In *The Saga of the People of Eyri*, it is Snorri Snorrason who takes over the farm after his father's death.

56. *many remarkable stories are told of him*: Gellir is mentioned elsewhere, including in *The Saga of the Confederates* and *The Saga of the People of Ljosavatn*.

57. *Arnor the Earl's Poet*: Described in *The Tale of Arnor, the Earl's Poet*.

58. *on a pilgrimage to St Peter the Apostle*: I.e. to the Pope, as St Peter's successor.

BOLLI BOLLASON'S TALE

1. *Tunga*: I.e. Saelingsdalstunga in the Dales.
2. *Arnor Crone's-nose*: Known from *The Tale of Svadi and Arnor Crone's-nose*.
3. *the wake attended by so many people*: A reference to the renowned funeral of Hjalti, held by his sons. More guests are said to have been entertained there than at any other gathering in Iceland. It is also mentioned in *The Book of Settlements*.
4. *declare Thorolf responsible for slaying the lad*: The initial step in a lawsuit after a killing was to declare the slayer responsible, after which the people who lived closest to the scene were called to bear witness.
5. *Starri of Guddalir*: Dueller Starri Eiriksson is mentioned in *The Saga of Christianity* and *The Book of Settlements*.
6. *when I turn the inside of my shield towards you . . . The shield is white on the inside*: Presumably the shield has different colours on the inside and exterior. A white colour on a shield usually denoted peace, and red, warfare.
7. *Gudmund the Powerful*: Lived at Modruvellir in Eyjafjord, and was one of the principal characters of *The Saga of the People of Ljosavatn* and is mentioned in many other works such as *Njal's Saga*, *The Saga of the People of Eyri*, *Valla-Ljot's Saga*, *The Saga of the People of Vatnsdal*, *Killer-Glum's Saga* and the kings' sagas. According to the chronology of the earlier sagas, Gudmund should have long been dead when these events occur.
8. *Hellu-Narfi*: Also mentioned in *Valla-Ljot's Saga*.
9. *began to take hay to give their horses*: According to older laws, travellers were forbidden to feed their horses with hay belonging to others, but *Jónsbók* (the Icelandic code agreed by the Althing in 1281) contains stipulations allowing this.
10. *Helgi then pronounced another summons, charging Bolli with vagrancy*: Helgi's summons is based on the provisions in 'Grey Goose' about vagrancy. The law was strict about vagrancy and punishment was severe, entailing fines or even exile.
11. *a man named Ljot lived at Vellir*: The protagonist of *Valla-Ljot's Saga*, where his clothing is described in much the same way.

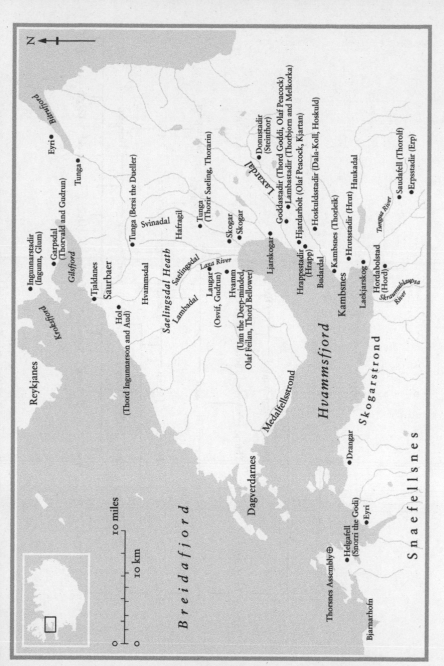

Laxardal

Family Ties in Laxardal

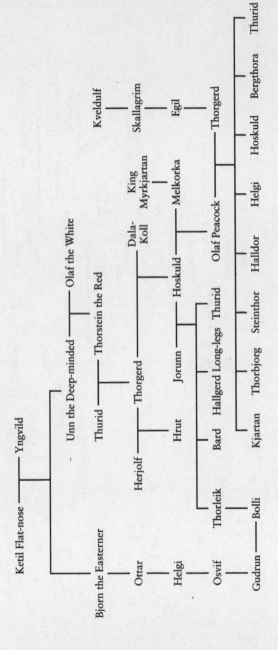

Gudrun's Family and Husbands

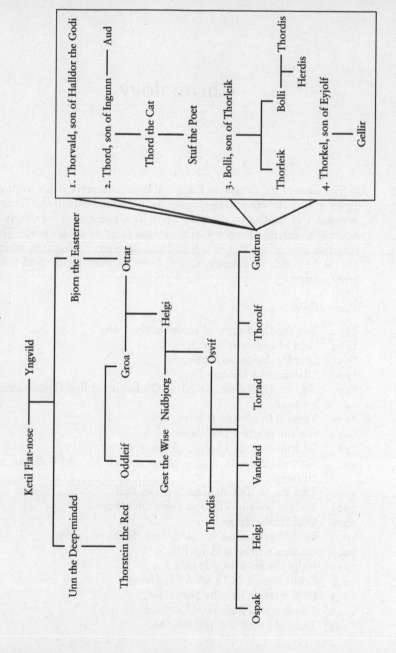

Chronology

In *The Saga of the People of Laxardal* time invariably yields to principles of fiction. Nevertheless, using the presumed date of the Christianization of Iceland in the year 1000 as a point of reference, it is possible to determine when various events in the saga take place. The tentative chronology below is based on numerous conjectures, which are marked with an asterisk. Other dates included are derived from other sources.

Year	Event
*890	Unn the Deep-minded settles in the Dales.
*915	Hrut Herjolfsson is born.
*938	Olaf Hoskuldsson is born.
*960	Olaf marries Thorgerd.
*970–74	Gudrun Osvifsdottir, Kjartan Olafsson and Bolli Thorleiksson are born.
*979	Thorkel Eyjolfsson is born.
*985	Gudrun marries Thorvald.
*987	Gudrun marries Thord Ingunnarson.
997	Kjartan refuses to take Gudrun abroad. He and Bolli sail for Norway.
1000	Christianization. Gudrun marries Bolli.
1003	Kjartan is slain. Thorleik Bollason is born.
1006	Olaf Hoskuldsson dies.
1007	Bolli Thorleiksson is killed. Bolli Bollason is born.
1008	Gudrun moves to Helgafell.
1019	Helgi Hardbeinsson is killed.
1020	Gudrun marries Thorkel Eyjolfsson.
1025	Bolli marries Thordis Snorradottir.
1027	Thorleik and Bolli travel abroad.
*1035	Thorkel Eyjolfsson is drowned.

*1039 Bolli Bollason returns.
*1050 Gudrun Osvifsdottir dies.
*1086 Gellir Thorkelsson dies.

Social, Political and Legal Structure

The notion of kinship is central to the sense of honour and duty in the sagas, and thereby to their action. Kinship essentially involves a sense of belonging not unlike that underlying the Celtic clan systems. The Icelandic word for kin or clan (*ætt*) is cognate with other words meaning 'to own' and 'direction' – the notion could be described as a 'social compass'.

Establishing kinship is one of the justifications for the long genealogies, which tend to strike non-Icelandic readers as idiosyncratic detours, and also for the preludes in Norway before the main saga action begins. Members of the modern nuclear family or close relatives are only part of the picture, since kinsmen are all those who are linked through a common ancestor – preferably one of high birth and high repute – as far back as five or six generations or even more.

Marriage ties, sworn brotherhood and other bonds could of course create conflicting loyalties with respect to the duty of revenge, as exemplified by Bolli Thorleiksson in *The Saga of the People of Laxardal*. A strict order stipulated who was to take revenge within the fairly immediate family, with a 'multiplier effect' if those seeking vengeance were killed in the process. The obligation to take revenge was inherited, just like wealth, property and claims. Patriarchy was the order of the day, although notable exceptions are found. Likewise, the physical duty of revenge devolved only upon males, but women were often responsible for instigating it, either by urging a husband or brother to action with slurs about their cowardice, or by bringing up their sons with a vengeful sense of purpose and even supplying them with old weapons that had become family heirlooms. When vengeance is exacted, many of the female characters in *The Saga of the People of Laxardal* go to extreme lengths beyond those of a typical woman in other sagas, for example when Thorgerd Egilsdottir keeps urging her sons to avenge the slaying of Kjartan, and then rides with them almost in a supervisory role when they attack

Bolli Thorleiksson (ch. 55), or when Breeches-Aud sets off alone to seek revenge when her brothers fail to perform their duty (ch. 35).

The legal status of women under the Commonwealth (930–1262) is frequently reflected in the sagas written down around the end of that period. Wealthy widows generally had a large say in their own affairs, the more so the higher they were placed in the social scale. In the thirteenth century, when *The Saga of the People of Laxardal* was written, women sometimes inherited political power on the death of their husbands, which may colour the saga's portrayal of Unn the Deep-minded. However, most women had to bow to the authority of men, and disputes repeatedly arise in the sagas because they have no say in their choice of husband, but are married off to bolster the position of their family or clan. A woman who divorces a man may suffer the loss of her wealth, as in the case of Vigdis, the wife of Thord Goddi, who takes 'nothing but her own belongings' with her when she leaves him (ch. 16). On the other hand, a widow inherits from her husband, but under the law can only betroth herself to another man in exceptional cases. Thus it is not merely a coincidence that the build-up to the marriage of Gudrun and Bolli is described in the following terms:

> Osvif then approached Gudrun and said that Bolli Thorleiksson had arrived, 'and has asked for your hand in marriage. You are to answer him. I can say without hesitation that if I were to decide, Bolli would not be turned down.'
>
> Gudrun answered, 'You've been quick to decide this. Bolli brought the question up once with me and I tried to discourage him, and I still feel the same way.'
>
> Osvif then said, 'If you refuse a man like Bolli many people will say that your answer shows more recklessness than foresight. But as long as I'm still alive, I intend to direct my children's actions in matters where I can see more clearly than they.'
>
> Since Osvif opposed her so, Gudrun did not, for her part, refuse, although she was very reluctant in all respects. Osvif's sons were also very eager for her to make the match and felt it was an honour for them to have Bolli as their brother-in-law. (ch. 43)

Osvif invokes his legal right, overrules his grown-up daughter who already has two marriages behind her, and in doing so enjoys the support of his sons, who aim to consolidate their social position through the marriage ties with Bolli.

Iceland was unique among European societies in the tenth to thirteenth centuries in two respects in particular: it had no king, and no executive power to follow through the pronouncements of its highly sophisticated legislative and judicial institutions. The lack of executive power meant that there was no means for preventing men from taking the law into their own hands, which gave rise to many memorable conflicts recorded in the sagas, but also led to the gradual disintegration of the Commonwealth in the thirteenth century.

The Althing served not only as a general or national assembly (which is what its name means), but also as the main festival and social gathering of the year, where people exchanged stories and news, renewed acquaintances with old friends and relatives, and the like. Originally it was inaugurated (with a pagan ceremony) by the leading godi (*allsherjargoði*) who was a descendant of the first settler Ingolf Arnarson, in the tenth week of summer. Early in the eleventh century the opening day was changed to the Thursday of the eleventh week of summer (18–24 June). Legislative authority at the Althing was in the hands of the Law Council, while there were two levels of judiciary, the Quarter Courts and the Fifth Court.

The Law Council originally comprised the thirty-six godis, along with two thingmen for each, and the Lawspeaker, who was the highest authority in the Commonwealth, elected by the Law Council for a term of three years. It was the duty of the Lawspeaker to recite the entire procedures of the assembly and one third of the laws of the country every year. He presided over the meetings of the Law Council and ruled on points of legal interpretation.

Quarter Courts, established at the Althing around 965, evolved from earlier regional Spring Assemblies, probably panels of nine men, which had dealt with cases involving people from the same quarter. Three new godords were created in the north when the Quarter Courts were set up. The godis appointed thirty-six men to the Quarter Court and their decisions had to be unanimous.

Around 1005, a Fifth Court was established as a kind of court of appeal to hear cases which were unresolved by the Quarter Courts. The godis appointed forty-eight members to the Fifth Court and the two sides in each case were allowed to reject six each. A simple majority among the remaining thirty-six then decided the outcome, and lots were drawn in the event of a tie. With the creation of the Fifth Court, the number of godis was increased correspondingly, and with their two thingmen each and the Lawspeaker, the Law Council then consisted of 145 people in all.

Legal disputes feature prominently in the Sagas of Icelanders, and the prosecution and defence of a case followed clearly defined procedures. Cases were prepared locally some time before the Althing, and could be dismissed there if they were technically flawed. Preparation generally took one of two forms. A panel of 'neighbours' could be called, consisting of five or nine people who lived near the scene of the incident or the home of the accused, to testify to what had happened. Alternatively, a party could go to the home of the accused to summons him during the Summons Days, two weeks before the Spring Assembly but three or four weeks before the Althing.

The accused generally did not attend the Althing, but was defended by someone else, who called witnesses and was entitled to disqualify members of the panel. Panels did not testify to the details and facts of the case in the modern sense, but determined whether the incident had taken place. The case was then summed up and a ruling passed on it by the Quarter Court.

Cases were often settled without going through the complex court procedure, either by arbitration, a ruling from a third party who was accepted by both sides, or by self-judgement by either of the parties involved in the case. Duelling was another method for settling disputes but was formally banned in Iceland in 1006. A number of sagas describe ordeals that were undertaken when evidence was lacking. Generally this involved holding red-hot iron; if the person doing so remained unharmed, the Almighty had deemed that he was telling the truth.

In *The Saga of the People of Laxardal*, some characters blatantly sidestep the law, or attempt to, in various ways. Thorkel Scarf arranges for men to disrupt a test of his own truthfulness; Thord Ingunnarson probably accuses Breeches-Aud wrongfully in order to gain a divorce from her; and Hoskuld Dala-Kollsson refuses to pay his brother Hrut his rightful share of his inheritance. Such actions are evidence of weaknesses in the social structure, where the executive authority was not sufficiently strong to enforce the law.

Penalties depended upon the seriousness of the case and took the form of either monetary compensation or outlawry. A confiscation court would seize the belongings of a person outlawed for three years or life. Two types of outlawry were applied, depending upon the seriousness of the offence: lesser outlawry (*fjörbaugsgarður*) and full outlawry (*skóggangur*). According to the legal code 'Grey Goose', a lesser outlaw enjoyed sanctuary in three homes in Iceland, no more than one day's passage from each other, and safe passage along a direct route between them, but was obliged to leave the country as soon as possible for three years' exile. A formal request for passage abroad also had to be made on his behalf and a fine of one mark was levied on the outlaw – *fjörbaugsgarður* means literally 'life-ring enclosure' and the penalty was originally a silver ring to be paid to the godi in charge of the court as a token to save the offender's life, while the enclosure was his safe route into exile. A sentence of lesser outlawry was converted to full outlawry if he returned to Iceland before three years, if no passage was requested on his behalf, or if he could not arrange to leave the country within three summers after sentence was passed on him. Full outlawry meant that a man lost all his goods and rights, and was not to be fed, helped on his way or sheltered – it was tantamount to a death sentence. The full outlaw often had no recourse but to live in the wilds, as the term for him, *skógarmaður* ('forest man') implies. A full outlaw could be rightfully slain wherever he was found, in Iceland or abroad, but the killer did not always earn much renown from doing so and sometimes ultimately paid with his own life in revenge.

Glossary

The Icelandic term is printed in italics after the head-word, with modern spelling.

Althing *alþingi*: General assembly. See 'Social, Political and Legal Structure'.

arch of raised turf *jarðarmen*: In order to confirm sworn brotherhood, the participants had to mix their blood and walk under an arch of raised turf: 'A long piece of sod was cut from a grassy field but the ends left uncut. It was raised up into an arch under which the person carrying out the ordeal had to pass' (ch. 18).

Autumn Meeting *leið*, *leiðarþing*: Held after the Althing and generally lasting one or two days at the end of July or beginning of August. Proceedings and decisions from the Althing were announced at the Autumn Meeting, which had no judicial role.

bed closet *hvílugólf*, *lokrekkja*, *lokhvíla*, *lokrekkjugólf*: A private sleeping area used for the heads of better-off households. The closet was usually partitioned off from the rest of the house, and had a door that was secured from the inside.

berserk *berserkur*: (Literally 'bear-shirt'.) A warrior who could assume the might of a bear during a kind of induced trance in battle which made him apparently immune to the effect of blows from weapons. In his *Heimskringla* (*History of the Kings of Norway*), Snorri Sturluson attributes this power to a blessing by Odin, the chief god of the pagan pantheon: 'Odin knew how to make his enemies in battle blind or deaf or full of fear, and their weapons would bite no more than sticks, while his own men went without armour and were as crazed as dogs or wolves, biting at their shields, and as strong as bears or bulls. They killed people, but were impervious to both fire and iron. This is called "going beserk".' By the time of the sagas, berserks had lost all religious dignity and tended to be cast in the role of brutal but simple-minded villains; when heroes do away with them, there is usually little regret, and a great deal of local relief.

Closely related to the original concept of the berserk (implied by its literal meaning) are the shape-shifters.

bloody wound *áverki*: Almost always used in a legal sense, that is with regard to a visible, most likely bloody wound, which could result in legal actions for compensation, or some more drastic proceedings like the taking of revenge.

booth *búð*: A temporary dwelling used by those who attended the various assemblies. Structurally, it seems to have involved permanent walls which were covered by a tent-like roof, probably made of cloth.

compensation *manngjöld, bætur*: Penalties imposed by the courts were of three main kinds: awards of compensation in cash; sentences of lesser outlawry, which could be lessened or dropped by the payment of compensation; and sentences of full outlawry with no chance of being moderated. In certain cases, a man's right to immediate vengeance was recognized, but for many offences compensation was the fixed legal penalty and the injured party had little choice but to accept the settlement offered by the court, an arbitrator or a man who had been given the right to self-judgement (*sjálfdæmi*). It was certainly legal to put pressure on the guilty party to pay. Neither court verdicts nor legislation, nor even the constitutional arrangements, had any coercive power behind them other than the free initiative of individual chieftains with their armed following.

cross-bench *pallur, þverpallur*: A raised platform or bench at the inner end of the main room, where women were usually seated.

directions *austur/vestur/norður/suður* (east/west/north/south): These directional terms are used in a very wide sense in the sagas; they are largely dependent on context, and they cannot always be trusted to reflect compass directions. Internationally, 'the east' generally refers to the countries to the east and south-east of Iceland, and although 'easterner' usually refers to a Norwegian, it can also apply to a Swede (especially since the concept of nationality was still not entirely clear when the sagas were being written), and might even be used for a person who has picked up Russian habits. 'The west', or to 'go west', tends to refer to Ireland and what are now the British Isles, but might even refer to lands still further afield; the point of orientation is west of Norway. When confined to Iceland, directional terms sometimes refer to the quarter to which a person is travelling, e.g. a man going to the Althing from the east of the country might be said to be going 'south' rather than 'west', and a person going home to the West Fjords from the Althing is said to be going 'west' rather than 'north'.

dowry *heimanfylgja*: Literally 'that which accompanies the bride from her home'. This was the amount of money (or land) that a bride's father contributed at her wedding. Like the bride-price, it remained legally her property. However, the husband controlled their financial affairs and was responsible for the use to which both these assets were put.

drapa *drápa*: A heroic, laudatory poem, usually in the complicated metre preferred by the Icelandic poets. Such poems were in fashion between the tenth and thirteenth centuries. They were usually composed in honour of kings, earls and other prominent men, living or dead. Occasionally they were addressed to a loved one or made in praise of pagan or Christian religious figures. A *drapa* usually consisted of three parts: an introduction, a middle section including one or more refrains, and a conclusion. It was usually clearly distinct from the *flokk*, which tended to be shorter, less laudatory and without refrains.

earl *jarl*: A title generally restricted to men of high rank in northern countries (though not in Iceland), who could be independent rulers or subordinate to a king. The title could be inherited, or it could be conferred by a king on a prominent supporter or leader of military forces. The Earls of Lade who appear in a number of sagas and tales ruled large sections of northern Norway (and often many southerly areas as well) for several centuries. Another prominent, almost independent, earldom was that of Orkney and Shetland.

east *austur*: See 'directions'.

fire hall *eldaskáli*: In literal terms, the fire hall was a room or special building (as perhaps at Jarlshof in Shetland) containing a fire, and its primary function was that of a kitchen. Such a definition, however, would be too limited, since the fire hall was also used for eating, working and sleeping. Indeed, in many cases the word *eldaskáli* seems to have been synonymous with the word *skáli*, meaning the hall of a farm.

follower *hirðmaður*: A member of the inner circle of followers who surrounded the Scandinavian kings, a sworn king's man.

foster- *fóstur-, fóstri, fóstra*: Children during the saga period were often brought up by foster-parents, who received either payment or support in return from the real parents. Being fostered was therefore somewhat different from being adopted: it was essentially a legal agreement and, more importantly, a form of alliance. None the less, emotionally, and in some cases legally, fostered children were seen as being part of the family circle. Relationships and loyalties between foster-kindred could become very strong. It should be noted that the expressions *fóstri/fóstra* were also used for people who had the function of looking after, bringing up and teaching the children on the farm.

freed slave *lausingi, leysingi*: A slave could be set or bought free, and thus acquired the general status of a free man, although this status was low, since if he/she died with no heir, his/her inheritance would return to the original owner. The children of freed slaves, however, were completely free.

full outlawry *skóggangur*: Outlawry for life. See 'Social, Political and Legal Structure'.

games *leikar*: *Leikur* (sing.) in Icelandic contained the same breadth of meaning as 'game' in English. The games meetings described in the sagas would probably have included a whole range of 'play' activities. Essentially, they involved men's sports, such as wrestling, ball games, 'skin-throwing games', 'scraper games' and horse-fights. Games of this kind took place whenever people came together, and seem to have formed a regular feature of assemblies and other gatherings (including the Althing) and religious festivals such as the Winter Nights. Sometimes prominent men invited people together specifically to take part in games.

godi *goði*: This word was little known outside Iceland in early Christian times, and seems to refer to a particularly Icelandic concept. A godi was a local chieftain who had legal and administrative responsibilities in Iceland. The name seems to have originally meant 'priest', or at least a person having a special relationship with gods or supernatural powers, and thus shows an early connection between religious and secular power. As time went on, however, the chief function of a godi came to be secular. The first godis were chosen from the leading families who settled Iceland in *c*.870–930. See 'Social, Political and Legal Structure'.

godord *goðorð*: The authority and rank of a godi, including his social and legal responsibilities towards his thingmen.

hall *skáli*: *Skáli* was used both for large halls such as those used by kings, and for the main farmhouse on the typical Icelandic farm.

hayfield *tún*: An enclosed field for hay cultivation close to or surrounding a farm house. This was the only 'cultivated' part of a farm and produced the best hay. Other hay, generally of lesser quality, came from the meadows which could be a good distance from the farm itself.

hayfield wall *túngarður*: A wall of stones surrounding the hayfield in order to protect it from grazing livestock.

high seat pillars *öndvegissúlur*: The high seat was often adorned with decorated high-seat pillars, which had a religious significance. There are several accounts of how those emigrating from Norway to Iceland took their high-seat pillars with them. As they approached land they threw the carved wood posts overboard. It was believed that the pillars would be guided by divine forces to the place where the travellers were destined to live.

homespun (cloth) *vaðmál*: For centuries wool and woollen products were Iceland's chief exports, especially in the form of strong and durable homespun cloth. It could be bought and sold in bolts or made up into items such as homespun cloaks. There were strict regulations on homespun, as it was used as a standard exchange product and often referred to in ounces, meaning its equivalent value expressed as a weight in silver. One ounce could equal three to six ells of homespun, one ell being roughly 50 cm.

horse-fight *hestaat/hestavíg*: A popular sport among the Icelanders, which seems to have taken place especially in the autumn, particularly at Autumn Meetings. Two horses were goaded to fight against each other, until one was killed or ran away. Understandably, emotions ran high, and horse-fights commonly led to feuds.

hundred *hundrað*: A 'long hundred' or 120. The expression, however, rarely refers to an accurate number, rather a generalized 'round' figure.

knorr *knörr*: An ocean-going cargo vessel.

Law Rock *Lögberg*: The raised spot at the Althing at Thingvellir, where the Lawspeaker may have recited the law code, and where public announcements and speeches were made. See also 'Social, Political and Legal Structure'.

Lawspeaker *lögsögumaður, lögmaður*: Means literally 'the man who recites the law', referring to the time before the advent of writing when the Lawspeaker had to learn the law by heart and recite one third of it every year, perhaps at the Law Rock. If he was unsure about the text, he had to consult a team of five or more 'lawmen' (*lögmenn*) who knew the law well. The Lawspeaker presided over the assembly at the Althing and was responsible for the preservation and clarification of legal tradition. He could exert influence, as in the case about whether the Icelanders should accept Christianity, but should not be regarded as having ruled the country. See also 'Social, Political and Legal Structure'.

leather sleeping sack *húðfat*: A large leather bag used by travellers for sleeping.

lesser outlawry *fjörbaugsgarður*: Outlawry for three years. See 'Social, Political and Legal Structure'.

magic rite *seiður*: The exact nature of magic ritual, or *seiður*, is somewhat obscure. It appears that it was originally a ceremony that was only practised by women. Even though there are several accounts of males who performed this (including the god Odin), they are almost always looked down on as having engaged in an 'effeminate' activity. The magic rite seems to have had two main purposes: a spell to influence people or the elements (see ch. 37, pp. 78–9), and a means of finding out about the future. There are evidently parallels between *seiður* and shamanistic rituals such as those carried out by the Lapps and Native Americans.

main room *stofa*: A room off the hall of a farmhouse.

mark *mörk*: A measurement of weight, eight ounces, approximately 214 grams.

north *norður*: See 'directions'.

ounce, ounces *eyrir*, pl. *aurar*: A unit of weight, varying slightly through time, but roughly 27 grams. Eight ounces were equal to one mark.

outlawry *útlegð, skóggangur, fjörbaugsgarður*: See 'Social, Political and Legal Structure'.

quarter *fjórðungur*: Administratively, Iceland was divided into four quarters based on the four cardinal directions. See 'Social, Political and Legal Structure'.

shieling *sel*: A roughly constructed hut in the highland grazing pastures away from the farm, where shepherds and cowherds lived during the summer. Milking and the preparation of various dairy products took place here, as did other important farm activities like the collection of peat and charcoal burning (depending on the surroundings). This arrangement was well known throughout the Scandinavian countries from the earliest times.

slave *þræll*: Slavery was quite an important aspect of Viking Age trade. A large number of slaves were taken from the Baltic nations and the western European countries that were raided and invaded by Scandinavians between the eighth and eleventh centuries. In addition, the Scandinavians had few scruples against taking slaves from the other Nordic countries. Judging from their names and appearance, a large number of the slaves mentioned in the sagas seem to have come from Ireland and Scotland. Stereotypically they are presented as being stupid and lazy. By law, slaves had hardly any rights at all, and they and their families could only gain freedom if their owners chose to free them, or somebody else bought their freedom: see 'freed slave'. In the Icelandic commonwealth, a slave who was wounded was entitled to one third of the compensation money; the rest went to his owner.

south *suður*: See 'directions'.

Spring Assembly *vorþing*: The local assembly, held each spring. These were the first regular assemblies to be held in Iceland. Held at thirteen sites and lasting four to seven days between 7 and 27 May, they were jointly supervised by three godis. The Spring Assembly had a dual legal and economic function. It consisted of a court of thirty-six men, twelve appointed by each of the godis, where local legal actions were heard, while major cases and those which could not be resolved locally were sent on to the Althing. In its other function it was a forum for settling debts, deciding prices and the like. Godis probably used the Spring Assembly to urge their followers to ride to the Althing; those who remained behind paid the costs of those who went. See 'Social, Political and Legal Structure'.

sprinkled with water *vatni ausinn*: Even before the arrival of Christianity, the Scandinavians practised a naming ceremony clearly similar to that involved in the modern-day 'christening'. The action of sprinkling a child with water and naming it meant that the child was initiated into society. After this ceremony, a child could not be taken out to die of exposure (a common practice in pagan times).

steward *stallari*: A high-ranking follower of the king, empowered to act as his representative at important meetings. The stewards were also responsible for preparations for war, and for overseeing other king's men.

temple *hof*: In spite of the elaborate description of the 'temple' at Hofstadir (literally 'Temple Place') in *The Saga of the People of Eyri*, ch. 4, and other temples mentioned in the sagas (see ch. 19, pp. 35), there is no certainty that buildings erected for the sole purpose of pagan worship ever existed in Iceland or the other Scandinavian countries. To date, no such building has been found in archaeological excavations. In all likelihood, pagan rituals and sacrifices took place outdoors, or in a specified area in certain large farmhouses belonging to priests, where the idols of the gods would also have been kept.

Viking *víkingur*: Normally has an unfavourable sense in the Sagas of Icelanders, referring to violent seafaring raiders, especially of the pagan period. It can also denote general bullies and villains.

west *vestur*: See 'directions'.

Winter Nights *veturnætur*: The period of two days when the winter began, around the middle of October. In the pagan era, this was a particularly holy time of the year, when sacrifices were made to the female guardian spirits, and social activities such as games meetings and weddings often took place. It was also the time when animals were slaughtered so that their meat could be stored over the winter.

Index of Characters

Thurid Asgeirsdottir 84, 121
Thurid Eyvindardottir 5
Thurid Olafsdottir (Peacock's)
    49, 59–61, 99, 102
Torrad Osvifsson 63, 113
Tungu-Odd Onundarson 10
Turf-Einar Rognvaldsson, Earl 6

Ulf Ospaksson 118
Ulf the Squinter 8
Ulf Uggason 59
Ulfheid Runolfsdottir 173
Unn Ketilsdottir the Deep-
    minded 3, 4, 6–9, 8–10
Unn Mardardottir (Gigja's) 35

Valgerd Thorgilsdottir 173
Vandrad Osvifsson 63, 113
Veleif the Old 13
Vermund Thorgimsson 5, 62, 86
Vestar Thorolfsson (Blister-
    pate's) 5
Vifil (slave) 8
Vigdis Hallsteinsdottir 14, 28,
    29
Vigdis Ingjaldsdottir 14–15,
    22–7, 34
Vigdis Thorsteinsdottir (the
    Red's) 8

Yngvild Ketilsdottir 3

PENGUIN CLASSICS

EGIL'S SAGA

'The sea-goddess has ruffled me,
stripped me bare of my loved ones'

Egil's Saga tells the story of the long and brutal life of the tenth-century warrior-poet and farmer Egil Skallagrimsson: a psychologically ambiguous character who was at once the composer of intricately beautiful poetry and a physical grotesque capable of staggering brutality. This Icelandic saga recounts Egil's progression from youthful savagery to mature wisdom as he struggles to defend his honour in a running feud against the Norwegian King Erik Blood-axe, fights for the English King Athelstan in his battles against Scotland and embarks on colourful Viking raids across Europe. Exploring issues as diverse as the question of loyalty, the power of poetry and the relationship between two brothers who love the same woman, *Egil's Saga* is a fascinating depiction of a deeply human character, and one of the true masterpieces of medieval literature.

This new translation by Bernard Scudder fully conveys the poetic style of the original. It also contains a new introduction by Svanhildur Óskarsdóttir, placing the saga in historical context, a detailed chronology, a chart of Egil's ancestors and family, maps and notes.

Translated by Bernard Scudder

Edited by Ornulfur Thorsson

THE STORY OF PENGUIN CLASSICS

Before 1946 ... 'Classics' are mainly the domain of academics and students; readable editions for everyone else are almost unheard of. This all changes when a little-known classicist, E. V. Rieu, presents Penguin founder Allen Lane with the translation of Homer's *Odyssey* that he has been working on in his spare time.

1946 Penguin Classics debuts with *The Odyssey*, which promptly sells three million copies. Suddenly, classics are no longer for the privileged few.

1950s Rieu, now series editor, turns to professional writers for the best modern, readable translations, including Dorothy L. Sayers's *Inferno* and Robert Graves's unexpurgated *Twelve Caesars*.

1960s The Classics are given the distinctive black covers that have remained a constant throughout the life of the series. Rieu retires in 1964, hailing the Penguin Classics list as 'the greatest educative force of the twentieth century.'

1970s A new generation of translators swells the Penguin Classics ranks, introducing readers of English to classics of world literature from more than twenty languages. The list grows to encompass more history, philosophy, science, religion and politics.

1980s The Penguin American Library launches with titles such as *Uncle Tom's Cabin,* and joins forces with Penguin Classics to provide the most comprehensive library of world literature available from any paperback publisher.

1990s The launch of Penguin Audiobooks brings the classics to a listening audience for the first time, and in 1999 the worldwide launch of the Penguin Classics website extends their reach to the global online community.

The 21st Century Penguin Classics are completely redesigned for the first time in nearly twenty years. This world-famous series now consists of more than 1300 titles, making the widest range of the best books ever written available to millions – and constantly redefining what makes a 'classic'.

The Odyssey continues ...

The best books ever written

PENGUIN 🐧 CLASSICS

SINCE 1946

Find out more at www.penguinclassics.com